I0831327

MOON CLAIMED

SUPERNATURAL BATTLE: WEREWOLF DENS

KELLY ST. CLARE

Moon Claimed
by Kelly St. Clare

Edited by Hot Tree Editing
Cover design by Covers by Christian

ABOUT THE AUTHOR

When Kelly is not reading or writing, she is lost in her latest reverie.

Books have always been magical and mysterious to her. One day she decided to unravel this mystery and began writing.

Her works include *The Tainted Accords, Last Battle for Earth, Pirates of Felicity, Supernatural Battle,* and *The Darkest Drae.*

Kelly resides in New Zealand with her ginger-haired husband, a great group of friends, and whatever animals she can add to her horde.

Join her newsletter tribe for sneak peeks, release news, and disjointed musings at kellystclare.com/free-gifts/

MOON CLAIMED

1

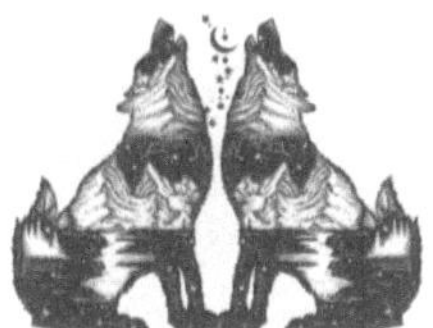

This emptier version of myself was a stranger, but we could agree on some things.

Werewolves existed, and one well and truly fucked my life.

My mother wasn't my mother. My father was her brother. My cousin was my sister. And Sascha Greyson, tribe enemy number one, wanted me for his baby mama.

Just another Sunday in the existence of Andie.

I jerked at a soft knock.

The office door opened, and Tiptoe Eleanor poked her head in. "Andie? Meeting with the Luthers in ten."

I forced my cold lips to work. "Thanks."

The death of a leader warranted a week off Grids for mourning. That grace period had officially drawn to a close.

Glancing around the manor office that Herc once occupied, I stood and twitched my grey sweater dress into place. The slight tremble of my hands only spurred my anger higher. Any weakness would be seen by our enemy.

I headed for the opposite end of the manor, and a shadowed form pushed off the wall.

"Hey," I said, a slight warmth permeating my chest.

My sister smiled. Rhona was a loyal heart under barbwire. Not a cute feisty barbwire. *Layers* of the stuff. Her barbwire was now gone. Her defences had been stripped away. Her smile showed me how crappy she felt.

"Head Steward." Rhona fell into step beside me. "You're sure about this?"

My stomach churned. I wasn't sure of anything, but Herc sort of prepared me for this moment without me realising. If I was a Luther, I'd be circling for the kill. They'd see a young leader who barely knew the game.

They'd see the perfect time to strike.

My job was to show everyone our tribe was as strong as ever.

That we were confident.

"Absolutely," I said. "This is the best path to take."

I nodded at a few stewards who gawked at us, then glanced at her. "Are you ready to face the pack?"

"You're asking if I'll lose my shit?"

Yes.

My sister was, to all external purposes, my twin aside from the year separating us. I grew up scraping for a dollar and she grew up... here. Life had taught me that *losing my shit* only worked if I had nothing to actually lose. That wasn't the case here. The tribe needed us. "I'm asking if you're ready to look at the Luther who murdered your father."

She sucked in a breath.

"They want to see you crumble." With Rhona, a challenge was the way to make her perform. Especially when it came to pride. How Herc could have injured that pride so badly blew my mind. Then again, I doubted he intended to take the truth to death.

Closing my eyes, I cleared my mind. I couldn't afford any distractions against *this* wolf.

Rhona met my gaze after. "I won't let you down. The only way to beat them is to stay together."

She felt a different version of the same revenge wedged in my heart. I gripped her shoulder. "Together, we'll drive them into the ground."

Her lips curved. "Sounds like a good time."

I entered, greeting the head team members. Some I knew the names of prior to ten days ago. Most I'd met over the blur of meetings since life took this… turn.

With the reading of Hercules Thana's will, a wrecking ball crashed into my already scattered life. For the first time ever, I couldn't just add the lie to Mum's overflowing pile.

Because I didn't belong to her—or anyone—and everyone who could tell me *why* this had happened was fucking dead—or killed by the Luther bastard.

Sascha Greyson would pay for what he did. The life he'd taken, and those lives he'd ruined. Oh, the irony that fate put me in the perfect position to do just that.

I'd win Grids and exile werewolves from Deception Valley.

Rhona took a seat on my right.

I'd once attended a meeting like this. I was thankful for the accidental experience Herc mistakenly—or purposefully—gave me.

Drawing from memory, I said, "The objective is to show the Luthers we're a unified and strong front. We are operating as usual. We have taken the change of leadership in our stride."

The head team hadn't given me trouble—something I could thank ingrained tribe tradition for, as well as myself. Well before Herc's murder, I threw myself into learning everything about Grids. That didn't go unnoticed by anyone, and it had earned me an unofficial probation period when I inherited head stewardship.

"Would you like me to put the call through?" Roderick asked.

I thrummed my fingers on the table. "I think not."

Herc always put the call through—was the bigger person. He'd waited for the Luthers to pick up the phone at their leisure.

Roderick's lips twitched. "Very well."

The call was scheduled for 10:00 a.m.

10:01. A phone symbol appeared on the large blue screen before us.

My heart leaped into my throat. I'd asked Rhona if she was ready.

Was I?

Sascha and I hadn't faced each other since the will reading. What would he do? He could reveal everything about the breeding meets and our *mating*, which would see me firmly booted from this job. My only security was that he wanted to be my sperm donor.

Jesus, Dr Phil would have a field day with this shit.

Hardening my expression, I listened to the phone ring for the fifth time.

Seven.

Nine.

"Answer," I said calmly.

Roderick did the honours, and the fucker himself appeared on the screen.

His gaze found me.

I took in his scraggly shoulder-length brown hair and liquid-honey eyes. The asshole stood front and middle of his team, and I broke our staredown to look at Leroy, Hairy, Mandy, Grim, and Lisa. *Alpha, beta, delta, gamma, and omega.*

"Luther," I said.

Mandy's eyes narrowed.

I had no fucks to give her. She'd have to pre-order one.

"Miss Thana." The smooth syrup of his voice trickled in warm, slow drips down my back.

Yeah, the meets we'd completed so far did a few things to me. Each time, I felt *more*. The capture meet had ramped things up again.

I fisted my hands beneath the table. *Focus.* Sascha was far more experienced at swordplay. I couldn't dance with this monster. Best get to the point. "We've made our choice for the next grid."

We lost Sandstone by a few points but won the grid back as

reparation for Herc's murder, so the choice for Wednesday's battle was all ours.

My choice was an unusual one.

The werewolf considered me.

What did he see? Hair that should have been washed three days ago, dark circles under my emerald eyes, and a gaunt expression because I was too heartsick and stressed to eat?

"What's the decision of the head steward?" Gravel entered his voice.

My ire swelled for Greyson's—my nickname for his wolf—presence in the meeting. Sascha and Greyson were one and the same, but *Greyson* led the capture meet. He'd been in charge when Herc ran to save me. *He* was the murderer.

Yes, I blamed Sascha.

I blamed Greyson more.

A smile graced my lips. "We'll see your pack in Water."

Nothing betrayed his surprise. I mean, the Luthers currently held three grids—Water, Clay, and Timber—so my choice wasn't groundbreaking, but traditionally, we were weakest in Water closely followed by Clay. Therefore, the tribe usually chose Timber first.

I'd played the game in two grids so far—three if you counted my unlucky experience with the fake laser tag in the forest.

Water was our biggest weakness. I had to know it better.

"Very well," Sascha replied. "The game will fall outside of the new moon this month. Three days after."

The wolves' power had everything to do with the sun. At the new moon, when sunlight wasn't reflected off the moon, the Luthers became most volatile. "The game will obviously go ahead."

"Obviously." The gravel in his voice strengthened. I couldn't glean a thing from his expression, but his eyes didn't shift from mine. If he had a straw in his mouth, I'd say he was drinking me in.

"Unless there's another obvious point you'd like to make, Luther, there are other places I'd like to be."

Leroy's eyes narrowed, but Hairy nudged him like a good little beta.

"Until Wednesday, Miss Booker." Honey eyes bore into me.

My chest tightened. Never again. I'd *never* let myself fall for those eyes again. "I go by Miss Thana."

I nodded at Roderick, and the screen blanked, cutting off Sascha's reply.

Twisting, I eyed Rhona's murderous grip on the armrests. "You alright?"

"I killed him ten times in my mind."

"Therapeutic."

Her mouth crooked in a smile. "It will tide me over until I can do the real thing."

My stomach twisted, and I ignored the magic voodoo telling me Sascha's death should be avoided at all costs, even with my own life.

"Now to win a grid we've never won," my sister murmured.

I stood. "Win? No. Learn? Yes."

Luck wouldn't help me destroy Sascha Greyson. And I didn't *want* to win with luck. *No*.

When the Luther pack went down, it would be because I controlled the puppet strings.

2

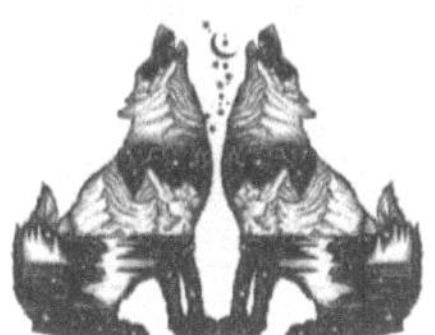

I stared at my buzzing phone.

Unknown number.

We need to talk

I strongly disagreed.

Sascha had shown his true colours, and I could only feel stupid for believing some of his act. I never had a problem with the wolves before, not really. Part of me even felt for their situation at one stage.

Now.

If I'd sometimes winced at Herc's blatant disgust toward the Luthers, *that* Andie had learned her lesson.

Another message arrived.

His last words. They're pack secrets.
He shouldn't have known them.

Red fury blinded me, and I dropped my gaze to where my hands strangled the phone.

Herc's last words. Which fucking ones?

I'd rather lose a grid than see this happen to her.

I've seen this before.

I won't fail again.

You can be fixed.

Your death won't kill her.

I deleted Sascha's messages and blocked the number without replying. His information gave me nothing about what I truly wanted to know.

Why did Mum steal me from Herc? If I knew *that*, maybe I could feel warm again. Maybe...

I'd understand how she could have hurt me so badly.

Only one port of call came to mind. Scrolling through my contacts, I turned the speaker on.

"Baby girl, what can I do you for?"

With Wade, the sexual innuendo was always intended. "Hey, do you know the Freys?"

"Sure do. Gotta say, they're not the biggest fans of your family. They causing trouble?"

I didn't get bad vibes during my short conversation with Margaret, but good to know. "They're my—" *Fathers*... "Well, my, uh, Mother was with a Frey when she left the valley. I'd like to ask them questions."

"I'll set it up. How soon?"

"As soon as they can." The faster I put this plaguing curiosity to rest, the better I'd sleep, and the more energy I could dedicate to Grids.

My phone buzzed. "Someone else is calling. I'll catch ya later."

Hanging up, I checked the name. "Roy. Good news, I hope."

I needed rid of Mum's debt *yesterday*.

In two months, I'd accumulated nearly four thousand dollars in interest. The debt was getting beyond what the house sale could cover. Another month would screw me.

"Good news," he said. "There's an offer. Young family. One child and another on the way. Looking for a house with a bit of a yard."

If they bought the house, they could be flying pigs for all I cared.

"Offer is three ninety-nine."

My heart sank. "That's less than I expected."

"Remember that's the initial offer," Roy rushed to say.

I needed 416,000 to cover conveyance fees, the commission Roy would take, and the new interest. "I can go down by four thousand. That's it."

A brief pause. "They have some wiggle room, but probably not that much."

I got paid an allowance for leading the *Ni Tiaki*. The money pulled from the trust that contained Deception Valley land and this manor. The allowance was better than my saxophone gig at *The Dens*, and I no longer had any living costs. I could pay off a thousand dollars in the next month. If I sold short of the debt amount, I'd still have a fight against interest, but it would only be calculated on a few thousand as opposed to hundreds.

I could win that fight.

I leaned back in the office chair. "If they're willing to pay a higher deposit and can authorise release of that deposit to me immediately, I can meet them at 412,000."

"I'll take that back to them." His grim tone told me what the answer would be.

Dammit. "If they're willing to meet me there, I'll throw the house furnishings in too."

Storage was a cost I didn't need, and I just wanted everything to do with Queen's Way gone. The new owners would be doing me a favour.

Surprise coloured his voice. "Could you send a list of the contents?"

Could I squeeze that between three hours of meetings, study, overseeing Sandstone, Iron, and the council of this valley, managing disputes between stewards, and the endless documents requiring my attention?

Herc had once asked Rhona and me how we'd juggle such a load. I'd given a beautiful answer. A textbook answer.

What an idiot.

This had to take priority. I was drowning in problems. "Give me until the end of the day and you'll have it."

Rhona entered without knocking as I slid my phone away.

"Done with study?" she asked.

It was midday so I had to be. And I'd done approximately none. The situation grated sorely at my straight-A pride, but I couldn't do much about that. Only a pass was realistic. "All done. Are you alright?"

She blew out a breath, taking the seat opposite mine. "I've thought more about the last two weeks. There were signs I should have picked up on."

I tensed. *Sascha killed your father because of me.* "Like what?"

Rhona licked her lips. "I think Dad tried to tell me the truth a few times—about you. He was acting weird, you know?"

I refrained from wiping the beading perspiration from my brow. Working undercover in *The Dens* had taught me subtlety at least.

"There's something I need to come clean on," she spoke to her hands. "When you first arrived here, Dad said that we needed to do everything we could to ensure you stayed."

I blinked. "What?"

Rhona met my eyes briefly. "He told me to introduce you to people our age. I was meant to show you our community without being too pushy. He said you didn't have much money, so I asked you to drive my friends around to eat into what you did have. Dad said you'd be a great addition to the team, and he'd never done that before. I figured it was because you were a Thana. But it was wrong."

What the fuck. "He orchestrated all that?"

Herc offered me a rent-free apartment and a job within a minute of me expressing interest in remaining here. He and Rhona were a big part of my decision to stay.

They'd made me feel so welcome.

And it was all fake.

My mouth dropped. "Was he dangling that information about Mum on purpose too?"

I'd hesitated about playing the game before he informed me Mum was a star player. And he said Mum's friend couldn't talk until Tuesday when I'd expressly mentioned departing on *Monday*.

Is there any way you can extend your trip?

"Why?" I asked.

She lifted a shoulder. "Because you were his long-lost stolen daughter, I suppose. I didn't ask at the time."

"Were Wade and Cameron involved?"

"I saw them introduce themselves at the lake. You seemed to get on well, and I told Dad..."

Who then used Wade and Cameron too.

At least they'd had nothing to do with it. Rubbing my temples, I sighed. "There's so much I want to ask him."

"Do you ever wonder if he was training you all that time?"

I could lie to her. *Jesus*, this had to hurt her so much. I'd rolled in and pushed her off the podium in a matter of weeks.

Herc was the one to replace her, but I looked like the shitty person.

I had to conceal what happened with Sascha in Sandstone, but otherwise, I refused to disrespect Rhona that way. "The day we switched, Herc figured it out, but only told me after the meeting and asking me leadership questions."

He'd expressed concerns about Rhona's ability to lead the stewards on multiple occasions. Personally, I thought he was wrong on that count. What I'd give to switch with her now. Give me the role of advisor any day. Chuck me in an office somewhere. Anything that removed this terrible pressure to succeed.

"The date on the will was a week prior to his death," she said quietly.

"I heard." My heart hurt for her.

The date was unmissable. Seven days before Sascha snapped his neck, Herc changed his will to name me as heir. He'd only informed Pascal as she had to marshal the document, and she hadn't said anything else on the matter thus far.

Rhona stared at her hands, and a familiar fury rose in me, creeping over my jaw.

"He loved you, Rhona. Never forget that. People fuck up."

"That's a big fuck up," she whispered. "Why lie for so long and then spell out the truth in a will? He could have left it buried."

Because I came back and started asking questions. "I think the answer has to do with why Mum and Murphy left with me. I want to find out what happened."

"She wasn't your mother."

I swallowed against the stabbing pain under my ribs. "It's hard to think of her as anything else yet."

To go from Mum to Aunty Ragna seemed physically and mentally impossible. And to think of Aunty Savannah as Mother was stranger still. I'd made the switch from cousin to sister with Rhona, but we'd forged a bond prior to this mess that made that leap easy.

"Are you angry at her?"

My mind flashed to sitting with Mum in the garden. "I can't feel more anger. If I could, I'd be angry at all three of them."

They'd *all* lied. The person least to blame was ironically the person I'd blamed since three years old. Murphy.

"Ragna stole you though."

"Savannah gave *birth* to me. Don't you think it's strange that none of the stewards saw a massive pregnant woman waddling around? How did no one know I existed? I mean, Mum fucked up too many times to count in my life, and I'm well aware of that. But something bigger is going on. People don't just steal babies."

Rhona rose, rounding the desk. "Have you searched in here? I haven't. Maybe there's something that could help us. A fifty-page letter detailing all the answers we want."

I arched a brow. "Yeah, right. And I feel like an imposter sitting in this chair. So no."

Rhona elbowed me out of the way. "Get over it. You're the eldest. Tradition is tradition."

This woman had an odd, kind of brutal way of lightening my heart. I opened the drawers to my left as she started on the right.

In the top drawer, I found a list of the stewards. That could come in handy. Digging underneath, I found another folder titled *Importer Contacts.*

Also handy.

The next drawer down was filled with stationery. The last drawer had a change of clothes and some toiletries. Couldn't blame him. There was a definite pressure to appear put together in this position. Maybe I should do that too.

"What are these?" Rhona straightened from searching the bottom drawer, two books in her hand.

My mouth dried. "They look like the journals Mum used."

She'd used a black, leather-clad journal each year. I'd read until age seventeen and assumed there weren't more. Herc had purposefully concealed these.

Rhona handed them over.

The first was titled *I'm 18* and the second *I'm 19.*

If Herc concealed these, the journals had to contain truths he hadn't wanted me to learn.

"What's wrong?" Rhona gripped my arm.

I hovered my fingers over the page corner of the first, arrested by fear. Mum left at nineteen with me and Murphy. Was I ready to learn the truth? "She lied to me so badly. She's not even my mother, and I should hate her for pretending. But she was the only person I had. How could she do that to me?"

Why did she hurt me? Again and again.

And why did I always forgive her?

Since her death, wedge after wedge had been slammed between me and the memory of her. I couldn't take another hit without losing her completely.

Rhona whispered, "I guess the answer is inside those journals."

I cast her a look. "Herc kept these journals from me, Rhona. What if there's something more in here? Something worse."

I couldn't fathom what could *be* worse, but anything was fucking possible at this point.

My sister paled.

Exactly.

I shut the cover. "I'm one blow from emotional knock out. We need to get through Grids this week. Whatever's in here can wait."

Until I could handle it.

"Just promise me, Andie, no matter what's in there, you tell me. No matter how hard the truth is, I want it. I'm so sick of the lies."

Guilt slammed into my chest. I inhaled slowly, hating myself. "I promise."

3

I parked Ella F outside the riverside apartment. The short time spent living in town and making my own way at *The Dens* before werewolves existed haunted me.

Stewards were at dawn training, and this was officially the first chance I'd had to get out of the manor. People were always around, asking questions, clamouring for my thoughts, wanting something.

I just needed one hour of alone time. Especially with the Tuesday night gathering tonight. If I didn't decompress somehow, I'd end up shaving my head or something.

I walked up the stairs and down the hall, then stood in the doorway, studying the small, open-plan space.

Yep. Really fucking bittersweet.

And I just needed to get over it.

First step, moving out.

Wade and Cameron transferred my clothes to the manor after Herc's death, but everything else was here. Setting the flattened boxes on the table, I set to work.

Stripping the bed, I shoved the load in the washing machine and made up the boxes. Everything would fit in Ella F—the only new additions were the cleaning and cooking supplies. I couldn't quite bear to leave them behind after having forked out the money for them.

Habit was still a big bitchhole.

Packing felt the same as emptying the house after Mum's death.

Like I was touching someone else's stuff.

This Andie played saxophone at a bar and had normal problems—well, mostly normal. I glanced at the saxophone case on the two-seater couch. After the will reading, I gave it to Wade to ditch here.

That was part of old Andie's life too. She'd played it for her mother.

Tearing my gaze from the instrument, I boxed my few books and threadbare towels.

The floor creaked.

Heart leaping into my throat, I whirled to find a man in the doorway. *Him.* How the fuck did he have the audacity to show his face here?

Sascha Greyson, dressed in jeans and a forest-green flannel shirt, looked at me from across the room.

"You aren't this stupid," I told him.

He took a breath.

Oh? He *was.*

"*Get out.* This is an unsanctioned meeting."

The Luther stepped into the room instead. "And when the marshals ask why I came to your apartment, will you tell them what nearly happened on that bed two weeks ago?"

His face between my legs.

Not that anything *did* happen, but what went down was without doubt the most erotic experience of my life. Every time I relived it, I felt like a disgusting piece of shit.

I set the full box on the dusty kitchen table. "That's a mighty bluff. The truth would be just as bad for your people as mine."

"My people know everything," the werewolf said without missing a beat.

There was a reason I didn't try to best him with words. "You could try it, I suppose."

"You know I won't."

"You killed my father. I think we can agree there's no limit to what you'll do."

Sascha lowered his head.

I'd had enough interactions with him to recall that was a sign of submission, but the werewolf lifted his head again and took another step inside.

"Get out," I snapped. "I mean it. The only time I want to see you is on the other side of a screen."

The werewolf circled the table toward me. "The mating meets will continue."

Incredulous laughter left my lips. "I fucking dare you to try."

His eyes darkened, and my mouth shut with an audible click. Greyson loved nothing more than a challenge.

I'd learned that the hard way. "You've catalogued my scents, right? Then have a good whiff. I loathe you. The sight of you is repulsive. What nearly happened between us in the past *revolts* me. I find you and your kind vile in every way. I was a stupid girl who didn't believe what a monster you really were. *What* a wake-up call. Get the fuck out and stop trying to ruin what's left of my life."

The Luther was carved from stone. Why couldn't I be like that? Why was my breath shallow and erratic?

Why were *my* eyes burning?

Sascha lifted a hand to my face, and I reeled away.

"Touch me and I will do my best to murder you with my bare hands." Icicles dripped from every word.

Shock coated his handsome features.

Seemed fitting that the worst monsters had the prettiest packaging.

"Hercules was wrong about one thing," he said low and fast. "When the seven meets are done, you have a choice to decline me as a mate. I've scented you already. We've met gazes and touched, and my wolf captured you. There are three more meets. Then you'll be free, and I won't be driven to obey the meeting call. If you still don't want me."

If you still don't want me.

"You're incredible. How can I say this so you'll understand? There is no possible future where I will not hate you. There will never be an us. I will never accept you."

His eyes glittered. "Then there shouldn't be a problem seeing it through to the end."

"I don't acknowledge rudimentary Luther rituals." I gathered one of the filled boxes. "Close the door on the way out."

A small growl built in his chest. "You're moving to the manor for good."

I didn't answer.

The werewolf followed me down the stairs. Opening Ella F, I shoved the box in, glowering when Sascha slid the remaining three inside after.

His honey eyes bore into my face.

The rage I felt toward him was almost shocking in its intensity. I wouldn't have thought myself capable of so much hate.

He inhaled.

Yeah, have a good sniff. That's undying fury.

"Would it help if I told you how sorry I was?" he said quietly.

My brows shot up. "You killed someone and you're *sorry*? Shit, that makes it all better."

"I wasn't talking about Hercules Thana. I won't apologise for his death."

My face slackened. "You're truly a monster inside, aren't you?"

"He intended to kill me. Do you know what my death would do to you?"

Ugh.

Considering Rhona had plans to tear Sascha Greyson apart, perhaps I should take notice of this. "What?"

"It would break you."

Herc's words came back to me. *Your death won't kill her.*

"But my death would kill you," I mused.

Sascha clenched his jaw. “You hate me that much?”

My upper lip curled. “I don’t hate *myself* that much. It is good to have the insurance with your killing tendencies.”

Black edged in on the honey. “He would have killed you too, Andie. Maybe not immediately, but in time, once he witnessed your reaction. I trust my wolf’s instincts implicitly. Hercules Thana was dangerous for you. Leaving him alive wasn’t an option. Not with the power he holds in this valley.”

I’d never wanted a protector. I never wanted any of this. “You’re doing so well looking after me, Sascha. Sign me up.”

He flinched. “I will prove myself to you. I will undo the hurt I’ve caused. I swear this to you.”

His hurt was a cool rain on the furious inferno filling my heart.

Nothing I said would get through to this beast.

His eyes searched my face. “You should know a mating call between a Luther and human is unusual. Unheard of in our pack and in others I’ve reached out to. So far as I can tell, you didn’t complete your side of the scent meet. I think it’s because you don’t possess the strength of our senses.”

Good. Something was going my way at last.

“Without it, you can’t make your final decision, and the mating process cannot end.”

My face hardened. “Again. I don’t acknowledge your rituals.”

His jaw clenched. “This isn’t going away, Andie. If an answer exists, we’ll need each other to figure it out.”

Yeah. Snort. I was sure that would work just fine with whatever he had planned for the next meet.

I turned my back on him to slam the boot closed. “How about we skip to the end? You’re unworthy, Sascha Greyson. There’s not a chance in hell I’d ever choose you.”

4

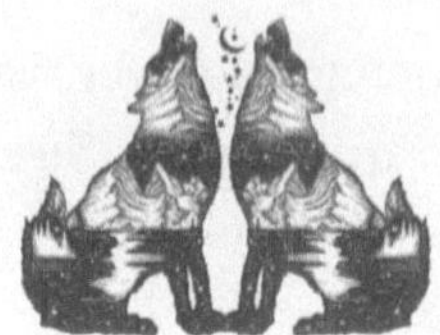

I paced inside Herc's office, breaths shallow. This was the first time I'd faced the stewards since the day at the lake. They knew I didn't belong in this position. And like Rhona, they didn't even know the truth.

I shook my hands out, exhale shaking.

The point of visiting my old apartment was to decompress. After the run in with Sascha, I was a mess.

I couldn't *be* a mess.

This was crucial.

Yet trying to not be a mess was just making me *more* of a mess.

Fuck.

The door opened, and Rhona stepped in. "Everyone's here. It's your turn."

No.

I'd reached my limit. "I can't do it."

Glancing over her shoulder, she closed the door. "That's unfortunate, because you need to get your ass on that stage."

"I've played in the grid *twice*. Why the hell would anyone listen to me?"

Why didn't I go with Timber? Something safe. Something I didn't need to justify.

I could see it now. A sea of blank faces as they wondered why I'd bitten off the hardest grid out of the gate.

"I fucked up." I thumped my forehead against the bookshelf ladder.

"You convinced the head team," Rhona said. "And me."

Except the anger fuelling me all week had chosen now to disappear. I'd used it all against Sascha Greyson. *Mothershitter.*

I sank to the floor, shoving my head between my knees. "I'm not doing it. Can you go out and make an excuse? I'm unwell."

"You can't be hearing yourself." She pulled my arms away. "All week, you've said we need to be confident and unified. What the hell do you think this message will tell our stewards?"

That I sucked. I was past caring.

This was my breaking point.

Gripping my wrists, Rhona clenched her jaw, scanning my face. "Get up."

I stayed put.

"Get up and put on my clothes," she said, sighing.

Jerking my head up, I took in her tight black cargos and long-sleeved, fitted top. She had a red cap on that read *Go Fork Yourself.*

My steel-grey full-length jumpsuit was about as opposite as could be from her outfit.

I rose on trembling legs. "You think it'll work?"

"No idea. But the tribe needs to see you tonight. And their looks of pity are grinding my gears. You be me. I'll be you. Win-win. What do I say?"

I rushed through the points of my intended speech, watching her nod at intervals as we switched clothing.

I raked my hair into a ponytail. She pulled hers free.

"You'll need to say it like me." I pressed my hands into my cheeks. *Shit,* this was ballsy, but I just needed to not be me for five seconds.

"I've heard you say this stuff at meetings already. Piece of cake."

Why the hell did Herc name me as heir? Rhona was perfect.

"You better head out first," she said.

I fixed the red cap on and set a scowl in place. Thinking of Rhona's expression, I injected some sadness into my eyes and left the manor. Tilting my chin, I strode through the midst of the gathered stewards.

Everyone was in attendance by the looks. Only one representative from each family was required on Tuesday evenings, but I couldn't condemn their curiosity or their need for reassurance.

People nodded at me, moving out of the way. *Crap*, what I'd give to be Rhona. The way people looked at her. They respected her ability in Grids. They knew her.

I wanted that so much.

Ignoring their adoration, I moved to the front and stood at ease beside Pascal. She slid me a look, but I didn't allow my mask to waver.

"Is she coming?" the grey-haired marshal asked.

I cracked my neck. "She wouldn't miss it."

Shame swirled in my gut for an instant before I banished it. Seriously, how much shit could someone take?

Just this once I wanted someone else to do the hard stuff.

There had to be some perks to having an almost twin.

The crowd quietened, and I watched Rhona walk out of the manor. She smiled at those gathered, stopping to talk with a few on the way. Shaking hands and touching shoulders, she moved through the crowds.

I mean, yes, I probably would do that...

But creepy.

What if we'd actually grown up together?

Oh, and I had to play my part. "Three cheers for our new head steward! Hip-hip!"

The first hooray was carried by those closest to me, but the second was triple the volume, and the third was a boom that rivalled the starting cannon in Grids.

Rhona reached me and we hugged.

"Did you just give yourself three cheers?" she whispered.

"Couldn't pass up the opportunity." I held her tight. What would I do without her? "Thank you."

"Always, remember?"

I squeezed my eyes shut. "Always."

Without a care in the world, my sister continued to the stage and microphone, and no one batted an eyelash.

She tapped the mic. "Stewards of the Ni Tiaki. Welcome to our tribal lands. *Welcome*. In the last two weeks, we have faced the loss of a much-loved leader. We lost a man who dedicated his life to this cause. Before we go further tonight, I'd like to lead a minute's silence for Hercules Thana. Please, link hands and join me."

Rhona deserved to say these words, not me.

I held Pascal's hand and turned to find Wade on the other side.

The minute was a slight breeze and a rustle of trees set against the last notes of bird song. Exactly what Herc deserved.

But Sascha's voice edged into my mind. *He was dangerous for you.*

Lie.

Herc wouldn't have killed me. He wasn't a killer.

"He's with us in the air and in the trees." Rhona's voice broke. She cleared her throat. "He remains with us in the company of our ancestors for all time. To my father, Hercules Thana."

I murmured his name with the other stewards, wondering if the horrible shame filling me would ever ebb.

Wade ran his thumb over the pads of my palm, and I yanked free, shooting him a glare.

"To this week's game." Rhona's voice boomed across the manicured lawn.

Was this how she saw me? How everyone saw me? If not, they wouldn't just stand there, hanging on her every word, right?

Seeing myself through another person was weird. Humbling. And I felt stupid for freaking out. My tribe didn't want to see me fail.

How easily I'd forgotten that we were all linked.

The stewards were my community.

My people.

"The Luthers expected us to choose Timber," Rhona said. "As you know, I chose Water. There's a wealth of knowledge within the head and strategy teams that I *must* adjunct with my own learning to truly serve you as a leader. That learning starts with Water. I can't deny that there has been massive change in our tribe. The wolves are circling, wondering if my father's death has weakened us. This week, I have an unusual request. *This* week, we won't focus on winning the grid."

Murmurs broke out.

Her voice swelled. "Instead, we will show the Luthers that we are one. That we are not shaken. That their vile actions in Sandstone have only brought us closer. Made us *more* determined. *This week*, we win by showing the Luthers we are united and strong."

She beamed at the cheering audience, and I watched on, heart stuck in my throat.

Valerie and Nathan took her place on the stage to run through the final strategies, and I released a breath, forcing myself to remain relaxed under Wade's rapt attention.

Bastard suspected a switch.

Behind Rhona, I strode back to the manor.

Closing the door, I turned to find her already stripping off. I tore off the red hat.

"You think they believed it?" she muttered.

I'd nearly believed her. "Yep, we're good. Thanks."

"You know that was a one-off?"

I nodded. Oddly, now she'd been me, my fear had dissipated. I was more than capable of addressing the stewards. "I just had a moment. It won't happen again."

Pulling up my jumpsuit, I waited for her to shove the cap on, and we exited the manor again.

Wade was there in an instant, taking my hand. He ran his hand over the pads of my palm again.

"Funny thing about you and Rhona," he whispered. "Rhona has callouses, and you have wimpy musician hands."

Dang it. "Yeah, I had a freak out. Keep it to yourself."

"I'm just upset you didn't get drunk and set the dummies up again."

So was I, but leaders didn't get the luxury of openly losing the plot.

Wade looped an arm around my neck. "Come on. The Freys are here to see you."

Oh, shit. I forgot about them. "Right now?"

"Right meow, baby girl."

What was I wearing? Why was I nervous? They weren't my real family anymore.

For a split second I had a great grandmother, two aunties, another uncle, and a grandfather—when Murphy was still my father.

Wade planted me in front of a small group.

I recognised Margaret, but her son and grandchildren were easy to spot. All of them had her straight nose.

I stared at the youngest man. He had to be in his late forties, nearly identical to pictures I'd seen of Murphy. My mouth dried as silence fell.

I just couldn't tear my gaze from the man.

All I'd discovered before the world imploded was that Murphy visited Deception Valley to *face his demons*. A week later, he'd died in a rock-climbing accident, and Mum let me believe he'd abandoned us.

Margaret limped forward, leaning heavily on her cane. "Andie. It's lovely to see you again."

I tore my gaze from her son. "Margaret. The same to you. I'm sorry we haven't seen each other sooner."

She rested a hand on my arm. "No apology needed. A horrible shock for you. For us too."

Of course. They'd lost a relative, too—their last connection to Murphy.

The surrounding groups quietened, and I squared my shoulders. "Will you join me in the garden? I have some questions, and I'm sure you have some for me."

The family exchanged a look, and Margaret's white-haired son stepped forward, linking arms with his mother.

"We'd like that," he told me softly.

Wade patted me on the shoulder. "Good luck."

I led them behind the manor where Herc and I first met to talk about Mum. Perching on the border of the herb garden, I waited as they sat at the wrought iron table. Some sat on the edges of the garden beds like me.

"I've always believed Murphy was my father." The words slipped from my mouth.

Margaret smiled sadly. "Since we learned of you, so have we. My granddaughter tells me you weren't aware of the subterfuge."

"As far as I was aware, Murphy left us when I was three and never returned."

The youngest woman—Murphy's youngest sister—cut in. "He'd *never* do that to Ragna."

Protective. I felt the same way about Rhona. "I know. But his commitment to her was also news to me. Mum always let me believe that he chose to leave."

Anger flooded the faces of his siblings, though his father and grandmother remained thoughtful.

They deserved to know everything. "I spoke with one of Mum's old friends who said she'd received a call from Mum after Murphy's death."

His father leaned forward. "Did Ragna say anything?"

"Asked where he was. Said he was meant to be gone for a week. To me, she only said that Murphy left to face his demons. That he couldn't ignore them. She hated talking about him, and always gave me that same answer."

The sister yet to speak burst to her feet. "How could she do that to him? Betraying him like that. He loved her so much. I thought she loved him too."

I lifted a shoulder. "It doesn't make any sense. Everyone says they loved each other more than anything."

Margaret looked up at the sky. "They did. I'd never seen love like it. From so young too. If your mother hated my grandson in the end, it was only because he left her alone when he died."

"You think so?"

"We can't truly despise someone without having loved them first. And the harder we love, the more we loathe. Hate is the food of broken dreams and betrayal, after all."

I wasn't sure I agreed.

The father said, "What I don't understand are these demons Ragna referred to. Murphy stayed with us during that time and never mentioned any issues."

My stomach plummeted. "I was really hoping he had mentioned something. I keep wondering why my mum left this place. But now I know she wasn't my mother at all, I can't stop thinking about what happened all those years ago."

"Murphy would never steal a child," the youngest sister spoke again. "He couldn't take the guilt. My brother was a good, decent man."

Was she implying Mum wasn't?

I took in her flushed cheeks. She missed her brother. "I wish I'd known him."

Margaret tapped her cane. "Perhaps that was the demon he'd come to face. Maybe he had to explain everything to Hercules."

"Do you remember who he went to see?" I leaned forward.

The son replied, "He visited all his friends, and Hercules Thana."

I didn't miss the way he'd separated Herc from *all his friends*. "Did Murphy say anything about the meeting with Herc?"

"Never, but I could tell he was out of sorts after."

"How many times did they see each other?"

"At least three occasions that I'm aware of." He lowered his gaze. "Before the last time."

Before Murphy died.

Margaret interrupted the heavy silence. "My grandson was an expert rock-climber."

"*Mum*," her son hissed.

She shot him a dry look. "I'm too old to not say what I want. Manners take time I don't have."

"What are you saying?" That sounded like an accusation.

Rhona walked into the garden. "Hey, I was looking for you. Everything okay?"

Wade said this family wasn't fans of the Thanas, and that was obvious by the sudden stiffness in their postures.

They hadn't liked Hercules, and Rhona was lumped in there too.

The talking was over.

"Thank you for telling me more about Murphy. I know it doesn't mean much, but I wish I'd had the chance to know him better. To every account, he was an incredible person."

"He was," the brother said hoarsely.

"If you ever want to know more—maybe see pictures—just let us know," the youngest sister surprised me by saying.

I smiled at her. "I'll do that."

The father approached as the family began to leave. He took my hands, leaning in. "No matter why Ragna and my son left the valley, I can assure you that Murphy intended to return to you both. He was leaving at 2:00 p.m. once their group returned from rock-climbing. There was *nothing* he wouldn't have done for that beautiful, kind woman. And though he never told us of a child, I have no doubt he felt the same love for you, regardless of who your blood father might have been."

This was all so fucked up. I'd hated Murphy for most of my life, then felt so hopeful after piecing together the timeline of his death. Now I just felt bitter that his death robbed my life of much-needed security. He'd left a blatant hole in this family's lives—and mine.

I'd filled that hole with anger for twenty-one years.

I wanted Murphy to be my father again. Then Rhona would be head steward, and everything would be fine.

Mum would still be my mum.

Rhona lingered in my periphery, arms crossed. She was either oblivious to the Frey's dislike or uncaring.

Probably the latter.

"Thank you." I hugged the man's middle tight and whispered, "Who went rock-climbing with Murphy and Hercules that day?"

He moved his mouth close to my ear. "One other steward."

"Who?" I breathed.

"Pascal."

5

I winced as another flag went up.

"That's six hundred," Pascal murmured.

From the high observation tower in the middle of Lake Thana, I watched the annihilation of our tribe in Water. The playing field was on a part of the lake tucked behind the hill where Herc's will was read.

"Six hundred and one," she said.

Ugh. Embarrassing.

You came here to learn. But still. Bet Sascha was having a fucking laugh over this. And his pack. Cheeks burning, I studied the surface below. The water was clear and with the calm evening, visibility was easy.

The Luthers used rope against us to great effect in this grid. My stewards had oxygen tanks, and the Luthers—stronger and faster swimmers—merely trussed up our players, safe in the knowledge they could breathe for the duration of the game.

Cliffs lined a small part of the lake's perimeter. The stewards stationed there were safe, and they could fire at any werewolves within range. Of which there'd been a paltry number.

Problem one: The cliff couldn't fit one thousand stewards. The battle had to occur in the water. Our weakness there in comparison to the Luthers was undeniable. The equipment needed to give us much-needed speed was horrendously expensive.

Herc had a Water savings account. I'd traced the equipment bought over the last two years. He didn't choose Water because he wanted some defence when they eventually came here again, but that shit was costly.

Problem two: Our method of communication didn't work here. Once my stewards slipped under the surface, they were on their own, so our plan couldn't be adapted.

"Six hundred and two," Pascal said.

She murmured, "Six hundred and three," a second later.

Fuckers.

We were literally sitting ducks. I could *see* the Luthers converging on groups of us but had no way to warn my units.

The werewolves moved from one area of the lake to another with clear direction. They'd altered in response to our strategy too. Sascha had to be guiding them somehow. The wolves could talk underwater. There was no way they could be in sync otherwise, but we'd put frequency generators underwater that should block their ability to hear.

A puzzle.

That I intended to solve.

"Do they always do the same thing?" I asked Pascal, who was frantically tapping on her tablet.

Looking at her, a person would never guess this woman knew far more than she let on. Pascal had known about the will change. She'd been there when Murphy died.

My grandson was an expert rock-climber, Margaret had said.

That's why the Freys hadn't liked Herc. They believed he killed Murphy. Even for stealing me, his eldest daughter, could Herc have done such a thing?

Sure, I'd seen him attempt to kill a werewolf. He was capable of the act against a Luther, but not against humans.

And even if he was, Murphy was Herc's best chance of finding me again. Yet he'd never shown up on our doorstep. Herc never found out where Mum and I were.

If his plans were to find me, why kill Murphy *before* getting information?

Nope.

The Frey's need to blame someone was understandable, but I didn't swallow that Herc killed Murphy.

"Yes," Pascal answered. "Always. It's effective."

She alone knew what really happened that day.

People had a sad habit of dying before answering my questions, but I had to handle this matter delicately. She was our marshal and part of the head team. Pascal held power in our tribe.

Being new around here, I couldn't risk alienating her.

"If it ain't broke, don't fix it." I hummed. That was exactly the mentality that nearly lost us Sandstone. When one side held a grid for decades, they got lax. Sascha included.

I could figure this out. I just had to think outside the box and do some digging on how the Luthers were communicating.

Boom.

The final cannon blasted through the sky.

"Can't say I'm sorry that's over." I blew out a breath.

She arched a brow. "Not the greatest morale booster."

Agreed. Still… "It was important for me to see that." Maybe we could have won Timber and had the choice of grid again, plus the extra income too. That path didn't help us long-term when we had to come up against Water to win.

For most of the last ten years, the two sides had fought nearly exclusively over Timber. Something had to change.

Pascal slipped her tablet into a waterproof sleeve. "I go with the Luther marshal to check the final tally now. I'll meet you back on shore."

I heard the approaching boat. "Okay. See you soon."

Clipping on my binoculars, I zipped my jacket against the slight chill in the air now that summer was leaving the valley. Only the tiniest sliver of the moon was visible in the night sky, and the sight gave me cheer. The wolves would stick to their lands for the next four or five days during the new moon.

Roderick said they were always a bit sluggish the following week. Hopefully they'd be thrown off their game.

Gripping the ladder, I started down, vision buckling and warping.

Note to self: take vertigo meds before Water next time.

I closed my eyes, blocking out the water below, and felt for the next rung.

Bang.

The observation tower shook, and I gasped, my foot slipping from the rung. I clung to the ladder with both hands and scrambled for a foot hold.

Bang!

The tower tilted. I had no chance.

Fingers slipping, I screamed, hurtling for the surface.

Cool water closed over me as I catapulted down. Bubbles erupted, and I twisted to get my bearings. A male Luther appeared before me, and I shouted in surprise, bubbles erupting again.

I relaxed. He couldn't touch me. The game was over.

He'd be penalised.

Kicking for the surface, I was stopped by a grip on my ankle. I glared downward, trying to see the Luther through the low light and flurry of white water.

Lashing out, I tried to swim for air, but his hold was unshakeable.

Not this again.

He couldn't actually intend to drown me. Yet suddenly, the penalty of losing a grid didn't seem like much protection.

I shrieked at a pain in my calf. Blood swirled around my leg and his mouth.

What the fuck?

Did he just bite me?

A familiar tightness squeezed my lungs. Still smirking, the dark-haired werewolf released my leg. Chest burning, I dragged my body upward to the surface, gulping in air when I made it.

Where was the tower?

Body heavy, I spotted the tower behind me. *So far.*

I paddled in that direction.

An engine roared at my back, and a boat circled me.

"Need a hand?" Leroy held the engine out of the water.

I ignored him, staring up into honey eyes. "No."

"How did you fall out of the tower?" Sascha Greyson asked, jaw clenched.

How was he *dry?*

"Someone shook it. I suggest you ask your pack." I choked on a mouthful of water.

Sascha stilled. "You're exhausted. Here."

He extended his hand, and I shoved it away.

Was the tower getting closer or farther away?

I yelped, dragged bodily from the water by a grip on the back of my shirt. Sascha deposited me in the bottom of the boat.

Mustering my strength, I tried to sit. Leroy, of course, chose that moment to put the propeller back in the water. Huffing, I sagged against the wall of the boat, refusing to return Sascha's intense perusal.

I peeked at the shore, groaning at the stewards lining it, all of them facing this way.

For fuck's sake.

Sascha crouched before me. "You said the tower was shaken."

I didn't answer because my heart was thundering.

A wolf just bit me.

On purpose.

What did that mean? I had to find out. And until then, I couldn't make a big deal about a Luther attacking me.

Questions would be asked.

Fuck! Were Luthers born or made? I seriously hoped werewolf movies weren't accurate on the bite front.

I thumped my head against the rubber side of the boat.

Leroy guided the craft alongside the pier, but Sascha didn't move from his crouch.

"You're terrified." He searched my expression.

I pulled myself to sitting. "Well, I'm in your company, aren't I?"

Leroy growled low, quietening at a sharp look from his leader.

With the grace of a cat, Sascha cradled me in his arms. I crossed my arms as he stepped up onto the pier.

Wade was the first to reach us.

"I'll take her from here, Luther," he said coolly.

Sascha froze, sniffing. "You're bleeding."

"You're hurt?" Wade took me in his arms. "I saw you fall."

"It's nothing," I said, feeling the exact moment Sascha smelt the *lie.* I was too close to miss his sudden tension. "The ladder caught my leg as I fell."

Rhona ran up. "What happened?"

"The tower was shaken. Someone wanted to throw me off." I avoided Sascha's gaze.

She spun on the Luther.

"I didn't see them." I cut her off.

Lie.

"Only one species here is strong enough to shake that tower," she snarled at Sascha.

My leg ached, and I couldn't risk anyone here seeing the wound. "I have no proof, Rhona. A penalty would be disallowed. But a penalty for you attacking their leader in plain sight would not go unpunished."

She cocked her head, slanting me a glance.

I looked at him then.

His body almost vibrated with the force of his anger. *Yep,* he smelt the lie, alright. Wade tightened his grip on me.

I wasn't the only one noticing his reaction.

"Thank you for bringing the boat over," I said. "Congratulations on the win."

Sascha's gaze darted to my leg and back. His fingers twitched at his side. "We both know you didn't intend to win that round, Miss

Thana. You won't find me a relaxed opponent despite your recent introduction to Victratum. I respect your cunning too much."

With a short bow, the werewolf returned to the boat. Rhona stared after him, fixing me with a curious look.

"Let's go," I muttered.

Wade carried me down the pier.

"Get everyone dispersed, please, Rhona." I sighed. "There was an attack on me, but we have no proof." That would fire everyone up. "They did well today, and the Luthers should fear the next time we meet them in Water."

Let's hope I could live up to that promise.

Or just live in general.

🐾🐾

"How's the wound?" Rhona asked, striding into the office.

I tensed at the mention of my injury. The wound had the appearance of a cut at least—the Luther's teeth must be razor sharp. I'd told everyone the metal of the ladder caught me on the fall.

I shrugged. "Fine. Bruising is turning yellow, and everything is scabbed over."

Thank fuck. The tribe's history only mentioned a werewolf's volatileness at the new moon. Two days into that lunar phase and I'd felt nothing at all.

No sideburns or extra hair.

No fangs.

No growl in my voice.

Only one thing wouldn't let me relax—the Luther's smirk. What was he so happy about? Scaring me? I wished I'd got a clear look at the bastard.

Rhona plonked into the seat opposite. "Got a moment?"

No. I was calling our main importers today to introduce myself and pass on the news of Herc's death. After that, I had an hour of study and a meeting with the head team.

I placed the importer's contact file aside. "Of course."

She frowned at her hands. "I was already on shore when the tower began to shake and tilt. Most of us saw you fall. Sascha Greyson was onshore too. He and the blonde ran for a boat when you screamed."

She fell silent, and I waited.

Nothing more came. "And?"

"Like *sprinted*."

I blinked. "I don't understand."

Oh, but I did. *Damn it,* Sascha.

Rhona fixed me with a serious look. "When the boat came back, he cradled you in his arms like some precious treasure. He wouldn't stop looking at you. And he *respects your cunning.*"

Okay. *Shit.* I could not risk Rhona growing suspicious. "I thought he was close by at the time. You think he was in on what happened?"

Her brows climbed. "No. Well, we shouldn't discount that risk, but no. I think the pack leader *wants* you. Like, is completely besotted with you. I don't know how I didn't see it before. He's obsessed."

I blanched. *Fuck.* "You're kidding me?"

She kicked her boots up on the desk. "Think about it. We always thought he was gunning for you because you infiltrated The Dens and he couldn't act outside of the game to get back at you. What if that wasn't the case?"

"I—"

"We could use this against him, Andie."

Exhaling quietly, I shook my head. "I don't know how we'd go about that."

"Tie you up as a sacrifice."

I snorted.

"Just a fake one, obviously. You could wear a white dress that gapes at the front. And you'd need to scream. It'll be like *King Kong*, minus the gorilla and plus a werewolf."

Laughing to cover my pounding heart, I leaned forward. She

was far too close to the truth. If she wanted to use me as a weapon, then Rhona would expect me to bring this to the head team's attention.

The theory would then spread to the entire tribe. That was a lot of scrutiny on an area that I couldn't afford questions.

I had to contain this.

Rhona pursed her lips. "You don't think it's a good idea?"

More lies. "We can use it. I think there could be something to your theory. My worry is that the tribe could easily misunderstand the matter. I've just become head steward, and that information could make them view me in a negative light."

"Right. I didn't think about that. You think we only tell the head team?"

"I think that we keep it between us for now. Let's brainstorm a way to use me to gaping-white-dress effect and take our plan to the head team then."

"We only have two grids right now. Shouldn't we throw everything we have at the Luthers?"

"Believe me, I intend to. What do you think they'll choose today?"

"They beat us in Sandstone last time, so that's my guess. Don't see why they wouldn't."

Unless we revolutionised our strategy in Sandstone, the grid would belong to the Luthers in a week, so if I were Sascha, Iron would be my pick.

Win the harder grid, finish on the easier battlefield.

Plus, Iron was the *Ni Tiaki*'s main source of income. Without that money, collecting gear for Water would be nearly impossible. We were already down 25 percent with the loss of Timber a while back.

Stretching, I yawned. "I'm going with Iron."

"Read any of the journals yet?" she asked.

"Just started last night. More of Mum being in love with Murphy. Can't say I'm enjoying it."

Once, I'd raced to devour Mum's journals. Now, reading them

was another chore—and one that made me feel so horrible. But I couldn't not read the journals either. Aside from Pascal, they were my only clue to the past.

Rhona closed her eyes. "I'm so angry at them. Mum and Dad."

She'd known her real parents, and perhaps that made their betrayal harder to stomach. Herc and Savannah never let her down in life—not until the end. My mother regularly let me down in life and this last lie was just the straw on the camel's back. "You have every right to be angry. You were old enough to hear the truth."

"Do you think after Mum's death, Dad didn't want to hurt me more or something?"

"I believe that was a factor. Maybe he didn't know how to tell us too. Whether that had to do with his fear of the fallout or him trying to find the right time, we won't ever know."

A tear slipped over her cheek. "I hate him so much sometimes. I feel like you're handling it so much better than me."

I smiled. "Don't believe what you see on TV, sis."

Rhona eyed me. "Right. Dad was good at hiding emotions too."

"What are you doing today?" Probably best if we didn't linger on that subject either.

"I took your advice," she said. "I'm working with Gerry and taking over some of the dawn trainings."

Once Gerry retired, I'd look after the strategy and Rhona would look after the execution of those strategies. Playing to our strengths made sense, and this job gave her responsibility. "Good. You'll be great at it."

"People are too afraid of me to mention if I'm bad. Anyway, I'll let you get back to ruling the world." She winked, leaving the office.

I scrubbed at my face. "Fuck."

That was too close.

Rhona wasn't the only smart steward around. If she thought the exchange with Sascha was weird, others could think the same.

Picking up my phone, I unblocked the number from the other day and dialled.

One ring.

"Andie."

I shivered at his smooth voice, hating myself for the reaction. "I thought you might be interested to know that your behaviour at the lake was noticed and commented upon. I don't care if I'm dying, drowning, or being mauled, *do not* pull that shit again."

His reply was immediate. "Impossible."

"This is the part where you make up some Luther bullshit to justify ruining my life, right?"

"I can't *not* protect you from life-threatening situations. We are an instinctual race, and in some situations, our wolves take the lead."

Greyson.

I rolled my eyes. "There's a new one. Now you're saying you *had* to kill Herc. It just happened. Give me a break, Sascha."

"My life is also tied to yours, as you know."

"So you say."

"If a male dies, his female mate must live on to care for any young she has birthed. If a female dies, nature deems the male's existence unnecessary as he will not sire more children.

Oh, brother.

"You always know what to say to turn me on," I quipped before hanging up.

His number flashed again, and I declined the call.

A message came through.

Remember.
I will make everything alright again.

Delete and block.

He was pretty fast at texting though. Couldn't deny that.

Turning to the list of importers, I dialled the top name. Something about it seemed vaguely familiar. *Le Spyre.*

Kind of fancy.

"Hello, you're speaking with Evie."

I double-checked the name. "Sorry, must be a wrong number. I'm looking for Basilia Le Spyre."

"I'm one of her secretaries."

One of. "Right. Is she around?"

"Mrs Le Spyre is a very busy woman. Can I ask what this call is in regard to?"

"I wanted to introduce myself as the new CEO of Deception Valley Exports. My father recently passed."

There was a pause. "Please hold."

The line was answered a second later. "Yello, this is Mrs Le Spyre."

"Uh, yello. I'm Andie Thana, the—"

"Yeah, I heard. Nice to meet you and all that."

How did she hear? This lady sounded young. My age, maybe a little older. "The same to you. I wanted to touch base and let you know that my father recently passed. I've taken over the CEO role of our export companies."

"My sympathies. And empathies. A similar thing happened to me not long ago."

This lady was eccentric, no doubt about it, but her words were heartfelt. "My sympathies and empathies back to you, Mrs Le Spyre."

"Real talk time. My mate says your family is at war with werewolves. True or false?"

My heart hammered. "What?"

"Oh, don't worry. I know about all the supernatural stuff."

She *did*?

Something else stole my attention though. "Did you say *mate*?"

"Kyros is a vampire. I am too. One week old."

What. The. Fuck.

Vampires exist?

My body chilled. I mean, I knew other stuff had to be out there, but this woman was from Bluff City.

Five hours away.

"So," she drew out in the silence. "Vampires—Vissimo—are

kind of territorial. And a little elitist. They're a bit snobby about discussing other races. What's the go with werewolves?"

Swallowing hard, my mind rushed for an out. For all I knew, she was recording this conversation. "You'll need to excuse me, Mrs Le Spyre. I only found out recently."

That was vague enough. I hoped.

Her voice lowered. "You didn't know?"

"Nope."

"And you grew up in the valley? That's bullshit. Been there, done that. Hated it. All I can say is that things do get better. If you need to talk, well, I actually am really busy and super rich, but leave a message with Evie and she'll pop a call through when I'm free."

Weirdly, my chest loosened at her offer.

She wasn't a steward. Was that it? I had so many secrets at this point and something to hide from everyone. Even Rhona and Wade. Talking about my troubles to an unbiased ear—someone who'd mated with a supernatural creature—would be incredible. "Thank you. That means a lot. Really. And if you have any business questions, don't hesitate to call. I'm busy, but not super rich, so leave a message and I'll pop a call through myself."

The woman laughed. "I like you. Gotta go, *Truth Ranges* time."

Billionaires watched that crap? The line beeped. I grinned. *Did she hang up?*

She did.

I liked her too.

The door burst open.

I sagged. "Christ, Wade."

He kicked the door shut. "Hey, baby girl. Busy?"

"Only extremely. Hey, do you know the name Le Spyre?"

"Basilia Le Spyre is the seventh richest person in the world. Like, crazy powerful. I want to use the word camp, but I'm not so sure I understand what it means."

Did you know she's a vampire? "Do you know other supernatural races exist?"

"Yeah. Vampires rule Bluff City. Big war there for a long time. Apparently, it just came to an end."

So casual. "Any other creatures I should know about?"

"Like, locally? Demons to the north, some say. There were rumours of a witch's coven out south at one point."

My ears rang. "What else exists?"

"I wouldn't rule out anything in books. I mean, you've seen what the Luthers can do. Best to just throw the rules out the window. On to more interesting things."

"I find this subject pretty interesting."

"When were you going to tell me that Sascha Greyson was the one to leave the record player in your room?"

My ears buzzed. "He didn't."

"You're a liar. And he did. Which is scary for a whole lot of reasons. Chiefly, that he snuck into the manor undetected. Wait, did he build the pillow wall between us?" he gasped. "He *did.*"

I stood. "Wade."

"Scandal sandals. How long have you known and—"

"*Wade,*" I snapped.

The six-foot-five male squeaked and plonked in the chair.

I rounded the desk and perched there as I contemplated him. *Mothershitter.* Basilia Le Spyre just gave me a taste of what it would be like to unburden myself. Wade knew too much already, and I could lie. I *could* lie to him like everyone else.

I was so deathly sick of the lies.

Sick of falling for them. Sick of treating others that way.

Maybe this would help.

Wade's face was serious. "As someone who told this very isolated and old-fashioned population that he was bisexual, you can be certain I'll never, *ever* judge you."

The last of my fear fled.

I pulled the other chair closer and grabbed his hands. "I've kept this a secret for so long. I didn't know what was happening at first, and then I thought everyone would misunderstand."

I closed my eyes. "Sascha Greyson believes I'm his mate."

I stole a peek.

Wade's jaw dropped, but my throat was uncorked. There was no stemming the verbal tide.

"He's driven to complete a series of interactions with me that he calls *meets.* The end result is that I either choose or don't choose him as a mate. For breeding purposes. For all time."

Wade blinked once. *Twice.* "What's a mate?"

"A one and only kind of arrangement. Like Jacob *Twilight* shit."

"Right. That's... permanent. Why the record player?"

I clenched my teeth. "He had to stalk me for the last meet. Learn everything about me. And then capture me."

He dragged in a shaking breath. "Have you... Has anything happened between you?"

"Nothing much, and that was before I knew werewolves existed." My cheeks burned and Wade searched my gaze.

The details would remain my dark secret.

"I guess I should ask if you return his feelings?" Wade said carefully.

"No," I spat. "He's a monster."

"Okay, we have that at least. I'm not gonna lie, there's being bisexual, then there's being in love with a Luther. There are some things the Ni Tiaki won't accept."

"Believe me, I know. When I found out about werewolves and the meets, I tried to stop them, but things don't work that way, so I'm told. Sascha and I must go through each of the meets so I can deny his ass at the end."

Wade freed his hands, running them through his blond hair. "First off, you need to know everything will be okay. I'm going to help you. Is there a reason you haven't told anyone the truth?"

How much could I say?

Fuck it. I was in this far. "Herc is dead because he interfered with the capture meet." I bowed my head. "I should have told Herc before Sandstone. I knew what Sascha might try in the grid, but I was so ashamed, Wade. I'd just found my family here, and I didn't want them to hate me. Herc is dead because of me."

Wade tugged me forward, and I pressed my face against his shoulder.

"You shouldn't shoulder everything alone," he whispered. "*Shh*, baby girl. I'm here. You're not to blame for any of this, I swear. You came to this valley knowing nothing about their kind. Sascha Greyson took advantage of you from day one, don't you see? There's nothing to be ashamed about. How were you to know what he was? Our tribe can't spout on about how much they hate the Luthers and then expect you to come running to them with this. Herc would have understood."

But he hadn't. What I'd done disgusted Herc through and through.

I sniffed hard. "Rhona doesn't know."

"And that was a hard decision you had to make for the good of the tribe, I'd expect. She's not known for her reasoning ability."

"Was it the right decision?"

He didn't pause. "As long as it remains a secret, yes. She's pepper, remember? You don't want to get that shit in your eyes. Seasoning only."

We were back to pepper analogies. "So after Water, Rhona has decided Sascha is besotted with me and that we should use the weakness against him in Grids. I convinced her not to share her theory with anyone."

Wade swore under his breath. "What's our plan? You need to remain our fearless and smart leader. That's imperative. It sounds like we need to get rid of these meets."

Dammit. "That's what Sascha said."

"When?"

Ugh.

I pulled away. "When he cornered me in the riverside apartment on Tuesday."

Wade paled. "I'd be shaking in my fucking Doc Martins. That bitchhole is scary as shit."

And dangerous as shit.

"What do the meets involve?" he asked.

"There's one teensy problem with that."

"Problems," Wade blurted. "I love problems. They're my favourite."

"Sarcasm is the lowest form of wit."

"Puns should be lower, in my peasant opinion."

I sat back. "The *problem* is that it's not normal for a wolf and human to mate. This is a first for the pack, from what I understand. Because I'm not a wolf, we haven't completed the meet that usually comes first."

"What happens in that one?"

"We sniff each other. Essentially."

Wade's brows shot up. "That's pretty strange. Butts or anywhere?"

"Anywhere, I sincerely hope."

"Are your senses too weak or something?"

I groaned, dropping my head into my hands. "Yes. Wade, what if there's not a way out of this mess?"

He squeezed my shoulder. "We'll figure this out, Andie. I'm going to discover what I can. You have enough on your plate. So, let's keep this between us at all costs. I may love this family, but they have a limit, and I have a feeling butt sniffing a Luther will be it."

6

Pascal slid a document across the table. “Please note an official letter from the Luthers. A request that future meetings occur face to face.”

I clenched my jaw. *Sascha, you mothershitter.*

Nathan sneered. “They must be joking.”

The marshal looked at him. “Do they usually?”

He wisely remained silent.

“Where would the meetings occur?” I asked.

“They’d alternate between the manor and pack lands.”

Taking the letter, I skimmed over the contents, lingering on the scrawled signature at the bottom. *Sascha Alarick Greyson.*

Aka Bastard.

The head team exploded into furious debate.

When they paused for breath, I cut in. “The pack leader has invited us to their lands tonight to hear the grid announcement.”

Roderick jumped in. “This is our chance to learn more about them.”

Valerie snapped, “Fat lot of good learning will do if they decide to kill the head team and our new head steward. Then there’s the recent new moon to consider.”

"Their proposal is a first. We shouldn't be so hasty to shut the door," Trixie added.

There was no situation where me entering pack lands was a good idea. This was clearly a design to get me close. How could Sascha complete the meets when I barely left the manor?

He was drawing me out.

If I only had personal considerations to make, the choice would be easy.

Except this wasn't just my life, it was the battle of generations of the *Ni Tiaki* and all who'd fought before me. I couldn't make this decision for selfish reasons.

What would I decide if the meets and mating bullshit were removed from the equation?

Dammit.

"We no longer have an insider at The Dens," I said, cutting off Nathan—my least favourite head team member.

"I hardly think the Luthers will show us everything we want to know while we're there," Stanley said gruffly.

He was mostly bark and little bite, but I valued his input. "And they didn't intend to show me anything at The Dens, and yet they did. It's about opportunity. If we're not on pack lands, we'll never learn anything. The wolves are communicating in Water somehow. We need to know how they're doing that or we'll never win the grid."

"The reverse is true though," Pascal said. "They'll enter the manor and have opportunity to glimpse our operations. With their senses, they'll have a larger advantage."

"Nothing frequency generators can't fix," Roderick said. "They come in the front door and straight to this room, then leave. No chance to see or smell anything they shouldn't. We'll get those on cleaning roster to douse the manor in wolfsbane ahead of their visit."

I eyed him. "You think there's value in this?"

Roderick pressed his lips together. "Yourself aside, no steward has entered pack lands in fifty-seven years. By understanding the wolves, we can *beat* them. And, if nothing else, that understanding can only improve relations between the two sides."

"Peace has always failed." Trixie blew out a breath.

Discussion exploded again, and I resisted the urge to rub my temples. I may not have a Luther's nose, but I suspected fear fuelled the counterarguments. The rest was long-held grudge.

"We can't beat the Luthers by doing what we've always done," I said in the next break.

They quietened.

"Sascha Greyson has proved that time and again." I curled my hands to fists. "We have *two* grids in our possession. Now isn't the time to play it safe. In saying that, I'll never gamble with any steward's life. That includes everyone at this table. Pascal, send a reply to the Luthers. Outline that if any harm befalls either head team in the opposition's territory, it will result in immediate loss of Victratum."

I faced the silent members, noting three sullen faces amongst the eight. "A small opportunity is better than none at all. Nathan, Valerie, and Stanley, do you have further comments to add?"

Stanley shrugged. "I don't agree, but I can see your argument. Things changed when Herc took the wheel, and it was always going to be the same with you."

The other two were pissed, but whatever, I wasn't here to make them happy. "Dismissed. We depart for pack lands in an hour."

I lifted my head as the stewards filed out. "Pascal. Could I have a word, please?"

She stepped aside, allowing Trixie to pass.

I waited for the last of them to leave and closed the door.

"Am I in trouble?" Her lips curved.

That was the thing with her. I'd never have guessed this woman kept so many secrets. Pascal held herself with a dignity and confidence that could intimidate, but otherwise, no one would ever look twice at the unassuming older woman.

I smiled. "I was wondering if you could help me with

something. Now things have settled somewhat, I wanted to ask you more about what Herc said when he changed the will."

And what happened to Murphy.

Her expression remained mild. "I was as shocked as the two of you. He asked me to keep the matter confidential and said he planned to tell you both before the will came into effect."

I'd have to tell Rhona that. "He never said why he suddenly decided to change his will and reveal everything? He could've left things as they were with no one the wiser."

Pascal regarded me. "I can't speak for your father, Andie. To a lot of us, it became abundantly clear, very early on, that you had what it took to lead us. Rhona could be taught to lead in time, if she chose to learn. Not only do you have the intelligence, but whatever you've faced in life before coming here provided you with resilience, objectivity, and compassion."

That comment would crush Rhona. "Both of us are very curious about the events that took me from the valley as a baby. I've tried to find out as much as possible about why my... well, why *Ragna* left. No one has a clue. I only know that Murphy came back to face some kind of guilt or remorse but died before returning to Queen's Way."

Pascal's face dropped. "A horrible, horrible day."

"The incident?" I sank into the seat beside hers.

"I've never heard someone scream like that. The sound as he hit the ground— I'll never forget the thud."

Chills ran up my spine. "I spoke with the Freys."

The marshal shot me a look. "Their conspiracy theories that Herc had something to do with Murphy's death only made matters worse. Even the best climbers can fall, but maybe it was easier for the Freys to believe Herc had a hand in things rather than admit that maybe their loved one made a mistake while climbing."

"I don't believe Herc killed him. Is there anything else you recall from that day? Anything Murphy said or did that stood out?"

She rested back. "He wouldn't answer any of my questions

about Ragna. I remember that. We all wanted news of her, as you can imagine."

"Herc said the same."

"Murphy didn't trust us for whatever reason. I recall thinking he was no longer a steward. Now, I realise his silence was because they stole you and he wasn't giving up any hint of your whereabouts. So why would Herc do anything to his only hope to find you? More likely, he planned to follow Murphy back to Ragna and yourself. Even the Freys have to admit that now."

My thought exactly.

"I'm reading her last two journals in the hopes of learning more." *Dang,* I'd really hoped she'd know more.

Pascal glanced at me. "Ragna kept journals?"

"Yes, until nineteen—the year she left. I just can't understand how one thousand stewards and their families missed Savannah's first pregnancy."

"Charise and Nicolas had been killed not long prior. Having Thana as a last name wasn't a healthy pastime."

I'd forgotten how soon after my grandparents' deaths this must have happened. "You think they decided to hide the pregnancy to keep me safe?"

"And Savannah safe too. That's my guess. She was a tall woman, like yourself. In later months, we received word doctors had diagnosed her with multiple sclerosis. No one thought anything of not seeing her for several months. To my knowledge, only her mother—your other grandmother—stayed with her."

That made sense. "Is Savannah's mother still alive?"

Pascal looked at me sadly. "No, Andie. I'm sorry."

I straightened. "Story of my life. Thank you, Pascal. I appreciate your honesty."

"I'm glad you asked. Secrets like that are a punishment to carry. If there's nothing else, I should communicate your request to the Luthers."

"That's all," I answered, mind already turning to the list of jobs to be done. "If you see Rhona, could you send her in, please?"

There were a few things she should know.

🐾🐾

Last time I entered pack lands, I had a thong for company. I really hoped that didn't come back to bite me on the ass.

"I'm going to protect the shit out of your virtue," Wade said from the passenger seat.

He was here in Rhona's place. If this was an ambush, then the stewards would still have a leader. "Stop saying virtue. But yes. That would be ideal."

The other head team members followed in one of the manor vans. I'd opted to bring Ella F instead of the silver Bentley.

Grim stepped from the tree line when we entered pack territory. I waved to him before thinking better of it.

He waved back, standing clear so our convoy could continue.

"Who's that hunk of meat?" Wade asked.

"Grim. Gamma wolf."

"What does that mean?"

I lifted a shoulder. "Smart. Bit unusual. Always seems slightly angry. Nice enough."

In the rear-view mirror, I caught Grim's smile. *Yeah*, I didn't have a frequency generator in Ella F.

Wade peered around in interest as we passed by the harvest fields. "Do I get a Guardian of the Vagina badge for doing this?"

Gripping the wheel, I didn't answer. Because honestly? He might earn one. My stomach was doing a progressively intense aerial workout the closer I got to Sascha.

Wade looked at me. "You'll be okay."

"They can hear us."

"Don't give a fuck."

I grinned, and he winked.

Taking a breath, I nodded. My Girl Guide sash was beyond full of badges. I could handle this. "Hey, were you a scout?"

"Sure was."

"Many badges?"

"I could wear my sash either side up and it was still full. I'll leave it at that."

We had this in the bag.

Get in. Listen to the announcement. Leave. No sex.

Wade made an appreciative noise. "Kind of pretty though, huh? All the bungalows."

I could agree with that. Pack lands looked like one big nature retreat.

Hairy was waiting outside the largest bungalow. One I'd entered previously in a thong.

I parked out front, tugging my cream cable-knit sweater down over black jeans. High-heel boots completed the non-descript outfit.

"Andie," the Luther said, catching himself when he started to bow.

I arched a brow at the slip. "Hairy."

"How are things with you?"

Fucking sarcastic werewolves. "Just peachy. We in here today?" I didn't need his confirmation. I could just *feel* Sascha was inside. Shit. That was concerning on a whole new level. I hadn't felt him until now.

Hairy smiled, displaying far too much tooth. "Sure are, sweetheart."

"That's Head Steward to you." Wade rounded the car.

Whoa, angry Wade. Didn't know that version of him existed.

"Guardian of the Vagina." Hairy *did* bow then. "What an honour."

Knew they were listening.

The two men were at eye level, and Wade wasn't backing down.

I glanced back as Roderick, Trixie, and the others left the safety of the van.

"Let's get this over with." I stepped around Hairy to lead the way.

The communal building had considerably less Luthers in it this time around. *Huh,* I'd been in here twice, actually. I didn't see the kitchen at the back during my thong visit, but I woke here after drowning.

The building was more of a hall—made of hand-cut logs. Thick rugs covered the floor.

At the far end, two rows of chairs faced each other. Those farthest from me were occupied by werewolves. I locked eyes with Sascha in his huge antler-decorated throne. Leroy, Mandy, and Lisa were in attendance too.

As I took the seat facing Sascha, Hairy filed past to sit in one of the two empty chairs.

Wade sat on my right, and the others took their usual seats, Stanley occupying the seat on my left.

"Thank you for agreeing to hold our meetings face to face, Head Steward," *he* said.

Why did his voice make everything better?

Scrap that, I knew why. But why did it *have* to?

What had I fucking done that I couldn't just hate him in peace? Why had the world tied us together in such a way when nothing could ever come of it? When I despised him?

It was torture.

I rested my hands on the armrests of the tall-backed chair. Only my chair and Sascha's were different from the rest.

His honey eyes didn't leave mine.

"Why doesn't my chair have antlers?" I enjoyed Wade's muffled snort.

The werewolf tilted his head ever so slightly. "I'll rectify that at the next meeting, Head Steward."

"We're here for the grid announcement." I shifted my eyes to his company in the hopes he'd do the same. The head team was made up of the most capable minds the *Ni Tiaki* had to offer. If Sascha wasn't careful, he'd fuck things up.

Again.

He stood, extending to his full height. "I'd like to officially welcome all representatives of the Ni Tiaki to pack lands. This is a momentous occasion, and—I hope—a step in the right direction. For myself, with my recent actions in Sandstone, I appreciate your willingness to accept change between our two teams."

A pretty speech. And a casual murder mention. I didn't need to look at Nathan and Valerie to know how they'd take it. Valerie nursed a serious sweet spot for Herc before his death. She took things extra hard. Nathan was Herc's best friend from what I'd pieced together.

I tilted my chin. "Our reasons for agreeing to meet are our own. Don't take our presence to mean your actions in Sandstone are forgotten."

Mandy snarled, her fangs lengthening. "Oh, none of us have forgotten what happened, Andie. Don't worry about that."

Sascha didn't look at her, but his low growl filled the room.

Mandy lost her glare.

"I apologise," he said. "As you know, it's harder for us to control our wolves at this time."

"An interesting time to invite the opposite team to your territory then," Stanley said.

"The game goes on. We are well accustomed to doing the same, no matter what our wolves may prefer."

Sascha sat—still the largest being in the room. "Let it be known that the Luthers select Iron for the next round of Victratum."

Knew it. This was ideal for us. We'd win, and I'd reclaim Timber after to get our full revenue back. That would help fund my ideas for Water and Clay.

"We'll see you there," I said, standing.

"A moment." Sascha's order boomed through the room, belying his quiet tone. "I wish to confer with you about the incident in Water."

My heart beat faster, and no one from the other side missed it. "Don't worry, Luther, we can't prove anything. You got away with this one."

His gaze was solemn. "I don't wish to *get away* with anything.

What I would like is to find which of my wolves was responsible. With your help."

Sure he did. This guy wanted me for my breeding hips and my breeding hips alone. "Ask your questions then."

"Would you do me the honour of discussing the matter in private? Leader to leader."

No. "Whatever you say to me can be said in front of my team."

"I thought they could take the chance to look around pack lands."

Oh, you clever son of a bitch.

I felt the immediate tension in my team. *This is what we came for*. "How thoughtful of you."

Roderick cleared his throat. "Given both side's willingness for change, I think we can entertain this additional small request."

Yeah, yeah. They wanted to nose around. Sascha wouldn't have left a damn Luther manual lying around.

"Very well," I said. "Wade will remain with me."

Suck on that.

I resumed my chair, exchanging a leaden look with Wade as everyone filed out of the bungalow.

Sascha picked up his throne and placed it before me. When he sat, our knees were just a whisper apart.

Wade eyed the proximity. "You know she doesn't want this. You could at least respect her wishes and maintain your distance."

If he was surprised that Wade knew, Sascha made no comment. "It's physically painful to be apart from her at this stage of the meets. Being close when I can allows me to resist the next meet for as long as possible to respect her wishes."

"Touché," my friend said after a beat.

I brushed my hair back. "Did you really want to discuss what happened at the tower or was this another ploy?"

Sascha drawled a smile that called to a heat simmering deep within me. One I hated. "Why not both?" His face grew serious. "You lied to your sister on the pier. You told her you didn't see who the wolf was. You did."

Not the only lie I told that day. "He wasn't wearing an oxygen mask, so I can surmise that he was a Luther. Why?"

"He acted outside pack orders. He attacked my potential mate. That is a grave offence. You are my vulnerability, Andie. My life was tied to yours from the moment we first met. Through you, a wolf could kill me."

I never thought of it that way. Sascha's hold on the pack seemed so infallible. "They want the top job? Surely the pack wouldn't follow someone who did that to you."

"Likely not. There's no honour in such backhand tactics, and a pack must respect its leader first and foremost. It doesn't change that my death would be catastrophic for our pack and our position in Victratum."

It must be so strange to talk like this knowing your entire pack could listen in. The wolf who bit me could be listening too.

I leaned forward. "Then why would someone do it?"

"Because my mate is human."

"Ouchies," Wade said.

"Our kind has long been persecuted by humans," Sascha answered. "Some think Andie is unfit to be my mate. Others believe the match means I am unfit to lead."

I said, "Luthers talk too damn much. But let me try to remember the guy's face."

There were bubbles everywhere that evening. And light was low. Everything happened so fast. I could only recall that damn smirk, really. The flash of his teeth. "He had black hair."

"Nothing else?"

"A smirk I wanted to slap off his face. White teeth."

Sascha rubbed his forehead.

"I know what you're thinking. It would be a lot easier if his teeth were blue."

Wade tossed me a grin, but Sascha just sighed. "We're a dark-furred pack. Aside from a few here and there, most of us have black and brown hair."

Crap.

"Was this a one off? Sascha, is my life in danger?"

Darkness edged into the honey shade. "Until the wolf fulfils his agenda, yes, your life is in danger."

I settled back. If the Luther's agenda was to change me into a werewolf, he'd failed. Did that mean he'd try again soon?

In no version of hell, did I want to become a monster.

"I'd like to station five of my most trusted wolves around the manor."

"Impossible," I quipped without delay.

"You're in danger," Sascha said, jaw clenching.

I didn't look away. "I can't risk the confidentiality of tribe operations just to protect myself. If your life is in danger, I suggest you protect it on this end."

His throat worked. "I'm trying to work with you on a solution. If I cannot do that, my wolf will take matters into his own hands."

"Tell Greyson to fuck off."

Sascha cocked a brow. "Greyson? You've named my wolf?"

"Yeah..." Wade turned to me. "You named his wolf?"

My cheeks burned. "Let's not get distracted."

Dammit, I did believe Sascha was attempting to figure this out. I just didn't want to accept anything from him.

If I didn't take this offer, Greyson would lose the plot and take matters into his own hands—stupid sigma fucker. My options were thin.

"Give me time to figure out another way," I said eventually.

"How long?"

"However long I *need*." I glared at the huge Luther, trying not to linger on the broad expanse of his chest. Mating voodoo.

Wade grabbed my hand. "The remaining meets. Care to fill us in on what to expect?"

But Sascha's gaze fixed on where Wade touched me. His nostrils flared.

Wade stilled—perhaps without realising he'd reacted to the silent charge in the air.

"You're very lucky that your smell doesn't change when you

touch her, boy," Sascha said, darkness nearly blotting out the honey. "Or hers."

Wade took a few seconds to answer. "She doesn't give me a boner, if that's what you mean, and I don't make her nipples hard. Just chimp tits. We've checked. It's a friendship miracle."

Sascha's growl exploded from his chest.

"Wade," I whispered.

He didn't stop. "If you really care for her, you'll be happy Andie has someone to talk to about this bullshit. You have no idea the state I found her in before learning all this. Back off."

I tensed in readiness to become a human shield. Sascha surprised me by blinking and leaning back, honey returning to his vision.

"For that, I thank you," he said stiffly. "The thought of her in pain keeps me up at night."

I wrinkled my nose. *Ugh.* "The meets. What are they?"

"You've changed your mind."

"It doesn't seem like we can get through the meets, Sascha. Part of me doesn't think we should bother. You said this far through the process, distance between us causes you physical pain. Will that get worse?"

"For the record, I wanted to tell you everything after you nearly drowned the first time," he said.

"I wasn't ready to hear it then."

Sascha searched my face, voice lowering, "I know, little bird."

My eyes misted at the aching in his smooth tones. Fucking bond shit. Wade would give me crap over the *little bird* comment later too.

I dragged a hand over my face. "Tell me now."

Sascha's eyes narrowed at the command, but he pulled his throne closer. His knees bordered mine, and I sucked in a breath as we touched.

"What was that?" Wade demanded. "You both relaxed."

Sascha's voice held a floating quality. "At first, scenting each other, eye contact, and touching carries the ability to heal your potential mate."

He blinked several times, fixing on me. "The effect is less in you, Andie, but you can feel some degree of what's happening. After the capture meet, usually a bond would be forged on both ends. We'd always know where the other was."

I stilled. "You don't, do you?"

He pressed his lips together. "I do."

That's how he knew I was at the apartment! "For fuck's sake."

"I'm guessing you didn't receive this gift?"

"Gift is a massive stretch."

"All supernatural creatures refer to powers developed through the mating process as gifts."

Vampires, demons, and witches included? "I knew you were in this building. But it only works at close quarters."

Sascha's chest rose sharply, but his expression didn't alter.

He liked that I could feel where he was. "You said *at first* about the healing stuff. What does that mean?"

"As the meets progress, the individual gifts knit together. Each gift begins to interact with the others. Our senses would become one over time. We could exchange physical strength and call to each other from great distances. If you choose to mate with me, the gifts are greater still. We would be able to see through each other's eyes and mind-speak outside of wolf form."

Mind-speak. I struggled to contain my excitement. "It's not normal for mind-speak to happen outside of wolf form?"

"Not in human form," Sascha said after a beat.

He'd said too much and knew it. *Got ya.* That's how wolves communicated in Water. They were partially shifting. Some of them anyway. Our heat detectors didn't pick that up.

"Is mating a senses thing then?" Wade ticked off his fingers, saying, "Touch, sight, and scent."

Sascha darted him a look before returning his focus to me. "Senses are crucial to our way of life, so those dictate the initial meets, yes. My wolf then controls two of the meets—the capture meet and the biting meet."

My eyes widened. "*Biting* meet? No way."

"It won't turn you into a werewolf," Sascha added.

I almost melted into a puddle on the floor in relief. Their bites didn't do anything. Thank fuck.

"It's a marking thing?" Wade asked. "The Luther version of Andie tattooing your name on her butt?"

The werewolf tightened his grip on the armrests.

"You doing okay there, furry?" I asked, ready to throw myself out of danger's way.

Sascha inhaled. "It's not easy to discuss this while keeping the mating urge at bay."

Oh, brother. I leaned forward, resting my hands on his knees. His exhale of relief was unmissable.

"Is the biting next?" I muttered.

"It's hard to say," he answered. "With the scent meet incomplete, I can't guess the order of the last three."

I stared, and he solemnly gazed back.

Dang, that wasn't a hilarious joke.

"If no one else is gonna ask, I will," Wade said, peering between us. "What's the seventh meet?"

I silently dared Sascha to answer.

"Sex," he said, smirking at me.

Yep, I called it.

Scowling, I snatched my hands back. "I'm not okay with either biting *or* sex. While we're on the subject, how am I meant to deny you if you're literally inside me?"

His throne skidded back. In a blur and snarl, Sascha was across the room, body shaking, his face contorted.

"Maybe the wrong thing to say, baby girl," Wade whispered.

No kidding. But logistically, how was that possible? I had to assume the cleopatra position thing and say the magic words. Not to mention keep my distance. The closer I was to Sascha after a meet, the stronger my reaction.

I circled my temples. "I don't see how this will work. Without the scent meet happening, we continue on at the risk of merely strengthening the bonding crap between us. If we can't complete the meets, our position will then be *worse* off. Or at least for you. Is there any way for us to get around the scent thing?"

His heaving back was to me. Gravel rode his voice. "Only one way is certain. You become a werewolf."

"Werewolves can be made?" I squeaked.

Mothershitter.

He turned, blinking away the black. "Yes, but assuming that's a hard no for you, our other path would be to continue through the meets and hope a strengthening bond will give you whatever's needed to finish the process."

There were a whole lot of maybes and what ifs in that. "Then what? What if we get all the way through?"

"Then you officially accept or deny me in a ceremony held after the seventh meet."

Deny. All the way.

"I need to process this. How long have I got until Greyson makes a move?"

Sascha dragged his gaze over my thighs, lingering on my breasts, before his burning gaze swept over my lips, reaching my eyes.

He looked at my face? *Such* a gentleman.

"I want to claim you. My wolf wants to claim you. We want you for our own."

My chest tightened. "I thought you *didn't* want this mating stuff either."

Sascha studied me. "Forgive me the lie. You have a habit of running when people get too close. You should never make the mistake of thinking I don't want you in all ways, Andie Booker. If it were up to me, you'd be chained to my side already."

7

"*If it were up to me, you'd be chained to my side already,*" Wade said in a deep voice.

I waved to Cameron at the manor gate. "Shut up."

His eyes slid to me. "What's running through your head right meow?"

I gritted my teeth. "It's just impossible, Wade. I want to *not* be squished between two boulders for a change. I can't recall the last time I didn't feel stuck, and it's always other people doing it to me."

Wade opened his mouth, then squeaked as I parked. "Incoming angry Rhona. Three o'clock. You're on your own."

He was out the door in a flash.

I sighed. The guy would face werewolves but not my sister.

Turning to *three o'clock*, I blanched at the sight of Rhona charging down the manor steps.

Maybe I'd take Sascha over her too...

I got out of the car. "Rhona. What happened?"

"*You* happened," she snarled.

My stomach hit the floor. She knew. She'd figured it out. She—

"You took the head team to pack lands and fucking left me behind. What the hell, Andie?"

The head team trickled to join us.

Rhona's cheeks were flushed, and auburn hair flew about her face. "I deserved to be there. I deserve to stare down the piece of shit who killed my father. I can't believe you'd do that without me."

Shoulders heaving, she drew in another breath.

I'd never seen her lose her shit like this. I mean, the *potential* of the storm was always there with Rhona. That's what put people on edge. But this was a new one for me, and it had to be navigated with care.

"I appreciate what you're saying," I told her. "Those are points I considered before making my decision. They were outweighed by the fact that if anything happened to me in pack lands, you'd need to lead the stewards."

"And what? I'd just get the news that you'd been killed like Dad? You didn't even tell me you were going."

Pascal stepped forward. "We received the invitation an hour before leaving. Andie sent me to tell you, but no one knew your whereabouts."

Rhona closed her mouth.

Bet she was somewhere with Foley.

"Now that you're here," I said, feeling the unsettled stirring of the head team around us. This shit did not look good. "The head team will meet the Luthers for the grid announcement each week. You're welcome to sit in on the meetings that occur at the manor."

She burst out, "Why are you meeting them at all? How can you bear to look at them after what they did?"

"I can't lead this tribe by what I can *bear*, Rhona. I have to do what's best for them. Visiting pack lands gives us the opportunity to learn about our opposition."

"And what did you learn this time?" she said sarcastically.

I smiled. "I learned how they're communicating in Water."

The head team turned to me as one like we were in some dramatic stage production.

Roderick's grin was broad. "You did?"

No idea what to do about the information, but that's what

strategy teams were for. "I did. I'd like to discuss the matter immediately. Please gather in the meeting room in twenty minutes."

The head team dispersed, and my shoulders relaxed. I watched as Valerie clasped Rhona's shoulder.

"Is there anything else you'd like to say, Rhona?"

She was still angry. We definitely shared our temper—if not the way we managed it.

"I'm serious," I said. "Get it out now."

Rhona blew out a breath. "Okay, I lost my shit."

"I can see why. It does hurt my feelings that you assumed the worst."

"Bad habit," she muttered. "Maybe I was afraid of losing you and having no control. Like with Mum and Dad."

For Rhona, that took a lot to say.

I took her hands. "If bad things ever happen to me—ever—know that none of it was your fault. You can't take on that burden. Not for anyone. We all have a choice."

She swallowed. "You're the only person I have left."

Tell me about it. I hugged her. "That's why I left you here."

"Next time, I want to come to pack lands."

"I love you."

Her shoulders shook. "That's a no."

"Our people come first. That's what it means to be us."

"I don't always like being a Thana."

"Does anyone like who they are all the time? I sure don't. Can you do me a favour though? If you have an issue with me, talk to me in private, and please don't shout at me. I'll listen to you at normal volume just the same."

Her smile was sheepish. "Sorry."

"So am I. Now, let's go figure out how to fuck shit up in Water."

My phone rang. "You go ahead. It's the realtor." I answered, heart beating fast, "Roy. Hi. What did they say?"

"Andie, how is it? Sorry about the delay. They were on holiday, but I got hold of them last night."

Rhona hadn't budged, and I closed my eyes. "Well?"

"They'll meet you at $412,000 once they've viewed the furnishings. It took some talking, but they're happy to pay a 20 percent deposit upon signing."

I considered that. "I can send you the key for the storage shed. It will take a couple of days to get there. Could you visit the shed with them?"

"Happy to. They have finance preapproval already. The wife is a builder and is satisfied with the condition of the house. We've given them the council report, so with the condition of finance, this deal is looking cut and dried."

I was currently over four thousand dollars short of paying everything off, but that was far more doable than ten times that number. "I'll need the settlement to be as short as possible."

"They need two weeks for the bank to process finance and lawyers to do their thing."

Two weeks would bring me up to five thousand dollars. Just under with their deposit in my bank account. This deal was as good as it got. "I can swing that."

"Great. I'll leave you to get in touch with your lawyer then," Roy said. "Congratulations on selling your house, Andie!"

"Thanks for your help," I said softly. "I realise you've gone above and beyond with this sale." If I could have afforded to give him more, I would. Maybe I'd send him a thank-you card with the key.

"You're welcome. I'll be in touch."

I hung up, unwilling to trust in the excited bubbling in my gut. Until the house went unconditional, I couldn't give hope a voice. Better to believe that everything could fall through tomorrow.

Anything more was an unexpected bonus.

"Someone made an offer?" Rhona asked.

I nodded. "It will nearly cover Mum's gambling debt."

"I thought the sale was meant to cover the whole thing?"

"Yeah, well, interest has accrued in that time. Once Roy's commission is taken out and lawyers are paid, I should only have five thousand left to pay off. I can manage that."

Her expression turned downright murderous.

"It's fine. Really. If this all goes through, I'll have one less problem to worry about."

"You have so much on your plate already," Rhona murmured.

She was angry on my behalf, and that meant the world. I lifted a shoulder. "I'm unsure if I've ever *not* had anything on my plate. Maybe one day. Think of the two of us suntanning on some island after winning Grids."

"We're redheads. We'd burn and peel. But Andie, you know the tribe is here to help you, right? Not just for *you* to help *us*. You'll need a lawyer for the deal. We've got at least seven stewards who are lawyers. And why pay interest on the outstanding amount when you could borrow from the tribe and pay back what's owed?"

I shook my head. "I couldn't do that."

"Because you like to do everything alone?"

My lips twitched. "Ouch."

"It's true."

Wade excluded... *yeah,* okay. Herc pointed that quality out as my weakness almost immediately. "Point taken. Wouldn't that be kind of unethical though?"

"You can't fight a battle on two fronts."

Three fronts, at least. "I'd pay it off as soon as possible. We could have a steward lawyer draw up a contract, so everything is legally binding."

This would save me *so* much money. I could be free of Mum's debt in a matter of months.

Rhona looped an arm around my neck. "Whatever. Do what you gotta do. But we're here for you too."

I kissed her cheek. "Love you, sister-cousin."

She laughed. "Dad-uncles. Aunty-mums. How the fuck did we end up in this shit pile?"

Good question.

We walked up the manor stairs.

"I talked to Pascal before leaving for pack lands," I said low.

"She said Herc intended to tell us the truth before his will ever went into effect."

Rhona missed a step, but quickly recovered. "I *knew* it."

"He didn't mean for you, *either* of us, to find out that way."

"But he still chose you." She frowned.

I shoved down the memory of Pascal's other words. "Maybe he just couldn't stand concealing the truth anymore. Oh, and Pascal wondered if our grandparents' deaths convinced Herc and Savannah to hide the pregnancy. No one saw her for three months and assumed it was to do with her MS diagnosis."

"That's... I mean, I can almost understand that mentality. I want to hide you. I don't want you in the spotlight or for you to be under so much stress. But why not come out with the truth when you were stolen? Or even years later."

I understood the pressure of maintaining image better now. "Because they'd already hidden it for so long. Secrets get like that. You become more scared of the time that's gone by than the secret itself."

"Sometimes you say stuff and I imagine you with a beard and a staff."

"Like Gandalf?"

"Who's Gandalf?"

"That's disgusting. Educate yourself." I paused outside the office. "Hold on, I need to grab my jacket. The meeting room gets cold."

I strode into the office, rounding the desk. I paused at the sight of partly open drawers. "Someone has been in here."

Rhona pushed off the doorframe. "You left them closed?"

"I didn't have a lot of space in my bedroom back in Queen's Way. Unless I closed the drawers all the way, I'd always bang my hip. It's just a habit now, but I'm certain everything was closed. I mean, not that anything in here is secret."

My mouth dried, thinking of the journals. I extracted the key from my pocket and crouched to unlock the locked drawer. I exhaled loudly.

They were still here.

"I don't like that someone was digging around," Rhona said, eyes narrowing. "It's not that they would have found anything. It's that they did it at all. Does someone think you're hiding something?"

If they were smart. "Maybe they knew more of Herc's secrets."

"You think Dad had other secrets?"

No matter what Pascal recollected from the rock-climbing incident, the words Herc exchanged with Murphy were still a mystery. "Doesn't everyone?"

"I'm an open book."

I pulled the journals free. "You're anything but an open book. No one would ever know you have a gooey interior."

"I'm not sure about that."

"I am." I locked the drawer again. Checking the contents of the top drawers, I clutched the journals tight to my chest.

Rhona followed me to the door. "You gonna lock the office door?"

"As long as nothing goes missing, I hope the person finds whatever they're looking for."

I'd check the hall cameras to see who came in. If someone was suspicious of me, I had to know who. "Look. Could you go on ahead to the meeting? I just remembered something."

"Only because I yelled at you and feel remorse."

Watching her leave, I asked for directions to the security office, and let myself in. A woman sat in there who defied the IT stereotype almost entirely. She turned and I caught sight of her *Star Trek* slogan tee. *Well, nearly*.

"Hi, I'm Andie."

"I know. Nice to meet you. I'm Heather. Heather Sullivan."

"Lovely to meet you."

"Ha!"

I jolted, peering behind me. "What's funny?"

"Nothing. Nervous thing. How can I help you?"

Maybe my initial judgement was way off base. "No problem. I'd like to look at the footage outside my office in the last three hours, please."

"You got it, dude." Typing rapidly, she cast me a look. "Remember *Full House*?"

"Uh, no. TV show?"

"Ha!" she barked. "Yep. More of a *Truth Ranges* fan myself."

Hated that show. "Oh, cool. I'm not a big TV person."

"*Well*, someone's frozen eggs just got stolen. Like, *egg* eggs. Only the town serial killer can find them. I really hope he decides to help despite the murder addiction. I want her to have kids, and it's nice to see a bit of redemption now and then, you know?"

She twiddled some intense-looking gear and pointed to a screen in the middle. I could see the entire hall. Herc's office was halfway down.

"I'll set it to triple speed. Let me know if you want me to stop," she said.

"What are the security measures on the manor?" I watched the screen.

"Frequency generators, obvs. Heat detectors. They span the entire north side of the valley, covering all steward homes. There are cameras throughout the manor, and around. Everywhere but the bedrooms and bathrooms—because sex and nakedness. Ha!"

I blinked several times. "Of course. The grounds themselves?"

"Just the perimeter. Same with steward homes. Too expensive to have cameras everywhere. We just enclose our territory. Personally, I think it'd be nice to have audio capabilities on our security, too, but that's another expense. Guess people deserve their privacy, but it would make my job a whole lot more interesting."

Props to Sascha. He got through all that stuff undetected. "It'd be like real-life *Truth Ranges*."

"Ha!" She covered her mouth. "Sorry. Not sure why that happens. People, I think."

I struggled to keep a smile at bay. She had a disarming manner.

On the screen, someone entered Herc's office. "Stop there."

She paused the footage, rewinding a way.

I leaned forward and identified the person. “Oh, that’s no problem,” I lied. “Keep going.”

The footage kept rolling to the end, and I faked interest.

“Sorry you didn’t find whatever you were looking for,” Heather said.

But I did. “That’s okay. I really just wanted to pick your brains on security anyway. If you have any ideas on how to tighten the manor against werewolves, I’d be happy to hear them. We can’t have Luthers sneaking in.”

“It’d be pretty impossible for them to penetrate our defences, but I do have some ideas.”

Mmm-hmm. Impossible.

“Could you speak with Eleanor to arrange a time?”

“Ha!”

I’d take that as a yes. Leaving the security office, I strode away, clutching Ragna’s journals tightly.

Reaching the meeting room, I entered without preamble and sat, setting the leather-bound books on the desk.

She took the bait. Pascal’s eyes went straight to them.

And no wonder.

I’d mentioned Ragna’s journals to her in passing just before the head team left for pack lands. She’d either rushed straight to the office—forgoing the search for Rhona—or raced to search prior to this meeting while I was outside.

She was desperate enough to take the risk of entering despite the cameras in the hall.

I glanced at her, and she met my gaze with the same mild expression the woman always wore.

I smiled before shifting my focus.

Pascal wanted the journals.

Which meant there *had* to be something in them she didn’t want me to know.

8

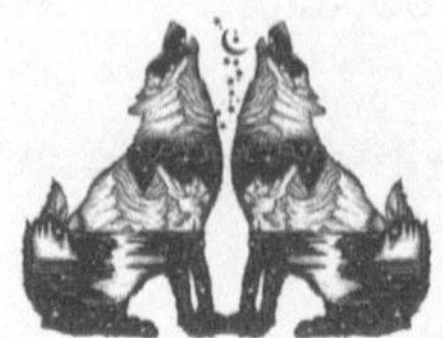

I rubbed my eyes again.

"It's easier than usual to find you unattractive," Wade said.

"Thanks." I sent him a withering glare. "I was up late. Not feeling so great."

I'd finished the *I'm 18* journal and learned not a single thing. The start of *I'm 19* had so far proven to be mostly grief from the loss of Mum's father. I must have fallen asleep in the early morning.

"You need more sleep," Cameron said from his other side. "I can bring you some camomile tea, if you like?"

If I chewed on an entire packet, would it solve my problems? "That'd be great."

Wade nudged Cameron. "Where've you been lately, anyway?" He gasped. "You have a lover."

Snatching her hands, he stared into her eyes. "Forbidden. More real than anything you've ever felt."

Cameron wrenched her hands free. "No lover."

"Whatever. My power is foolproof."

I shoved my hands in my pockets, watching stewards assemble for the Tuesday night rundown. "Gotta say, he was bang on about Logan."

"He's wrong *this* time," Cameron muttered, walking away.

"It isn't easy to carry so much power," Wade said. "I better go schmooze. She's a grudge holder."

I watched him leave, waving at the Freys. There was a never-ending list of stewards to know—Geralds, Ryans, Trenthams, Lees. I had no idea how I'd remember them all. Pretty sure I'd offend several people tonight by not recalling their names.

"You good to go?" Rhona said, joining me.

I'd rather not.

Turned out, while I had no problem playing my saxophone for crowds, talking wasn't the same. I forced my thoughts away from the stupid instrument. "Yeah."

I startled at the harshness of my voice.

"Whoa." She grinned. "Intense. You sick or something?"

I forced a laugh. "Something caught in my throat."

"Just saying though, the name Andie works no matter your gender."

Shoving her, I climbed the stairs.

Channelling Rhona from last week, I tapped the microphone. Things like this were so much easier if I pretended to be her. She didn't take shit from anyone. Squaring my shoulders, I waited for the tribe to quieten.

Last week, Rhona commanded them, pretending to be me.

I could do this.

"Stewards, welcome to our tribal lands. Welcome." Totally borrowed that line. "Thank you for your effort in Water last week. It's never easy to face failure, but I can assure you the next meeting in Water won't end the same. Next week's battle is in Iron, and I've heard this is a particular strength of ours."

The crowd exchanged smiles.

"I look forward to seeing the Luthers retreat, tails between their legs." The harsh darkness returned to my voice. *Jesus*, maybe I'd come down with something. I cleared my throat. "We've always dominated Iron, but the real danger to us in this grid is complacency. Face this grid as you'd face Water. The worst thing we can do is assume a win. I wager that the leader of the Luthers is taking the opportunity with Iron that I took with Water. He wants to seek out our weaknesses. Don't let him find any."

I let the seriousness of my words sink in. Their smug smiles were gone. *Good.* "The strategy teams have outdone themselves in readiness. Soon, Valerie and Nathan will take you through final strategies, and I hope our plan excites you as much as it excites me. Before they do that, I want to take the chance to thank each and every steward for their ongoing effort. Your job, whether in our various businesses, in deliveries or security, or in strategy, is *crucial.* I will never be unaware of that—and I will never be complacent—even if I don't know all your names yet." I slanted them a grin as chuckles arose.

Walking back to Rhona's side, I fixed my outward attention on Valerie and Nathan on the stage.

I couldn't wait for sleep tonight; My eyes felt scratchy. My body ached from holding the damn book up for hours on end. Despite that, I'd read the journals tonight until exhaustion claimed me again.

"You okay?" Rhona whispered.

"Might have to see the doctor."

"It's not the wound, is it?"

I froze.

Oh.

Fuck.

"It could be infected or something," she added.

Sascha said werewolves could be made, but not from biting. I forced myself to breathe. "The wound is pretty much gone now. Just stress, I'm sure."

"You know," she said hesitantly, "if you need me to take on more responsibilities, I'm here for you."

She'd already taken on a huge job. "Honestly, once the debt is gone, that will clear a lot of emotional space for me."

"You spoke to Neve then?"

Neve was a lawyer who'd dealt with a lot of the Thana's legal matters over the years. She drew up the papers for the transfer of funds yesterday. Another lawyer was working on conveyance for the house, so that would save me over a grand. "Yeah, I'll transfer the leftover balance from the manor accounts after house settlement. Not gonna lie, I can't wait to be free of that shit. Thanks for helping me with that."

She pressed her lips together, and I could almost hear the angry outburst about Ragna on her lips, though she swallowed it back.

Even now, I couldn't help feeling a loyalty to the woman who'd raised me.

Even calling her Ragna felt disrespectful.

Calling Herc my father felt like a lie.

But I had a sister. I had to remember that.

Valerie and Nathan finished, and I listened to the energetic murmur rising from the stewards. *Perfect.* I didn't want to dampen their spirit with the *don't be complacent* speech, but arrogance was a certain way to lose a grid in my amateur opinion.

Now, there was an edge in the air that told me they were ready to bring their A-game.

Wade approached with a middle-aged woman on his arm. "Andie, have you met Harlow Greene? Let me introduce the two of you."

Switching on my *head steward* smile, I shook her hand.

An hour of introductions passed before I managed to escape to my room. I dragged the last journal from beneath the tallboy. After Pascal's office search, I didn't want to take any chances.

There *had* to be something in here.

Changing into my threadbare pyjamas, I ducked under the covers, adjusting the bedside lamp to shine on the page.

"Child-Ragna, give me something solid, please. People around here be lying."

I see my friends together, but it's just nothing like what I feel for Murphy. It's like we're one.

"Oh, brother." Flicking through ten pages of loved-up teen life, the details of their latest sexapades, and Grandmother Charise's death, I slowed at another passage.

> *Mother and father are gone, and Herc is so busy now. He's so short-tempered, and I'm trying to be the person he needs me to be, but I feel so alone. If Murphy left, I couldn't go on. What are we even doing playing this game? What's the point when everyone I love dies? One person holds my happiness in his hands. And that's so terrifying that sometimes I can't speak.*

I paused at two frantically written words on the next page.

Murphy's sick.

Sitting straighter, I scratched at my aching calf.

> *He came down with it last week and it's getting worse. I'm so angry he concealed this! He knows I can't live without him, but—of course—he didn't want me to worry. He's aching all over and has a sore throat. He's downplaying how bad things are, but my Murphy is always cheerful. Now, he looks so tired. If he doesn't get better tomorrow, I'll call the doctor.*

An overreaction for the flu, but she'd been clear on what Murphy meant to her. Margaret Frey wondered if Ragna never forgave Murphy for dying and leaving her alone. It seemed strange at the time, but more and more, I believed the theory could hold weight.

But what about me?

Savannah had to be heavily pregnant with me right now, but there hadn't been any mention of her in the journal. They really did hide me from everyone. Did that speak for the lack of trust between Herc and Ragna, or the lack of trust between Savannah and Ragna? Savannah was only mentioned in the fondest terms in the journals, so if so, the problem was one-sided.

My heart stopped at the next passage.

> *Murphy lied to me. He knows why he's sick.*
> *We can't see a doctor.*
> *No one can know.*

I turned the journal toward the light to better see, but the three following pages were a mess of emotional ramblings and no specifics. "Come on, Child-Ragna. Give me something." My urge to figure this out passed healthy curiosity weeks ago.

I had to understand.

I was *desperate* to understand.

> *Herc and Savannah can't know.*
> *Especially with the baby due next week. They'd never see our side.*

"You *did* know about the pregnancy," I murmured.

I'd never felt less like sleep as I focused on her words. "Come on. Tell me what happened."

Even after everything. This was still about her.

Still about me missing her.

The light illuminated four words.

I read each of them, heart hammering. And I knew the words were now burned into my mind forever.

Tears had blurred the ink on the page twenty-one years ago. I traced the uneven, smeared words with a shaking hand, *feeling* her dire hopelessness through the coarse page.

Murphy's becoming a Luther.

"Andie?"

I peered over the readying mass of stewards. They'd dressed in a dusty red that would allow them to camouflage against the iron ore. Protective vests and helmets on, we otherwise tried to keep bulky equipment to a minimum in this grid.

The bottom of the circular quarry was a lake. And this was to our massive advantage. The grid entry point was into the water. From the lake base, tiers rose up steep and fast for one hundred and fifty metres like an amphitheatre for giants. The result was a vertical height nearly three times the height of sandstone.

The Luthers had never taken Iron from us.

I couldn't lose this grid today, or I'd lose standing with the stewards in a big way.

"Andie?"

Focus. That's what I had to do.

But how could I after what I read last night?

> *He was bitten in Timber two weeks ago. By one of them. At first, he didn't think anything of it, especially when the new moon came and went. But last week, he started to feel different.*

An aching body. Changes in his voice. Fatigue.

Panic cloyed my throat.

> *I didn't say anything, but sometimes, if I mention telling others, he gets angry and his eyes go dark.*

I'd read her mounting terror as Murphy displayed more and more signs of an imminent shift. Anger. Outbursts. Growls and snarls.

The last entry helped me figure out much of the rest.

> *We're leaving. We can't tell a soul. Herc won't understand. He'll cast us out.*

The Luthers hate my family. No one will help us. We need to go.
Murphy is leaving on a delivery tomorrow. I'll leave the day after while Herc's in meetings. Nothing could part me from this valley but Murphy.
I'll hide these journals with the hope that one day we'll return to our home. One day, when the game is over.
Brother. Savannah. And my little niece, Andie.
I love you all so much.
I fear you all so much.
My heart is breaking.
Goodbye.

She'd said goodbye to me, so she didn't intend to steal me at that point. So what changed?

Someone shook my shoulder roughly.

Jerking, I looked into Rhona's eyes. "What?"

"Where are you? I've been calling your name."

I'm turning into a Luther. "Sorry, I'm trying to think whether we missed anything."

She scrutinised me. "Did you sleep last night?"

"Maybe?"

Rhona grabbed my arm and pulled me aside. "You need to take better care of yourself."

"I know," I retorted sharply. "I will."

Her brows shot up. "Alright, keep your hair on."

"Sorry, just tired. What can I help you with?"

She released my arm. "Came to tell you that everyone is prepared, and they completed the new manoeuvres without issue."

"Thank you. How's the training going?"

She hummed. "Good. Really good. But it doesn't feel like I'm doing enough."

Gripping her hand, I squeezed. "You're helping more than you know. Keep doing what you're doing."

"It's just—"

"Andie," Wade hollered. "Speech!"

The chant was taken up on the muddy shore of the lake. I sucked in a breath at the assault on my ears.

My *really* sensitive ears.

Tears pricked my eyes. Something was happening to my body. I was becoming something I hated.

The new moon passed. I thought I was safe.

Sascha said biting didn't make werewolves.

Rhona would never forgive me for my part in Herc's death, and the stewards wouldn't trust me if they knew about the mating call with Sascha. But a *werewolf* leader?

I might not understand so much about Ragna's decisions, but I understood why she ran instead of staying.

Hate ran deep. And it would turn on me. Without doubt.

I couldn't even tell Wade.

No one.

Mum always dated her journals, and I spent the hours before dawn figuring out what phase of the moon Murphy was bitten during. *Waning Gibbous.* Just after the full moon. They left before he actually changed. The speck of desperate hope in my heart wanted to believe that meant nothing ever happened.

But then why didn't they return?

No. Murphy changed alright. Then he came back to explain everything to Herc.

And Herc killed him.

I'd reasoned that my *father* wouldn't hurt a human, but I'd seen first-hand he had no qualms about killing Luthers.

I climbed atop a rock with Billy's help.

Eager faces stared up at me. One thousand of them.

I was an imposter.

A fraud.

A letdown.

I had to leave them. And they'd never know why.

From Murphy's timeline, new werewolves didn't shift at the new moon when they had the least power. I felt stupid for missing it.

The *sun* gave Luthers their power.

The full moon would be my last day as a human.

“Stewards,” I said, pitching my voice higher. “Naatira Thana said something on the cusp of a battle in this grid one hundred years ago, and during my readings on tribe history, her words have stuck with me. I say them for you now. *Flow fast water, flow down valleys and roads. Flood everything, but do not pretend that your actions are undertaken with purpose. Yours are the fumbling actions of a beast. Move with intent. Surge forth only with knowledge. Hold strong against the rising tide knowing you forged the path that water can only flow upon.*”

I took a breath. “There’s a reason our strength is Iron. There’s a reason the Luthers’ strength is Water. Tonight, we show them the difference. Move with our intention. Surge forth only with knowledge. We forge the path for another day in thousands as those before you have done. The Luthers can merely flow upon it.”

Did they hear the nerves in my voice?

Why were they silent?

A few shouted “Head stewards” from the back renewed my courage. I raised a fist, unsmiling.

In a wave, a sea of fists raised to the sky. The air thrummed with determination that tore me apart as surely as it made me.

Next week, I’d no longer be one of them.

I stared at the one thousand people who would soon hate me.

Boom.

A well-oiled team, the stewards headed for the murky water. The lake looked border-line dangerous to swim in, but I’d been assured it was impossible to drink enough to take in harmful levels of iron.

The fastest swimmers had to make it to the farthest side. The weaker swimmers were already climbing the nearest tiers. We didn’t use many traps in this grid, but that had to change.

Sascha wouldn’t pull punches, and neither would I.

When Pascal joined me, I resisted the urge to demand answers. Maybe she knew how to cure this. Maybe she could help me.

But if she'd guessed what was in the journals—that was one thing. If she'd *read* the journals, then she was aware of the symptoms displayed by a human changing into a Luther.

She could ruin me if I mis-stepped.

I had to be very, *very* careful.

"Nice evening out," I said cheerfully.

She arched a brow. "Indeed."

Indeed.

9

Unknown number.

Just what I needed. Shouldn't have unblocked him.

"What?" I snarled into the phone.

"Andie," Sascha's voice tipped over me like warm water.

My rage spiralled higher. "To what do I owe this honour?"

"The honour is mine, mate," he replied. "Congratulations on the win."

Yeah. Yeah. We both knew Water and Iron were pretty much assured victories for either side. "Thanks."

He paused, and I hated that part of me just wanted to be with him. Touching him. Kissing him. *Talking* to him.

Simply because I'd feel better for it. I wanted to feel better.

My body was tired.

I was at my wit's end. The galloping approach of the full moon was like a noose around my neck.

"Have you thought any more about the meets?" He said low. "I'm not sure I can keep away from you for much longer."

The words weren't a threat—just truth. If I didn't act, Greyson would.

Yet I couldn't. Not until I figured *something* out.

Leaving town. Surely, I had to leave town. How could I hide this from the tribe, let alone Luthers?

I closed my eyes. "My situation has changed. I can't go through the meets with you."

A leaden silence met my words.

"What changed?" He asked so softly my sensitive ears nearly missed the question.

Some people, like Rhona, got louder when angry. The thing about Sascha... he didn't have a tell. With him, I could throw the dice with very little idea which emotional square they'd land on. He could be murderous, contemplative, or worried right now and he'd *still* speak in that quiet, controlled voice.

Without this mating call, I never would have peeked beyond his mild exterior. Even *with* this crap, I rarely saw him lose his cool. Freaky didn't begin to describe it. "Nothing that concerns you."

"It very much concerns me, Andie."

My ears twinged. Was that an undercurrent of desperation or anger? "This isn't what you wanted to hear, but it's how things have to be. I'd appreciate if you could contain Greyson on your end."

Impossibly, his voice lowered further. "You know Greyson doesn't play by the rules, little bird. You know he'll kill to get to you. If I put my people between you and me, I put them in harm's way. The same for any of your people. What could possibly be more important than preventing further bloodshed between both sides? Tell me what has happened since we last spoke."

He was lecturing me on the lives of others. Fucking rich. "That's my decision. You don't have to like it. Let me say right now that if you attempt to harm any of my stewards, I will kill you myself—whether it breaks me or not."

Sascha sucked in a breath that I'd associate with someone who'd been kicked in the chest.

He swore a moment later. "How did things get this way between us?"

I gripped the top of the tallboy, staring into the mirror. "I met you. That's how."

Blackness crept in on my emerald eyes, and I reeled back.

"Andie?"

Oh my god. I'm a monster. "Got to go."

Breathing hard, I gaped at the stranger in the mirror. *Me.* How could that be me? I tried blinking the darkness away. When that failed, I turned to the black fury inside.

Breathe, Andie.

Watching closely, I deepened my exhales, casting my mind to the forest as I so often escaped to when playing the saxophone.

My heartbeat slowed.

The pounding blood left my cheeks.

Darkness ebbed, leaving misted emerald behind.

A tear slipped over my cheek. What the fuck was I going to do? What if my eyes did this in a meeting?

I had to practice.

Focusing on that unshakeable fury, I let it out again, barring my teeth as black edged in once more.

Drawing my rage in, I forced the shadows away.

I wasn't a Luther yet, but maybe doing this would help me control the effects.

But would my smell change when I shifted? If so, the pack would know immediately.

Maybe if Rhona could take my place in meetings… I could think of some excuse. Sascha and the other Luthers would assume that was me avoiding the mating call.

In the grids, I kept out of the fighting, away from werewolves.

To consider staying was *madness*, but I'd lost so much. I'd fought so hard.

I couldn't give up now.

Becoming a monster didn't mean I had to become one inside. I could still fight for the right side. And maybe, *maybe* if I could show the stewards that they were my ongoing priority, I could share my secret one day without fear.

A growl slipped from my lips, and I doubled over as pain

erupted in my fingertips. I fell to my knees, crying out and clawing my hands.

Needles were trying to press from the inside out.

I panted in a heap on the floor until the stabbing agony faded. What the hell was that?

Knock, knock.

"Andie?"

It was Wade.

I didn't answer until the door handle turned. "I'm busy right now!"

"Oh my giddy aunt, are you getting some?" came his muffled reply.

I had bigger fucking problems.

I winced as a deep ache throbbed in my teeth, around where I assumed fangs would explode into existence one day. I dashed away another tear. "Go away."

"Are you okay?'

"Jesus, Wade. Leave me alone!"

Scrambling for the mirror, I stared in horror at the darkness looking back at me. I watched the shadow of his feet under the door and reached for my mental forest.

"Okay... Sorry to interrupt."

The shadow disappeared, and I listened to his retreating footsteps, sinking down to the floor, dark eyes and all.

No.

This couldn't be my fate.

I *refused* to let this bite and transition determine my future. I couldn't lose everyone and everything. This place was part of me now, and *no one* would ever forge my path again.

Picking myself up, I made sure my eyes had returned to human norms and sat next to the window.

There was a way out of this.

I just had to find it.

"I realise it's an irregular request," I smiled slightly.

Nathan frowned. "That's one word for it. It will send a message that you want to be separated from the stewards."

Forest, forest, forest.

My teeth ached something ferocious. I could assume they wanted to sink into Nathan's neck.

"Only if we portray it that way," I pressed. "Cast in another light, I could just wish to experience life as they do. I could be one of them."

Roderick hummed. "You'd be outside the protection of the manor."

"If stewards' houses are less secure than the manor, then that is of concern to me," I said coolly.

Every emotion had to be cool and calm. Not white hot and furious. I couldn't let frustration take over. Or any strong feeling.

Not now. Not ever again.

That's when my Luther symptoms ramped up.

"You know what I mean," he replied. "You have a larger target on your head than most. We can't forget the attack on you in Water."

"Tell us why again," Pascal said in the quiet wake.

Shocked was an apt description of how they'd been since I mentioned moving out of the manor. There were two free cabins—I'd checked with Eleanor. One sat at the far outskirts of our territory.

There, I'd have a shot at hiding the truth.

I spread my hands on the table. "I'm not used to so many people around all the time. It's affecting my focus. I can't sustain a healthy balance this way, so I have to alter something. I'll be at the manor from dawn until dusk each day, and available at all hours of the day by phone. But for me, living away from the manor creates a clear line in my mind that will allow me to switch off in the evening. I'm not sleeping. What sleep I do get isn't restful. My mind isn't leaving work, so to speak."

"That's why you're not sleeping?" Rhona asked.

She didn't believe me. "I'd be lying if I said the events of the last two months aren't affecting me too. I lost my mother—or the woman I assumed was her. Then the father I thought was my uncle. I'm processing their deaths and their lies, but I need space to do that."

The others fell silent.

My move didn't look good—Nathan was right, for once. But I couldn't transform into a Luther in the damn manor.

If this compromise was made, then I could stay.

If it wasn't, I'd leave tonight.

I held Rhona's gaze, clinging to my invisible forest. *Please understand.*

"I don't like it," she said. "You're too vulnerable out there."

Fuck.

She straightened. "I'll live out there with you."

"We can't put both of us at risk."

"Just you, right?" she drawled.

Fury slammed into my chest. I stood and turned from the head team. *Inhale. Exhale.* When the ache receded from my throat and teeth, I answered, "That's right, Rhona. If you needed this, then I would support you. I know your disagreement stems from your fear for my life, but I won't live in fear." Opening my eyes, I looked into the reflection of a picture to check them.

No black.

I faced them again. "I *will* live my life for this tribe, but it's with this caveat. And it's *for* the tribe. I know my own limits. I know how to manage them."

Stanley rumbled, "I don't see the issue of you moving out myself. Couldn't stand people milling around at every hour of the day. If the stewards take issue, it's because they're too damn nosy."

My lips twitched. "Thank you, Stanley."

"I'm against it, but then, I don't believe you were asking for our permission," Valerie said, glancing at my sister.

Yeah, Valerie didn't like me one bit. I addressed her. "The head team are representatives of the tribe. Concerns you have will be shared by other stewards. Of course, we must be united in how this is presented."

Pascal leaned forward. "You know your limits. You're a strong believer in maintaining your wellbeing for the betterment of the tribe. Even if that baffles some, they'll respect it. Some will talk." Her eyes slid to Nathan and Valerie. On purpose?

I couldn't figure that woman out.

"I'm in agreement. If you need this to balance the stresses of head stewardship, then we'll support you," Roderick said.

The others murmured their assent.

Mostly.

"If you can't *handle* the stresses of head stewardship, you should delegate more tasks to others," Rhona exploded.

When I played this through in my head, Rhona didn't kick up the most fuss. I should have known better, but my heightened temper *really* wanted to forget that she cared about me.

"That's exactly what I wanted to talk to you about." I tilted my head when she glared at me. "Will you join me on a walk outside? I've been cooped inside all day."

My skin literally itched with the need to be outside—another Luther trait, I could assume.

Rhona stormed for the door, and I followed her out, halting in the doorway. "You're dismissed. Please return to me for individual reports on strategy developments by the end of today."

Timber was next, and I'd passed my ideas on to the teams.

We *had* to win this grid. I needed a damn good thing to happen.

Rhona was waiting for me in the herb garden. I should be happy she didn't make me run to prove my love.

We fell into step.

"Why are you really doing it?" she burst out.

This required quick thinking and another fucking lie. It was true what they said—telling one lie led to another and another.

I slid a look at her. "You were right about Sascha Greyson."

Her eyes widened. "That he's obsessed with you? How do you know?"

"I watched him when we went to pack lands. There's something to your theory. And I've thought of a way to use it to our advantage."

Rhona stopped. "You want to lure him to the cabin."

"Yes. Any unwilling touch between Luther and steward outside of Grids will result in a penalty point. Five penalty points and the Luthers lose a grid. We have cameras all through our territory."

Her face worked. I didn't know if being sisters made reading her emotions easier, but I'd never had the ability to read anyone like Rhona. I could almost hear her inner battle.

She didn't want me in danger's way, but she loathed Sascha Greyson with the fires of a thousand hells.

She smirked. *Hatred won.* "You'll need to gear up to protect yourself. I'd be on speed dial, of course."

"That's why I need to be at the outskirts. Though, I'm really not lying, I need this for myself too."

She kicked at the ground. "I know."

"Are you sure? Because you managed to make those words sound like *fuck you.*"

She snorted. "It's a skill. I'm sorry. I keep biting off your head without meaning to."

This wasn't just temper. This was her truly worrying about me. And more. "I can handle anything the Luthers throw at me. You know that, right? I've *got* this head stewardship under control. I'm almost bored."

Her head lowered and the movement only reminded me of a werewolf's submission.

"It's just that..." She bit her lip. "I could do it too. That's the problem."

I stiffened, and Rhona shook her head, holding up her hands. "It's a daddy issue. That's all. I'm taking it out on you. I have this need to prove myself to show him what a mistake he made. All the while, I *agree* that he made the best choice in you. I would choose you too. Seriously, don't worry. It's fucked up."

Gripping her arm, I said fiercely. "You would have made a *great* head steward, Rhona. Don't ever doubt it. We know Herc didn't mean for things to come out this way, but please don't doubt that he believed in you. You could lead the stewards in a heartbeat. I know it. You know it."

Her eyes shone with unshed tears. "I'm being silly. It's nothing."

Wounds like this weren't nothing. I really hoped she came to terms with this one day.

"Also, ouch." She tugged free. "Your grip is strong considering you stopped training."

Oops. "I want to start again soon. Once I have things in order. I feel better after Iron. Give me a few months, and I'll be an old hat at this." I remembered my real reason for this talk. "Listen, I want you to do something. I have a feeling you'll be happy about it."

Rhona's brows climbed. "Do I get to kill Sascha Greyson?"

My stomach lurched and I gritted my teeth against the voodoo before forcing a smirk. "Well, it's a start."

10

I heaved the last suitcase from Ella F onto the small table in the kitchen. *Dusty*. And worn.

I didn't care.

This run-down cabin was officially my safety net.

"We're going to have so many parties here." Wade burst inside with my cleaning supplies from the car.

"Hey," I greeted him. "Didn't hear you pull up."

"Walked here," he said. "You're really isolated. Are you sure that won't bother you?"

The full moon would begin tonight, and—impossibly—I could feel energy stirring under my blood like a beast waking from slumber. I just hoped the change happened tonight and not during the grid *tomorrow* night.

I crossed the creaking floorboards. "Wade, listen. About the other night when I yelled at you. I'm sorry."

He pursed his lips. "What was it about?"

"Everything. And nothing I want to get into. I just needed a moment alone."

Wade pulled me into his arms. "Being a hermit out here will give you a lot more of that. Forgiven, baby girl."

"Thank you."

"Do you want me to stay with you tonight?"

Hell fucking no. "I appreciate that. But I'd like to be alone."

His hold tightened. "*I'd* like to pull apart whatever you're holding inside, but I'm going to be an adult about this."

Drawing away, I peered up. "Uh, thanks?"

"You should thank me. Adulting is something I prefer to avoid. Just please promise there's nothing to worry about."

I eyed the cabin. "The only thing to worry about is the state of this place. You have perfect timing."

He groaned. "I fell into that one. Before I forget. The accommodation team want to start letting the riverside apartment again. They found your saxophone inside. I put it just outside."

My mouth dried. "Okay."

"I'll grab it. I know you have an unhealthy relationship with it."

"No, no. It'll get dusty with this mess. I'll grab it later."

Fucking thing can stay out there and rust.

Wade started with the broom and dustpan as I grabbed a rag and surface spray. I listened to his singing, rolling my shoulders that perpetually ached.

I was so sore that feeling terror was almost impossible. Almost. I'd seen Sascha shift to four-legged form. The sickening squelching, cracks, and pops. The movies depicted nice versions of these creatures shifting in a shimmering haze. They weren't anywhere close to reality.

My entire body would break apart as it changed to another *species*. My chest tightened and I inhaled thinly, turning from Wade as the throbbing at the base of my incisors ramped up.

In the last two days, I'd found my gums and knuckles always hurt when my eyes started darkening. It was a good warning sign for me to regain control.

My phone pinged, and I checked the email. "*Yes.*"

"Porn?"

I rolled my eyes. "Not everything is porn."

"Respectfully, I disagree."

"The house deposit was paid into my account." *Huh,* and the payment from the manor account to cover the outstanding debt balance.

Rhona must have done it. I wasn't going to do that until settlement.

I slipped the phone away.

"You can't tell me selling your house isn't worthy of a few drinks tonight," Wade said.

"My aunty-mum left me a nearly half-a-million-dollar debt. My ex-boyfriend tried to sabotage the sale by smashing windows. I just want the debt and house gone and to never think about it ever again. Until that happens completely, I can't celebrate."

Wade's smile slid away.

"I just... don't want to talk about any of this. I want to clean this cabin and be alone."

"That's fine for a while," he said eventually. "After what you and Rhona have been through, it's even expected. As long as you know that can't last. You're head steward, Andie."

I whirled. "Do you think I've forgotten that?"

"I know Ragna fucked up, but you loved her. *Love* her. Selling the house won't... well, I don't think that will make the pain better, baby girl."

"I don't need a reality check. I need people to understand the words coming out of my mouth. I want to be alone."

After a beat, he nodded. "I can do that."

His shoulders were tense as he turned away to resume cleaning.

Fuck. I was taking this out on the wrong person. Wade had been there for me. "Sorry. Again. Just—don't take this the wrong way. I value you a lot, but I'm in a shit mood. Could you leave me to this? Forget I was a bitch for the second time."

The itching under my skin was driving me fucking crazy. I pulled at the bottom of my sweater.

Wade ran a hand through his blond hair. "People only lash out when they're hurting. I'll leave you alone tonight. You better believe I'll be back tomorrow morning."

I blinked several times. "I don't deserve you."

"You deserve the very best. Of which I am."

I kissed his cheek and hugged his firm middle. "Don't come too early. I haven't been sleeping well."

"Is that why Rhona's doing the Timber announcement to the Luthers right now instead of you?"

"That's me sending a message to Sascha. I've decided not to keep going with the mating meets."

Wade stiffened, holding me at arm's length. "Since when?"

"Since two nights ago when I told him."

He searched my face. "Andie. Is that smart?"

I closed my eyes in case things got charged again. "I'm sick of it. The mating stuff is his problem."

At his silence, I cracked an eyelid. "What?"

Wade shrugged. "Never thought I'd agree with a Luther." Before I could snap again, he squeezed my shoulders. "I'll lecture you tomorrow. Tonight is yours."

I grimaced. "How about we don't do the lecture at all?"

"I'm the best, bitchhole. Not perfect."

Ditching the rag and spray, I walked onto the porch to watch him leave. The closest cabin was a ten-minute walk according to Rhona.

Leaning on the balustrade, I scanned the area. A visit to Heather told me two frequency generators covered this space. A camera was fixed fifty metres to my right. Another, one hundred metres to the left. They faced outward to cover the road and forest bordering our territory. There weren't any cameras beyond them.

A heat detector was stationed not far from the cabin. I'd need to be at least sixty metres from that when I shifted. Safer to be well away before that time. To my knowledge, partial shifts didn't register as abnormal on the detectors, but I couldn't rely on that to remain hidden.

Maybe first shifts were different.

I was going in totally blind.

Returning to the house, I set to ridding the small cabin of dust and dirt. Mopping the floor for the third time, I made the bed with linens stolen from the manor and unpacked my things in the small drawers and wardrobe.

I'd done it.

The first part of *remain in Deception Valley as a werewolf*.

Time for phase two.

Dragging out my phone, I texted Cameron.

Hey, everything at the cabin is good. Just cleaned stuff up and it's looking cosy.
I want you to see it, but I won't lie, tonight I'm chilling out.
This girl needs a few hours to herself.

I clicked Send and messaged Rhona.

How did you get on? Notice anything?

Cameron replied.

You deserve it.
Rest up. I'll come see the place tomorrow!

This felt so much like a goodbye.

Did everyone survive the transformation? With so much else to organise, it struck me that I may not even be *alive* tomorrow.

This could kill me.

The only alternative was to get Sascha involved... but I just couldn't give him more power over me. His presence wouldn't change the outcome.

This would be my dirty secret for as long as I could manage it.

I read Rhona's reply.

Yeah, SG noticed straightaway. Smelt it maybe? All of them did.
He was pissed.
They didn't say anything though.

Part of me expected Sascha to, well, *cry wolf* to the head team. I'd relied on the guilt Sascha still held about Herc's death and his desperation for me to view him as worthy. Looked like it worked.

I typed back.

Thank you. Love you.
I'll see you tomorrow.

She replied.

Please be careful or I'll never forgive you.

My single wish would be for Rhona to know everything and still love me the same. If there wasn't a slim chance of that, I couldn't say whether or not I'd still be in the valley.

A pain stabbed me in the stomach, and I gasped, phone tumbling from my fingers.

Another followed, and I sank down, clutching my torso.

Eyes streaming, I peered up to the full moon peeking between the thick trees.

Fuck.

Stumbling inside, I grabbed my prepared pack. It contained a change of clothes, soap, a towel, a first aid kit, food, water, and spare shoes.

Snatching up my keys, I tried to remain upright and casual on the way to Ella F in case Heather was watching.

I had to get far enough away so no one could see or hear me.

I gunned the engine as a fresh bout of agony ricocheted through me.

This is it.

A cold dread settled over me, and I just knew.

It was happening.

Wrenching at the wheel, I barrelled down the road.

Past the heat detector.

Past the cameras and frequency generators.

Out of tribe territory.
Away.
I had to get away.

11

I screamed as my leg bowed under the brutal and invisible force.

Snap.

Thigh bone.

My toes followed suit in a wave of snaps that stole sanity from me.

My vision ebbed. This had happened before. The breaking and the blacking out. Many times. One of the other times, twilight was here. Now, it was pitch-black. No birds sang. Maybe I just couldn't hear them over the weak shrieks ripping from my raw throat.

Time had passed and I couldn't remember being here before.

Tears fell from my scratchy eyes as I panted, noting the pressure of fangs either side of my chin.

Was it still my chin?

I felt like paper mâché. Like pulp. Like someone had added water to me and let a toddler do their worst.

My body was broken and *still* breaking.

Arching, my feet slid through the sandy shore of Lake Thana. My cry turned guttural and deep, animalistic. Breaths chuffed from a chest that didn't feel the same shape.

As my ribs popped and squelched again, I couldn't care.

This had to end and take me with it.

The invisible force flung my thighs to my chest, and I shrieked again as my knee reversed in a splitting of ligament and bone.

I tried to move my limbs. It worked. A little.

A whining filled my chest as I was thrown forward, but I didn't sprawl in the sand. My lower body supported me.

In horror, I stared at my human hands bunched in the sand, then to the hairy legs folded beneath me.

I was half wolf.

More than half.

Coarse red hair covered my naked, bleeding, pulpy torso, spreading down my arms. I stopped breathing as my fingers shattered and pulsed, reforming into paws also covered with red fur.

Mostly wolf, I sank into lying. But auburn strands waved in my peripherals. Was my face still human?

No more.

Please.

The pained moans from my lips turned to high-pitched whines as the pressure in my face mounted. Mounted until my human shape could no longer contain the bulging shape pushing to escape. My cheekbones cracked, chin dissolving away as my mouth pushed forward, shoving aside my skin to lengthen to a snout.

Throwing my head back, I *screamed...*

... and mourned the howl that left my curled lip.

I trembled in the sand, a wolf, waiting for the next onslaught.

So weak. I listened to the whine escaping my animal face.

Hello, Andie Thana.

Intruder. I couldn't even spare the energy to yelp. I inhaled instead, tasting the scents on the air.

Good water. Stone. Sand dirt. Little food. No danger.

Wait, what was I doing? This was crazy. Yet my nose hadn't lied. I wasn't in danger.

I was alone.

Mostly alone, yes. Except for me.

I froze as my ears picked out the familiar tones of the voice bouncing inside my head. Was that *my* voice?

My brain was talking to me.

I am your wolf, Andie Charise Thana.

Frozen, I couldn't move. Tuning inward, I could feel a... a foreign presence inside. I couldn't say exactly where—in the same way I couldn't describe myself as coming from one part of my body.

This thing was just *in* me. I mean, Sascha and Greyson were so different, but I'd always viewed them as Jekyll and Hyde. Different sides of the same coin. But *this* was another entity within me. A living, breathing, and thinking entity.

This was bad. I should find out more.

You consider Luthers your enemy? she asked.

Should I talk back? Could she hear all my thoughts? *Uhm, hey. And yeah. Luthers don't like me. It's returned.*

Would that offend her? Him?

Good. I don't like rules.

I closed my eyes. *You're a sigma.*

The world was laughing at me.

Your labels are pointless. I don't acknowledge them.

So that was a big, fat yes. *Are you inside my, uh, body forever? And are you female?*

Who knew how this stuff worked?

I am made for childbearing like you, yes. And I will be with you until death.

Crap, crap, crap! *You kind of just stay in the background and talk?*

In this form, I am most active. In two-legged form, I will assert myself if you anger me. I can talk to you in both forms if I choose, but human interactions are beneath me.

The wolf had a huge ego.

I inhaled, checking for enemies again. Or were *we* doing that together without me realising? My ears twitched at the sound of hooves in the distance. Medium prey judging by the tread. Enough meat to sustain me for a week.

The childbearing thing, I replied after this influx of messed-up information. *I'm not down with that.*

You don't have to be. I am made to have children. If I don't do that, then I have no purpose and I must die.

"Jesus." At least I tried to say the word. A chortling question mark sound came out instead. *You said that you don't like rules, but you're sticking to a pretty big tradition there.*

Talking to her was helping somehow. Or maybe it was a time thing. I felt stronger. The shaking had stopped.

I should figure out how I got here.

Where was Ella F? The last thing I remembered was slamming on the brakes when my arms first broke.

Her harsh words filled my mind again. *It is a good argument if not a pointless one. I am what I am.*

Okay, cool. How do I get back to two-legged Andie?

You want to leave this form already?

Her displeasure and disappointment were plain. Her emotions had that same foreign tinge to them—I could just tell they weren't mine.

If you don't respect my presence, she said, *I will take over entirely.*

That couldn't happen. *How do I respect your presence?*

Seriously, I had no idea Luthers had a running conversation in their heads all the time.

I like to run. I like to chase prey. I don't like others of my kind, especially the one you call Greyson.

Ha! We can fucking agree on that.

I will kill him when he arrives, but we should find a better battlefield.

My eyes widened. Odd, really, how many things wolves could do. *He's coming here?*

I drew him with our howl. Men are led by their breeding parts. I told him that we were eager.

She didn't. *That was a dick move.*

You won't say that when his blood coats our fangs and fur.

Gross.

I'm taking control now, she said.

Half a yelp left me before she slid into the driver's seat. Just like that, I had no control over this form. I was a passenger, able to feel the movement of my four legs and the expansion of my ribs, and able to process scents and sounds and tastes, while being an absolute observer at the same time.

I didn't like it.

You'll get used to it. As I will in our two-legged form.

Claustrophobic was the word.

We whined as my panic mounted.

That will drive us both insane, she snapped. *Relax into our movement.*

No, I snapped back. *Give control to me.*

She laughed in her dark, guttural voice. *This is my form. You have control in the other. That is how we exist, Andie Thana.*

I got how this was meant to work, but it just wouldn't. With me. *That's a no, not an I can't. It's an I am not capable of doing that.*

Our breath became shallow and erratic.

We stumbled through the bush even as our ears picked up the whisper-soft sigh of a large predator racing toward us.

I felt weak and drained—so different from a minute prior. What was happening?

This form is mine, she snarled.

This is my body. Our body, if you're here, too, now. We share everything. This form and the other. I won't be locked out ever.

Whining again, we flopped onto the ground in a shuddering heap. The sudden divide between us was draining our energy away. It was the only thing that had changed.

Black crept across my vision and the impossible strength I'd felt building on the shore was a forgotten thing.

We share both forms, she mused. *It is unnatural and will take practice. But I am fond of making my own rules. I will do this thing, so you don't kill us both. If a wolf and human cannot co-exist, then nature has no need for us.*

I sighed as the black retreated and power flooded back into my body, filling my lungs with air and sharpening my mind. *I feel stronger than before.*

Yes, she answered, her amusement plain. *It seems meeting halfway was right.*

I moved a paw. *How is sharing going to work?*

You tell me.

Rolling to stand, I tried to walk forward, face-planting when my four legs tangled together. *Shit. Okay, how about you handle our movement. I'll handle the senses for now. We can play around with things later.*

She didn't reply before taking off at a loping run that was nowhere near as fast as the huge bounds of the beast closing in. I twitched our ears and pinpointed him behind us. *How far away is he?*

I don't know how to tell you.

Crap, okay. *A metre is the length of that branch. How many metres away is he?*

Around a thousand of those.

A kilometre. Okay, thanks. We could only count on a couple of minutes.

We wound up a small rise and found a cave at the top. She smirked inwardly as I scanned the dark for company, inhaling. Rats? Small prey. Nothing more. And they'd already scattered because they wanted to live.

Hey, I asked. *What should I call you? Do you have a name?*

I live, I eat, I breed, and I die. I have no need nor desire for a name.

I had a feeling a lot of our conversations would be this way. *What's the plan with Greyson?*

Kill him and eat his heart.

That actually made me emotional. *Thanks for hating him too.*

His wolf murdered a member of your pack.

She didn't consider the tribe her pack. Then again, she didn't like others of her kind either. Sigmas were usually lone wolves, so that must be it.

Don't take this the wrong way, but Greyson is kind of big. How are we playing this?

He won't hurt us. We are his weakness.

Twisted. I liked it. *I might just give you the reins for this one. I'm a bit rusty on wolf-to-wolf combat.*

She didn't snort as I'd expected. Instead, I felt her agreement in my mind. Or wherever she resided.

I won't betray your trust, Andie Thana.

Just Andie will do.

I had so many questions. Mainly about how she sounded so wise and old when she was less than an hour old. Did she know where Luthers came from originally or anything about them? I'd known Luthers could speak to each other in wolf form, but not that they actually *spoke* to their wolves. Was my wolf limited to what I knew? She seemed to come into existence knowing how to survive. In which case, she could help me against the pack. This could be a far stronger advantage than I ever expected.

Maybe I shouldn't look at this development as a negative.

Your incessant chatter distracts me.

Oh. Sorry. I focused on Greyson. He'd slowed and circled us with a deliberate tread not intended to hide his presence.

He completed a lap, paused, and then retreated before stalking forward a way.

My wolf shuffled us forward to the edge, draping our paws over so we could glance to the bottom of the small rise.

I listened to his breathing, peering into the trees where I knew him to be.

We *inhaled.*

Pine. Musk. River water. Sweat.

The scents hit us one after the other like brick walls. *Pine, musk, river water, sweat.* We staggered from the force of the smells, and a panicked *yelp* left our snarling lips as we clawed at the crumbling rock ledge.

Nope.

Yelping, we rolled down the crumbling, rocky hill. I didn't care.

Pine, musk, river water, sweat. Pine, musk, river water, sweat. Slamming to a halt against a thick root, the smell barraged our senses, filling us with need.

Pine, musk, river water, sweat.

He's coming, my wolf said with difficulty.

We struggled upward as Greyson stalked into the clearing. Sinking down, we snapped and growled our warning, ears pressing back. Our claws splayed in the forest floor, ready to provide traction, eager to slice and tear.

The wolf took a step closer, and our snarl intensified. *Pine, musk, river water, sweat.*

Take another step and I will kill you, my wolf boomed.

Full of shit. We were disorientated to say the least. We shook our head, but the scents kept bouncing around in there.

You are mine, she-wolf, Greyson answered.

We will never belong to you. You murdered a member of her pack.

Greyson tilted his head. *She was in danger.*

She can handle herself. Leave. Or die by my fangs and claws. You are no mate of mine.

A whine slipped from our teeth as his scent swam around us.

What's wrong? he demanded.

We didn't answer as our legs gave out and we trembled on the ground. I listened absently to the cracking of bone and ripping of sinew, thankful it wasn't coming from me.

The one I like is here, my wolf purred.

I cracked open an eyelid and took in a very naked Sascha. *You're fucking kidding me. We don't like him either!*

I do. A lot.

Fucking traitor.

"You're okay, little bird," Sascha said in a low voice that *one* of us liked far too much.

Don't come any closer, I mentally snapped at him.

He won't hear us in two-legged form, she told me.

He sank to a crouch and held both hands up. "I need to get closer to see what's wrong."

Maybe the gnashing teeth gave away my mood.

There's nothing wrong with the way he smells. Mmm. She inhaled deeply.

What is it? I demanded.

The scent meet. On our behalf anyway. Judging by his lack of reaction, he's already scented us.

Oh, fuck. She was right. *Where's the sex part?*

Both of you must be in two-legged form.

"You need to shift back." Sascha shuffled closer.

He's right. Her voice echoed in my head. Our head.

Whatever.

Panting, I moved away, stopping when my butt hit the crumbling hill at our back.

"Easy, little bird. *Easy.* You need to focus on what you look like as a human. Imagine the way your body moves in that form. The way you see and smell. The shape of your ears and mouth. The feel of your fingertips."

Not doing it.

My wolf snorted. *You will not be a normal companion, I see. This time, I will trigger the shift. But I prefer this form and will not help you again.*

Don't you dare. The heat!

Her thoughts seized mine. Hands through sand. Hair tickling my lower back. The long, graceful movement of two legs.

Crack.

Short nails. Warm toes.

Pop.

Upright. Soft voice.

Crack, crack, crack.

The invisible force took over, and we whined as it flung us forward again.

Human arms.

Human body.

Auburn hair, not red fur, plastered against my sweaty forehead.

In a crouch, my legs reversed and lengthened with a series of sickening crunches and groans so much faster than my descent into the other.

My face drew in, shortening, sharpening, and I jolted as my whine morphed to panting gasps. Knees to my chest and hair in a tangled curtain between me and Sascha, I struggled to get my bearings from my crouched position before him.

Oh my god. I was back.

My breath hitched.

"Andie," Sascha said, his voice filled with wonder. "*Beautiful wolf.*"

My senses were sharper.

I felt strong. Powerful. Fast. I could hear the trickle of where the closest stream met Lake Thana.

They weren't as attuned as in wolf form, but I was...

I was a predator.

I was alive.

Inhaling, I froze. Wrenching my head upward, I locked eyes with Sascha as heat filled me. A heat I knew.

A heat I wanted.

Crying out, I rested forward on my knees, widening my thighs in invitation as my hands swept my body. "Sascha."

His voice choked, and he *came* for me.

As I wanted him to.

A smile crossed my lips.

He found me, hands gripping my ass to bring our naked bodies flush. The feel of our skin touching was bliss. The inferno in me climbed higher as his lips brushed my neck, inciting heatwaves that rocked me to my very core.

"Inside," I ordered in a hoarse voice.

Gazes locked, Sascha blinked a few times, body shuddering. "Mate—"

"Not mate." I brushed my hands across the broad expanse of his chest. We'd fit perfectly—him inside me. The ultimate pleasure awaited, and my legs trembled where I sat on his lap, ankles hooked at his lower back. Even pressed against him like this, the sensation was otherworldly.

My head tipped back, a desperate noise leaving my lips. "I need you, Sascha."

"You—"

His voice choked again, and I frowned, anger sweeping through me. I gripped his face, straightening to scowl at him. "Now."

He tried to turn his head away and I dragged him back, grinding down on him.

Black flooded his eyes and he shoved me away.

Sprawled on the forest floor, I snarled up at him, attempting to stand on wobbling legs so I could pounce on the naked male.

Naked male.

Hold on.

I—

I lifted a hand to my forehead, steadying myself on the rise behind me. The inferno firing my body was almost painful.

Only one person could help it go away.

Shaking, I looked at Sascha. Black eyes. He was shaking too.

"No," I whispered. *I didn't want this.* This was the mating call. The heat!

Legs folding—or more collapsing—into the kneeling position, I forced my weakened arms to assume the cleopatra position.

The words.

What were the fucking words?

My voice failed me, but I shoved the words out of my raw, aching throat. "*Doore koh e baka.*"

Shuddering, I crumpled on the shingled ground, unable to help myself as my head slammed into a thick root.

Frantic footsteps.

The most *intoxicating* smell I'd ever experienced. I inhaled deeply, unable to stop myself.

Hands swept my body, turning me.

"Andie. How—?" Horrified honey eyes stared down at me, and I was too tired to look away.

His hands trembled as he gathered me in his arms.

"Beautiful wolf, what happened?" He sounded close to tears, and a fat tear of my own slipped unbidden over my temple.

I shivered as he cradled me closer. "You weren't meant to find out."

Black closed in on his vision and I watched him battle it back, more than aware, *now*, of the war raging within him. Sascha didn't completely win. Gravel rode his voice hard. "The wolf in Water did this? This is why you hid from me and changed your mind about the meets."

A furious growl ramped in his chest, and a wrinkle formed between my brows at the way the sound made me feel.

Safe.

In a word, with my new ears, Sascha's voice was *wondrous.*

His smell. His touch. The way he sounded.

They made me realise I'd never marvelled before.

I squeezed my eyes shut, repeating, "You weren't meant to find out."

"You went through your first shift alone." He sounded broken beyond words. "You could have died. You should be dead."

That opened my weary eyes again. "Really?"

"A wolf can't shift without their alpha in attendance. The entire pack usually calls to the new wolf to help them. But I have no link to your Luther form." His expression blanked. "Your wolf is a sigma."

Clever cookie. Knew he'd put two and two together. "She is."

He squeezed me to him gently. "Do you know how lucky you are? Any other status and you'd be dead."

Which meant he'd also be dead.

My eyes drifted closed. "I need to get back. What's the time?"

"Just past midnight. Your howl woke me. And the pack. *Fuck*," he whispered into my hair. "I thought it was a dream. Your howl is the most beautiful sound—I couldn't believe my ears. You're a wolf."

The glee in his voice was unmistakeable.

"This doesn't change a thing, Sascha. Aside from us moving through the meets now I've scented you or whatever."

He started walking us back through the forest, and I couldn't summon the energy to care that he was holding me.

"Your wolf form is exquisite," Sascha said after a while. " You stole my breath away. What colour are you?"

The pleased feeling rising through my chest was foreign. *Your crush will never see the light of day,* I told her.

Displeasure replaced the pleased feeling, and my arm jerked, fingers squeezing Sascha's bicep.

My eyes widened. *Stop that.*

You're the one that wanted to share both forms, she taunted.

"She's red," I said in a strangled voice.

"I've never seen a red wolf before."

Probably because he'd never seen colour before at *all.*

He ducked us beneath a low-hanging branch. "Do you feel anything else around me after shifting?"

We were back at the lake, and he was thankfully not going to mention the small bicep-groping incident.

I stopped fighting my eyelids. "You sound good. And smell good too. It feels good to touch you."

Understatement of the millennium.

"Thank you."

"Not a compliment."

His lips brushed my forehead, and I let him do it. Kind of impossible not to at this point. My body was packing up for the day. Or night. But one thing bothered me. "Thank you for stopping me. Earlier."

We'd be three orgasms deep by now if he didn't shove me away. From what I understood, a female Luther's heat completely took over a male. I couldn't imagine how much control it took him to separate us.

What if the male wolf didn't want the female? I'd always looked at this as Sascha using his power and knowledge to take advantage of me. Really, women got the most choice in this. What if Sascha hadn't always wanted me? He'd be a slave to the heat regardless.

My heart panged.

I fucking hated these meets.

"I'm glad you weren't forced to do anything you'd later regret and hate me for," he said mildly.

Blood crept into my cheeks. "I'm glad I didn't force *you* to do anything you didn't want to do."

"There's no danger of that, beautiful wolf. I assure you."

Looked like sleep wasn't happening just yet. I slitted my lids to watch him. The harsh line of his jaw was just visible through the tangled strands of his shoulder-length brown hair. My stomach clenched and I tensed at the surge of need.

That felt way more intense than usual. Almost like the pain I felt in the heat.

Sascha's nostrils flared and he stopped short, staring at me.

Even I could smell my… want. Lust? Fucking embarrassing was what it was. That his lust rose hard and fast in response only lessened my mortification by a sliver.

"That's just, uhm, leftover." I pressed a hand to my cheek in case Little Miss Grope took over again.

The massive werewolf didn't stop his stare. "Is it?"

Was he asking himself that question or me? "It feels kind of like the heat, but I'm not mindless."

His eyes rounded a fraction.

"What is it?" I asked. Was this unusual or something?

Sascha pressed his lips together. "We're not ready for sex, little bird."

That's a shame. Because in this state—vulnerable, tired, and horny as hell, I was more than ready to make a delicious mistake. "Why? Out of interest?"

Sascha walked us to a boulder lining the lake and sat down, still holding me close. "From what I witnessed between you and Logan, you use sex as a weapon. Or at the very least, you don't view sex as emotional. More a need to be fulfilled rather than something…

more."

My mouth dried. An angry retort balanced on my lips, but I refused to give it voice. That wasn't how I used sex at all. I *liked* sex. Sex was fun. It felt good.

And boy, had it been a long time. My eyes narrowed. *Are you influencing me somehow?*

My wolf didn't answer.

Dang. This was all me.

I looked up at him. "I thought you wanted me."

"I want you so much that I cannot take that gift from you yet. Not like this. Not until we are one in other ways."

Yeah, he really wasn't getting the memo on that front.

I winced as the ache between my thighs became acute. Seriously, it was out of control.

I needed to get home to deal with it myself.

"But I am a man who takes care of his mate's needs." Sascha's voice hitched.

Warmth pooled in my belly. "What do you mean?"

Please mean what I think you mean.

His expression was solemn. "If it comes down to me having front row seats to what will inevitably happen or imagining what you're doing to yourself for the hour after I drop you home, I choose the front row seats. No sex doesn't mean we can't touch."

My chest rose, and I processed for the first time that we were both naked. He'd been clinical until now, but that dam broke as he dragged his gaze to my breasts and across my stomach.

"Andie," he said softly. "It comes with conditions."

"What?" I breathed.

I wanted his hands on me, his mouth on my breasts, and his fingers crooking in just the right spot.

Now.

He didn't do it. "You tell me, truly, that it's what you want. That you won't regret it."

"Yes."

"Yes, what?"

I bared my teeth, feeling my claws lengthen, and he grinned. "Easy, beautiful wolf. You know this is important."

A foreign agreement, and my claws receded. *You're an absolute sucker*, I told her.

"I want this. And I won't hold it against you after," I said.

This wasn't the magic-mating voodoo forcing us together. This was me, horny as hell and after a solution from a male that I'd always found attractive. I didn't have to agree with what he was or who he was to get off.

Sex was a business deal.

I traced a finger over his pec muscles, sucking in a breath at the sensation.

"Second condition," he said hoarsely. "You let me help you learn to be a Luther."

"No. I can figure it out." My wolf agreed with that—and no wonder with her stance on rules and others.

"*Yes*," he breathed. "Or I won't bury my face between your legs."

I stared wide-eyed at him as the visual of that pulsated exactly where he intended to relocate. I'd always been easier to convince when horny. "I shifted by myself."

Sascha lay me back over the boulder. He put distance between us, and I closed my legs as he left the frame of them. "There are things you must know. For your safety. The pack's safety. For humans' safety too."

And to help the stewards in the game. Really, I shouldn't turn this offer down. "It will be hard to get away from tribal lands."

"You've moved to a cabin on the outskirts. We'll manage."

Of course he knew about that. *Sigh.* "Once it's done. Once I've learned what I need to. Things will return to normal. We'll get the mating call over with. Things between us will officially end. None of this ever comes to light. Not me being a Luther. Not anything we've shared. Not the mating call. *Nothing.*"

The full moon didn't leave room to miss the sadness in his honey gaze. "You shouldn't feel ashamed of what you are, little bird."

Shame?

Yes, I was fucking ashamed. Out here like this? I could marvel at the powerful creature I'd become. I could be curious about the new presence within me and what she might offer.

When I stepped onto tribe land, that stopped. I could only hide what I was from those who would view me as a monster.

Shame?

I felt so much shame that adding another piece of it right now was nothing.

"I've agreed to your terms, Luther." I wet my lips. "Will you deliver?"

A growl rumbled in his chest. "I've waited months to deliver. You're certain?"

My need for completion was making sleep seem like a tiny whim. I couldn't rest until he touched me. "Make me come, Sascha."

I wasn't rusty in that department at least.

His eyes blazed. That was all I saw before he leaned over and took one of my nipples in his mouth. My lips parted and I slapped my hands down on the rock that would be cold if I wasn't running so damn hot.

"Oh my god," I whispered as he lapped and circled, biting softly.

The Luther smiled against my skin, fingers rolling my other nipple as he whispered scalding kisses across my middle.

Down.

My fingers found his hair, helping him, but he resisted my none too gentle pushes, turning his attention to my left knee. A kiss.

Right knee, just a little higher. A kiss.

Left, higher.

Right, higher.

He drew closer to my core at an excruciating pace, left to right, inching upward.

I whimpered as he kissed the crease at my inner thigh. "Please, Sascha."

"No."

Scowling, I tried to line my pelvis up with his mouth, and he clamped down on me.

As a werewolf, I was stronger than I could've ever imagined.

He was stronger.

Stronger than I could fathom. Unless he wanted to move me, I wouldn't budge an inch.

The pain was almost at exploding point. "You promised to help."

"Little bird," he hummed against the edges of my core, making me arch—the only movement afforded by his iron hold on my lower half.

Honey eyes burned over the flat plane of my stomach, between the valley of my breasts, to bore their way into me.

Sascha lowered his head, kissing my core.

My eyes fluttered shut as I *left* for a moment.

Heat flushed my body in a wave that promised the start of something unfathomable as I slammed back down.

Fuck.

He kissed me again, just as slow, and my thighs began to shake.

Once more.

"*Faster,*" I begged.

He watched me like I was his favourite show. I didn't want him to see me come apart like this.

"Close. Your eyes," I moaned.

Sascha arched a brow. "No."

My fangs and claws lengthened at the refusal, but my mind stalled as Sascha dragged his tongue from my ass *all* the way up.

A desperate cry left my lips and I felt that initial step from pain to pleasure. I needed him to lick me for all he was worth.

I needed fast. Hard.

Over.

Done.

Another slow lick. Actual *tears* welled in my eyes. "Please. I can't take it anymore."

Sascha latched directly onto my clit and sucked *hard.*

I *screamed.* I screamed bloody murder, using my entire strength to buck against his face as my body catapulted into something so powerful, it couldn't possibly be an orgasm.

But it was.

God, it was.

He released his hold. Freed, I circled and ground against his mouth with abandon, using the tongue he so nicely kept out.

My hips jerked, slower and slower until I collapsed on the boulder. He followed me down, and I panted, writhing as Sascha continued sucking and lapping relentlessly.

Oh—

Arms wide either side, I shook from a violent aftershock as Sascha released my sensitive flesh.

I thumped my head against the rock, gasping for air.

I couldn't speak. There weren't words.

"I'm so fucking hard." Sascha rested his forehead against my thigh. "That was, without doubt, the sexiest thing I will experience in my life."

He regarded me, and I couldn't find the will to close my trembling legs. "You taste incredible, mate."

"Thank you," I said. More for the sexual favour than his taste buds' approval.

My core throbbed angrily. The pain there though less was still present.

I hesitated.

He stood, smiling. "More, beautiful wolf?"

I broke our stare. "It's okay."

If this was what the after-effect of a denied heat was now I'd become a Luther, I'd hate to actually go through a heat.

Sascha stopped me rolling off the boulder with a hand on my stomach. "I'm not done with you." He glanced down. "Do you mind if I deal with this at the same time?"

I fanned my lashes to look at his erection. "Oh. Okay. That's... fair."

"Does the thought make you uncomfortable?"

The amusement in his voice had me snapping my gaze up again. "Do what you need to, Sascha."

His lips twitched. "Don't mind if I do."

I watched as he took hold of something I'd ignored pretty well until now, given the size. I tried not to react as he moved his hand up and down in slow, firm strokes.

Not reacting was well and good until we could both smell my mounting approval of his actions.

Fuck my life.

Sascha was done laughing, however.

This time he didn't bring his head between my legs. He released himself, and pinned me again, working a large finger inside. I was so wet, his finger slid in, but—as before—he kept the pace excruciatingly slow.

Pricks of pleasure lit my body, tingling in my arms and spine. It was like someone slowly turning up the wattage.

I'd never felt *anything* like this.

"Are you going to scream again, Andie?"

My claws scratched against the boulder, seeking purchase. "I hope so."

His chuckle was deep. It filled me as surely as his finger.

He took himself in hand again, stroking slowly, in time to the sliding movement of his finger.

Was he making this feel like sex on purpose? My need just slightly outweighed my embarrassment, but I wished he'd stop looking at me that way. Timing the movement of his hips and the push of his hand between my thighs.

Look away.

Pretend this doesn't mean anything.

Because it didn't.

Sascha crooked his finger.

Air seized in my throat. "It can't."

"What can't, little bird?"

I choked on my words as he hooked his finger again.

"Yes, mate. Your body is mine to memorize and nurture. I will always give you everything you need. I'll give you what you never knew you wanted."

I needed what his finger could give me now.

I'd never admit that I wanted *him* specifically to fulfil that need.

A force so strong it almost scared me began to push upward from my core. A confused moan left me.

Sascha's shoulders bunched as he moved both of his hands, and the sight of him pleasuring himself was the sight that began to unravel me.

"You're close, mate," he murmured.

I nodded, unable to speak. I could only beg him with my eyes not to stop.

Never to stop.

"Let go, mate." His low voice rocked through me, and I was inwardly lifted and thrown into a place I could never return from.

12

Ouch.

Fucking ouch.

Groaning, I moved my legs through the blankets tangled around my body. Someone had driven a battering ram into my sides.

One hundred and two times by the feel.

"You'll be sore for a few days," a honey voice said. "The first change isn't easy."

I wrenched my eyes open and sat.

Across my cabin—*thank shit* I wasn't on pack lands—sat the man-beast who'd last occupied the space between my legs.

Very well if memory served.

I ran a hand through my hair. "What happened?"

"The part where you shifted alone, then I found you, and we nearly entered the heat? Or the part where you passed out from the best orgasm of your life?"

Yeah, that was 2000 percent gloating.

"You should be proud of yourself," I told him flatly.

His smug smile didn't fade.

Honestly? He could back it up.

Asshole.

"One day," Sascha rumbled, "I'll have you in my bed looking just like that. Tussled auburn hair, dazed eyes, and naked. After hours of sex."

Peering down, I eyed my breasts which were, indeed, popping out to say hello. Scowling at the Luther, I kicked the blankets away and wobbled over to my wardrobe. I yanked out a short dressing gown.

"The glare can stay too," he muttered low.

He likes our glare, my wolf gushed.

She was still here—then again, I'd felt her foreign presence within me as soon as I woke.

Ignoring her continued crush, I shrugged into the gown, tying it tightly. Last night dealt with my out-of-control libido, but it was a one-off.

"What's the time?" I croaked. "And where did you get pants?"

"Just after dawn. Hairy dropped them off."

He couldn't have dropped off a shirt as well? "You carried me here?"

"I found your car and brought us back in that."

I tensed. "The cameras?"

"Two of them. Don't worry. No one saw me."

Sighing, I filled the kettle and set it to boil. When I leaned against the bench, Sascha was sitting on the low couch, comfortable as pie as his gaze lazily roamed over me.

Did he watch me sleep all night? Heat flooded me at the thought, and his nostrils flared.

He wasn't smiling now. "How are you going to play this, Andie?"

Gravel rode my voice. "*Oh, I'd like to play with you.*" I clapped a hand over my mouth, blinking at him. "That wasn't me."

Sascha was still for a moment, then he threw back his head, rich laughter booming.

I rubbed my forehead. *Was that necessary?*

You're the one who wanted to share forms, she said smugly.

Something I'm regretting.

You shouldn't. The surge in strength afterward meant this was the right choice for us.

I'm trying to play it cool with Sascha. I can't be seen to... find him attractive.

No one else is here to look.

She could make a point. I'd give her that. *That's not enough with everything else he's done.*

Greyson did those things.

They're the same person.

Are we the same person?

Mothershitter, she was good. *I like to think that we'll take each other's considerations into account before acting.*

So take mine into account. I like Sascha's physical appearance and possibly his mind—though that's not strictly needed.

You also want to eat Greyson's heart. Sounds like a super healthy relationship.

Who said I wanted a relationship?

We could agree on that at least.

Snorting, I poured my tea as Sascha got himself under control. "Want a drink?"

"Thank you, mate. Yes. Just whatever you're having."

Didn't strike me as an Earl Grey tea man, but I shrugged, grabbing a second mug. There weren't many seating options in the cabin. Withholding a sigh, I strode to the couch but halted at the object occupying the other seat.

Sascha scanned my face. "I found your saxophone outside."

Yeah, I left it there on purpose.

He took his drink, focus never leaving my face as I moved the instrument without comment and sat as far from Sascha as possible on the two-seater. My hand burned where it had touched the case, and I forced my mind from it.

"We need to decide how this goes from now." He took a tentative sip.

Curious, I inhaled. The pine part of his scent retreated. He didn't like the tea? Was this how he catalogued my moods?

What did I smell like? "I'm going to keep what I've become from the tribe, Sascha. For as long as possible."

"They'll notice. New Luthers aren't known for their control."

A new Luther never had the incentive I did. "I'll practice."

"It takes years. Decades. As a sigma, you're more powerful than most because you don't rely on strength from a pack, but Luthers of our status face struggles of their own."

Tell me about it. "The lone wolf thing?"

"That. And following rules. It took most of my life to find a way for Greyson to accept my position and what came with it. Even then, the pack makes allowances for his nature. How will your wolf manage the confines of your position around people who have no idea about her and therefore make no compromise?"

My wolf was listening. *I don't like rules.*

I've heard. We'll find a way. I'm not going to shut you out. I promise. And I wouldn't. I'd expected to be quivering in fear after the shift, but it was like my mind and heart had doubled. I accepted her place inside me without question, something that surprised me most of all. I didn't depend on people. I depended on myself. Yet I was bizarrely okay with her permanent residence in my body.

Thank you, Andie.

You got it, wolf girl.

Don't call me that. I've told you that I have no need or desire for a name.

It just feels strange calling you my wolf all the time. She had her own mind.

I didn't receive an answer.

"I appreciate what you're saying," I said. "You know a lot more about being a sigma and a Luther than I do. I know what I won't give up, and that's my family."

Sascha held my gaze. "The family who might not accept who you are."

"Who may not accept what my enemy turned me into. You forget they'll sympathise. It could have happened to any of us."

His hands curled to tight fists. "I'll tear his throat out when I find him."

"Go ahead. How did this happen anyway? You said biting didn't change humans to Luthers."

Sascha glanced at me. "Not just any kind of bite."

I waited.

"It's purposeful," he said shortly.

That's all I'd get apparently. "Well at least me being a Luther serves your agenda too."

He glanced at me. "You think I'd change you against your will?"

"Perhaps not you. But Greyson, yes."

"Then you don't know him." There was a definite bite to the words.

I raised a brow. "Why are you upset about me being a Luther when it only serves what you've wanted this whole time?"

Sascha's jaw clenched. A slight growl filled the cabin. "Another Luther touched my mate. That's against our most sacred laws."

"Why?"

"Because we only have one mate. We can only have children with that one mate. We'll only experience such a connection with our one mate. Our mate is everything. They are not to be harmed. And with all that, it's against our laws to change a human without pack consent. I can't recall it ever happening."

I toyed with the handle of my mug and twitched my nose. The musk in his scent just increased to irritating levels. It smelled… dishonest?

Sascha was holding something back on the mate front. "Does your entire pack know about me now?"

"They'll put two and two together. Your howl and lack of mental link to the pack marked you as an outsider. My reaction will unlock the rest of the puzzle for them."

Fuck. "Will they keep their mouths shut?"

"Have they revealed anything else?"

True.

He regarded me. "That's your choice then? You'll remain in this cabin, leading the Ni Tiaki?"

I didn't flinch. "It is."

The musk in his scent muted this time while the river water smell intensified. I wanted to whine in response. This one was easy. He was unhappy.

Sascha set his mug aside. "Then here's what you need to know until we're able to meet again for a Luther lesson. The first shift is the only shift made at the full moon. Otherwise, you will be pushed to shift when there's least sun—during the nights of the new moon. The next one is in two weeks. During this time, I suggest you meet with my pack—"

I opened my mouth, and he held up a hand.

"—*initially*. This will prevent your wolf attacking anyone or anything she shouldn't."

I do like to chase things and eat hearts, she informed me.

Jesus.

But hundreds of Luthers watching and judging me? No thanks.

"The presence of your wolf, as you've probably gathered, grows stronger in times of high emotion. Meditation will help you to retain control in two-legged form."

I'd discovered that pre-shift and I'd practice in every spare moment. "Can I shift between new moons?"

"Yes, you'll need to. You can shift whenever you like, but I suggest waiting until you're fully healed before a second shift."

My stomach churned. "Will every time be as bad as the first?"

He paused. "How long did it last?"

I frowned. "It started somewhere around seven, I think. You found me at midnight? Five hours?"

Sascha jerked, fingers twitching on his thighs. "If you shift in the presence of the pack, the first shift should take no more than twenty minutes."

Minutes. My gaze flew to his. "Really?"

His expression was grave. "The longest first shift I've heard of is one hour."

I shivered. Right. Sounds like I brushed a little close to death. *Yikes.* "What if I shifted by myself again?"

"Not as long. Considering the length of your first, I can't guess." Sascha's chest rose. "Please don't shift without me near, little bird. I can help you."

No deal. I nodded, and he glared.

He leaned in. "I'll need to keep an eye on you."

"That's not creepy."

Sascha's lips twitched. "Not creepy if you know I'm there."

That. "I'm… not sure I can feel you anymore."

His face smoothed. "You can't feel me sitting here?"

"Maybe it will work when you're farther away?" *That* would be handy as shit. A Sascha beacon.

"Perhaps," he replied after a beat.

I inhaled again. *Unhappy.*

"There's one more thing," he said. "But I must ask that you keep to yourself at all costs. Telling you this could endanger my pack, and it's not a decision I take lightly. If ignorance of this didn't endanger your life… I'm asking you not to betray my trust."

Dang. This had to be good. "I promise."

Sascha took another sip of his drink.

Definitely didn't like Earl Grey tea. Cataloguing his scents was kind of like collecting Pokémon cards or something. I could see the fascination with it.

I watched him closely, hands still wrapped around my warm mug.

He rested back, closing his eyes. "Our pack travelled across the seas over two hundred and sixty years ago, before my birth. We were a much larger pack then. Ten times the size. My father had a disagreement with the alpha in our homeland, his brother, and the pack split in two. The responsibility landed on my father to find new territory for those who'd chosen to follow him. We landed in what's now known as Bluff City and were almost immediately set upon by Vissimo—or vampires as they're known to some humans. We ran, fighting a battle at our backs that took thousands of Luther lives—Vissimo being the stronger adversaries. We only escaped because of sheer numbers."

That didn't really tell me anything except that I should hire three hundred vampires as mercenaries to fight for us in Grids, which was probably against the rules anyway.

He shot me a look. "The Vissimo ceased the attack when we reached the area now known as Frankton Gorge, but the way forward was treacherous. The battle had weakened us, and our elderly and young couldn't face such dangerous terrain. To his error, my father turned north. There, our pack encountered the largest demon kingdom in the world and lost thousands more. Those who could, fled injured back to Frankton Gorge. We had only fifteen hundred pack members of *ten thousand* left. There was mass dissent. Those who'd followed my father across an ocean now struggled to be loyal to him through their despair. We hung by a thread, and my father knew we could not face another battle. We could go east or south, but what if those territories were claimed by another supernatural race? In the end, he chose the route no one in their right mind would take—the treacherous, rocky cliffs leading east that he'd turned from before. If Luthers, the most endurable of all supernatural races, shied away from entering this place, no other supernatural race would have sought to enter it before. He hoped."

I found myself leaning forward. "And he was right."

But fifteen hundred Luthers were left after the demon war, and yet the pack now numbered just over seven hundred and fifty.

What happened?

Sascha shifted in the seat, widening his thighs, and I swallowed. Why did he do hot stuff like that? It hardly helped.

I pushed back into the corner of the couch as he continued.

"We were welcomed to Deception Valley by a human tribe who deemed themselves protectors of the land. The area was bountiful and, really, we had no other choice but to lick our wounds for a time on the land loaned to us. Decades went by in this manner without issue, but then the humans discovered what we truly were.

Sensing the shift in the tribe, my father tried to broker the purchase of land here, but the tribe would not allow it. Owning land was against their sacred laws. They agreed to loan us the south side of the valley in return for their guaranteed safety. The relationship was tense, and my father worried for the future of our pack. He turned his attention to a new direction. South. A small group were sent to gather what information they could."

My mouth dried. "What happened to them?"

"Only one returned. Before he died, he told father that a witch's coven occupied the land to the south. They'd claimed the territory in the last ten years. Father had left the exploration too late—and the terrible sight of the dead Luther's body was enough to convince him not to start a war with witches. Now, only one direction remained. Farther east. Another party were sent there. They discovered that not only did the demon kingdom we'd faced fifty years before occupy the territory north of Deception Valley, but their kingdom wrapped around the base of this place too."

Vampires to the west.

Witches to the south.

Demons to the north and east.

Oh my god. "You're *trapped* here."

I'd never seen Sascha look so solemn when he replied, "We can never leave this place."

They'd wanted to own the land for security.

If my tribe won Grids and cast the Luthers out, they'd be slaughtered. "Shit, Sascha."

But that didn't explain how they'd lost another half of their pack.

Was that to the *Ni Tiaki*?

He looked at me. "That's not all. We can't leave Deception Valley, Andie. That means our mates can't get in either. And we can't have children without finding our mates. Some of us have been lucky in the last two hundred and sixty years—very few. Some were already mated prior to coming here."

"What does that mean?" I croaked.

Sascha glanced away. "It means my pack is dying. Any pups are few and far between."

"But you're immortal."

"Immortality is given to mates only. Nature only protects those of us able to reproduce. The lifespan without finding your mate is around four hundred and fifty years. Many of the pack were at least one hundred before they arrived at Bluff City."

Shit.

Being contained like this was literally killing them.

I mean, four hundred and fifty years was over five times the life expectancy of a human, but that seemed so harsh, to kill wolves who couldn't reproduce.

And to never find a mate because they couldn't leave the valley… that put so many things into perspective. How desperate Sascha was when we first met and I mentioned leaving. How intense he'd been.

He probably expected to die without finding his mate.

Yet he'd never forced me to stay here either. Nowhere near as much as Herc and Rhona.

I frowned, aware that feeling pity and sadness for my enemy wasn't a great idea. "Does anyone outside of the pack know?"

"I'm sure you can see why we keep it a secret?"

In a word, *yes*. The tribe could simply wait for them to die. My thoughts drifted to the pup I'd saved in the river. I'd only ever seen that one pup on pack lands. And he'd nearly *died*. That would have devastated them. "Your parents are mated, so they're immortal, right? Your father must still be alive then. How are you the leader?"

"I became stronger than my father when Greyson decided to work with me and the pack."

How nice of him.

Quiet fell as I processed that.

My heart squeezed. *Fuck.* That's why he told me. This was my fate, too, now. I couldn't ever leave the valley. I squeezed my mug harder. Sascha could get in line. The fucker who bit me would die by my hand. Or claws.

Or he'd hurt at least. I wasn't sure murder was my gig.

I can never leave this place.

My wolf answered, *We love it here.*

Except running was always my plan B. If the tribe discovered the truth and exiled me, then obviously it would hurt and suck, but I'd be able to leave the area.

Not anymore.

My wolf didn't seem too worried. *Guess we better not get caught.*

I rubbed a hand over my face.

"It's a lot to take in," Sascha said.

"I can handle it."

One corner of his mouth lifted. "There doesn't seem to be anything you don't take in stride. I have a strong mate."

Ugh. "I need to get to the manor."

His musk smell faded. "You can't take the day off to recover?"

"Good joke. Do you get days off?"

Sascha arched a brow. "Touché. When can you next meet?"

Never. Though I couldn't deny the advantages of Luther lessons—even knowing Sascha would use the time to grow closer to me. "End of the week. Friday or Saturday."

"Done. If you unblock my number again, I'll contact you."

I set my cup on the offensive saxophone. "I'll consider it."

Sascha took my hand. "Please be careful, little bird. Promise me."

"I'll promise myself. How about that?"

A hint of sadness stung my nostrils before Sascha directed his attention to the small table behind me. "Have you had time to play?"

I glanced back. *The saxophone.* "No."

He released me. "Well, now you're out here, you could."

"Maybe." *Not happening.*

Sascha didn't follow me to the door.

I turned back, crossing my arms. "What?"

He regarded me in silence, and I couldn't fail to notice it *wasn't* awkward. I didn't feel the need to fill in quiet moments with him.

"Could I hold you for a moment?" he asked, rubbing his jaw.

I skimmed over the tight bunching of his shoulders and the slight glaze to his honey eyes. He hadn't slept all night, and to my memory, we had a biting and screwing meet left that he was trying to resist.

Wish he wouldn't, my wolf hummed.

I've gathered that much.

"Okay," I said.

Sascha closed the gap and engulfed me in his strong arms. I hugged his middle, resting my cheek against his firm chest. His hands splayed against my back, and a deep rumble filled him as he buried his nose in my hair and inhaled. I couldn't resist the urge to do the same as liquid warmth filled me, sweeping away the bruised ache left from my first shift. My worries faded, replaced by a feeling of contentment that had to be fake because I'd *never*—not once in my life—experienced anything like this.

Hugging Sascha wasn't just a hangover cure any longer. I could *feel* our bond thing fixing me, *healing* my wounds. It felt so right that the thought of stepping back left my mind almost entirely.

"Why aren't you playing your saxophone?" Sascha whispered in my ear. "You love it."

Anger twisted sharp in my gut and the spell was broken. I stepped back. "None of your business."

"Is it because of your mother?" His eyes were clear and sharp again, and a languidness hung over his previously tense shoulders.

A humourless smirk curved my lips. "Which mother?"

"The one you knew and loved."

I brushed my hair back. "Let's get something straight, Sascha. I'm grateful for the help last night, and the orgasms, but don't believe for a second that things between us have otherwise changed."

Sascha stalked closer and caged me against the door.

I glowered up at him.

He tilted my chin, exposing my neck. "What will you do when you realise outrunning me is futile?"

He'd uttered a similar version long ago, and my answer was still the same. "It's not a matter of outrunning you."

"I agree," he murmured, drawing closer until a bare sliver separated us. "You're running from your past. But I'm not your past, Andie. I'm here to stay. You will *always* have me. So stop running."

My chest rose, and his focus dipped to my breasts.

"No person stays forever. Everyone has their limit. Even you."

He stared into my eyes. "Time will show you, little bird."

I tore away from his intense perusal, trying to even out my shallow breaths. My new senses made standing close to Sascha torturous. The bond wanted me to go to him, to wrap my legs around him, to rest my cheek against his chest again, and to never let go.

Was this what Sascha always felt?

It was fucking overwhelming.

"Time *will* show me," I replied in a trembling voice.

Sascha led a trapped pack. His parents were immortal. *Literally*, no one could leave him because the pack couldn't leave the valley. He had no idea how shit abandonment felt, regardless of his age. He didn't understand that people weren't reliable, and that I wasn't angry or bitter about that. It just was.

Fact.

Done.

Reaching behind me for the handle, I twisted and pushed.

Sascha's reactions were too quick to fall on his face, but the look of shock on his features didn't quite mesh with what I'd done. Smirking, I turned, jolting at the sight of Rhona.

Her shock equalled his.

"Rhona," I said calmly. "Sascha Greyson was just leaving."

My sister's emerald eyes moved between my short dressing gown and the Luther leader's bare chest.

Okay, this didn't look great.

Her shock morphed to rage. She blinked several times and met my eye once again.

I spoke over my shoulder. "Goodbye, Luther."

"If you change your mind, let me know, Head Steward," he said.

My heart squeezed. The words were nonsense. He was trying to give me a way out of this.

But I already had one.

Even with *that* excuse, this looked bad.

"Not a chance," I replied. "Rhona. Come in."

She shouldered Sascha while obeying, but only a slight sorrow flickered in his eyes at her rudeness.

Yeah, he'd killed her father. Sascha was lucky Rhona didn't attempt to return the favour.

"Head Steward." He moved to the stairs and glanced back, searching my face

"I've got this," I mouthed. Aloud, I said, "Luther. I'll see you in Grids."

He hovered on the top step, focus sliding to the open entrance.

Making the choice for him, I entered and shut the door.

White-lipped fury about summed Rhona up.

Shit.

Leaning over the couch, I gazed out the window, watching Sascha stride away.

"What the fuck?" Rhona seethed.

Half turning, I held a finger to my lips.

"You *slept* with that fucker?" she exploded.

I winced as her voice boomed in my ears. I could probably hear that from around a kilometre away, so there was no chance Sascha didn't catch it even with the frequency generators. "You're making a series of assumptions. I suggest you listen first instead."

The words were harsh, yes, but I'd changed into a fucking wolf last night, so she could suck it up.

She inhaled sharply for another go.

"*Rhona.*" My voice cracked like a whip.

Her mouth snapped shut. I doubted she'd ever been spoken to in such a way.

She tests our authority, my wolf silently spoke.

My fingernails sharpened and extended. *We've got to stay cool!*

Forest, forest, forest. Calm.

Why? my wolf enquired.

I gave her a quick rundown of Rhona, the stewards, and my position and felt her boredom seep through me.

Human politics. I will leave you to them.

My claws receded and the pressure in my gums disappeared.

Sascha's footsteps cut off suddenly. He'd moved past the frequency generators. I could still see him walking away through the trees though.

It had to be the frequency generators.

"If we speak quietly, he shouldn't hear," I said, doing a final check for any wolfy body changes before facing her. "Let's clear one thing up. I did not sleep with Sascha Greyson. No matter my agenda for the tribe, I'm not willing to go that far."

Her face didn't change.

"You don't believe me?"

"You're naked beneath that gown," she hissed.

I shrugged. "I showered and fell into bed after hours of cleaning. The Luther woke me up when he arrived. I expected you, Wade, or Cameron, so I just put the gown on. When I realised it was him, of course I wasn't about to change—not with the theory we're currently testing."

She chewed on that, but for the first time—maybe ever—Rhona didn't give me a shred of reluctant acceptance.

Dang, she was really upset.

"He came the very morning after you moved out here?" She looked at the two mugs. "How did he know?"

Crap. My heart thumped. "I believe he's stalking me."

"Why?"

I opened the closet and dragged out loose shorts and a comfortable T-shirt. This gown was chaffing me. Long sleeves and pants weren't a great idea today. My professional appearance would need to take a hit until I wrapped my head around the new sensitivity of my skin. "Because he often turns up where I am. I went to collect my things from the apartment recently and he arrived not long after I got there."

"Why didn't you tell me?"

I pulled on underwear and a bra, drawing on the silk T-shirt before pulling up the high-waisted linen shorts and fastening the large brown buttons up the front. "Because he'd just killed your father, Rhona. You don't like to worry me, and I don't like to worry you."

"If I hadn't come across the pair of you, would I know about *this*? I asked Heather to alert me if she spotted anything unusual on the cameras. He avoided them somehow."

I nodded grimly. "Heather never called me either. Obviously, I didn't expect to wake up with a Luther at my door. If they're able to wriggle their way onto tribe territory, we need to tighten security."

Rhona considered me. She'd tucked her rage away, but a hardness remained.

"Something's worrying you," I said softly. "You knew this was the plan, Rhona. You knew I intended to use this infatuation against him. It was your idea."

Rhona faced the window. "He was *inside* your cabin, Andie. That's another thing entirely. Did he… did he *touch* you?"

Thank fuck she was facing away. Blood rushed into my cheeks because, *uh*—yes—touching ensued. Some really nice touching that couldn't happen again.

"He's playing a game of cat and mouse with me. For now."

Rhona shook her head. "*For now*. Then what?"

"That's what we need to decide in the upcoming weeks. For Grids. Together."

She faced me, and I couldn't notice any dent in the hardness.

"Maybe we should call it quits on this strategy right now. You seem upset, and nothing is worth that to me. Say the word, and we'll move on."

That got to her at last.

The tension in my shoulders eased as she exhaled.

"You've never betrayed my trust," she muttered. "It's just that Dad never did either. Until he *really* did, you know?"

My stomach churned. "I know. Just please remember that I would do anything for you, Rhona. Always. Anything, seriously."

She forced a smile. "I know. It's just... there's never been anything between you and the Luther before now, right?"

Here it was. The opening to reveal all and tell her the sordid truth—that Herc's death was partially my fault. That I could have prevented it.

Was there anything I could tell her without revealing too much? "That's everything, sister. If it means a lot to you, I'll fill you in on the small things from now on."

"I'd like that," she answered after a beat.

I wrapped my arms around her, waiting stubbornly until she gave up and hugged me back.

"Ready for Timber tonight?" she asked.

Nope. "Bring it on."

13

This grid brought back a whole heap of memories—and regrets. I might never have encountered Sascha if not for entering Timber on the wrong night.

One fucking sniff. That's why I was here.

The thought made my gums ache, so I forced my attention to the here and now.

"Visibility is an issue in Timber as you see," Pascal said from beside me. "We wait here until the end. Tallying the points takes longer as we must go through the grid after, but there's nothing for it."

The less people I could see, then the less people could see me. *Ideal.* Because the high emotion was getting to me—the mounting tension and smell of adrenaline urged my wolf to the surface.

She wanted to run in the trees. To chase and catch prey.

Let's get through the next two hours, I pleaded with her again. *Sascha said not to shift until we've healed, but if you can wait a few hours, we'll go for a run after Grids.*

But I could just go now, she answered in a matter-of-fact tone.

You could. If you want me to be hurt.

Human politics?

Yep.

She sighed. *After the game then.*

Thanking the presence in my head, I replied to Pascal, "How long until the Luthers enter?"

"Five minutes."

The stewards were currently split into four teams. One team was fixing traps that the Luthers located and tampered with between times. That wasn't something we usually had to deal with —what with normally having Timber in our possession between games.

Gentle rolling hills made up this terrain. Those hills were crammed tight with the oldest trees Deception Valley had to offer. Virgin forest splayed out, the master of this place since far before my birth. Thick roots jutted and dipped under the thick layer of leaves and pine needles blanketing the ground. The canopy was so thick barely any of the remaining sunlight could make it through.

I could feel my power to resist four-legged form dwindle as twilight deepened, and I inwardly kicked myself for being so confident after a day without issue in the manor.

The sun was my power, and the growing darkness called to us both. It wanted to sharpen our senses. To protect us.

I'd be stronger in four-legged form.

Boom.

My ears picked up the distant sound of seven hundred running Luthers even over the frequency generators. That meant human ears could pick up the sound too. The footsteps came from the south and north where the pack entered the grid.

Tonight, I'd use my new senses to better understand their strategy. The frequency generators limited me, but I had my sight and sense of smell, and one day as a Luther had shown me smell was my most powerful tool.

Correct, my wolf said.

Can you help?

All the better to eat Greyson's heart with.

Whatever floats your boat. I felt her slide to occupy my nose, ears, eyes. Without knowing exactly how, I understood she navigated those systems now, leaving me to control movement and speech. Which was for the best. A quick test revealed she was as bad at walking in two-legged form as I was in four-legged, and no matter what she sounded like in my mind, she didn't actually speak any form of human.

As she took over my senses, I realised how exhausted I was from controlling everything all day. Sharing like this did feel easy and right.

We couldn't do this all the time, but...

Maybe once I get used to four-legged form, I can work on letting you have complete control for stints too, I told her.

I'd like that.

I didn't want to always lock her up. For all I'd said to Sascha that morning, there was now one being that wouldn't leave me.

We inhaled deeply, and I caught a curious look from Pascal.

Easy with the sniffer. We have company.

Our enemy are advancing and creating a line from the river to where they entered. Like a crescent moon.

It's what they did last time too. It was a favourite of Sascha's—to unify his pack on the battlefield and work through the grid systematically.

I distanced myself from Pascal and clicked my walkie-talkie. "This is Big Red. Luthers forming a crescent front from north to south along east ridge. Prepare for phase one. Over."

Three team leaders responded with "*Roger that, Big Red.*"

One did not.

I pressed my lips together. Rhona.

Should I read into that?

Turning from Pascal, we inhaled again.

Their scent is strengthening, my wolf growled.

Moving closer?

Fifty of the metres you showed me.

Let me know when they're another fifty, please.

I checked Pascal and found her tapping away on the tablet.

"*This is Reindeer. Circling now. Over.*"

The north team was nearly in position.

"*Snow. In position.*"

West and east should already be in position too. I received confirmation from the third team a minute later.

Not Rhona.

I clicked the walkie. "*Big Red. East in position? Over.*"

Silence.

For fuck's sake. I thought she was over this morning. Chills ran down my spine. Unless she was in trouble.

Your pack is in danger? My wolf growled, hackles raising.

Maybe. Maybe not.

They're fifty metres closer.

I clicked the button again. "Initiate phase one."

If the Luthers wanted to congregate in a nice, tidy group, then we'd use that to our advantage. My stewards were about to funnel them into a gulley that three teams spent an hour rigging with every kind of quick set-up trap we had in stock.

I heard muffled shouting in the distance as my stewards opened fire to drive the pack into the gulley. Other than that? Nothing.

I shook my head. Those generators were fucking annoying.

Adrenaline, my wolf growled.

The smell of prey rose from my trapped enemy.

They're running, Andie. Closer to us.

Into the trap. Good. They just had to keep going. If the north and south teams could hold the exit point at their end, and east and west could do the same, then the traps in the gulley would do the work.

A howl rocketed through the air, and I gasped, fangs and claws exploding. I strode farther from Pascal.

It's him, my wolf said in fury. *Greyson.*

Not here! I frantically tried to assemble my mental forest. Stepping farther into the trees, I grappled with her for control.

"Andie?" Pascal asked.

My wolf was losing the plot. I had to get out of here.

Forcing my fangs away with every scrap of energy I possessed, I blurted in a rough voice, "Change of plans. I need to see what's going on. I'm entering the grid."

"You're certain?"

"I'll see you afterward."

That was all I could manage. My fangs slid back into place as I gave up the battle for control.

I broke into a human-paced run. I had to get away from Pascal.

And fast.

Another howl. Sascha could make the sound in his two-legged form, but that was 100 percent Greyson.

His call was impossible to deny. To turn from it would be like leaving the pup to drown at the river. His howl forced a reaction from me.

Not the need to protect.

Kill.

I licked my lips and focused on keeping my wolf at a human-paced run until we were far enough from Pascal.

Then I just let go.

Oh my god. We were too weak to run last night. This felt...

Glorious didn't sum it up.

This was freedom. Elation filled every part of me. For a moment, the need to tear Greyson apart took second place.

It feels even better with four legs, she grumbled.

I look forward to shifting after the grid. Smelling a steward nearby, I slowed to a lope and veered west.

But you said Luthers lose points for shifting in the grid.

I halted behind a tree, scanning for company. *You're evil. And smart.*

Thank you.

Glancing around once more, I sniffed hard. Nothing except small prey.

"*Wizard here. Phase one successful. Over.*"

I jerked at the jubilant message from west and hastily clicked on my walkie. "Big Red. Initiate phase two. Over."

"Roger."

Three replies.

Again.

You're worried about your sister.

She could take care of herself, but the protocol was clear. If Rhona went down, the closest member of the unit took over communication. I should have heard from Billy, Foley, or the others by now.

My gut churned.

Ripping off my clothes, I crouched. *Okay, shift. Quickly though. I need to get back to the walkie.*

Greyson's distant howl hammered in my chest.

My pleasure.

My gasp was more from shock as my human body split into a thousand pieces. Last night, I felt every breaking bone and every snap of sinew. Tonight, my mind couldn't process the rapid breaking and reforming.

FurLegsSnoutFangsKneeBendTeeth.

An ancient strength infused us, *filled* us, completed us.

Mmm, my wolf said, shaking her coat.

She wasn't wrong. I felt invincible. *We should walk close to a heat sensor to make sure they lose a point for a shift.*

If you like. She took off at a lope through the forest.

This was our best speed. Not a sprint as I would have assumed prior. We could keep up this loping pace for weeks on end if our tummy was full. Nothing in the world could rival our stamina.

Nothing could outlast us.

I focused on our senses, relying on memory of the grid. *There's a sensor to the left. There's no way it missed our shift.*

I'm glad for you.

Okay, let's go back. I need to be by my walkie.

I think not.

I blinked. *Now is not the time to go off on a vendetta. If you attack Greyson, my pack comes to harm.*

If any are near, they will only see a wolf attacking another wolf.

And you think the Luthers will just allow that to happen? I rely on their secrecy.

Human politics.

Politics that keep me safe.

Greyson must die.

Then I hope you enjoy watching Sascha die too, I snapped.

She shrugged, and I focused on forcing us back to human form. What was I meant to do? Imagine my human legs. My ears... and... *Where are we going?*

I'm drawing him out.

Of course. He could feel where we were. *You have access to my memories and knowledge then?*

No, those I must earn in time, as you must earn mine. I listened to your conversation with my Sascha this morning. It is bothersome that I can't also feel where he is.

My wolf circled around the north and south team. I could smell the barricade of their human bodies and knew the tribe were holding strong.

If I didn't fuck it up, we may have another grid in thirty minutes.

It is time, she announced.

Time for what?

Resting on her haunches, she bared our throat to the waning moon and howled.

I shrivelled and died inside. *You didn't!*

She did it again, and I caught Sascha's hypnotic scent. It stood out from the chaotic smells of his pack like a red flag in a sea of black.

He can't get to us, she cackled. *He's stuck.*

Another howl burst from our snout. This one was filled with glee.

Don't forget my pack will hear that and try to take you out. I smelled for company and located a small group advancing from the north.

We took off south, settling our pace after a brief sprint. My wolf howled again, laughing as Sascha's smell remained within the gulley to our right.

Greyson is listening to Sascha, she scoffed. *He's trying to do what's right for the pack. Loser.*

It's nice to know that's possible, I scowled. *This isn't funny. I need my clothes and to direct my team. You want to kill Greyson, that's fine by me. We're meeting him in two days. Let's do it then.*

They'll lose another point if he shifts.

Not everything is about points, I said angrily. *It's about winning the game, not the battle. It's about keeping what we are a secret.*

This will get him out.

She yelped, injecting pain into a short howl.

My jaw dropped. *You faker!*

I inhaled. His scent was growing stronger. Fast.

For fuck's sake. *He's coming.*

Yes, my enemy is coming to die, and he's not alone. Four wolves.

Despite myself, I couldn't help tallying the points they'd lose.

Boom. The final cannon exploded.

In control of our body, she took off at full speed south. Without her speaking, I knew we were looking for high ground. An ideal place to fight.

We were small but very quick.

I studied the forest. *We're approaching one of the Luther's entry points.*

I want his people to watch him die.

Oh, was that all? Her Greyson hate was nice and all, but it didn't gel with her girl crush on Sascha. *I'm not sure I'm down with the public death thing.*

I really wasn't sure killing was my thing at all.

We left the last frequency generator behind, and less than ten seconds after we'd sprinted past, the distinct tread of four wolves reached our ears.

One was lighter than the others, fast like me.

We found a narrow path between two rock faces and my wolf turned.

This is crazy, I hissed. *His pack won't let you eat his damn heart.*

They won't have a choice. The stronger wolf will lead. This could end all your problems.

I stopped at that. *That's ludicrous.*

Is it? You lead one pack. Why not two?

We stopped bickering as the largest damn wolf I'd ever seen padded into sight. It was the third time I'd seen him.

Greyson.

His luscious dark brown coat had thinned for summer. Honey eyes blazed into mine from across the space. He was a strong wolf. Able-bodied. Sharp teeth. Powerful contender for breeding.

You're kidding me, I snapped.

Doesn't mean I like him.

I took in the white wolf on his right. *Leroy.* A shaggy black wolf to his left. *Hairy?* And a smaller wolf I'd seen at the reading of Herc's will. *Mandy.*

Mate.

The word was pushed into my mind by force.

We flattened our ears, snarling a warning.

You've come to fight me? He seemed amused.

Is that what we just said?

At a look from him, the wolves relaxed their stances and strolled away, looking at us from rocky perches.

They're taking us super seriously.

When I have my teeth at his neck, they will, she whispered back. *And when his blood dribbles down our chin, they will bow to me.*

I swallowed back queasiness. *This is going pretty far.*

More wolves spilled into the clearing now Grids was over. Some snapped my way, but most just obeyed looks from their leader, taking up onlooker positions around the clearing.

Fuck me. Just get it over with. I sighed wearily.

Like a catapult, we hurtled across the clearing. Greyson lowered, waiting to strike, but at the last second, we zigzagged, biting his back leg as we passed at a blur.

He didn't make a sound, but his pack stood as one, hackles raising.

We loped around Greyson, careful not to get too close. His strength beat our speed.

In another burst of speed, we dragged our claws deep in his left flank.

It will take hours to beat me this way, beautiful wolf, Greyson said.

You killed a member of her pack. I do not care how long it takes.

Hercules Thana would have killed her.

You treated her as though she had no say. You killed him before giving her second thought. You are not a worthy mate.

I did not know they were father and daughter.

Uncle and niece wasn't enough?

He bared his teeth. *I only thought of protecting her. I could smell murder on his skin. I was in peril. You know what that would do to her. There was no other choice, even if you both hate me for it now. I knew that was the risk, but I can live with her hate. I cannot live with her death.*

I cut off my wolf's reply. *The murder on his skin was for you, Luther.*

Your father was revolted by you. How long before he turned the gun in your direction? He may have done it after my death when he saw your reaction. He could have blamed me for your death while he was at it.

Theories aren't a good enough reason to kill someone, I exploded. *You took him from me and my sister. You took him from our tribe.*

If you expect me to regret the decision, little bird, then you are talking to the wrong part of me. We are alive and whole because that human is gone. I will always regret your pain. I regret that you no longer trust me as you once did. Though I can live with it, I regret the hate you feel when you look at me.

I'd never trusted him.

I regret, he kept going, *that your heart was broken. That is also mine to protect, and if there was another way, I would have protected you in all ways at once, rather than sacrifice one part for another.*

Growling, my wolf went for him, and I had no qualms with

giving her complete control. Claws extended, we went head to head with Greyson, slashing through fur and flesh.

He batted us away with a great paw and pounced.

Teeth gnashing in warning, Greyson snarled an inch from my throat.

Good plan, I told her sarcastically.

She didn't answer.

Hello? I called.

Where the hell did she go?

I kicked and scratched at Greyson's underbelly, refusing to expose my throat. He lay on top of me and brought his teeth to my neck, gripping it.

Fuck you, I spat.

He shook me slightly, and whatever his leader status gave him, the power battered at my mind, ramming into my refusal to turn my head.

I will never submit to you.

Little bird, beautiful wolf, I would never want you to.

He released my neck and stepped back. I launched at him, latching onto his throat.

Greyson froze.

I didn't dare relinquish my lethal grip on his throat. I felt more than saw the frantic pulse of his watching pack. I listened to their whines and relished their fear.

I could end their leader with a single bite.

His blood *would* drip down my chin.

The thought slammed into me.

Andie, Greyson said wearily, *I cannot submit. While Sascha has the ability, like your wolf, I do not. You must kill me or release me.*

If I killed him, I'd lead both the pack and stewards. My wolf was right. This could all be so easy.

But the images my wolf had painted of Greyson's death were graphic. The thought of his heart in my mouth. Of crunching through the artery held between my teeth.

It made me feel...

Vile.

Filthy.

Diseased.

Releasing him, I backed away.

Thank you, Andie, she whispered.

Oh, *now* she was back?

What the fuck was that? I seethed at her.

Sascha and Greyson cannot be separated.

That's what I was telling you the entire time!

You cannot deny the existence of one.

I bared my teeth. Whoa. What?

That's not what she'd said up until now. She was all about hating Sascha's wolf. She— *This was a fucking set up.*

Liking Greyson is not a must. It is something he must work for. Acceptance of his presence is a must. Today you admitted to yourself, to Greyson and Sascha, and to this pack that the loss of him is beyond you.

I'd never wanted to attack myself. She'd betrayed me. An actual *part* of me had betrayed me. She'd lied the entire time and put me in danger. Not just me, my tribe. *I thought you were on my side.*

There really wasn't anyone I could rely on.

My mistake.

I—

Forcing her into a box, I threw my mind at my human form, away from this farce; this joke I fell for last night.

The shift back was rapid.

Naked, I crouched in front of Greyson and lifted my head before standing.

"I apologise," I said stiffly. "My wolf decided to take over."

The enormous creature blocked my attempt to step around him.

Crack. Pop.

Sascha unfolded, naked, to stand over me, and I was so fucking angry at my wolf that his scrutinising look bounced straight off me.

"The marshals are tallying the grid. That's not a great place to be right now," he said eventually.

"That's where my clothes are."

His wolves were shifting back and stared on in condemning silence. Whatever. I didn't give a flying fuck what they thought.

Sascha strode past me to a bag. He drew out a flannel shirt, tossing it my way. "Take this."

Circling, he glared at the watching wolves, a warning growl rising from his throat. They found other places to look.

He barely gave me enough space to shrug into the huge shirt. "Thanks," I grunted, moving away.

"What was that?"

I couldn't look at him. "You deserve an explanation, but I can't give it to you. My wolf isn't who I thought she was."

The pine was intense. Heady. Sascha shoved his curiosity back. "I'll drive you back to the manor."

The manor? He knew perfectly well I wasn't there anymore. I peered around...

But his pack didn't?

Interesting.

"No." I could find my cabin. Ella F was there. It shouldn't be far. I'd change and head back to the manor.

Hopefully people weren't searching for me.

Sascha gripped my arm, and before I knew it, I'd whirled, my claws fully extended under his chin. I latched onto the strange calm inside me and lowered my fangs as I stared up at him.

Gasps rang from those watching, but Sascha smiled widely.

"Clever wolf," he whispered.

"Don't touch me without permission," I bit out.

He released his hold, and I retracted my claws and fangs, eliciting further gasps from his pack.

Ignoring them, I took off at a fast clip to the river that I could follow toward my cabin.

Hopefully this night hadn't exploded in my fucking face.

14

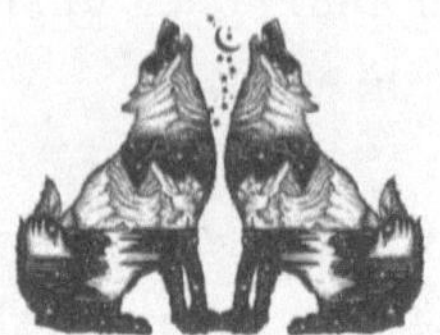

If no one looked closely, they wouldn't notice the different outfit. I inched Ella F into the last available park at the manor and listened to the thrumming bass rocketing from the stone building.

Party time, apparently.

I jogged for the steps. I had to find Rhona.

"Andie!"

My heart jolted. "Pascal, I've been searching for you. What's the verdict?"

A smile curved her thin lips. "A convincing win. They lost five points for shifting in the grid. The final tally was 145 to 110. The bottleneck strategy was a success."

And something that wouldn't work again. "That's great news."

At last. Talk about a week from hell.

"I was worried," she said as we walked up the steps. "Not long after you entered the grid, a Luther shifted ahead of you."

Thankfully she had no idea my faster speed meant that was me. "Yeah, the wolf chased me, but I managed to outsmart it just before the final cannon sounded. I didn't get a chance to reach the gulley."

She nodded, but that meant nothing when it came to this woman.

"Sounds like quite the party," I said as we entered the manor.

"It's your first turnover win." She cast me an amused look.

I supposed it was. In Iron, we just held the grid. This was the first time I'd won one back. "Hey, have you seen Rhona?"

"Yeah, she was around just before."

My chest loosened. I'd started to assume the worst.

Cameron grabbed my hand, spinning me. "The victor is here, everyone!"

A chorus of loud cheers rang out, and I grinned.

I *did* put in the work to bring in this win. The funnel idea was mine.

So I'd shifted into a wolf the last two nights. That didn't mean I couldn't claim this moment and this victory. I did all that work for these people.

I could enjoy this.

Cameron shoved and yanked until I clambered onto a seat. Giving up, I called to the room, "Your effort in Timber was nothing short of incredible. I'm so very proud of what we managed to do. You should all congratulate yourselves on reclaiming a grid. We're back at three!"

Mostly, I was impressed some of the stewards seemed drunk already. Guess intense training and adrenaline would lower a person's tolerance.

Wade wrapped an arm around Cameron and me. "How are my two favourite ladies?"

"Tired," I said honestly.

What a fucking night.

"I thought you were resting up last night?" Cam leaned forward to look across Wade at me.

... About that. "Maybe I feel worse for getting more sleep."

"Well, how about we relax tonight and have a drink before you go?"

I couldn't think of anything worse than a drunk, newly shifted Luther set loose on the manor. "Just one can't hurt."

When they looked away, I'd chuck it.

Wade and I watched Cameron dance to the drinks table.

"Is she weirdly happy recently?" he murmured. "We haven't hung out nearly as much."

Perhaps she'd met someone. "She'll tell us when she's ready. The person she's seeing may not be out or something."

"And you? How are you really?"

I looked into his beautiful grey eyes. "I've decided to start the meets again."

"Bit of whiplash never hurt anyone."

I nudged him. "Shut up."

"It's the least he deserves. For what it's worth. I think it's the right choice."

I rested my head against his shoulder. He smelled like salted caramel and the scent comforted me. "You're worth a whole lot to me, opinions and all."

"I support you."

"Don't ruin this."

"You do you."

Cameron returned to find us laughing. She crooked a brow. "Do I want to know?"

"We support you," I told her solemnly.

Her smile faded. "What?"

What did I say? "Wade's being crazy. Nothing."

Spotting my head team, I untangled myself and approached them. "A win!" I said.

Roderick wasted no time clinking his glass against mine. Valerie was a beat behind the others as always, but Nathan surprised me with hearty cheers. His approval was like a beam of sunlight shining directly out of his ass.

But I'd take it.

"I didn't think we'd get the Luthers in there." He shook his head.

Stanley eyed him. "We know. We had to listen to you all week."

I chuckled with the rest.

Nathan waved us to silence. "I was never happier to be proven wrong. We have the majority again." He raised his glass to me. "To our innovative leader's first turnover."

He tossed his drink back.

Pride filled my chest, but I was careful to taper it. Happy emotions worked just as well as angry emotions when it came to shifting—though my wolf hadn't uttered a peep since betraying me earlier.

Good riddance.

I'd been an idiot to trust her so quickly.

"Thank you all," I said. "When Herc was murdered, you got me as a replacement. I know how that looked—me hardly here a month and with the barest understanding of Victratum. I appreciate you giving me time to prove myself. I can't deny I'm relieved at the win, but it's just the start. I won't rest until the stewards have all five in their pocket."

And what would that mean for over seven hundred and fifty trapped Luthers?

I forced the thought away. They were my enemy, and the tribe was here first. Only one could win, and I could only worry about so much.

I took a fake sip. "Has anyone seen Rhona?"

"In the spa last I saw," Valerie piped up at last.

Her fruit smell took on a sour edge that took me by surprise. *Wow,* Valerie really didn't like me. Well, I'd give her two weeks to fix her attitude, then the grace period was at an end and I'd find a replacement. Her grief over Herc's death shouldn't be redirected toward me. Even if I deserved it more than she knew.

Walking through the manor wasn't a quick task. Everyone wanted to talk. Halfway there, I waved at the Freys, absorbed in listening to a play-by-play by Reindeer—aka Brooke Sarson—my north team leader.

Now I'd sealed a win and gotten my head around the process, meeting every steward should become a priority.

"Hey, Wade?" I asked when he joined me at the patio above the pool.

"Baby girl?"

He wrenched to a stop at the balustrade, staring down at the spa. "Are you seeing that?"

I squinted in the same direction before remembering I had no need to squint anymore.

"Foley and Laura," he hissed. "Sucking face."

That was one way to say it. They looked to be doing everything *but* having sex. They'd scared everyone else out and the pool area was rapidly clearing.

"I thought he was exclusive with Rhona," Wade said.

"So did I."

My sister's dark auburn ponytail was nowhere in sight, and a low anger unfurled in my stomach at Foley's blatant disrespect. Even if they'd ended without my knowledge, this was bullshit.

I passed Wade my drink.

"Oh, shit," he whispered.

Marching down the patio steps, I took hold of the calm, forest feeling cultivated through many hours of playing the saxophone. After forcing my wolf into a box, I knew that calm feeling was powerful and could be trusted. I was strong enough to control my wolf's guest appearances.

My gums didn't ache. My fingernails were normal length.

I crouched by their heads. Unnoticed.

Gross.

"Foley, dear," I said sweetly.

He jerked away from Laura, and I smiled down at them.

"How are things going?" I asked.

Laura spoke female and established a convincing distance between them without delay.

"Have you seen Rhona?" I addressed the red-faced and, in my opinion, spineless man.

Foley stammered, "She broke up with me. This morning. Whatever you're thinking."

My brows climbed. "You sound angry about that. Is that why we're getting this display in the pool? As payback."

"No," he burst out.

I didn't need the telltale flush of his cheeks with my new nose. The earthy component to his scent took on a rotten edge.

His words were false.

Laura folded her arms.

"You're a free man, Foley," I said. "But this behaviour is beneath you. You may also consider that the stewards need Rhona to be on her best game, and something like this may distract her from fulfilling her roles. We have three grids now. It could be four, but everyone needs to put themselves aside to make that happen."

He averted his eyes. "We'll find a room."

Laura scoffed and in a flurry of droplets left the spa.

Unfortunately, Foley did *not* speak female.

"Laura, wait," he called.

"I'm sorry your heart is hurting," I told him. "If you need to talk, it doesn't matter that Rhona's my sister, I'm here to listen and give what advice I can as your head steward too."

Kudos to him, the guy managed what Rhona rarely could—to swallow his temper. Genuinely.

A wrinkle appeared between his brows. "Thanks, Andie."

I stood and peered at Wade, who raised both of our glasses in my direction.

Couldn't blame Rhona for making scarce with that display, but I didn't hear from her during Grids, and now she was nowhere to be seen. She came over this morning and didn't mention anything about the breakup—or that she intended to end things with Foley.

Don't panic.

It meant nothing.

She was safe.

The first level hall was crammed with younger stewards who'd snuck in alcohol. Too absorbed with hiding their drinks, they didn't draw me into conversation.

I'd check Rhona's room. She may have retreated to punch something.

Passing my office, I backstepped and poked my head inside.

She was sitting behind the desk.

My entire body sagged against the door. "Rhona, here you are."

She didn't lift her head, absorbed with whatever she was reading.

I entered, and the voices outside muffled as I shut us in. "I was worried."

"Why?" she asked.

Uh. "You weren't answering my orders in Timber. I couldn't find you afterward. Why are you in here?"

"I got sick of the party."

Her tone was off. And her smell. Something was up.

Oh, duh. Of course.

I perched on the desk. "I heard about you and Foley. He was being a dick in the spa, but he's stopped now. He was only doing it for your attention."

Crap, Foley, Rhona, and Laura were in the same unit. I'd need to monitor them in the next grid and split them up if necessary.

"I don't care about him."

I studied her. "People fall out of love all the time."

"I chose him because I'd never love him."

Smart choice. I stilled at the thought and her words struck me in the gut. Sascha's accusation flashed in my mind.

You use sex as a weapon.

Was there something to his words?

Rhona didn't like to say goodbye. I didn't like to be said goodbye *to.* Neither of us got in too deep. We specifically chose men that would allow us to get what we needed without posing a threat. Looking back, I could say that I chose Logan for his body. But if I was honest, I chose him because he annoyed me outside the bedroom.

Nothing would have ever come of it.

Shit. I really did do that.

Rhona leaned back, and I caught sight of her reading material. "You're reading Mum's journal."

"Is there a problem with that?"

She was angry with *me*, that much was clear from her flat tones.

Why?

She was reading *I'm 18*. "Not at all. Maybe you'll find something in them that I didn't. I'm finishing up with the last one."

I had to break the news about Murphy to her soon—before she got her hands on *I'm 19* and discovered what he became. It wasn't ideal for her to get a look at the symptoms of a werewolf transformation though… maybe I'd remove some pages to protect myself.

"If you want the first six journals, let me know. They're out at the cabin."

"The cabin," she echoed in a strange voice.

I crouched and tried to peer at her face. She rarely wore her hair down, and the long curtain hid her face. "Seriously, Rhona, what's up? I thought we sorted out the Sascha thing."

She finally met my gaze. "So did I."

Her scent was bouncing all over the place. Her words weren't false, that's all I could glean. Other than that, I'd guess that she wasn't sure what to feel. "You need to help me out here. I have no idea what you're upset about."

"I felt bad for going to Heather after our chat this morning," she said, hardly blinking. "I sent her out of the security room and felt like a piece of shit for looking over the footage. Like doing that was a betrayal to you."

Shit.

Rhona knew what I was.

I said nothing, unwilling to condemn myself.

"You said Sascha Greyson turned up this morning. That you'd cleaned for hours last night and fell asleep naked." She laughed, shaking her head. "What a joke. You left your cabin in your car just before seven."

Leaning forward, she extracted her phone and unlocked it to reveal a picture. Of me in Ella F. Dated and with a time.

Not that I didn't already know she was right.

But what *else* did she know?

"You returned at one in the morning," she continued, "And you weren't alone."

The next picture was of the back of the car. The person driving wasn't visible, but there was clearly a large person driving and a smaller person in the passenger seat.

Fuck.

I stared into accusing emerald eyes. "What are you asking me, Rhona?"

"I'm not asking you anything. Not anymore. I can see how adept you are at wiggling out of tight spots. You spent the night with the Luther that killed my father. All night. You drove to see him, and he returned with you."

It spoke volumes of my life that I was just relieved she hadn't uncovered the biggest secret of all.

"It's not what you think." I stood. "I went to the lake for some alone time. While I was there, the same wolf who attacked me in Water came—"

"Where are the signs?" She scanned my body. "Attacked by a Luther again, and not a scratch on you. How lucky."

"It is, actually." I should be covered in scratches and bruises after my first shift. I assumed an accelerated healing ability was to thank.

Rhona rose, too, managing to stare me down though we were the same height. "I returned to the manor entry point after the game. Pascal was there. She said you'd gone into the grid."

"I believed you were in trouble because you weren't answering my orders." *Lie.* I shook my head. "Are you telling me that you weren't answering on purpose? You know better than to let your personal issues affect the game."

"I was fulfilling your *orders*, Head Steward," she said sarcastically. "I just didn't feel like speaking with a traitor. Nothing comes between me, my stewards, and the game. *Nothing.*"

"So much anger, Rhona," I said quietly. "We've been through so much already. Please don't let this confusion tear us apart."

"*I'm* not coming between us." The unnatural flatness she'd

maintained split apart with shocking suddenness. My breath hitched in my throat.

"I trust what I feel," she shouted. "You're trying to convince me nothing's the matter. You're trying to make me feel stupid and irrational."

She advanced on me, and that usually would have made me scramble back, but her last words froze me to the spot.

Oh my god.

I *was* doing that to her.

Each time she'd asked for the truth or lost her temper, I made her doubt her judgement and instincts. I'd laughed off her worries or piled more lies on top.

I professed to love my sister, and to put her above every other person in this valley, and yet I was destroying her self-confidence—abusing the trust between us.

I cut her off. "You're right. That is what I've done."

Rhona stared, but regained her anger in short measure. "Tell me the truth. All of it. How long have you been luring in Sascha Greyson?"

That was the real kick in the chest. Part of her still believed I was doing this for our so-called plan. She was this angry because she thought I'd concealed something to do with *that*.

Closing my eyes, I circled the table and sat in one of the visitor chairs.

I had to tell her everything.

The truth about Herc.

About me and Sascha.

Making her feel less because of my own past mistakes was just as bad as leaving her. I couldn't do this anymore.

"You'll want to sit," I rubbed my forehead. "This goes back a while."

She didn't. No surprise.

"It started the first night I entered Deception Valley." I watched her with tired eyes. "That night, Sascha Greyson smelled me for the first time. And something started that I wouldn't learn about for a while yet—something that Luthers call a mating call."

Rhona sucked in a harsh breath.

I ploughed on, bitter relief tinging my words as truth rushed from my lips. "Luthers have one mate in their lives. It seems I am Sascha Greyson's."

Disgust twisted her features.

I couldn't stop now.

"I didn't know that back then. I noticed how strange he behaved around me when offering the job at The Dens. A couple of times, when we first looked at each other and first touched, I collapsed. The weirdest feeling came over me. Soon after, I learned werewolves existed, and sometime after *that,* I returned to The Dens. Sascha confessed we were moving through a series of meets designed so he could prove his worthiness to me. I would be able to deny or accept him as a mate at the end of these seven meets."

I could tell Rhona wasn't registering everything and recalled how long it took me to wrap my head around the concept.

She lowered into the head steward chair and found her voice. "When I asked why you were doing extra shooting practice, you said Luthers at The Dens were acting strangely."

I flinched in memory. "I'd just found out the truth. It was after I saved the pup from drowning and woke on pack lands. He told me that another meet was coming soon. His wolf would learn everything about me, before chasing and capturing me."

She snorted.

"I was a steward at this point," I said softly. "I believed in the plight of the tribe. And I'd just met you and Uncle Herc. I knew what you both thought of the Luthers. I didn't want to lose either of you because of this thing that had been done *to me*. I just wanted the mating call to be gone. So I practiced with the tranquiliser gun and I moved to the manor for better protection before realising that would just present a bigger challenge to Sascha's wolf."

Her face was a wall. "You knew he'd do the next meet in Sandstone."

Closing my eyes, I forced the horrible guilt out at last, "I wondered if he would. It presented the largest challenge to his wolf."

"You knew he'd shift, and you said *nothing*. Did you think Dad and I would just let him chase you without coming to help? You have to know one or both of us could be in danger."

Her words slammed into my chest. "I wasn't sure of anything then. I was scared. Of Sascha. Of your reactions. I just thought if I could get through the capture meet—"

"You decided not to accept help." She withered.

I'd never heard a voice so cold. "Yes. I was scared—"

"You're a fucking coward," she shouted in my face, half standing.

Tears sparked my eyes. "I realise my mistake, believe me."

"And then you did it again." She swept everything off the table. "You lied to me about my own father's *death,* you piece of shit. Dad's will fucking stung, but I could rest a little easier because *you* were head steward. You..." She looked straight through me. "This is what you really are. A pathetic liar."

I stood, clinging to my depleting calm with everything I had. "I've wanted to tell you so many times. Sascha and I had already completed the capture meet when Herc found us. He had a gun. Without me saying anything, he knew what was going on. Maybe he'd already suspected. Why else have the gun? And he tried to shoot Sascha, too, even knowing what it would do to me."

The words rocked me. It was the first time I'd blamed Herc for what might have happened.

She rolled her eyes. "And what would happen?"

"Break me, apparently. Sascha will die if I'm killed. That's why another Luther is after me now. He thinks Sascha's connection to a human mate shows he's too weak to rule the pack. Rhona, you have to believe that you're the person I love most in the world. I can see how upset and angry you are. I understand that coming back from this could be impossible. Either way, I'm glad you know the truth. It's nothing less than you deserve. I don't think you're stupid or irrational. I just didn't know how to tell you."

"Bet getting all that off your chest will help you sleep at night." The cruel words slipped from her clenched teeth.

I absorbed the blow. "Do you have any more questions?"

She laughed—a harsh noise that would give me no shortage of nightmares. I'd never heard such a devoid sound except for the mournful echoes of my own heart.

"I know enough now to make a decision I should have made the moment Dad's will was read." Rhona's face twisted.

My growing fingernails dug into my palms. I spun from Rhona in case my eyes darkened. "Don't let this come between us. Please be smarter than me. You have a right to be angry and to hate me. But, in part, I lied to protect you."

"Get out."

I couldn't leave things like this.

My fangs pierced my gums and told me I was mistaken. Shifting into a wolf would be the straw on the camel's back. "Rhona—"

She screamed, "Get out!"

"I'm not leaving you," I lisped with the slight protrusion of my bulging incisors. "When you've had some time. When you have more questions. Or when you need me. I'll be here. I love you, Rhona. *Always.*"

Her voice lost the whip-like edge.

In its place was a dark voice I'd never heard from a human mouth.

"You're no daughter of my father's. You are no Thana. I reject you as head steward. The stewards may accept you for now, but you have no dominion over me any longer. You are no sister of mine."

Her words struck at the very oldest of my wounds and the most acute of my new fears. I gasped as my fangs surged.

"Get out," she whispered.

Eyes blurring and hands over my mouth, I stumbled from Herc's office.

15

I walked into the manor at dawn, waiting for the stewards to chase me out with pitchforks.

Rhona had all night to spread the sorry truth.

This was my mistake, my fuck up, and I'd come to face the music. Closure. Something no one had given me in my life. People deserved the chance to rant and rave and be furious.

But dread filled me.

The entranceway was empty of Tiptoe Eleanor, and I ducked through the kitchen to look out the window, scanning the training pavilions crammed with stewards.

Well, they were still focused on winning. That was good.

I should leave everything in order for Rhona in the office.

"Morning, Andie," Roderick said cheerfully.

Jerking, I glanced at him. "Oh, hey... How are you this morning?"

"I feel better than most. Not much of a drinker. Are you ready to capitalise on the win? Everyone is itching for a fourth grid."

He didn't know. That much was obvious. "Uh. Absolutely ready. I'll see you guys at eight."

What the hell was going on?

Grabbing an apple, I walked to the office in a daze.

In Herc's office, not a single book remained on the mahogany shelves. I'd seen Rhona sweep the desk clear, but she'd upturned the chairs and torn the curtains from their rails after I left.

I'd made her lose control to that degree. Just like Herc destroying her pride, I'd destroyed what was left of her. And from personal experience, I knew losing control to her temper would leave Rhona feeling like shit.

Closing the door, I set to work putting things to right. I could do that much. Maybe after, the way to setting things right with Rhona would be clearer.

By the time I'd finished, 8:00 a.m. loomed. I took a minute to ensure I had a hold of my forest calm, then dragged my ass to the meeting.

This was it for sure.

"Sorry, I got caught up." I entered the room.

The team didn't turn as one to glare at me. There were no ropes or burning pyres. Hope twinged in my gut. Did Rhona really put her feelings towards me aside for the good of the tribe?

Or did she think things through and see my side?

That seemed impossible after our argument last night, but what other explanation was there?

I scanned the head team, finding her in my chair, legs kicked up on the desk.

Stanley frowned at her. "You're in Andie's chair."

She shrugged.

I stared, and she stared right back. She hadn't told the stewards... but sitting there was a pretty clear declaration of her view of me. To everyone.

Whatever. I could handle a few petty jabs—I deserved no less.

"It's disrespectful is what it is," Stanley boomed.

Rhona didn't answer.

Put her in her place.

My wolf hadn't spoken since the grid last night. Ignoring her was harder when she spoke, but I'd fucking manage.

"It's okay, Stanley." I smiled. "I don't need a particular chair to get the job done."

I took the seat next to Rhona and glanced into mostly shocked faces. Pascal's was blank. Valerie appeared to love the show. Under my attention, she schooled her features.

I said to the table, "Personally, I'm here because I want to win another grid. If everyone is in agreement, I suggest we move on."

Dissent between the Thana sisters was a huge deal. It would confuse the head team and that would trickle down to the stewards. Rhona held my future in her hands. At any moment, she could tell all. Did she want to make me sweat? Was that it?

Regardless, by challenging my authority, she wasn't putting the tribe first as I'd expected.

"Personal problems have no space in this room," Pascal said to Rhona. "We can't expect to do our best for the tribe if we don't put our differences aside."

My sister leaned forward. "So we have Clay and Water to choose from."

The command in her voice was clear.

My mouth dried as I realised what her angle was. She was trying to lead the meeting. Rhona wanted my spot. She might not have outed me for my part in Herc's death and the mating call yet. She could have told the stewards everything and simply stepped into the top spot. Instead, Rhona planned to tear me down to become head steward.

Ouch.

"Clay is the obvious choice," I took over. "Even with our new plans for Water, revealing operations there before the time is right would be a mistake. In contrast, Clay is a more even footing. Operations there aren't as versatile, but they carry less cost to carry out. Plus, the tunnelling strategies we've considered will take time to put in place."

"I disagree," Rhona announced.

Roderick, who'd been about to speak, closed his mouth and gaped at her.

Yep, I was right. "Is there a reasoning behind your disagreement, Rhona?"

"The stewards are high on a win. That means something. We should use it to tackle Water again. See if we can chance a victory."

"I hardly think that's a solid plan. We can't rely on luck to win," Nathan said.

His words seemed to shock her.

She studied the other head team members, her mountain air scent pulsing. Weird. What did that mean?

"What are the other thoughts on Clay versus Water?" I asked.

Pascal replied, "Clay is the logical choice."

"We're not ready for Water," Stanley grumbled.

Roderick quirked a smile. "Your stewards are eager to return to Clay after your debut there."

They wouldn't be so eager to take my side if they knew what Rhona knew. "Clay it is. Moving on, we have Timber back. This is the first time I've been here for a grid turnover. What happens with the businesses?"

Trixie leaned forward. "That's my role. I put all Timber employees on standby before the game. They should be heading to their desks and jobs for a smooth takeover as we speak. Luthers are required to leave everything in acceptable order."

"Good. Thank you. Out of interest, where do the Timber stewards work when we didn't have that grid?"

"We absorb some of that number in Sandstone and Iron. The Timber crew rotate shifts in those grids and otherwise use their accumulated holiday leave. At that point, caring for them comes out of the tribe funds."

"I see. If we were to win Water and Clay, would we have enough staff to cover all five grids?"

She tapped a finger on the table. "We'd have to pull staff from our three grids to cover the head positions in the new grids. Being stronger and faster, the wolves don't hire any outsiders to help with work, whereas we'd definitely need to hire from the general valley population which makes things very tricky if the grid is switching back and forth between the tribe and pack. It's likely that people would need to move here from neighbouring regions to work for us. There'd be the question of accommodation for them."

Complicated. About what I expected. "Trixie, I'd like you to form another team, please. Your objective is to ensure that if we win Clay next week, there's a clear path for filling staff positions. One recommendation would be to book out tourist accommodation in town for any new workers. Not only will this help us relocate them, but it will create a dent in how many tourists can visit and spend money at The Dens." We owned all accommodation in town.

She jotted a few words in a notebook. "We can advertise jobs and delay the starting date if needed. The team can troubleshoot too."

"Please confer with Stanley regarding marketing costs. Stan, I trust that's something you'll have no problem with?"

He grunted.

I'd take that as a *yes*.

I ignored Rhona simmering beside me. What did she expect? To walk in here, click her fingers, and have the head team members jumping to her side? "I've read over the Victratum contract. It clearly states that care of the land must be exhibited at all times by the side in possession of each grid."

"What are you insinuating?" Rhona snapped.

I noted several annoyed expressions around the table. *Dammit.*

Sighing, I faced her.

Her eyes flashed.

Yep, she hated me alright, and it was like a burning dagger to the gut. "Rhona, I love you dearly. I value your input and your presence at my side. Whatever lays between us cannot affect the game. I know you're aware of that. I also know that sometimes shitty things happen in life, and it's hard to put feelings aside. If you're unable to do that today, that's okay. But if so, I'll need to ask you to leave this meeting. There's a job to do."

She pressed her lips together so hard they turned white. "You'd like that, wouldn't you?"

I waited for her to reveal everything. I could see it in her eyes—the indecision.

It was her right to tell whomever she wanted. To my error, I tried to control her without really knowing the consequences of doing such a thing. What happened next was her choice. I'd made my bed.

Rhona shoved her seat back.

"Please meet me in my office in twenty minutes," I told her softly.

Study would be skipped for the day. Pretty sure I was a hair's breadth from failing as it was, but some things couldn't be helped.

The room shook from the force of her slamming the door.

"I've never seen her like that," Valerie gasped. "What happened?"

Pascal saved the day. "I heard she broke up with Foley last night and caught him fooling around with Laura in the spa. She wasn't happy."

"Wade said you spoke with Foley after," Roderick said to me.

I swallowed. "I did."

"She's got a lot on her plate." Nathan peered to the door. "I'm worried about her."

"Something else must have happened," Valerie pressed.

"I'll speak to my sister after the meeting," I said. "Otherwise, I agree with Pascal's earlier words. Personal problems have no space in here."

Scanning each of them, I gave space for their disagreement.

They didn't give any. Probably because steam was coming out of my ears.

"Back to my point," I said. "I'd also like to restart a team that Mrs Frey tells me once existed. This team will brainstorm ways we can display greater care of the land in our grids. The team was disbanded ten years ago, and I can't help wondering, with the progression of environmentally friendly technology in recent years, if we're doing everything possible to ensure the wellbeing of this valley. This is a fundamental clause in the contract, and I don't want to give the Luthers any excuse to challenge us in the future."

"The team could analyse the Luther's grid care for weaknesses too," Trixie said.

With half a mind on the discussion around me, I released a pent-up breath.

Stretching my hearing in the direction of the office, I listened for sounds of Rhona's breathing or pacing, unsurprised when I didn't hear signs of life.

Rhona was making a stand for head steward.

And she held the ace in her hand.

"Shit and fuck." Wade gaped.

I flopped on the bed. "Tell me about it."

Ironically, turning into a wolf was the easiest part of my week. Rhona had made the last three days a living hell. She'd ignored my summons to talk and evaded attempts to track her down. She'd returned to head team meetings with barely veiled animosity but had set her intention to contributing to the best of her ability. I could tell some of the head team were impressed at the sudden change.

"That explains a lot." On the couch, he sipped on a cider.

I wouldn't mind a bottle of gin right now. Sabotaging myself had never held such appeal. "Like what?"

"Uh, she's sprouted some weird views in training the last couple of mornings. That we should take a more violent approach with the Luthers. That the wolves were able to handle a literal landslide and with the two hardest grids coming up, we can't restrict ourselves to a soft approach."

I stared at the wood ceiling. There was no doubt that more violence would be popular to some stewards. "Right. Dare I ask what the reaction was?"

"She has her supporters, but like me, most people were uncomfortable with her comments and a little confused. She was almost criticising you, but just falling shy."

I'd always maintained Herc was wrong about Rhona. She had the capacity to lead. Her weakness, in my eyes, rested in her lack of subtlety when it came to managing people.

Because, in short, people didn't *like* to be managed.

It wouldn't be her weakness forever though.

"Hopefully her words don't gain momentum," I said after a beat. "I'm not here to kill Luthers or maim them. Maybe she's right though—about the soft approach. I mean, I never would have cleared the landslide operation, yet that won us Sandstone."

Perhaps Rhona was the right leader. Maybe I was resisting a change of leadership that would benefit the tribe. Didn't I believe her to be the better choice from the start?

Wade dragged me to sitting. "No way. Don't do that *maybe she's right* bullshit, Andie Thana."

"I'm Andie Booker though," I whispered.

Wade set his cider down and gripped my shoulders. "I'm all for choosing whoever the hell you want to be, but never for a minute think someone else can choose that for you. If you want to be a Thana, then you're a *Thana*. Rhona's hurting. And yes, maybe you could have handled things differently. But what's done is done. You're the best person for the job. I'm not telling you that because I'm your friend. I'm saying that I'm your friend because of it."

I glanced up at him. "What?"

"I like powerful friends. Don't distract me. I'm trying to say that you can't doubt yourself. Any doubt from you hits the stewards. They look to you for reassurance and guidance. Rhona must be managed and not left to her own misplaced and bitter devices. If she plans to reveal everything, then we'll change our plan down the line, but perhaps reminding Rhona of what her actions would mean for the tribe is a good idea."

He's right, my wolf said.

Go away.

Your stubbornness grows wearisome.

Stones and glass houses, I snapped back.

Wade muttered, "Did you just fart? Your face went weird."

I wished that was all it was. "What do you suggest? That I tell everyone the truth?"

Part of me believed Rhona wouldn't tell everyone what happened. That now a few days had past, she'd see more clearly. Or at the very least, I believed that she loved the tribe more than she hated me. Unsettling them with another leadership change wasn't in their best interest.

Wade blew out a breath. "You're the game mastermind, not me, but I say we save that for worst-case scenario."

I flopped back again, tired beyond reason. I'd refused to let my wolf in whatsoever for three days. Exhausting couldn't describe the feeling of shutting her out. It was like someone had opened a plug and I was draining in a steady torrent.

She'd put me in danger. She'd humiliated me in front of my enemies—*and* Sascha and Greyson.

She wasn't on my side

Incorrect.

I growled low.

"Do you make that sound during sex?"

Oh my god. I cleared my throat. "Only during the really good stuff."

"That would be a massive turn off for me. As we both could have assumed."

He was working so hard to make me happy. "Glad to hear it."

"What's our plan then?"

"Fighting back is to stand against her. I don't want to fight with my sister. I can't. And I won't tell more lies to get myself out of the hole I dug. I'll just handle whatever new tactic she tries in the moment and try to talk sense to her."

"What about when stewards notice she's not Team Andie?"

I shrugged a shoulder. "I'll deal with that too."

My phone rang, and Wade snatched it up.

"Unknown, huh?" He slid me a shit-eating grin, light dancing in his grey eyes. "This is Andie's phone. Oh, *Sascha.* Hey, boo. No, she's in bed with me right now. Could you call back? We're kind of busy."

I grabbed the phone, trying and failing to glare at him. "Sascha."

"Is that true?"

"Greyson. None of your business. Why are you calling?"

"We arranged to meet for a Luther lesson."

I brushed my hair back. "Right. I forgot."

"Is everything okay, mate?"

"Don't call me that. Does it have to be tonight?"

"I have a commitment tomorrow that's come up."

I listened intently to his gravel-ridden voice for the truth but couldn't pick it out from his voice alone. I was so deathly tired. "Where and when?"

"I'm free for the rest of the evening. How about the manor?"

"Very funny," I said a beat too late.

"Ask Wade for directions to Broderick Falls. We close the road there to tourists at sundown. We'll be alone. I'll see you in thirty?"

The sooner I went, the sooner I'd be in bed. "Got it."

Hanging up, I flipped the phone in my palm. "Where's Broderick Falls?"

Wade's jaw dropped. "You're going to the falls where teen pregnancies occur and the back seats of cars are never the same? What on earth are you meeting there for?"

It spoke for my tiredness that I nearly mentioned Luther lessons. "Sascha and I need to discuss the remaining meets." Bastard picked that spot to put Wade in his place.

His eyes were round. "All the better to bite you with, *little bird.* Will another meet happen tonight?"

"Dunno. Probably not." I dragged a heavy jacket out of my closet, selecting dark jeans.

"Don't bother with underwear just in case," he said. "It disappears at Broderick Falls anyway."

This was just a meet up for Luther lessons.

None of *that* would happen.

Again.

16

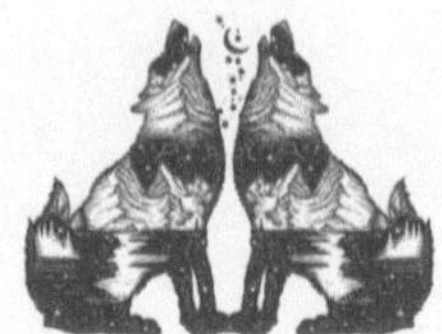

Shoving both hands in my jacket pockets, I followed the path to the falls. Did he mean for us to meet *at* the falls or back where I left Ella F?

I couldn't detect his scent. A curious spice mixture reached me instead. Very faint. Whatever it was from, the animal was far away. Even faint, the scent made me want to sneeze.

Enemy.

I ignored my wolf. She'd broken her silence earlier, and it seemed there was no return to blissful quiet. She'd made several comments on the way here.

Ahead, water pounded against rock, and behind me, a car pulled up to where I'd parked. Circling, the car left again, probably put off by the gate reading *Closed.*

A predator pounded from the east through the trees. The weight and tread of the four-legged gait were recognisable.

Greyson.

I craned my head to see the entire plunge waterfall. *Beautiful.* I'd never seen a waterfall in real life before. Well, Queen's Way had a waterfall that was about one metre high and dry half the year. And there was a three-step cascade into the Deception Valley town, I supposed, but this looked like a real waterfall.

My first waterfall and I felt separate from the beauty before me. I could appreciate how the mossy oasis might have seeped into my heart once.

A growl filled the clearing.

Glancing back, I cocked an eye at the dark brown wolf. "Greyson. In a mood tonight?"

I'm sure he had some retort, but we could only mind-speak in wolf form.

Hmm, actually. This was the ideal chance to confirm a theory.

Releasing some of my forest calm, my fingernails shot out into lethal claws, fangs sliding down either end of my chin. My vision sharpened and my hearing range burst outward to five times the radius, my smell stronger still. A trickle of energy returned to me, like dipping a foot into a hot bath.

I'd always found it weird that Sascha spoke of personal issues in the hearing of his pack, but with the sheer range of a Luther's senses, there probably wasn't another option. It would be impossible to drive twenty minutes away each time a person wanted to have a private conversation. Even the idea of lying to another Luther was ridiculous. *Ugh,* suddenly, my whole *infiltrate The Dens* ploy was laughable. They'd have known the minute I re-entered the casino.

You couldn't drive? I thought hard at the wolf.

His answer filled my head. *We never drive if we can run, mate.*

Pulling back my forest calm, I shoved my wolf away, trying to conceal my triumph. Wolves *could* mind-speak in a partial shift.

Facing the waterfall again, I focused there instead of on the cracks and pops behind me.

"You're happy with yourself? Why?" Sascha's smooth voice washed over me.

"You know, driving has its perks. Mainly that you'd be wearing clothes right now."

"I didn't think nudity bothered you," he said, walking toward me in his birthday suit. "Or is it just my nudity that makes you squirm?"

He had to use that word in particular.

Turning, I fixed my eyes on his mocking face. "What are you teaching me today?"

He stopped before me. "Why do you smell like sorrow and stress?"

"I told Rhona the truth of what happened during the capture meet. And about the meets and what it means. She's not happy."

Dang it, I couldn't help glancing down. He was a work of art, for shit's sake. Hard abs were the bridge between wide shoulders and hips that were built to fulfil all types of fantasies. There was no other word for his powerful physique than gorgeous, and I couldn't help but notice *this* beauty didn't feel distant and cold like the waterfall at my back.

"I've waited a long time for you to look at me like a woman looks at a man," Sascha said softly.

I politely returned my attention to the guy's face. "I appreciate nice bodies."

"Nice bodies or just mine?"

He could smell a lie. "I've always appreciated men's bodies. I have the power to look but not touch."

"Can you think of another man after what we shared?" He stalked closer. "It's been impossible for me to look at another woman since I first saw you. After tasting you, it's like women no longer exist."

"Doesn't that bother you? That you've magically been told to want me and so you do? If you were really attracted to me, then you would have been after Rhona long before I arrived."

His mouth crooked, and I tilted my head back, challenge in my gaze.

"Rhona smells like cut grass—"

"I love that smell," I shot in.

"—that's been in the compost heap for three weeks."

My mouth snapped shut. That didn't sound so pleasant.

"You—" Sascha wrapped his hands around my upper arms. "—do not. Your actions tell me that you have a beautiful mind and heart as well as an exquisite body. I don't know how I got so lucky."

Someone was counting their chickens before they'd hatched, but his slightly baffled tone made my stomach feel strange. "What do I smell like?"

He placed his mouth next to my ear. I swayed into him, feeling some of my exhaustion seep away.

"Like vanilla and oranges." His words warmed my insides. "Like liquorice and pumpkin spice."

All food. Typical.

Giving up, I rested my cheek against his chest. I just needed a little zap of energy after the last few days.

"And me?" he asked.

The word *compost* lingered on my lips, but if I insulted him, this contact would end, and I needed it. "Pine. Sweat. Musk. River water."

He hummed and the pine and river water scents intertwined.

"Are you happy right now?" I murmured.

"Yes."

Huh. "What does it mean when a scent pulses?" The description didn't jive with my human notions, but it was the best way to describe Rhona's sudden shift in scent during the head team meeting three days prior.

He pressed his nose into my hair, inhaling deeply. We were bodily pressed against each other now. "Shock, perhaps."

Shock would suit what happened. I was certain Rhona had realised in that moment that the head team weren't at her beck and call.

"If something smells rotten, is it a lie?"

"No," he answered, and I wrinkled my nose as his pine smell decayed.

Lie.

I shifted on the spot, worming closer. "I'll take that as a yes. Are you the only person who has four smells? Apart from Rhona, everyone else I've sniffed only has one."

Like Wade's salted caramel or the animal who smelled like spice.

"Sometimes family members will have two—or even three scents if you're very close. Lovers can have two after a while. To my knowledge, only mates share four."

Interesting.

"Magic voodoo," I murmured.

"The mating call drives my wolf and me through the meets, but it does not make me like you, nor make *you* like *me*. That's why there are seven meets, so we can determine the other's worthiness. Like an arranged marriage, respect is something that comes if both sides are willing. The mating call is simply nature telling us that we are compatible for producing children. Nature isn't concerned with how we *feel* about doing that. Anything more, love and trust... respect... is up to us—if we should wish it."

Then what was this feeling right now? I stiffened.

"An initial attraction to you and an undeniable drive to move through the seven meets is the only part triggered by the mating call," he continued. "The rest is all me and all you." Sascha's hands moved. "My hands sit perfectly at the curve of your hips." His breath hitched. "My hands nearly circle your waist. *Breasts* I'll never stop paying homage to except for the rest of your body tearing at my attention. *Fuck,* if you were mine, I'd never get anything done."

Warmth pooled between my legs, and my chest rose.

Now was the time to step away.

Sascha pulled me firm against his body.

I looked up.

"The slope of your neck when you submit," he growled low, "the angle of your jaw when you don't. Your lips, beautiful wolf. Made for kissing."

Logically, I knew a waterfall was pouring in a torrent at our back, but I could only hear the beat of his heart and mine. I could only smell the new way our scents tangled together.

"Sascha—"

"*Nature* does not care about such things," he said in a ragged voice. "Nature is not romantic. It is cold and clinical. None of what I've just described is necessary for the job that nature wants us to fulfil. My attraction grows of my own accord, as does my respect for your mind, and my awe of your heart."

This was too much. "It's pointless."

Why doesn't he hate me?

I'd worked against him from almost the first moment. This thing between us was doomed.

With all my strength, I stepped back. "Okay. Just. Let's cool it."

Sascha's jaw clenched. "You feel it too. We wouldn't feel this connection if you'd already decided against me. We wouldn't feel better when we touched. You wouldn't have felt a small version of the heat after scenting me for the first time. Even though you denied me, your mind and body must accept me on some level. Otherwise, you wouldn't have needed that gratification."

What? Was that true?

I took another step back. "I don't feel where you are at all times though. If I was really into this, then I'd have that."

"You weren't a wolf until recently. That could have altered things. Regardless, part of you finds me acceptable. That's enough for me."

I snarled at the slight decaying pine scent. He wanted all of me. "I've done nothing but push you away. Openly. To your pack and to you. Why haven't you decided against me?"

I couldn't put more distance between us without going for a swim.

Sascha crowded me against the ledge but didn't touch me again.

"You wouldn't push so hard if you didn't feel something. I'd rather work with love, but if love can become hate, then hate can do the reverse too. And the words Greyson once said to you are right, little bird."

This was too much. I pressed a hand against my cheek. "I don't remember."

"If the world wasn't between us, we'd already be in each other's arms. Our situation keeps us apart."

I couldn't say if that was true or not, but he was right about the world between us.

It was like a bucket of water over my heat. "Exactly. One of us loses Grids in the end. This doesn't have a happy ending. So why bother?"

He gripped my hand and gently tugged it away from my cheek. "Is that why you're holding back? You're trying so hard it kills me to watch. Always trying so hard, little bird, for everyone but yourself."

"What's that supposed to mean?" I glared at him.

"Trying hard for your mother. Trying hard for your father. Trying hard for your sister and tribe. At which point have you tried hard for yourself?"

I set my jaw.

"I'll tell you, shall I?" he whispered, gaze settling on my lips. "It was when you played at The Dens. Before you knew what I was."

There should be too many elements to our combined smell to make it appealing, but the aroma made me dizzy. He said nature gave us the urge to go through the meets. That it didn't make us like each other or feel more than initial attraction. So our scent made my mouth water because of *me*.

This wouldn't be happening if part of me didn't accept him. Sascha had said as much, and I'd smelled the truth in his words.

He was right.

And how did I switch that off? I wasn't aware of when it started.

For fuck's sake.

My lashes lowered as I studied his lips. I'd felt them between my legs, but we'd never kissed. Not once.

A wrinkle formed between my brows. "Don't you find it strange that we've never kissed?"

"It's one of the meets—usually, the next." He tensed.

It was? Did I miss that?

He had such a full bottom lip. "May as well get it over with then."

Sascha moved back, and I was doused with cold water, literally, as I felt the spray of the waterfall on my back.

I stared at him, heart hammering. "What is it?"

"Not tonight. Tonight is about teaching you how to manage your wolf—though you greatly impressed my pack with your show of control last night. That's no easy task. Some wolves never manage a partial shift."

That's what they were gasping and muttering about. I inhaled. "Why does that make you sad?"

He glanced back in surprise. "Well done."

I waited, trying to shove back disappointment that his lips weren't on mine.

"The answer to that can wait for another time."

He was usually so open with me. "If you won't tell me that, let's get the kissing meet over with."

"No," he said brusquely, striding back down the rocky path.

I marched after him. "Why? It's a quick kiss. We'll get it over with and only have two meets left. *You* wanted this."

His river water scent intensified once more, and when he halted, I studied his ass.

Sue me.

"I've dreamed of finding my mate for a lifetime," Sascha spoke, his back to me. "Since I found you, you've slipped through my fingers time and again. Nothing has turned out like my dreams at all—in fact, my nights are spent tossing in terror wondering what could befall you without me there. I could kiss you now, little bird. I could cave to the pressure building around us and claim you in all ways on a whim." He sighed heavily. "It is, perhaps, just a kiss. And I am, perhaps, just a fool. But I want one part of my dreams to be true. When I kiss you because no one else exists for me any longer, I want you to kiss me back just the same."

Wordless, I couldn't reply as the Luther half turned.

His cheeks reddened, and he dropped his gaze. "You're exhausted. Let's do this another time. Maybe you could stay behind after the meeting on Sunday?"

His words bounced back and forward between my ears. What did all that mean?

That there was lovin' talk.

"Sure?" I croaked.

"Okay. Goodnight." Sascha, still red-faced, shifted into Greyson, who sent me a long look before leaving.

Something tugged under my ribs, and I covered the spot with both hands.

What's that?

My wolf answered, *It's him.*

The tugging pulled taut, like an elastic band drawn tight, and I sucked in a breath.

Oh my god. Sascha was on the other end.

I had a Sascha beacon.

Now we can find him anywhere, she said quietly.

That's not what worried me.

Apparently, I just accepted the Luther a little bit more.

17

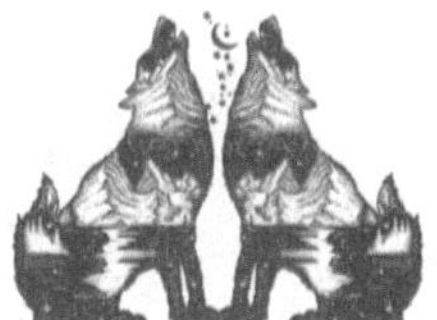

The sister is coming, my wolf said.

She'd reduced Rhona to *the sister* in the last two days.

I glanced behind to see that indeed, Rhona stormed our way. I managed nearly a whole day without any antics too.

"I'll meet you there," I said to the head team.

Roderick walked towards the van, but Valerie pointed over my shoulder. "Is Rhona coming too?"

Fucking. Valerie.

I turned. "Rhona. Can I help you with something?"

"I'm coming to pack lands."

Put her in her place.

"We've been through this," I said, ignoring my wolf *again*. "You must remain at the manor in case something happens to me."

She grinned and hurt spliced me at what the grin implied—*if only we were so lucky.*

"The Luthers have shown themselves to behave on two occasions," she countered. "I have a right to see pack lands as a Thana."

I tilted my chin. "Every steward in this tribe has a right. And yet I see none of them here. Would you leave them leaderless?"

"Not at all. You stay here. Just like last week when I took your spot."

Trixie broke the leaden silence. "What?"

"Andie and I swap places sometimes," Rhona lifted a shoulder. "Sometimes, she's too scared to give public speeches on Tuesday nights. And she needed a break last Sunday, so I stepped in for the grid announcement."

Wow. She went there.

She really hated me that much.

I scented the subtle shift in scent of those at my back. Facing them, I nodded. "Rhona's right. Twice, we've switched position. I'm afraid my confidence was lacking in the first week. Last weekend, I learned what happens when duty and health aren't balanced. I apologise for myself and for Rhona for not informing you of the switch. The first instance was last minute, and I admit, I was too ashamed to tell you the truth. The second, well, there's little excuse for that except health."

"And that theory we were testing," Rhona piped up behind me.

My stomach lurched. "My main objective was to recoup, but perhaps we can present our theory to the head team after the meeting on pack lands. We'll be late if we don't leave."

"And I'm coming," she said.

My gums ached, but I stepped in front of her, tilting my chin. Her lips curved, and I didn't hesitate to let her see my sadness and pain.

"Because I care for you and this tribe, my answer is no."

"Perhaps we could put it to a vote," Valerie said, the sneer evident in her voice.

I glanced over my shoulder. "If you want every decision to be a group vote, Valerie, we'll soon suffer from gross lack of efficiency."

"Even so. Given the circumstances with Herc," she simpered.

My wolf was bursting under the surface to take charge of the situation and put Valerie in her place way at the bottom. For a furious moment, I considered letting her do just that.

Tightening my hold, I focused. "I'm disappointed at your lack of confidence and trust in my decisions, Valerie. Some of that is on me too though. Something I've done has clearly made you feel that way. In the future, I hope you're able to support your head steward."

Her cheeks flushed.

"Those who believe Rhona has a right to visit pack lands on this single occasion, raise your hand," I said in a ringing voice.

Yep, I already knew the answer.

The majority of hands rose, including Rhona's.

"Damn selfish, I think," Stanley said, glowering at the others.

Bile rose in my throat at the sickly sweetness of Rhona's vanilla glee. "Rhona will come to pack lands. The two of us will meet the rest of you there."

"I'll ride with the head team." She shouldered me on the way to the driver's seat.

No one missed the blow.

Valerie smirked, and I turned away before my wolf decided to chomp through her jugular.

"See you all there." I moved toward Ella F.

Wade was coming down the stairs to make up Rhona's position on the head team. I waved him away, mouthing, "Not today." His grey gaze shifted over my shoulder to Rhona, and he stopped short.

Yep.

I just lost that round big time. Rhona wasn't just coming to pack lands. She'd won a powerplay with the head team.

No sooner had I pulled out of the manor gates, waving at Cameron, when my phone buzzed.

"*Oh my god,*" Wade said. "What happened? The tension was crazy."

"You know how Rhona and I switched a couple of times? She just told the head team."

He swore long and hard, then turned his ire on Rhona.

"What she's doing is mean, yes," I said, sighing. "She's only doing it because I hurt her so much."

"You don't have to call her what she is, but I certainly will."

I shook my head. "I've got a bigger problem. She also told them about the theory she had."

"The one where Sascha had the mega hots for you?"

"She's trying to make me sweat. More. I've delayed discussing the theory until after meeting the Luthers, but it will come up as soon as we're back. She could be telling them about it right now."

The line was silent. "Baby girl, I don't mean to be a butthole, but you need to stick up for yourself."

"Nothing she's saying is untrue. We did switch places."

"Exactly," he exploded. "*We.*"

"Only one of us is head steward."

"This fight has to end or the tribe loses. You need to make her back down."

Didn't he understand? I couldn't do that to my only remaining relative. My *sister*. She grieved for a father and mother who'd lied to her. She grieved the loss of a position she'd always believed would be hers. She felt alone and adrift. Me fighting her just proved to her that family wasn't forever—that the term *sister* didn't mean anything.

I refused to do that. "No."

"You cannot be hearing yourself."

"I am, Wade. Fighting or not, I lose either way. If push comes to shove, I choose to lose the head stewardship over my family."

"Alright," he said just as I wondered if the signal had dropped out. "I don't think that's best for the tribe though. Moving on, what will you tell the head team about Rhona's theory? She's trying to raise their suspicions about a connection to him without telling them outright."

"Why though? That's what I can't figure out. Why not tell them what she knows?"

Wade hummed. "No idea on that front. My advice would be to state the facts and to include Rhona in the conversation. There's no doubt the team will watch you after this. Don't suppose you happened to complete all three remaining meets last night?"

I groaned. "He's holding out."

Wade's voice darkened. "You're kidding me. He was the one

working so hard to convince you to keep going."

I couldn't repeat Sascha's explanation about the kissing. It felt too personal. "I know."

"What did you guys do out there for two hours?"

Erm. "Argued, pretty much. It's a shame there's not a meet for that."

He snorted.

I tilted my head, picking up sounds ahead. "I'll need to say goodbye. Meet at mine later?"

"Deal, baby girl. I know this is shit right now, but it's going to work out, okay? I love you."

My chest squeezed. No one had said that to me in so long. "I love you too."

I wound down my window when Grim stepped from the bushes. "Hey, Grim."

He bowed slightly. "Andie."

The van pulled up behind me. "Listen, can you make sure Sascha knows my sister, Rhona, is here? There's a chance she'll stir trouble up—not with violence, but she's angry with Sascha and with me. Could you let him know to be on his guard?"

Grim nodded and melted back into the bushes. He was a strange one, but I liked him for some reason.

I drove on, collecting my thoughts as I directed the team to the largest bungalow. This time Sascha waited outside.

"Head Steward," he greeted.

"Pack Leader," I replied, deciding to drop the Luther routine. It was fucking rude, and I was better than that.

The team piled out of the van behind me.

"Welcome to our territory," Sascha said.

Rhona scoffed, "Your territory? This is our land."

"The land belongs to itself," Sascha said mildly. "Or has your tribe changed its mind regarding ownership?"

"Don't mince words, Luther," Rhona spat, coming to my side.

"Rhona." I cut her off. "While here, we have a very easy and specific job to do for our tribe. How about we get to it?"

I didn't wait for her answer.

Sascha stood aside to let me enter and gave Rhona his back as he filed into the bungalow after me.

Dipping my head at the row of already seated Luthers, I missed my chance to take my seat. Rhona slid into the middle chair which Sascha had adorned with antlers between times. My lips twitched despite Rhona's move.

I took the seat next to her.

"Thank you for welcoming us to your territory," I said as Sascha took his throne.

He held up a hand. "Excuse my interruption, Head Steward, but I believe your sister has mistaken the seating arrangement."

"There's no mistake," Rhona said, smirking.

"Rhona," Stanley hissed under his breath. "Not here."

She ignored the old man.

"It's Luther custom that the leader sit in the correct chair," Sascha said in the thick tension.

Bullshit.

At least someone cares about establishing order, my wolf muttered.

You don't recognise the concept of pack or family, I replied, *who are you to judge me?*

I don't judge. I merely care.

"Then I see no reason why we can't proceed," Rhona said.

I really didn't need to say anything. That was a pretty clear declaration of her motive. Gasps rang out from my head team.

"Rhona," Valerie hushed. "I thought you came here for... well..."

To face her father's murderer in his own home? That's how I once looked at this meeting and playing Grids—as a standoff and a show of strength for Herc.

More and more, I saw that Herc wasn't exempt from blame. He drew a gun on Sascha too easily. Something happened to Murphy, and I was willing to bet Herc had a hand in his death. I saw the disgust in his eyes when I screamed at the idea of Sascha dying. It was the same disgust I'd directed at myself when I didn't kill Greyson. Things between Herc and me would never have been the same after that moment. Maybe he *would* have hurt me eventually. His own daughter.

And for what?

Because I was reacting to a magical bond I knew very little about? Because I was tainted by association? Because I didn't hate the Luthers enough?

Maybe what Sascha was scared me really bad at first. That fear had generated a cold contempt that Herc's death strengthened to loathing.

In hindsight, allowing my fear to condemn an entire race seemed so...

Ignorant.

The Luthers were trapped in this valley. And that evening in Sandstone, Greyson protected me, just like Sascha was doing right now against Rhona.

I could admit that now.

I couldn't hold Sascha or Greyson to that sad, regrettable moment anymore. I couldn't use Herc's death as another shield for the feelings and thoughts I wanted to avoid.

Because those things weren't going away.

I wasn't sure I wanted them to.

"When you're ready to assume your proper seat," Sascha was saying, "the meeting can resume."

Rhona ignored him.

"Would you like to swap?" I asked. "You know it doesn't matter to me what seat I lead the tribe from, but it would be rude to ignore the customs of our hosts."

I met her blazing emerald gaze and sadness filled my heart.

"I refuse to talk with dogs." Rhona burst to standing.

"That's the only language I speak," Sascha said. "Woof."

He didn't. *Oh my god.*

I rubbed a hand over my mouth to conceal my traitorous grin as Rhona stormed out.

Inhaling, I noted the sudden muting of the head members' scents. They were trying to hide. Embarrassed?

Correct, my wolf said.

I rose. "On behalf of the Ni Tiaki tribe, I sincerely apologise for my sister's behaviour. She finds it difficult to be in Luther company after her father's death."

"We found it very difficult to be in steward company after her father threw a landslide at us, but we managed." Mandy glowered. "Children have no part in the managing team."

Oddly, I gathered that she was trying to help me.

Valerie scoffed. "You had it coming."

Just like that, my good mood expired. "Valerie. Please join Rhona outside."

Her jaw dropped. Beet red, she stumbled from the bungalow.

I surveyed the wolves and bowed this time. "Another apology is needed. You can be assured that violence against your kind will not be condoned under my leadership, as per the rules of Victratum."

"I would request that your sister is absent from future meetings between our people," Sascha said.

Smelling his fury, I could only marvel at the lack of it in his voice.

"The head team will take that into consideration and deliver our decision by Monday evening." I sat in my antler throne.

His honey eyes bore into mine. I'd have thought the shorter distance would make the elastic band sensation under my ribs better, but it was almost worse to see and not touch him.

"Your choice for this week's grid?" he murmured.

I rubbed the area under my ribs and saw his gaze dip to the movement. His eyes widened slightly, and his attention snapped to my face.

"Clay," I said. "We'll see you in Clay."

The head team didn't look at Rhona as they filed into the van. Stanley took the driver's seat while Nathan took hold of Valerie's arm and dragged her to the vehicle.

They drove off, and I waited by Ella F.

"Are you coming?" I asked Rhona.

Her options were to come with me, walk, or stay here. She approached the car and gave it a swift kick.

"Whatever you may feel toward me right now, don't ruin my possessions because of it. I happened to work hard to buy this car, and if you can't respect that, walk back to the manor."

"You'd probably like that, wouldn't you, dog lover?" she hissed, wrenching open the door.

Growls rose around us, but I highly doubted she heard.

"They're your legs, not mine. Be my guest, if that's what you'd prefer." *Forest forest forest.*

Let me out, my wolf growled.

Not the time.

If you don't respect my needs, we will die, Andie Thana.

I just need you not to burst out right this second, I snarled.

That's not how this works. Sascha was right. I do not care for the confines of your pack.

Too bad.

"Do you feel like a whore when you let him inside you?" she hissed.

The growls ramped up.

Her words were for Sascha's benefit as much as mine, and his growl inside the bungalow was about the most menacing thing I'd ever heard. "I wouldn't know. What I do know is that you're embarrassing yourself."

It was the wrong thing to say, and I knew it before uttering the words. *Yep,* she'd officially gotten under my skin.

Her fist clenched as I gunned the engine.

"Hit me if you like, Rhona. It may make you feel better for a little while."

"Perhaps," she said. "Except there's nowhere to wash my hands after."

"You can say what you like to me," I directed us away from the bungalow. "I'll be here through it all. I won't say goodbye to you."

She laughed as we left the buildings behind, but I knew every wolf in over a kilometre radius could hear us.

My phone rang, and I fumbled to grab it.

Rhona swiped it up and turned on speaker. "Hello?"

"Hey," Wade said. "How did she go?"

Ah, shit nuts.

Thunderstorms closed in over Rhona's face. "*She* went fine."

Inaccurate. I'd tell Wade the truth later.

"Oh, heeey, Rhona."

I coughed. "Wade, Rhona is driving back with me."

"Apparently."

"You know everything," she said.

"Huh, what?"

She gripped the phone hard. "Don't fuck with me, steward."

Wade was silent for a beat. "Yeah, Rhona, I know. And guess what? Andie made a mistake, but you're being a massive bitchhole about this."

I groaned inwardly, squeezing the steering wheel. "Thanks so much for the input, Wade. I'll see you later."

Now she'd think I was bitching about her. He'd just made things ten times worse.

Wade squeaked and hung up as we rolled past the harvest fields.

"When did you tell him?"

"He came across me in a down moment a few weeks ago."

I hadn't thought she could be angrier at me, but yep, it happened before my very eyes to a startling degree. The rage spilling everywhere was methodically tucked in and frozen until a chilled shell remained in the passenger seat beside me.

"Rhona, I'll always love you," I whispered. "I know this doesn't make sense, but we can survive what's happening. I'm not going anywhere. I promise."

She glanced out the window. "Love from someone like you doesn't mean much when all you *can* do is love others. I mean, you could hardly love yourself."

18

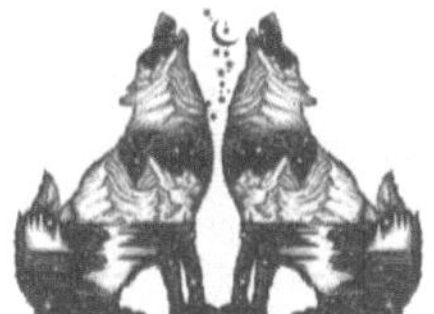

"I wasn't sure at first, but he turned up at the riverside apartment when I was there once," I said for the fifth time.

Rhona was nowhere to be seen and the head team wasn't inclined to involve her in this discussion after the display on pack lands.

I was on the verge of fainting from exhaustion. I had to shift and yet this talk had to happen while I had their sympathy. From most of them anyway. Valerie was off Team Andie for good.

"We can use this to our advantage," Roderick said. "He put antlers on her chair. The pack leader is inclined to be softer where Andie is concerned. I think there's truth in this."

That was a nice way of saying Sascha had a boner for me—which was essentially what I'd said.

"Why are we only hearing of this now?" Pascal asked. She'd been silent for the last half an hour.

I sighed. "Because I'm new to the valley, new to being a steward, new to head stewardship, and new to basically everything here. I thought this information could be detrimental and cause division between the stewards. I didn't really know any of you, even when Herc asked me to sit in on your meetings for Rhona sometimes. I thought this could harm the way stewards and this team perceived me. It was a risk I didn't want to take."

"You sat in on head meetings?" Trixie asked.

I lifted a shoulder. "I thought Herc was embarrassed Rhona wasn't around at the time, but now I wonder if he did it on purpose." I looked at them. "What are the thoughts moving forward?"

Nathan looked around the table. "I'm inclined to agree that this should be kept from general steward knowledge. We can strategize in private."

"The stewards have a right to know what their head steward is up to."

It was time to put Valerie in her place. My patience for her bullshit ran out sometime last week. "Valerie, while you offer valuable contributions to this team, I will always, no matter how you feel about me personally, listen to your opinions. *As long* as your opinion is made with the welfare of this tribe in mind. I understand that you loved my father, and that you greatly prefer his second daughter to myself. I understand that you dislike me so much it's very hard to keep it under wraps. But as long as you can keep your opinions of me separate from your advice, you'll find I don't care."

"What, like you're doing?" she sneered.

I smiled. "Can you name one instance where I brought my issues into this room?"

"Rhona—"

"Exactly," I cut her off. "Rhona."

Valerie's jaw set.

"Do you understand what I'm telling you?" I didn't move my gaze from hers until she glanced away. And I had a feeling that my wolf got involved there.

"Yes," she muttered.

I glanced at the others. "Today has upset us all, me included. In the interest of keeping the tribe strong and in the interest of protecting Rhona's feelings, I'd appreciate everyone keeping what happened to themselves."

"The pack leader asked that Rhona not be present in future meetings," Pascal said as I rose. "We need to vote."

"So we do." I locked my shaking legs and leaned forwards on the table.

We need to shift, my wolf urged.

Five minutes.

"All in favour of the pack leader's request?" I called.

Keeping Rhona from future gatherings would make life easier, but her anger would spill out in other areas. I may not be present in those areas to damage control.

"Andie? Your vote?"

An even number of hands were in the air and flat on the table. *Dammit.* With Rhona absent, my vote would be the decider.

Hoping I didn't come to regret it, I placed my hand on the table, ignoring Trixie's surprised murmur.

"Rhona is a Thana and she's a valued part of this tribe. We can't allow the Luthers to weaken her stance in our community in case something happens to me. However, I suggest that Rhona only return to these meetings and those with the Luthers once we've witnessed stability in her behaviour."

Everyone, even Valerie, seemed on board with that.

Thank fuck. I staggered to the door.

"Are you alright, Andie?" Roderick called.

We need to shift. My wolf was alarmed.

I know. And I really did. "Fine. Thank you. Just tired."

Not waiting for their response, I wobbled down the hall, ignoring cheerful greetings. I had to get out of here.

Gasping, I made it to Ella F and fumbled for the keys.

I can't wait any longer.

No! I shoved the keys in, and gunned the engine, tearing away from the manor.

I couldn't go back into town. I flattened my foot on the accelerator, blinking through the black darkening my eyes.

Just wait, I pleaded with her.

If I do not shift, we will die. I shouldn't have left it this long.

I ripped the wheel down and parked on the shoulder. The handbrake was barely up before I pushed open the door and fell to the ground. Kicking the car shut, I half crawled, half rolled to the edge of the road and didn't hesitate to throw myself down the steep forest slope.

It happened immediately.

The shift took over.

... But then it didn't.

My snout shortened and lengthened; shortened and lengthened. It should only move one way.

I arched, crying out. The cry morphed to a howl before cutting off to a pained cry yet again.

Flung forward, rocks and roots jabbed my half-shifted form as I tumbled farther down the steep slope bordering the north valley road.

It isn't working, I panted.

We are too weak, she replied grimly. *I waited too long to respect your wishes. I failed you.*

I felt my leg break and choked on a scream. *What now?*

Nothing. Now we die and our mate will soon follow.

Sascha and Greyson would die.

Yes.

I didn't know this could happen. She'd told me, but I hadn't understood how quickly things could spiral downward.

You felt that I broke your trust, and you shut me out. I did not realise my efforts to prove our feelings for Greyson would affect you so deeply, and for that I am sorry.

I vomited, unable to turn my head to do so. *I needed the wake-up call. It hurt, but I was in denial about Herc. This is my fault.*

No, Andie. But it will be over soon. I promise.

It was nice to meet you before the end, I whispered.

And you. I would have loved an existence with you.

A tear leaked over my temple as I stared up at the canopy, anguish overriding the agony.

Sascha would die.

Greyson too.

Was he dying as I died, or would it happen suddenly to him when I passed? Seeking comfort, I felt for the elastic band under my ribs.

Funny… I could feel it happening—death.

Cold.

I pulled at the elastic band, disappointed when I encountered complete resistance. I pulled again.

Stupid idea.

I closed my eyes.

Something cool moved over my skin, and I frowned, mumbling.

"Just covering you with a sheet, young wolf," a warm voice said.

The woman smelled like pine.

I didn't know her, but pine was safe.

Forcing my eyelids open, I blinked the room into focus.

Sascha's bungalow.

His bed.

How—?

We almost didn't make it, my wolf said wearily.

I stilled as she blasted images at me. Me tearing out of the manor. Rolling down the slope. Half shifted.

Dying.

My heart hammered. *How did we get here?*

Did we black out or something?

He found us. You pulled him to us through the bond. He forced you to shift and brought us to enemy territory.

"Shit," I said.

"That about sums it up," pine woman said.

I rolled to my side.

She sat on the wicker furniture, knitting. At first glance, the woman appeared around my age, maybe younger. A quick sniff told me she was old as hell, her pine scent earthy and rich.

I peered closer, noting the unusual golden hue of her irises. "You're Sascha's mother."

She dipped her head, continuing to knit.

Naked and in her son's bed. Well, this was about ten out of ten awkward.

"What happened?" I asked. "Sascha found me."

"With his help, you made the shift," she murmured. "You remained in wolf form until ten minutes ago. You shifted back in your sleep."

We nearly died, I croaked to my wolf.

My fault.

Our fault, I said firmly. *We both made mistakes, but we won't let it happen again.*

We must figure out how to make this work, she said.

"Is Sascha around? I should thank him before I leave." I wrapped the sheet around me.

She put her knitting aside and met my gaze. "You may find it difficult to leave. My son is very angry."

I dragged a hand over my face. "He deserves to be. I didn't realise what was happening until too late. I put his life in danger."

Her lips curved. "That's not why he's angry."

I stared. *Nope,* I didn't have the energy to leap down that rabbit hole. Standing, I tied the sheet in a knot over my boobs. "I'll find him."

A snarl rose from the hall. A lucky thing—or maybe not—that the doorway was so wide because a dark-brown wolf stalked into the room to loom over me.

"Greyson," I said.

His hackles were raised, teeth bared as he advanced.

He won't hurt us, right? I asked my wolf.

... No.

It would be awesome if she sounded certain. “Greyson, I was coming to find you.”

He leaped forward, teeth snapping an inch from my cheek. Heel catching in the sheet, I toppled back onto the bed. He lowered his head under my legs and tossed them onto the mattress.

Right. Guess this was where I was meant to stay. “Uh…”

The heavy, wooden bed groaned in protest and he leaped up and lay bodily on top of me.

I wheezed. “Get off.”

He is a very powerful male, my wolf said.

Oh, brother.

I gave up pushing at his underbelly because, honestly, I was tired beyond words. Closing my eyes, I waited for him to relax and get off.

Mmm. He was really warm.

The whole healing thing still worked with him in four-legged form. I sighed a breath, relaxing further, and felt my breaths deepen.

His bed was miles more comfortable than my shitty cabin one.

A warmth crept over my mind as the lull before slumber took me.

“If she’s resisting the change, she won’t live long.”

Greyson growled.

“Why is she doing it?”

I wanted to reassure Sascha’s mother the non-shifting saga really was a mistake, but my body was past responsiveness.

Snap. Crack. Sascha sighed. Not a wolf sound. Did he just shift his snout to a human mouth to talk—because that visual was gross.

He spoke, “She fears losing her people. Her sister and friends. Why else do you think she’d managed a partial shift already? She’s deathly afraid.”

Well that explained why he was simultaneously proud and sad about my ability to partially shift. It did sound kind of pathetic when he put it that way.

"Just kidnap her for the remaining meets, dear," his mother said. "It worked wonders for your father and me."

He snorted. "Thanks, Mum."

"The younger generation overthinks everything. What did your father say about her not shifting?"

"That it proves she isn't worthy."

"Though he did kidnap his potential mate, so keep that in mind."

That's where Sascha got his quirky humour.

Darkness blanketed my mind, and I tried to resist, but Greyson had known what I didn't.

I was past exhaustion. I barely caught her next words, and they slipped away as quickly as I registered them.

"Will you keep her here?"

"Against her will? Never."

I startled awake and bolted upright, clutching the sheet to my chin. The first strands of daylight streamed in through the open bifold doors.

"Andie," Sascha said in a low voice, striding to me from outside.

His mother was gone.

Relaxing, I dragged my fingers through my messy hair. I had to stink. "Sascha."

He sat on the bed, and I hesitated before placing my hand in his.

"I'm so sorry. There's no excuse for my behaviour but ignorance."

Sascha squeezed my hand. "Your wolf didn't tell you what would happen?"

"She mentioned dying, but there was never a good time..." I averted my face. "That sounds really stupid. I'm just sorry. To both of you."

He shuddered, honey eyes blazing. "We got there in time. Just. I thought you were dead. The only reason I didn't give up on the spot is because I was still alive."

My wolf whined in my mind.

"You made me shift somehow?" I rasped.

Sascha leaned across and passed me a glass of water. The cool liquid soothed my throat.

I must have screamed at some point. For a while.

Shadows crossed his face. "I lay next to you for a time to give you strength, but I had to force your shift in the end. Others helped."

"Who?"

"Those you know from The Dens. It took an hour, but once you got there, your natural healing took over."

I was out for all that? "Sascha?"

He briefly met my gaze.

"I owe you my life."

Sascha stood abruptly. "There's no debt between us. But I didn't realise you weren't shifting. You should do it once a day after recovering from the first shift. Doing so helps you find balance with your wolf. The more you shift, the closer you will become."

Will we get stuck again? I asked her.

No, we are stronger now, she answered.

I dragged the sheet with me as I stood. "Okay. Let's shift now. Then I need to get back."

A terse nod was my answer. I followed him to the stream and wrenched to a halt when Sascha undressed.

Oh...

Uhm. Over to you? I told my wolf, dropping the sheet.

Despite the horrendous snapping noises, the shift was like sliding into silk pyjamas. The rapidness of the transformation made it impossible for my mind to process the pain at all. My senses and brain were overwhelmed—like watching a movie in quadruple time—and then it was done.

On all fours, we shook, glimpsing the deep auburn fur covering our forelegs. Trotting to the stream, we peered down at our reflection.

Shit! We're a wolf.

Yes, Andie, she replied patiently.

Okay, but it's still a shock to be a wolf. We're pretty. Are we good-looking for a wolf?

What do you think?

I bared our teeth in a grin as she faced Greyson. She snarled, a polite warning not to fuck around, and then approached, smelling him.

If you sniff his butthole, we're done.

Human sensibilities. What do your handshakes tell you? Nothing. I can learn a whole range of things from the secretions of another wolf's anal glands—his breeding status and health, diet, and current emotion.

Sounded illegal but handy. *I'm of the opinion that if a task involves anal glands, it's a hard no.*

She huffed and, thankfully, left Sascha's butt alone.

Greyson lowered his head to look at me. He was around two thirds bigger than me, around the same size difference as our human forms.

I wondered if Sascha was talking to Greyson about buttholes too.

See if you can keep up, beautiful wolf. His words echoed.

Over to you, I told my wolf, giving up everything for the time being. It was only fair with my behaviour of late. After saying I'd never stick her in a box, I did just that. Even if I felt she went over the line to prove a point, reacting that way showed how strongly I'd refused to admit the truth.

The sun touched my fur and energy poured into me, soaking into my tired bones and filling them. Greyson set into a steady lope that I mimicked. When we cleared the stream and left the cabins behind, he took off without warning. Flattening our ears, we took off after him, bounding over fallen trunks and roots. He weaved between ancient trees, pine needles and dirt flying up behind him.

We ran straight, trying to head him off.

Snapping at his heels, we only just avoided smacking into a tree.

Greyson's laughter rang in our ears, and we set off in pursuit again.

Silence.

He's hiding somewhere, my wolf hushed.

Crawling on our belly, we panted, listening for signs of life. He had to be close.

A muted thud sounded to our right and we readied for his attack.

Boo! Greyson erupted from the trees at our back.

Yelping, we leaped directly up, scratching our way onto the lowest sturdy branch.

A very human roar of laughter rang out.

Flopping over the branch, we glared down at Sascha.

"A tree-climbing wolf," he gasped, naked and covered in dirt. "That's a first."

What else were we meant to do? He startled us, I said to her.

He tricked us.

Sascha had never looked more carefree as he continued laughing, but my sidekick wasn't happy about the slight.

She pounced from our branch and bowled him to the ground, standing over him, teeth gnashing over his throat.

He exposed his throat more. Reaching up, he threaded his fingers through our fur. "Sorry, beautiful wolf. That was unexpected is all. I admire your creativity."

That feels good, she slurred.

It really, really did.

Sascha scratched behind our ears.

Oh god, I moaned.

Tell me about it. Let's stay for a bit.

We lay on top of him and let the man continue.

"I've never seen anything like you," he crooned.

She huffed, twitching our tail.

You know he's flattering you, right?

She didn't answer.

Who knew wolves were vain?

"What do you know about Luthers, beautiful wolf?" he asked.

She rested our head on his chest.

"Our pack has a legend of a she-wolf," Sascha murmured. "She was chosen by the sun to bear an immortal pup who would create an army for a god. Any offspring that pup sired were given the name Luthers in recognition of their purpose for war. Unlike their sire, they only received immortality if they could reproduce and expand the god's army. And *unlike* him, they were not a slave to the beast that resided inside them, ready to burst out and defeat their foe when the order was given. The immortal sire grew jealous, seeing himself as savage and weak in comparison. He began to kill the young of his children and his children's children. The Luthers revolted, feeling his actions went against the very power that granted the she-wolf his life. They joined forces to kill their sire, and since that day, Luthers have governed themselves. None had his power, so none could unite the race as a whole. We broke into smaller groups, small enough that the strongest wolf could maintain harmony across the different statuses within our kind."

My wolf was grossly interested in his words. And why wouldn't she be? This was an explanation for her existence.

"Of course," Sascha continued, "we could discuss the obvious inbreeding implications of such a legend. And who was the god? Then there's the whole sun knocking up a she-wolf thing. Bit hard to swallow. But it's a nice story, and maybe parts of it are true."

My wolf snorted.

He stared at the sky. "When I was young, I imagined a rainbow shooting into the mother wolf's heart to make her pregnant. I didn't know where pups came from."

We laughed, the sound coming out as a series of short panted huffs.

I sniffed. *Spice.*

We stilled.

Enemy, my wolf snapped.

Careful not to dig our claws into Sascha, we launched after the smell, a snarl ripping from our curled lips.

I smelled that at the waterfall. What is it?

Another wolf, she hissed. *Bad wolf.*

Greyson sprinted in pursuit, but we drew to a halt before long. The scent was gone.

It was only faint to begin with.

How do you know it's an enemy? I asked.

Itchy aroma. He wants to hurt us.

Greyson caught up.

What is it? He circled me, hackles raised.

Something that didn't smell good.

His circles grew tighter. *Not good how?*

Made us want to sneeze.

He turned his attention outward. *I can't smell anything amiss.*

Nothing?

My pack frequents this area. Male Luthers have a stronger sense of smell than she-wolves, but I do not smell an enemy here. Only my pack.

I probably had a lot of enemies in the pack. And those enemies likely loved Sascha—which would change their scent for him.

Though an attack on me would certainly harm him. So this wolf had to be one twisted mothershitter.

Greyson, I've smelled that scent before. At the waterfall before you arrived.

A furious snarl ripped from his mouth. *Why didn't you tell me?*

I thought it was a random animal. Could it be the wolf who changed me?

It made sense.

He brushed his body around mine, focus turned outward. With gentle shoves, he herded me back the way we came.

Stumbling back, I tried to hold my ground to no avail. *Are we doing this all the way back? Because I have a better idea.*

Rounding on me, he snapped. I snapped right back and whirled to walk away, batting him around the face with my tail.

Do what I say, Greyson boomed.

Fuck you, my wolf replied.

Oh, shit, I said in glee. She learned that one from me.

We sashayed out of the clearing and settled into an easy lope back to Sascha's bungalow. Back on the patio by the stream, we lay flat on our stomach.

Over to you, she said.

I promise we'll run again tonight or tomorrow morning at dawn. I won't make the same mistake again.

I know, Andie. Neither will I. It's my job to alert you, just as it's your job to make time.

Alright, I hadn't really done this part without being in a rage. I drew forth the image of my legs and arms, the way they bent and swung. I remembered how it was to be upright and feel the tickle of my hair across my back.

The change wasn't as rapid, but I straightened after a minute and walked to my sheet, swiping it up.

"Not bad." Sascha leaned against the balustrade.

I cocked a brow, tying the sheet around my body. "The view or the shift?"

His lips curved, and he approached, not answering.

I tilted my chin, narrowing my eyes.

Sascha cupped my jaw, thumb brushing my cheekbone. "Running with you was an unbelievable turn-on."

Yeah, he wasn't alone in that. The latent thrum of adrenaline wanted me to do all kinds of wild things.

Lowering his head, Sascha trailed kisses down my throat. My head tipped back, and a sigh escaped my parted lips. I trailed my fingertips over his chest, leaning forward to place a kiss in the middle. He caged me against the bungalow wall and hooked my leg around his hips. His hands bunched in the sheet and a growl built in his throat.

Placing one hand over his, I captured his full attention and slowly traced his lips. Completing my torture, I ground into his erection at the same speed.

"Andie." Honey eyes burned brighter than ever before. His gaze snagged on my lips, and I moistened them.

He dragged a thumb over my bottom lip, a favour I'd return in short duration.

Just as soon as he kissed me.

"Where is she?" a voice bellowed.

A slap wouldn't have worked half so well. "What is Wade doing here?"

"I texted him off your phone a few hours ago to let him know what happened," he answered.

"Wade doesn't know I'm a wolf!" I scented the slight decay of Sascha's pine.

He knew that.

"Such a dick move." Pushing past, I ran into the bungalow for my clothes.

Fuck, I didn't have any.

"Andie Thana, get your ass out here!"

Dread curling around my heart, I gave up the hunt for clothes and trudged down the hallway in my sheet.

Outside, Wade folded his arms when he saw me. He'd driven Ella F here.

"Hey." I crossed the distance.

"You're in a sheet."

"I... ruined my clothes."

"When you shifted into a wolf," he said coldly.

I lowered my head. *Dammit, Sascha.* "When I turned into a wolf, yes."

"That fucker bit you in Water." He began to pace. Wade stopped abruptly, fists bunching. "When did you first shift?"

"Night before Timber." I'd never seen him this furious. Holy shit.

"The night you wanted time to yourself. That's why you moved out to the cabin. What the *fuck,* Andie?"

I closed my eyes. "I didn't want to put you in a position where you had to lie to the tribe."

"I *already* lie to the tribe for you."

"I know. But this is another level. I couldn't face you."

He squared his shoulders, grey eyes flashing. "You didn't trust me."

"I trust you."

"You didn't trust me *enough*."

I remained mute. "Stewards are raised to hate Luthers. Even if they don't learn about the wolf part until later, I hear the way mothers talk about the *people on the south side* to their kids. It's not that I didn't trust you enough. It's that I feared..."

"What?" he said, unfolding his arms.

We looked at each other.

Wade didn't budge. "If I had to wake up to that shitty text and drive over here believing you were dead, then you can say the fucking hard words in front of this pack."

My lips twitched.

His eyes narrowed. "Don't you smirk at me."

I crossed the gap. "I didn't know if your love for me would be greater than a lifetime of prejudice."

Wade's shoulders sagged, and I hugged him around the middle.

His arms didn't come around me. "What do you think now?"

I peeked up. "That you *might* love me more than a lifetime of prejudice?"

"Don't look at me with those eyes. You know I can't resist them." He returned the hug tightly.

Swallowing hard, I said, "I'm sorry."

"You will be."

My stomach plummeted. "Why? Who else knows?"

He pulled away to glare. "You think I'm stupid? You can't tell anyone else—well, maybe Cameron, but definitely not your bullshit sister."

"Don't say that about Rhona."

His mouth bobbed. "Wait, *this* isn't why she's so pissed, is it?"

The thought of her discovering *this* truth made me feel sick.

I shook my head.

Wade swore. "Whoa. She definitely can't find out then. Can you imagine her reaction? Talk about the Kardashian episode to end all Kardashian episodes."

Yep.

She couldn't ever find out.

A tear slipped over my cheek and I ducked my head as more followed. *Crap.* I sniffed, and Wade held me at arm's length.

Horror painted his features. "Oh fuck, are you crying?"

I didn't think he'd still want to be my friend. I gulped in air as sobs wracked my chest.

"What do I do?" Wade said frantically.

Sascha spoke from behind me. "I don't know. Make her stop somehow."

"I don't speak female, wolf man. You want to bone her on the regular, *you* make her stop."

He all but shoved me into Sascha's arms, who held me close, resting his chin atop my head. Our good juju seeped under my skin immediately, and I recovered the strength to close my tear ducts.

Embarrassing.

Maybe overdue.

And maybe I'd hide here for a while.

"Thank you," Sascha said.

Wade's salted caramel took on a slight burned tinge. "It wasn't for you. And I've heard that you're holding out on the final mating meets. That's bullshit. You know Andie wants them over and done with."

A few growls rose around us.

Sascha didn't share that tidbit with his pack?

"That's between Andie and me," Sascha said stiffly.

Did he think I'd told Wade the reason why? I hoped not.

"Actually, as leaders, this is between you, Andie, our tribe, and your pack. Pull your head out of your ass, Sascha. Your lives don't just belong to you."

Big ouch.

Sascha didn't say anything, and a quick sniff told me he was considering Wade's remark.

There was something undeniably sexy about men who could do that.

I think so, my wolf rushed to say.

I rolled my eyes, untangling myself.

Wade dug around in Ella F and held up a bag. "Clothes for you. Because I'm a genius. You can thank me alongside begging for my forgiveness when you organise and execute a King Wade Day in my honour."

I meekly took the bag and padded past the silent Luther to change in the bungalow.

When I returned, the pair stood in silence.

"Cool." I cleared my throat. "I apologise again for risking your life, Sascha. I won't let it happen again."

He nodded vaguely.

"You risked his life?" Wade said.

"She nearly killed herself by avoiding the shift."

Wade's gaze landed heavy on me. "That true?"

"Yep."

Wade directed me to the car and peered back at Sascha. "Maybe your head isn't up your ass, Luther. Maybe it's only your finger."

My grin faded as Sascha walked around to my open door.

He braced against the car, and though he'd put on sweatpants, the front-row seats to his ab show were more than enough for my libido.

Holy fuck.

Wade slid into the driver's seat and cocked a brow at Sascha's stomach, then my flushed face.

Ugh.

Sascha crouched, resting a hand on my thigh. "Please be careful, little bird."

I heard what he *didn't* say. No matter that he didn't smell an enemy during our run, I did. Someone was following me.

"I will. I'll also add that you're very lucky this worked out or I'd never have forgiven you."

The Luther tapped his nose. "Your smells intertwine when you're together. Not luck. You needed a friend, whether you believed it or not."

"We have a friend smell. Cute," Wade said.

Sascha leaned closer. "About the meets. We'll continue without delay. It's selfish of me to do otherwise. Message when you're free."

Hesitating, he kissed my cheek.

Fresh heat poured into my face. I didn't even need to look to know Wade's smirk was dialled to Cheshire cat.

Sweat licked my palms. Should I do something? Stay like this?

Sascha released my thigh.

His honey eyes locked on mine. "I'll see you soon."

19

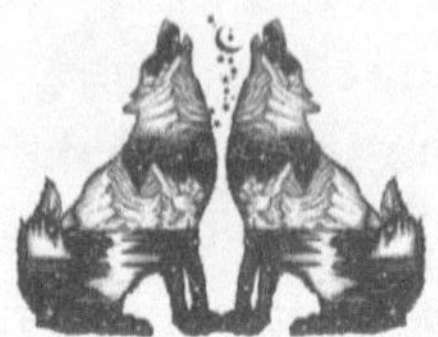

"What's her name?" I asked.

Wade took the car keys from me and pocketed them. "Jessi Angell."

Sounded like a boutique sports clothing brand. "Anything I should know?"

The time for making an effort to meet every steward had started today. Tuesday afternoons were now blocked out for the job. For someone who wasn't big on most people, Wade knew *everyone*, which made him the perfect person for introductions.

I knocked, and a short woman answered.

"Head Steward," she gasped.

"Jessi, isn't it?" I held out a hand that she automatically took, blurting a "Yes."

Wade intervened. "The head steward is trying to get around to meet us all. Do you have ten minutes for a quick introduction?"

The ten-minute hint was appreciated. The first four visits took over two hours—I couldn't blame stewards for wanting to ask the same questions, but I felt more like a politician with each passing second.

What are your plans for the tribe?

Do you think we can win?

We were so shocked when Herc's will was read.

How is Rhona doing?

We followed Jessi inside.

Whoa.

Plants took up nearly every available space in the cabin. A potted tree behind the flower-print sofa was so large it now grew sideways along the ceiling.

"You like nature," I said after a beat.

She flushed. "Well, yes. I think it's our duty to love nature. I've always felt a call."

That was something I could appreciate. "I felt the same when I set foot into this valley."

"Sometimes, when I'm upset, I just go out and hug the trees. Makes me feel good inside."

Wade coughed into his water.

I schooled my features. "If it makes you happy, I'm all for tree hugging."

Her gaze turned dreamy. "Yes. Happy and peaceful." A wrinkle formed between her brows. "Rhona's made concerning comments at trainings—about a more violent approach to the game."

Dammit.

I tapped a finger on the threadbare side of the sofa. "I'm sure you can appreciate that my sister has lost two grandparents and her father to Luthers. Her views are a way of expressing her current grief. I assure you that there are no plans to take a more violent approach against our opponent."

The training propaganda was an issue, but I'd started waking at 4:00 a.m. to cram study, shift, and run. I made it to the manor for the first head team meeting at 8:00 a.m. when dawn training ended. I wasn't sure how to stomp on the problem without being physically present.

Jessi sighed. "I'm glad to hear it. Do you think I should talk to Rhona about hugging trees?"

Wade piped up, "Please do. I think she'd greatly benefit from it. Don't you think so, Head Steward?"

Bastard. I nodded, shooting him a death look. "Absolutely."

A few minutes later, Wade interrupted our conversation on whether dirt had feelings. We walked to the door and I shook her hand in both of mine.

"Andie," she said. "I mean, Head Steward, it's so nice of you to stop by and see me. I don't play a big part in Grids—I never much liked shooting the tranquiliser gun—but this tribe means everything to me."

"Jessi, you're an essential part of our tribe and the game. I mean that with complete sincerity. If you ever have a question or concern, my door is wide open."

We left to her repeated thanks.

"Sweet lady," I murmured.

Wade slanted a look at me as I pulled Ella F out of the bumpy driveway. "You know, you're kind of amazing at this."

I scoffed. "Whatever."

"I'm serious. You connect with people so easily. That double-hand handshake is inspired. I'm almost envious."

"Don't be. A connection is easy to fake. Very few of my relationships progress past that—and most that did ended in a burning ball of flame."

"Your mum and Herc?"

They were the two main ones. "Yes."

"To be fair, I'm not sure they could have lied more than they did."

I blew out a breath. "Tell me about it. And that's not all." Now the dog was out of the rucksack, it made no sense to hold anything back.

I filled him in on Murphy and my suspicions about Pascal and the journals.

Wade blew out a breath. "You think Herc killed him? That's really hard to imagine."

Unless Pascal fessed up, I'd never know for sure. "It's a possibility I can't deny after how easily he drew a gun on Sascha."

"Since you brought up the werewolf himself, what's happening there?"

I sighed. "I keep going back to what happened in Sandstone. Herc knew that killing Sascha would hurt me, but he still fired. So, did Herc come to protect my life at all? Or did he come to protect the *image* of me as a Thana and his eldest daughter? On one hand, I feel like I lost Herc too soon, but I also don't stand with slaughtering someone you hate or disagree with. I've let go of enough anger to see that Sascha was defending himself and me too. In my mind, that's an acceptable reason for what he did. I believe Herc was in the wrong that night."

Wade chewed his lip. "That's a lot to process. Baby girl… you may not find the tribe very open-minded on that front."

"Don't worry—that's between us." I took the manor turnoff.

"Does that change things between you and Sascha?"

"Wouldn't the thought of me being with him disgust you? Seriously, you're so unjudgmental, it's almost off-putting."

"Thank you. Flattery will get you somewhere with me, but don't think you're getting out of King Wade Day."

I grinned. "Wouldn't dream of it."

"Well then, I'll tell you what I saw a few days ago. I saw a woman wrapped in a sheet come out of Sascha Greyson's bungalow. And her nipples were hard."

Ugh.

"Something that's never happened around me, I might add," he said. "I saw that same woman stop crying when Sascha Greyson held her. *Then*, I saw her blush like a schoolgirl meeting One Direction after a certain Luther kissed her on the cheek. Her *cheek*, no less."

I groaned. "Stop."

Wade turned dancing grey eyes on me. "You like Sascha Greyson."

I frowned. "I don't know if *like* is the right word."

"What's the right word then?"

"I *understand* him. His position. His burdens. I understand that things might have been different if we weren't who we are, and certain things hadn't happened. But they did. So I just... understand him."

Wade's nose scrunched. "That's the biggest load of horseshit I've ever heard."

"I'm telling the truth."

"Pfft. You *think* you are, Miss *I Only Make Connections.* You're lying to yourself big time."

I waved to Troy at the gates. "So what? Maybe I'm doing that because nothing can come of us. Why would I ever pursue Sascha Greyson?"

He hummed. "Wild sex isn't a good enough reason?"

It always was before. "He won't have sex with me."

A screech filled the car. I checked my foot wasn't slammed on the brake.

Wade screeched again. "Sascha isn't putting out?"

"He says I use sex as a weapon."

Wade's mouth rounded. "Holy shit. I really haven't given him enough credit. Ingenious."

"What's that mean?"

"It means I saw the way you went for Billy that one time. He's absolutely right. By denying you, he's forced you to take one of two other paths. You either turn him down entirely, *or* you accept that to be with him, a deeper and *real* emotional connection is required. *Ingenious.*"

Wade just joined Team Sascha.

Cars blocked me from my usual car park in front of the manor. The normal Tuesday night briefing wouldn't start for another hour. "What's going on?"

I spotted a small group of stewards by the stage set up for the gathering tonight. The sight of auburn hair made my stomach plummet.

"That don't look good none," Wade muttered.

I parked, rolling down my window.

The microphone shot Rhona's voice across the clearing—and probably the entire manor property.

"Grids has continued without end for over two hundred years," she said. *"We have two centuries of data that tells us our approach isn't working. What we're doing is insanity."*

I gritted my teeth, swinging the door open.

Wade fell into step beside me. "This is the stuff she's saying at training."

Rhona had supporters. Around fifty. Those were just the ones brave enough to show up.

Shit.

She spotted me and smirked.

I stood beside the crowd and folded my arms as she continued. She'd timed her rally to catch stewards arriving early for the gathering. I *could* pull out the microphone power supply, but every steward here was welcome to have their say if they believed me to be lacking.

This was within Rhona's rights as a steward and Thana, no matter that it was very much a personal attack.

As she wrapped up, I joined her at the mic.

"Rhona," I greeted her.

She walked off without a word—something no one missed.

I studied the crowd that had doubled in size. Those at the front peered back with stony expressions while those at the back seemed highly uncomfortable.

"Look around you," I said quietly.

The request surprised those in the front row at least.

"Look into the eyes of the stewards around you. That person is who we risk by adopting a more violent approach. There's a reason our ancestors played the game this way. There's a reason we've maintained a place on the gameboard for two centuries. That's because past leaders cared about your lives. To purposefully injure Luthers is to risk losing points and *our* place in this valley. We'd risk their potential retaliation. I will never accept such an extreme stance because I care about your lives. Anyone in this tribe is welcome to express their views to me at any time. I want your feedback. Your opinion will not be buried or disregarded, I promise you. I simply ask that you consider how important it is that stewards stick together at all times when you express any opinions. United, we can win."

"They weren't your ancestors," a woman called.

I didn't even know her. "What's your name, steward?"

She cocked a hip. "Dakota."

"Dakota has just shouted that the ancestors of this tribe weren't mine." Talk about a punch in the gut.

The woman lost some of her cocky edge.

Yeah, try standing in front of a mic instead of melting into the crowd, you coward.

"I can only say that the woman I thought was my mother stole me from Hercules and Savannah Thana as an infant. I was raised away from this wondrous place in less than ideal circumstances. When arriving in Deception Valley, I thought I'd entered a dream. I don't trust easily, but I never questioned the bond I felt to this land even before meeting Herc for the first time. *That* was the strength of what I experienced. While I've only known about our ancestors for a short time, Dakota, I'd thank you not to take them from me—as others tried to do. Those who came before me are more precious to me than most people will ever realise."

She was a healthy shade of purple.

No fucks given.

"This evening's gathering will commence shortly." I dipped my head to the gathered stewards.

I descended the three stairs and Wade flanked me as we walked to the manor.

"What a *cow,*" he spat. "She doesn't care about our tribe. What she's doing can only split us apart."

"Hold on. I don't want anyone to overhear." We reached the office, and I pushed—

Locked. I never locked it. "Have you got my keys?"

He passed over the car keys, and I found the right one, shoving it in the lock. It didn't turn.

I stared at the mahogany door, sliding the key free.

"She did *not* change the lock." Wade took the key and tried, swearing when nothing happened.

Not only was Rhona organising rallies against me, she'd shut me out of Herc's office. I remembered one brief time where I didn't feel like an imposter for entering this room as head steward—the night of my first grid win, just before shit hit the fan. This fucking *stung*.

Wade kicked the door.

I yanked him back, checking the hall. "We can't make a scene. We'll go to my room."

"This is *bullying*," Wade said when we made it there.

"Tell me about it."

"*Do* something then." He rounded on me.

I rubbed my forehead. "Like what?"

"Be the fearless Andie Thana everyone knows and loves," he shouted.

Whoa.

I lowered my hand. "Wade... what's going on?"

"You know what I hate most in this world? I hate people who treat others like shit. Do you know what it was like being a young bisexual in this valley?"

My breath caught at the tears in his eyes.

Wade sniffed hard, dragging an arm across his face. "I'll tell you what, Andie. It was shit. I see the faces of my bullies every night in my nightmares, and I tell them exactly how weak they were to judge someone who never hurt them. But you know what that means?"

Mute, I shook my head.

"*Fuck all.*"

Wade sat heavily on the bed. "I've never *once* known you to be mean-spirited, but you never take shit. If you can't stand up to Rhona, then who will?"

I'd missed how much Rhona's behaviour affected him. He wasn't just cheering me on as a friend. He was really upset.

I wrapped an arm around his shoulders. "I didn't know this fight was hurting you so much."

He sniffed again. "Yeah."

"Who bullied you?"

"Not many from the tribe. Once we knew werewolves existed, it banded us together."

"The public then, huh? That makes it easier to exterminate them," I said conversationally.

He choked on a pitiful laugh.

"My position," I said carefully, "is that Rhona is my last relation and emotionally, I'm not sure if I can hurt her more than she's already been hurt. I *will* hold my ground, Wade, and I'm asking you to really look at the reaction to what she's doing. Who just came out on top just before?"

"My girl," he whispered.

"That's right. When she demanded to come to pack lands, who came out on top?" I continued without his answer. "As much as it pains me to witness, Rhona is only tearing herself down."

"Division in the tribe is a problem," he croaked. "And what about your office?"

"You know Tiptoe Eleanor?"

"Quietest walker in the tribe and maybe all history. Sure."

"She can pick locks. She'll get me in, no problem. I'll tell her I lost my key. Sorted."

Discontent in the tribe was another problem. Messing with that was a solid no for me, and Rhona was drawing precariously close to crossing the line.

She was off the head team already. Maybe I should consider relieving her of the training leader position until these antics stopped. There was a responsible and mature way to give an opinion, and it wasn't like that—which she was more than aware of.

"Sorry," Wade straightened. "You have way bigger problems. I didn't mean to add another."

I hugged him tight. "It's nice to know you need help sometimes. I will *always* have time for you. You're the best person I know."

He hugged me back.

"For what it's worth," I whispered, "kids can be fucking assholes when they're finding themselves. Anyone out of the norm presents an easy way for the most insecure teens to feel accepted. Their words will haunt them a lot more than they haunt you."

We were still for a time.

"Thank you, baby girl," he whispered.

I leaned my head on his shoulder. "Anytime."

20

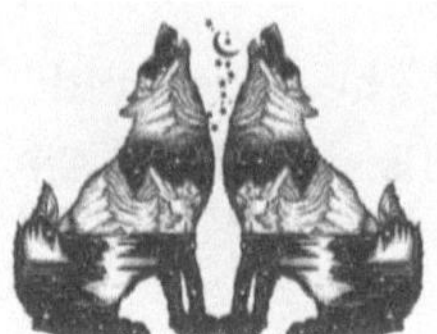

I tried to shrug off the itch crawling over my skin. The waning crescent moon—so Google had informed me—was a sliver in the sky. My long-sleeve top and jeans were irritating to the extreme as the slow strangulation of light created a dark hunger that wanted to consume me.

We'll need to shift after the game, my wolf said.

Agreed.

"The cabin seems to be working for you," Pascal said.

I glanced at the marshal. "I feel much better."

With our daily runs, we'd never felt stronger. We could snap through fallen tree limbs with a chomp of our razor-sharp teeth. Everything was *more* in wolf form, but even with two legs, I was unimaginably powerful. And so aware of my surroundings. Our raised position over Clay allowed us to see the detailed markings of a chickadee five hundred metres away. It was nothing short of incredible.

I'd looked to our morning runs as something I *had* to do. How wrong I'd been.

Each time, I learned something more about my wolf and

marvelled at some new connection to the land that my senses provided.

"If any of the head team remained unconvinced of your choice, I believe they've changed their mind."

Not Valerie. She put on an excellent show, but she couldn't fool my new nose.

"I'm glad to hear it," I said as the first cannon boomed. "It was an irregular request."

Pascal smiled at her tablet. "Perhaps irregular is what this tribe has needed for a long time."

I could not figure this woman out. "You think?"

"I do."

"Not as irregular as Murphy though?" I pretended to adjust my binoculars, relying on my nose for her reaction.

It didn't disappoint.

Shock.

Fear.

So much fear it rankled my predatory instincts.

"I wonder if Murphy told Herc he'd shifted to a Luther." I lowered the binoculars.

Pascal was as flustered as I'd ever seen. This could be a stupid course of action considering my allies grew thinner each day.

Perhaps I was sick of lies.

"I don't know what happened that day, Pascal," I said. "I don't *need* to know unless you'd like to tell me. What I would like to know is why you lied to your head steward. Herc is gone. Your loyalty is to me."

She closed her eyes. "What we did that day doesn't go away because Herc died."

And there it was.

"How did he do it?"

"Cut the rope. Made me swear to secrecy."

I couldn't imagine anyone forcing this woman to do something. She was marshal for a reason. Pascal upheld the rules above all. So what did Herc have over her?

"If you lie to me again, we'll have a problem," I told her. "And if you need something from my office in the future, you need only ask."

Pink tinged her cheeks. "Understood, Head Steward."

"Let's focus on Clay."

I returned my attention to the grid, scanning the area sans binoculars. They were a joke with my better sight.

The east and west team were busy digging. They'd dig as far into the clay rises as possible and then pack the entrances. Hopefully that would prevent Luthers from filling in our tunnels between times. We'd only know if the plan was successful the next time we played here.

Tunnels were a long-term plan. *Years,* really.

We'd had pitifully few ideas for Clay this week. Water was the real whammy for us, but Clay allowed so little room for new tactics. The terrain was gluggy and played against our physical strengths. The Luthers didn't allow us to make trap advancements from battle to battle.

My only thought was to use their own past strategy against them. The *sky* could be utilised. And then, like us, the Luthers could spend the next week picking up tranquiliser darts.

I checked my phone and clicked my walkie. "This is Big Red. Wrap it up. We've got fifteen left. Over."

Three confirmations came through. Nothing from Rhona—no surprises there. With next week off Grids because of the new moon, I'd give her two weeks to sort her shit. If I didn't see visible change, I'd relieve her of the dawn training position *and* her team leader position on the field.

A series of "*Clears*" reached me five minutes before the cannon.

Everyone was in position.

Boom.

My gums ached at the surge in adrenaline in the air, tangible on my tongue.

"You think they'll sweep the area like last time?" I murmured.

"After Timber, I'd be surprised."

The counter-strategy team thought so too. The terrain here could lend itself to the same strategy we used in Timber—and Sascha wouldn't miss that.

We were prepared either way.

The words *Operation Baking* lingered on my lips, but I swallowed the words back. I had to time it right.

"Looks like we were right," she said.

I squinted. "What are those things on their backs?"

The Luthers below unravelled hoses, climbing the uneven tiers formed by the extraction of Clay over time.

My mouth bobbed as they sprayed the top of the clay mounds. *Crap.*

"They're making it too dangerous to occupy high ground," Pascal said. "Smart."

Any steward up there had vacated on sight of the Luthers. Even with the wolves retreating to lower ground, my team couldn't return to occupy the highest positions in the grid.

And I couldn't use the drones too soon or the Luthers would recover from the tranquiliser dose.

We had another option.

I clicked my walkie. "Big Red here. High ground is too dangerous to occupy. Prepare for Operation Banh Mi. Over."

Hopefully, most of the stewards had done as instructed and kept an eye out for crevices and cracks during the first hour. Not everyone would find a place, but we needed a rapid change of plan now we'd lost high ground advantage.

I waited a full two minutes. "Big Red. Initiate Operation Bahn Mi. Continue for duration. Over."

"Will you go in today?" Pascal asked.

"No," I murmured. "It's not the day to test theories."

The head team wanted to see if Sascha would be drawn to my presence on the grid. With Pascal's vantage point, humouring their test was a big fucking no. I'd cater to their whims in Timber.

I ground my teeth as three more flags were raised.

Fuck.

"What's the tally?"

"Forty to twenty."

"Dammit." I chewed my lip. Should I risk sending the drones up early? I could follow up by ordering the stewards on a group sweep, but that was a huge risk. If the Luthers took cover and not enough went down, we'd just come head-to-head with a werewolf army stronger than us in every way.

A crack rent the air, echoing through the clay quarry.

"What was that?" I strained to hear.

Crack.

Crack.

It wasn't the *pop* of a tranquiliser gun or the sound of a shifting Luther. It was almost like a car backfiring.

Like—

My heart skipped a beat.

Crack.

Crack.

"Those are gunshots," I blurted. That's the sound Herc's gun made when he shot Sascha.

Pascal's exclamation was lost as I looked to the south to where the sound continued in a steady staccato.

"That's Rhona's position." I swore.

I grabbed my walkie. "This is Big Red. South team. Stand down. Stand down immediately. Over."

Crack.

Crack.

Crack.

They were shooting Luthers with real bullets. I covered my mouth and clicked a different button on the walkie that put me through to all stewards. "South team. This is Big Red. This is your final warning to stand down. Our tribe does *not* condone the use of real bullets in the grid against any being. *Stand down* or face the consequences. Over."

Five seconds was long enough to tell me they wouldn't stop.

I gripped the balustrade. "I have to do something."

"You don't have the gear to protect you against real bullets."

"This isn't what we stand for. She's putting everything at risk. Rhona has gone too far."

Pascal returned to her tablet, tallying the blue flags. Luthers in the south territory were falling like flies.

Sliding down the observation tower ladder, I ran around the grid outskirts, sticking to human pace by the skin of my fangs.

I slowed as the shooting grew louder. *What if Sascha is hit?*

We'll heal him, my wolf answered, a whine in her voice.

Bile rose up my throat as I saw the scene.

Luthers splayed on the ground, shot by the stewards concealed on the large clay rise to my right.

I watched three Luthers run for their injured from my left. They got halfway there before bullets tore through their bodies

Monsters.

And I wasn't referring to the werewolves.

I strode into the middle of the gun fight, tensing for a hit that may very likely come.

Stopping near the centre, I stared at the man groaning at my feet.

The gunfire stopped.

"Come to join the fun, have you?" Rhona slid down the bank, a small gun in each hand.

"You've gone too far. Real bullets. I wouldn't have believed you could do such a thing."

She scoffed. "You—"

"Look at them," I screamed in her face, making her jump.

I gestured at the Luther at my feet. "Look at him, Rhona. Look at what you've let your hate do. You foolish, foolish girl. They're *people*."

"That's exactly what I'd expect a dog lover to say," she hissed.

"I could no sooner treat a bear this way," I replied, digging my claws into my palms. "These people have families that want to see them come home. They have children and lives."

She opened her mouth.

"What would Herc say?" I asked her quietly, very much aware of the silence in front of me as well as behind.

"I'll never know." Loathing oozed through her emerald eyes like thick mud.

"You won't. That's because he used a gun on a Luther too."

Rhona's fist whipped out and only my new strength stopped me falling on my ass. My head rocked to the side, spinning me. Face to the Luthers, I battled to keep my wolf from ripping my sister's head off.

Sascha pushed through the row to stand in the middle. His gaze fell on his injured pack members. Over the blood and pain, I smelled his horror.

I'm not backing down this time, I reassured my wolf.

She hit you.

I know. Trust me on this.

The stewards left their hiding spots on the tiers. While everyone else spent the first hour digging tunnels for future plans, I could assume that this team—under Rhona's direction—made themselves a lovely battleground instead.

In control, I faced Rhona again.

Shooting holes in Luthers hadn't done it, but Rhona was aware she'd overstepped by hitting me. And in the eyes of her supporters.

Stepping around her, I planted myself before the stewards. The Dakota woman was here.

Valerie.

Billy. Laura. Foley.

Several others from Rhona's rally last night.

Fury filled my heart. "*Put. Down. Your. Weapons.*"

I stalked in front of them, meeting their gazes. "Now."

Foley was the first to cave. After that, the rest followed.

"Each of you will attend a disciplinary hearing in the next two days that will decide your continuing role in this tribe. Valerie, effective immediately, you are no longer part of the head team. Your part in this horrific plan fills me with disgust. All of you, wait for me at our entry point for further orders." My hands shook.

Turning from Valerie's pale expression, I ignored Rhona again.

I located Sascha and tilted my chin. "The Ni Tiaki forfeit this grid to the Luthers with our sincerest and deepest apologies. Most of us share your horror and disgust for what a small and idiotic number of our tribe decided to do today. Please collect your injured and let us know if we can aid you in any way."

Rhona exploded. "You can't forfeit—"

I clicked my walkie on. "This is Big Red. Due to the actions of the south team under the direction of Rhona Thana, our tribe has forfeited the grid. The battle is over, everyone. This is an order for all stewards to gather at the manor without delay."

She grabbed my shoulder.

I gripped hers right back. "I have a responsibility as head steward to protect this tribe. From our opponents," I gestured at the stricken Luthers, "and from other stewards. I love you, Rhona, but what you did tonight was very wrong."

She reeled back.

"Remember that what comes next I do as your sister and also as your leader. I hope you can accept that someday."

"Will I accept the orders of someone who helped to kill my father?" she hissed for only us and the Luthers to hear. "Over my dead body."

"You don't have to accept my orders," I told her. "But that choice will come with consequences. I've given you more than enough time to get a hold of your hate. Now you're hurting others and I can't stand by while that happens."

I strode to where Sascha crouched beside a screaming she-wolf caught mid-shift.

He gripped her chin, locking gazes with her. "Shift," he said in a gravel-ridden voice.

She sighed, completing the transformation to become a small brown wolf.

"Can I help in any way?" I said to his tense back.

He stroked the wolf's head, and I took in the matted blood covering the fur on her chest.

"No," Greyson answered. "Tribe presence here will create more problems than it will solve."

I agreed. "This won't go unpunished."

He didn't answer, and though I hadn't fired the guns myself, if I'd been in wolf form, my tail would have been tucked between my legs.

How could Rhona do this?

Leaving him, I pulled out my phone, taking pictures of those I passed—of their wounds and tear-streaked faces, along with some videos of screaming Luthers and loved ones shouting for help.

Most stewards had left when I reached the entry point. Those who'd covered the farthest area trickled in last, shock blanketing their faces.

"Return to the manor," I called. "All will be explained there."

Pascal joined me, along with the head team—barring Valerie.

"Is it true? The south team brought real guns onto the grid?" Roderick said.

I glanced at the guilty culprits who lingered, heads bowed for the most part. Their ringleader was nowhere to be seen.

"Rhona has gone too far. Her actions will lose us the game if unchecked. Her views on violence have gained momentum and need to be addressed to the entire tribe. I will do so tonight and need your full support on that front."

They were torn between shock and anger as I was, but every one of them nodded.

Rhona's actions were a slap for the tribe, yes. It was a larger slap to the head team, not only me. We'd banned her from meetings, and she'd retaliated in a horrific manner.

"Valerie was involved and is no longer part of the head team," I stated. "That is my decision and it is final. We cannot be seen to condone such behaviour on any level, particularly not in our leading positions."

No one made a peep, though Nathan's eyes shot to the guilty group.

"Are there any thoughts on how best to convey this to the tribe?" I asked next.

Stanley rubbed his jaw. "They'll feel as shocked as we do. Rhona's violence and your forfeit will certainly create a divide. People will feel they need to pick a Thana. We should take steps to lessen that impact."

"What do you suggest?"

"We have two weeks off Grids," he said. "Let's use that time to hold mandatory events to encourage team spirit and boost morale."

"Great idea." I mulled that over. "Okay, I need four of you to escort the group over there to the manor. The rest of us will brainstorm events on the drive back. I'd like to announce the first event tonight to provide everyone with positive focus."

"Where's Rhona now?" Trixie asked.

"She's done a runner. After the tribe is brought up to speed, we'll send a search party out. The Luthers could look for blood after this."

Part of me wouldn't blame them.

But even now, when she'd done something so heinous, I couldn't let anyone hurt Rhona. It just wasn't an option.

Not ever.

21

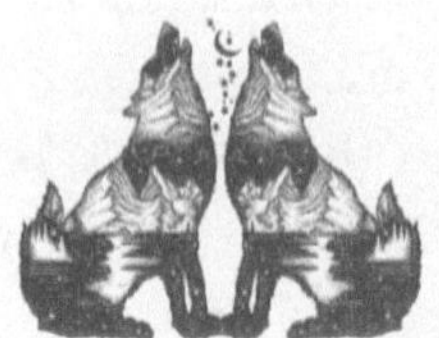

"There's a brewery in town," I said to Wade. "How about that?"

"Eh," Wade replied from where he sprawled on my bed.

Cameron thumped her head against the back of the sofa. "Why does he get a King Wade Day anyway?"

"Because I'm awesome. I want adventure *and* drinking."

I threw him a dry look. "Because that never led to disaster."

He grinned.

Cameron said, "Let's go river tubing Laos style."

I sat next to her. "What's Laos style?"

"Drinking while we do it."

"As someone who nearly drowned in the river while sober, I vote for drinking *after*." I'd have to fake drinking somehow, but I faked being human every day now. Fake drinking would be a breeze.

Wade hummed. "This would be an acceptable plan to King Wade."

Cameron rolled her eyes. "I'm so glad. I don't know about you guys, but I just really need chill out time with friends."

"Is everything alright?" I asked. Her scent carried an edge of worry and sorrow that felt serious.

"You're kidding, right? The tribe is crazy at the moment. Those pictures you showed everyone made me sick to my stomach."

Which was why I did it.

Seeing was believing. I hadn't let empathy for the tribe's comfort affect me whatsoever as I relayed the happenings in Clay. Valerie and Rhona's demotions were laid out for all to hear. The three units who'd combined to carry out the ambush were disbanded and relocated as individuals into teams selected by Roderick and Pascal. They were on a one-year probation to decide their participation in Grids and would be closely monitored. I promoted a woman named Catrina to team leader based on a recommendation.

"There has been a lot of change," I answered.

I may have asserted authority over Rhona, but the ground felt shakier than ever, especially with my new hearing.

Why didn't she wait?

She feels sorry for them and that won't help us win.

Rhona is a Thana.

I heard she didn't give Valerie any chance to explain herself.

I was the subject of growing conversation. I'd forfeited the grid, and stewards didn't care that we probably would have lost the grid for inflicting serious and sustained injuries anyway. Even if they agreed the entire tribe should be held to account for Rhona's actions, as the matter stood, my action was a small betrayal.

They were reeling, and I could only be as open as possible about what happened and continue to repeat myself until the heat died down.

"Maybe change is what we need," Wade said.

Cameron balled her hands. "It's past due."

I inhaled the slight decay of lime. "Cam, is this the only thing bothering you?"

"Tomorrow morning then." Cameron stood.

Uhm, blatant fob off.

"Works for King Wade." He glanced at me.

Dang. I'd hoped to start my trimester assignment tomorrow. It was due in three weeks and with the new moon coming up, I had the entire day free until the meeting with the Luthers.

Still, I owed Wade big time. “I’ll be there.”

She let herself out.

There’s a problem in her life, my wolf said.

I’ll keep an eye on her.

Wade took Cam’s place on the couch, running a finger through the layer of dust covering my saxophone case. “Messaged Sascha about the kissing meet?”

I sighed, reliving—for the hundredth time—the absolute horror on his face when he saw his wounded pack members. “He’ll have his hands busy managing the pack. It’s not the time.”

“The whole point of getting through the meets is because there *isn’t* a good time. Text him, meet somewhere, lay one on him, done. One step closer to being free.”

My heart twisted. “It’s not that simple.”

“Why not?”

“It just doesn’t feel that simple, okay?”

We both jerked at the harshness of my lowered voice.

“Yikes, baby girl. Think wolfy wants out.”

He’s right. The new moon is drawing too close. We’ll need to do several shifts a day. And longer runs.

We’ll make it work. “I’ll need to shift more often in the next few days. On Wednesday, the shift will trigger when the sun goes down and I’ll remain a wolf until morning. I don’t know how to get out of tribe night with things so bad after Clay.”

“That’s a tricky one.”

“Tell me about it.”

“What if you came down with a sickness? That would inspire sympathy and cover you.”

“I can only do that so many times before my absence every new moon is noticed.” The change of day would help a little, but after a few years, surely someone would notice my continued absence.

Wade hummed. “How about this? We form an extra security squad for the new moon in case the Luthers seek revenge for Clay.”

I considered that. "We could spread around the manor lands in pairs."

"I'd be your pair obviously."

A smile broke over my face. "You're a genius."

"I know. Now go run. I'm staying here tonight."

"Do I get a choice in that?"

He ignored me and, listening to the urging of my wolf, I grabbed my keys and slid into Ella F without further argument.

The lake again? I asked.

My wolf pondered. *That will be fine.*

We can run for longer tonight and explore something new.

That appealed to her more. It must get boring when there was an entire valley to explore. Directing Ella F along the dirt road that led to the swimming spot Rhona took me to so long ago, I scanned the area for company before stripping.

I want to try something, my wolf said.

We both loved a challenge. For the last week, we'd tried to complete our shift as fast as possible.

I'm not sure we can shift any faster. Well, not *into* wolf form. I still had work to do on the return shift.

That movie Wade was watching with the robot cars.

Transformers?

They shift in the air. I want to try it.

I laughed. *Like a run and jump thing? Sure, why not.*

Taking off at a sprint toward the lake, my eyes sharpened to see easily in the darkening night, I pumped my arms and legs, gaining speed. *Ready?*

Do it.

At a full bolt, I threw myself forward headfirst.

I shrieked as the shift took over, my flight adding a layer of chaos to the already hectic flurry.

Yelping, we landed and rolled through the dry brush.

We stared at the night sky.

That's not what Optimus Prime looked like, she wheezed.

My laughter came out as a series of huffs. *We'll work on it. You want control?*

You should work on our legs first.

I didn't like leg duty. Four legs were a lot to keep track of. I mean, two legs must have been an issue once, but *four* was crazy.

Rolling to our feet, I put a front leg forward, then the opposite back leg, then the other front leg, finishing with the last back leg.

I was a wolf doing the Cha Cha. *Shuffle, shuffle, shuffle.*

I tried to speed things up, aiming for a normal walking pace.

It was just a faster Cha Cha.

Would you like help?

Please. Take over.

No, you can learn. But here.

As she'd done once before, my wolf sent me a flurry of images. These were memories of her running. Of the rhythm. Through her memory, I felt the soft thudding beat of her paws on the forest floor.

Did that help? she asked.

I think so. I tried not to overthink the movement, allowing my body to mimic her memories.

We slipped into a relaxed lope.

I did it!

She smiled, and our tongue lolled. *Maybe you can show me how to walk on two legs.*

She struggled to balance on half the number of legs. *Deal. How do you send memories?*

The same way we talk to Greyson. Focus on what you want to tell me and push it through.

I'd give it a go when we shifted back. *Your turn to run. Go wild. We've got plenty of time tonight.*

My wolf took over, senses and all, and I let her at it, oddly glad for the chance to be a passenger.

We left the lake behind, and climbed the north slopes of the valley, then trotted along the ridge for an hour before descending.

My wolf paused. *This area smells like you and Greyson. And another man. Stale, powerful scents.*

I took notice of our surroundings. We were near Sandstone. This particular area had haunted me for a while. *This is where Greyson killed Herc.*

That explains it. Nose to the ground, my wolf covered the area, approaching the spot where Herc died.

We sneezed at the smell.

Spice.

Enemy, she snarled.

He wasn't my enemy. I disagreed.

Then why does he smell like spice?

I don't know. He may not have been the father or uncle I believed him to be, but he wasn't evil.

Was anyone truly evil?

Ragna wasn't evil, though others looking in might have made that judgement. Rhona wasn't evil, though she'd done a terrible thing. I wasn't evil, though my lies grew bigger by the day.

Gathering my memories of that night, I pushed everything at my wolf, showing her what happened. Seemed stupid not to share these things when we were in the same mind and body.

You were very angry, she said.

Part of me still *was* angry at Sascha over the loss of a family member I didn't get a chance to know. Even though I didn't blame him. Talk about messed up.

My anger was directed inwardly, too, and at Herc for bringing the gun.

You're angry at your mother, she whispered.

I didn't answer.

Most of all, she added.

I don't want to talk about Ragna. Can I have the senses now?

She handed over control without a word, and we started back, a delicious tiredness filling our legs.

Spice.

I wrinkled our nose, trying to get rid of Herc's smell.

That's not Herc. She dropped us to the forest floor.

Our ears twitched at the sound of movement behind us. *Spice.* Growing stronger. Fast.

Too fast!

Go, I urged.

My wolf burst upward, moving from stationary to a full sprint in seconds. We raced around the Sandstone quarry and through Thana Reserve toward the road.

The wolf was heavier—a male, but nowhere near the weight of Sascha which meant our speeds were matched too closely for comfort.

Forcing ourselves to maintain the sprint that was by no means comfortable for our endurance-inclined body, we stuck to the road for a time.

Claws on gravel. He'd reached the road too.

We abandoned the route in favour of the bush. We were more agile than him in denser terrain.

We'll follow the river, she panted. *We'll be lighter on the loose pebbles and the way is easier.*

He's gaining. How far away from the car are we?

We can't keep up this sprint the whole way back. He'll struggle to manage it, too, but we've been running for hours already.

No shit.

Should we call for Sascha's help? I could tug at the bond again or howl. Except after what Rhona did in Clay, asking him for help felt... icky. I'd made my stance on anything between us clear. I couldn't just mess with that whenever my life was in danger.

It's his life too.

We'll see if we can lose spicy first, I said.

The scattering of river pebbles spurred us faster. He'd exited the forest.

I want to see who it is.

That will cost us ground, she answered.

But she was curious too. At the next bend, we looked back.

A black wolf sprinted in our wake, fifty metres back, teeth bared and head down as he hunted us.

I didn't need to speak wolf to see he wanted to hurt us. *Bad.*

We renewed our sprint, weariness weighing our hind legs.

He's gaining, my wolf snarled.

I had to call for Sascha. We were still a good ten minutes from the car.

Swimming gets rid of our scent, right? I studied a narrowing in the river.

Only for a short time. Minutes.

I sent my idea to her.

I don't like the water.

Do you like dying? Because spicy wants a chomp out of our neck.

Not waiting for her approval, I tugged on the elastic sensation under my ribs as my wolf launched us into the river.

I took over paddling as panic swamped her. We'd barely reached the other side when I heard the telltale splash of the black wolf in pursuit.

In the tree line, as quietly as possible, I climbed a sturdy oak.

The elastic band under my ribs was loosening. Sascha was running to me, rapidly gaining.

We held our breath as the sopping-wet black wolf broke into a run past us. He stopped suddenly, and we didn't dare move as he sniffed the air.

The Luther circled backward.

Closer.

Shit.

The wolf reached our tree, where he stopped, cocking an ear.

Fuck.

The black wolf looked upward, and we snarled loudly, tail bolt upright in warning. He crouched in preparation of jumping, and we prepared to do the reverse and bolt for the river again.

Greyson's frantic howl filled the air, and I didn't possess the restraint to refuse an answer. Tilting my head back, we howled, my wolf giving him details with our call in a way I didn't yet understand.

His second howl was pure murderous promise.

The black wolf hesitated, and I renewed my snarling, standing on the branch to show him my full size.

He couldn't beat two wolves.

And he knew it.

The black wolf sprinted for the river and was soon gone from sight.

Up here, I called when Greyson paused beneath me.

His lip curled, exposing his fangs. *I thought you were in trouble.*

My wolf snapped, *We were followed through the river. Our attacker lost his scent.*

Greyson sat back on his haunches.

Schooled. I congratulated her.

We leaped down, shaking off excess water so it flew over the massive wolf.

Who was it? he asked in a politer tone.

Black male wolf, we answered together.

Greyson lay down. *That narrows things. There are around eighty black males in my pack.*

Eighty! I groaned. *You can't smell him here at all?*

I can only smell you and my pack. Lake Thana is a favourite running spot. I cannot hear him either, but he could easily hide with the noise of the river.

The world hated me. *You have no idea who it is?*

I will find out, mate.

We lay next to him and ignored his licking ministrations over our coat.

My wolf growled, *How are we meant to run and shift if you can't keep your pack in line?*

Eek.

Greyson stiffened. *I am both fearsome and fair. My pack are loyal, and my leadership is respected. Do not judge me by one male. Know that if you join me, your place as my queen will be secure. Our young will be safe. I will protect you, and my mother is ready to give over the rule of our she-wolves into your care without issue. You will want for nothing, female.*

Greyson's fervent words would make me explode into laughter if he wasn't so deadly earnest.

My wolf licked his snout, working up to his ear.

Uhm, I murmured to her, *are we okay with ear licking?*

I grimaced as she worked down his neck. *Please, stop.*

She sat back and studiously ignored Greyson.

Licking and then a cold shoulder. Is this a treat him mean, keep him keen thing? I asked.

Yes. To Greyson, she said, *I must leave now.*

I will run with you, she-wolf.

From the way she displayed our butthole as we loped back to the river, I'd wager that he'd responded correctly.

Nothing like showing a man your butthole as a reward.

What would you do if Sascha pleased you? My wolf paused on the river edge.

If Sascha called me female, he'd probably receive a slap.

Humans came her reply.

She yelped at a nudge from behind. We toppled, twisting, into the water. I took over and directed us to the other side, listening to her furious tirade.

Greyson just undid all his hard work.

Let that be a lesson about showing your butthole to men, I told her.

We were joined on the other side, and Greyson followed close in our wake as we trotted back to Ella F.

Nose in the air, I inhaled for company.

The black wolf was long gone. Coward.

I shifted back and opened the trunk. Sascha shifted, too, as I grabbed a towel.

"Thanks for coming," I said. "I know it's not the best time."

His jaw clenched, but it was all I could do to keep my attention on his face.

"I *want* you to bother me."

Lowering my lashes, I dried my hair. "I didn't mean to insult you. I just mean that I don't want to confuse things between us."

"I hardly think more confusion matters," he said.

Frowning slightly, I towelled my body dry. "I'm so sorry about Clay, Sascha. Is everyone alright?"

He sighed. "They all made it. Physically. Andie... my pack is furious. They want revenge."

Couldn't blame them. "We're placing extra security around the manor. Any recommendations?"

"I believe a formal apology would go a long way. Most of us are old fashioned, and gestures of this level are respected."

A formal apology would strengthen the stewards' whispers about me, but it could save their lives. "Done."

"They'll be in a clearer headspace after the new moon. Until then, extra security is a good idea. I worry about you living on the outskirts of tribe territory. I'd prefer you were with me at the new moon."

I grabbed an over-sized T-shirt from the trunk and slipped it on so at least my ass was mostly covered.

The heat in Sascha's gaze ramped up a notch. *Go figure.*

"I'm not sure being around a pack who wants revenge is a great idea." I closed the trunk. "But thanks. Is there anything else I should know about the new moon?"

He grimaced. "Don't be surprised if your wolf catches a snack. Or tries to."

Gross. "Right. And really, what should I do about running? That wolf is definitely stalking me."

Sascha growled. "I always ensure the pack remains on pack lands during the new moon. I'll have extra Luthers on watch to ensure nobody leaves. If you stick to the north side, there won't be any trouble that night. Otherwise, I'd like to request that you let me join you on daily runs until we find the culprit."

I played with the bottom hem of my shirt.

Like a regular meet up every day? That was a commitment. What did he mean by it? Or was I just reading too much into stuff? There was a male wolf after me, and Sascha's presence would ensure my safety. That's all he meant. "Uhm, sure. I mean, that makes sense. I run in the mornings usually though."

"So do I, beautiful wolf. It's no trouble."

I peeked up at his honey eyes. "Okay then."

A smile ghosted his lips which only served to increase the heat in my face by one hundred-fold.

As the tension mounted, he began to shake.

"Are you alright?"

Sascha grimaced. "Just the mating call. Nothing to worry about, little bird."

Oh. Right. "Guess we should do the kissing meet sometime..."

I watched the black edging in around his honey irises.

"Guess we should." The corner of his mouth lifted.

My stomach sank. "Unless, maybe it would be better after the new moon? Would that affect anything?"

He searched my face, and I scented his slight confusion. "We can wait until after. It's not far away. If you prefer?"

I cleared my throat. We'd gone this long. What was another few days? "Sure. Sounds good. I'll see you then?"

Sascha grabbed my hand and flipped it, resting a gentle kiss on the back. He lingered before straightening, and when his eyes met mine, I sucked in a breath at the curious warmth filling my chest.

Blinking, I drew my hand from his and spun on my heel, resisting the urge to smile like a fool *and* the urge to pull the bottom hem of my T-shirt down to cover my half-exposed ass.

My wolf snorted. *I thought we weren't meant to show our butthole as a reward.*

22

I rolled over and smacked my nose into a wall of muscle. "*Jesus.*"

"Nope. Just me, baby girl."

I located my ringing phone, scowling at the blurry name illuminated there.

Gasping, I sat in a tangle of sheets. "Roy. Hi."

"Sorry for the early call on a Sunday, Andie. Just wanted to touch base and make sure everything was done on your end."

Oh my god. The house sale. Thank fuck for lawyers. They'd sent through the final papers at some point. I remembered signing. "Let me just check."

Placing him on speaker, I logged into my online banking.

Please, please, please.

My heart leaped into my mouth.

$0.00

Zero dollars. I'd never been happier to see that figure in my life.

I was out of debt—well, I owed the tribe five thousand, but that would be paid in a matter of months. There were my student loans, too, but they were interest free for another year and a half.

"Everything is in order on my end." I could hardly believe the words. "You received the keys?"

Roy messaged when they viewed the storage shed, but I forgot to respond.

"Sure did. Congratulations, Andie. I'm very happy for you."

I was too. Or *would* be when the zeros remained—or ideally, became a positive balance. But right now, the house I'd grown up in was gone, and strangely, that was all I could think about.

Tears welled in my eyes. "Thanks, Roy. Please tell the new owners there's a week remaining on the storage shed. If they want to continue the lease beyond that, they'll need to make arrangements so the contents aren't carted away."

Thanking him again, I hung up.

Wade kneaded his toes into my back. "Does that mean what I think it means?"

"That I have significantly less debt now?"

He waited.

"Yes." I dashed away a tear, my back turned.

Selling the house shouldn't feel like another goodbye to Ragna, but it really did. And why I even cared was anyone's guess.

Wade dragged me up, harassing me until I bounced on the bed with him.

"Andie isn't as poor. Andie isn't as poor!"

Cameron burst in. "What the hell is going on?"

I rolled off the bed as Wade continued, "*Andie isn't as poor*."

Jerking a thumb, I said, "I'm not as poor. The house sale just cleared."

Cameron gasped. "Finally."

Dragging me onto the bed again, we all engaged in another round of celebratory jumping.

Crack.

The world slanted as I was thrown into Wade's thighs. He fell back onto the bed, and Cameron crushed the air from my lungs when she landed on top.

I wheezed. "RIP, bed."

"Who cares. You get paid big bucks for being head steward. You'll have enough to afford a new bed in no time."

Sure would.

I grinned into his inner thigh as Cameron extracted her face from my ass cheeks.

"Enough about me. Today is your day." Padding to the kitchenette, I proceeded to drag a cake out of the fridge.

"Are you insinuating that I'm the kind of person who eats triple... chocolate... fudge cake for breakfast?" he asked.

I pulled out three plates and flicked on the kettle.

Wade arranged himself in my bed as I presented him with the cake. I opened the bedside drawer and extracted the cardboard crown I made yesterday, settling it atop his blond curls.

"I hereby dub thee King Wade. Your orders are to be obeyed without question—"

"I'm not part of that," Cameron said around a mouthful of cake.

"—by *me*," I said. "May your twenty-four-hour rule be prosperous."

Wade dipped his head regally. "Thank you, wench."

Ugh. He'd enjoy this far too much. I made our hot drinks and settled into my slice of goodness.

Cameron had located tubes already, so we were sliding into her car in no time.

"Where will we leave from?" I asked as she drove west through town.

"We'll head out Frankton Gorge way. There's a spot there."

Shoot.

Could I go to Frankton Gorge?

In the back seat, I drew out my phone, pulling up Sascha's number.

My phone vibrated.

Speaking of the devil.

Where are you going?

I texted him back.

Frankton Gorge. Is that safe?

I pressed Send.

"Have you been tubing before, Andie?" Cam asked.

"Nope. Will I die?"

"Only from fun." Wade cranked the music.

They sang along to "Don't Start Now" by Dua Lipa, and I checked my phone.

[Your message was not delivered.]

No reception.

Fuck.

He definitely mentioned vampires in Bluff City, and a witch coven somewhere, and a huge demon kingdom.

I couldn't remember if the claimed territories included Frankton Gorge. That's where they gathered after the vampires and demons, right? Or did the witches control it now?

We left the *Welcome to Deception Valley* sign behind, and my chest tightened.

"I haven't left the valley in so long," Wade groaned. "Maybe we should keep going and have a bender in Bluff City. They have this new club, Forbidden."

Cam waggled her brows. "Sounds like my kind of scene."

That was a definite no. "I need to be back for the announcement. Just to be a party pooper."

"Boo," they chorused.

I focused on listening to our surroundings. I knew nothing about any of these supernatural creatures, and with Wade and Cameron along, a run-in could be disastrous.

"Here we are." She pulled over.

I didn't relax as we untied the tubes and pulled on suspiciously heavy rucksacks.

Cameron locked the car and tucked the keys on top of the tire. "Sonny and Dave are returning from a run to Bluff City. Sonny said he'll drive my car into town and leave it for us."

"Thanks for organising this, Cam." I felt bad that organising Wade's big day was my task and I didn't actually do anything except buy a cake and make a crown.

She threw me a smile. "It was more for me, believe me. I really need this."

I inhaled her worry and sorrow again.

I wish she'd tell me what was up, I whispered to my wolf.

She might in time.

I gave over control of my senses, following the others down a steep trail while clutching my massive tube.

No one is around, my wolf said after a beat.

My shoulders eased some. I'd clarify claimed territory next time I saw Sascha. He'd be so worried.

"Here's a dry bag for your phone," Cameron said.

No reception here either. I tucked the phone in and clipped the bag to my waterproof backpack.

Don't get us too wet, my wolf glowered.

Yeah, yeah. I settled my pack on my front, kicking out until I entered the rapids ahead of Cameron. Better that we go first to search for danger.

"So tense, wench," Wade called. "Relax. It's only water. We've done this dozens of times and a school group came through yesterday afternoon."

That did make me feel better.

"I thought we were drinking *after* tubing, King Wade." I eyed the beer tin in his grip.

He took a sip, righting his cardboard crown with one hand. "I did hear you say that. I thought it was a hilarious joke."

Cameron had a cider.

"Can we entice you to join?" she said.

I smiled. "Fine."

I'd pour it out on the way. Sometimes, I couldn't understand people my age. I wished relaxing and letting loose came easy, but the consequences of drinking in the water wouldn't leave me alone.

Coast still clear? I checked in with her.

All clear. Sascha is on the move west, but not fast. Just into the human building bubble.

You mean town? I grinned.

"Something you'd like to share with the team?" Wade asked.

Nope. "What's happening in your love life?"

He scowled. "Not enough."

Conversation paused as we clung on through a series of rapids. I wiped water from my face after, shaking my much lighter cider tin. This would be easier than I thought.

"No one catching your eye?" Cam said to him.

"Everyone but Andie catches my eye."

They laughed as I splashed him.

Wade overtook me so he led our queue. "I just find everyone here so limited. You know? I wonder sometimes if this is the right place for me to really thrive. But then, the game, I could never leave."

My smile faded. "If the game didn't exist, where would you go?"

He looked at the sky. "Bluff City. Maybe overseas. I've saved a good amount of money."

It was easy to get caught up in my own woes. Other people were making sacrifices too.

I relaxed more, confident my wolf was on the job. "What about you, Cam? If the game didn't exist, where would you be?"

"Right here."

Huh. Surprising.

"I always thought you'd be the first to go." Wade beat me to the punch.

"Things change." She swished her hand in the water.

Wade changed the topic after a leaden silence, and I counted the number of drinks they'd consumed, unable to resist laughing as their antics and comments took on a wild edge.

"Another cider, Andie?" Cameron asked.

I took another, handing back my empty which she shoved in her pack. She squealed, encountering the waterproof speaker in her bag, and soon the music was pumping.

"Your taste in music is *so* much better than Wade's," I moaned, half my mind on Sascha's location. We weren't so far away from him now, and assuming he was at *The Dens,* the tube ride would end well before Wade and Cameron drowned secondary to intoxication.

Wade scoffed. "You were born in the wrong decade, baby girl. Your taste in music is old as shit."

"Music is music," I disagreed.

"You know what King Wade wants?" He cut me off. "You to serenade me on the saxophone. Dressed as Lisa Simpson."

Not happening. I wouldn't play ever again.

I shut my eyes. A calm lulled me as we floated downstream.

Maybe I could get used to this.

Water pounded, and I sat up, peering ahead.

"You might want to put your pack on properly." Wade swung his behind and tightened the waist strap.

The pounding increased. "Why?"

Cameron was doing the same, tucking the radio and tins away.

My mouth dried as I hurried to do the same. "Where are we in relation to the start of town?"

"Just at the top of the cascade," Wade chirped.

"We go *down* those?" I shrieked, searching for the closest land.

We were moving fast, and more importantly, the others seemed set on going over.

"You guys are crazy!"

Cameron tossed her hair back. "Bet neither of you stay on for all three drops. Amateurs."

Oh my god.

We flew through the water, and I kicked faster to surge ahead of Wade. "You two are unbelievable."

They roared with laughter, and my stomach lurched as my tube shot out into thin air.

I screamed, struggling to keep the tube right side up as I plummeted down.

Water exploded as I landed and lost the battle to hang on. The tube shot from under me, disappearing, and there was only a second to see that Wade and Cameron had landed safely before the water forced me over the second drop.

A second scream and this time, I plunged underwater at the bottom.

You said we wouldn't get wet. My wolf panicked, kicking our legs senselessly as air escaped us.

Calm down.

I don't like it!

I seized control as Wade and Cameron landed behind me. I swam upward, lungs bursting.

The water dragged me over the third cascade, and I went, unable to scream because I needed air so badly.

I plummeted through the water and lost no time kicking for the surface. Coughing, I swam for the closest bank where we'd attracted a small crowd of tourists.

When I neared, hands heaved me from the water. The good juju gave him away. I panted on the rock, coughing.

"Claws, little bird," Sascha said, unclipping my pack.

Crap.

I tucked my claws away and checked in with my frightened wolf. *Are you okay?*

She whined in response.

We're okay, I told her.

Sascha helped me stand.

I shoved my sopping hair back. "Thanks."

I located Wade and Cameron down at the bridge. They looked back and I waved.

No idea where my tube was.

"What was that?" Sascha said, holding my pack.

Not Sascha. *Greyson.*

I looked up into black eyes. His grip on my arm was iron-clad as he hoisted me over the barricade. Fully suited, he jumped over the railing like an Olympic athlete and guided me down the street.

I craned to see back, but my friends were out of sight.

"I heard you scream," Greyson seethed. "I felt you moving away from Deception Valley."

"Where are you taking me?" I peered around, sincerely hoping a steward wasn't watching this exchange.

I shouldn't have asked.

We entered *The Dens,* and I grimaced at Hairy who, after one look at the Luther beside me, backed the fuck up.

Greyson marched me between tables of gaping patrons to the staff quarters. I yanked free when we reached his office.

"What's your problem?" I hissed. "There was no need for that."

"There's a need," he disagreed in a savage tone, dropping my pack.

I was crushed against his hard chest, eyes wide as his arms wrapped around me, palms splaying across my back.

Warmth pulsed between us, easing my tension. Chin on my head, Greyson sighed, stroking my hair and back in turn. That apparently wasn't enough to reassure him. Scooping me up, he took us to the green, leather couch lining the far wall, and sat us down.

"I'm soaking." But my grip on his suit jacket tightened.

Why did it have to feel so right?

And unlike anything I'd ever experienced.

Perfect.

Off-limits.

Doomed to fail.

"My friends will search for me." I pulled back, averting my attention.

Greyson captured my chin and forced me to meet his gaze. "I thought you were leaving the valley."

That's why they were so upset? "I can't leave the valley."

He glanced away. "I know. And even knowing that, we feared."

My reply was soft. "I see."

"I want to bite you, Andie," he growled. "I want to chase your wolf and claim her with my fangs."

I shivered, genuinely afraid at the thought. His fangs were fucking massive.

His nostrils flared, and his eyes blazed brighter still.

"You *like* my fear." I glared, crossing my arms.

Greyson didn't deny it. "The scent drives me wild. Wild to protect you. Wild for you. But I am of the understanding that biting you without permission could make you very upset."

Sascha had been at work. I almost smiled. "Yes, I would be upset. It's my body, and I get to decide when things like that happen."

Greyson kissed my forehead. "I will wait as long as I can, but I recognise neither human nor wolf custom, only instinct. What is offensive to a human is rarely offensive to a wolf."

I had a living, breathing predator within me now. She certainly didn't share my boundaries, likes, and dislikes. Especially pertaining to buttholes and who saw them. "Thanks for telling me, I guess."

His eyes darkened once more, and honey returned.

"Andie." Sascha's smooth tone curled my toes.

Our scents swirled, dancing and touching and merging. The combination made my head swim.

His lips were inches from me.

So painfully close.

Should I kiss him?

Would he let me?

I'd felt his mouth on my body, and judging by both our scents, we both wanted a repeat of what happened that night.

Thinking about it made it hard to breathe.

"Are you thinking of my head between your thighs?" Sascha whispered, pressing a kiss in the crook of my neck.

Straddling him, my legs trembled. "I could be. You?"

"I had a different point of view," he answered. "A delicious point of view. But yes, I'm thinking of everything you laid bare for me."

I had a dirty talker. My favourite.

I brought my lips to his ear. "You know, that was the wettest I've ever been. I was so ready for you."

His breath hitched, and his want threatened to consume me.

It was the perfect suspense. He'd agonise over me for days.

Pushing back, I left him on the couch. His gaze scorched me from head to toe in my one-piece swimsuit and drenched sarong.

"I have to find my friends." I walked to the door.

His arm around my waist stopped me short.

"I've got a different idea," he growled.

Sascha swept a hand up my side, and I gasped a moan as his thumb brushed my nipple. He swept back down, spinning me to face him.

The Luther watched me closely as he cupped between my legs.

My breath stalled as he hooked a finger in the crotch of my swimsuit, drawing it to one side.

"My idea is… we do a repeat of that night." He looked at me.

My body almost took matters into its own hands. His fingers were so close to something that had wanted him *bad* since I first shifted.

God, it wouldn't take long.

"Tempting," I whispered. "How about another time? Wade and Cameron will be looking for me."

Sascha's brows climbed. "Really?"

His surprise was a reality check. What did I say?

Oh, shit.

I'd just told him I was available for future orgasms and not just accidental ones.

"I…" I glanced away. "I don't know."

"And it's me you want to do that with," Sascha said, somehow more intent than he'd been seconds before. "Not just anyone?"

I tried to step back but stopped abruptly at a tearing sound.

We stared at the crotch of my swimsuit.

What used to be a crotch.

"Sascha," I groaned, grabbing the two ends of my suit. "I have nothing else to wear."

He choked. "Take my jacket."

"It's not funny." I scowled up at him, "I'm just supposed to wear your jacket? And how did my suit break?"

He grinned. "You're very creative."

I pushed him. "It's not funny!"

Sascha tugged me around his desk and drew a stapler out of the top drawer.

"You're fucking kidding me."

His honey eyes danced with mischief. "It's a solution."

Laughter trembled on my lips. "You're such a... Do it."

I propped my bare foot up on his thigh, and he stilled, staring at my torn suit—or, more likely, what the tear revealed.

"What did I do to deserve this torture?" he asked the room.

Clearing my throat, I focused everywhere but him as he held the ends of my suit together.

Click. Click. Click.

I gave up and started to laugh. Sascha's rich chuckle was quick to follow, and by the time he'd finished, I was wiping tears from my eyes.

I walked experimentally. "Okay. Not totally comfortable, but that will hold for a bit."

"Do you want to take the stapler with you?" His shoulders shook.

Biting my lip, I snatched the stapler. "Actually, yes."

Swiping up my soaking pack, I marched out of his office, heart skipping a beat as his deep laughter echoed down the hallway after me.

23

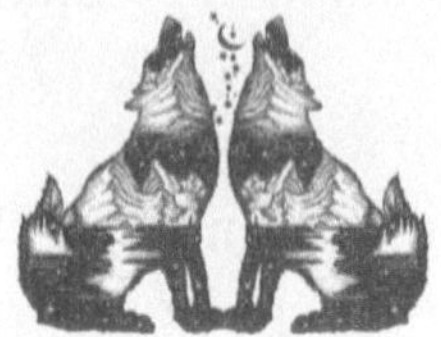

"Got everything?" Wade asked.

Change of clothes, food, water—and a toothbrush after Sascha's critter comment the other day. "Pretty sure."

We hiked through the thickening forest to our sentry point. We'd selected the farthest position with only one camera to avoid.

"Are you nervous?"

"Yes."

You shouldn't be. My wolf sniffed.

Well, I was. Mostly that we'd hurt someone—and that I'd wake with rat organs in my teeth.

The sun was quickly sinking, and I clenched my teeth against the wild urges cloying my thoughts. They wanted me to shift, to run, and to *hunt.*

"You're looking pretty wolfy, Andie." Wade glanced at me.

Reaching up, I felt the tips of my fangs peeking out from beneath my upper lip. "Oops."

"They're cute. Is that the biggest they get?"

We were *both* insulted this time. "No," I spat. "They're massive."

He held up his hands. "Wrong question to ask. My bad."

I sighed. "I'm antsy. Sorry."

"No surprise after the crotch-stapler incident."

Yeah, Cameron wasn't bothered by my disappearing act, but Wade didn't swallow the *I went to buy a towel* cover story—probably because he'd seen the contents of my bank account and towels cost more than zero dollars. And I didn't come back with a towel. There was that.

"That's not why," I retorted.

Though the stapler incident didn't make the tension better over the last three days, particularly with seeing Sascha each day for a quick run. Every night since, I'd deleted a draft booty call message.

And I wasn't even sure why I deleted the messages instead of sending them.

I knew he'd come and give me what I needed.

... It just didn't feel right.

Not because of what he was or our situation.

I didn't know. I should stop overthinking it.

"I can't wait for this to be over."

Wade strode ahead of me up the slope. "Ditto, baby girl. But don't stress. I'll hold down the fort until you return."

"Hopefully I'm back by dawn."

"No stress, remember? We're the farthest out. No one will think anything of us taking our time back. Half of the tribe think we're a couple and I've encouraged the rumours because of your Sascha issue." Wade consulted his map and stopped. "This is us."

I inhaled. "Camera twenty metres to the right." Like all the perimeter cameras, it was facing outward. "We're out of sight."

As he set up the tent, I strode over and waved to Heather through the camera in case someone was watching—Rhona.

She'd been relatively quiet since returning to the manor the day after Clay. She'd kept out of my sight, and I didn't trust her quietness—though it was also a welcome reprieve.

My fangs lengthened more, and I shuddered. "I better go."

"Could you just—" Wade took a look at me and blanched. "Never mind. Off you go. See you in the morning."

"Be good," I told him.

"Or be good at it," he quipped.

I passed behind the camera and ran at a sharp angle until I was out of sight. Pausing, I sniffed for more cameras.

Clear.

The sun dipped to the east and I picked up the pace, bursting through the forest for thirty minutes.

I inhaled. Small prey. Water nearby. Something rotten.

Please don't eat that.

My wolf mentally shrugged.

That didn't seem like a promise.

"Guess there's nothing for it." Delaying the moment, I took out my phone and read the message there from Sascha.

There's nothing to be afraid of.
I won't allow any wolf to leave pack lands. I swear to you.

I grinned like a goof before realising what I was doing.

Shuddering at the mounting darkness within me, I texted back.

Thanks. About to go in.

Seriously. How did he text so fast?

Please message me tomorrow.

Warmth filled me.

I will.

My wolf growled. *Just whenever you're ready.*

Sorry. I placed the phone in my bag as the last of sunlight disappeared. My body began to tremble.

Oh, shit.

Three missed calls from Sascha.

I put the phone on speaker as I dug out my spare clothes.

"Andie," he answered after a ring.

"Hey, everything went okay."

Untangling twigs and leaves from my hair, I vowed to bring a hairbrush and a face cloth next time. I'd woken in a bed of leaves, dirt all over me.

He exhaled. "I'm glad to hear it. How do you feel?"

A smile broke over my face. "Really good." By comparison, I could feel how tense the last five days were.

Languidness filled me. A warmth. Energy.

Positivity.

The tribe assumed that Luthers were tired and more likely to make mistakes in the grid after the new moon. That was total bullshit—something the pack had to be faking. Because I'd never felt sharper. *Wiley wolves.*

I could hear the smile in Sascha's voice as he replied, "It's a nice feeling. You probably won't need to run for a couple of days. We'll meet again on Friday?"

My heart panged. *Oh.* A whole two days away. "Okay then. Any headway on the other issue?"

I'd keep things vague. Who knew if black wolf was around him?

"None yet. It's a delicate problem to navigate."

"The pack has that mind link. Can't you just hear their thoughts?"

"We choose what others can hear through that link. I can assert my power as pack leader to search for truth, but it's viewed as a betrayal of a kind. I must be almost certain of guilt before taking that route."

Dang. "I see. Well… I need to get back."

It was just after dawn, but I needed to return and hear how Trixie and Stanley did with our latest morale boosting Tribe Night.

"Have a good day, little bird."

"You too." Hanging up, I frowned at the screen.

That conversation felt entirely too normal.

So did him calling me little bird.

We were literally on opposite sides. How the hell did we get to the stage where I called so he wouldn't worry? I mean, the situation was as unique as it got, but even with boyfriends, I never did that.

"Crap," I muttered.

Making quick work of backtracking to Wade's salted caramel scent, I shook his tent, grinning at his alarmed shout.

A mussed-up Wade poked his head out, glaring. "I could dislike you."

"Good luck. I'll make breakfast."

"We only brought granola bars."

Dammit. My stomach complained. Granola bars would not cut it.

By the time he'd dressed, I was on my third bar. Pursing my lips, I pushed the remaining three at him.

Wade took one. "You have the other two. I'm worried you'll eat me."

I snatched up the two bars and, well, *wolfed* them down.

Less than an hour later, we started for the manor.

"So?" Wade asked.

"Don't remember a thing." I smiled.

He glanced over his shoulder. "Did you find mushrooms of some description while out there?"

"I just feel so much better."

He turned back as we wound through the forest. "Shifting sounds like a period."

I scrunched my nose. *Damn,* it pretty much was. "Does that mean I get two periods each month?"

"Yes. What if they both happen at the same time one time? That'd be like a double whammy. Will you eat children?"

I really didn't want to find out.

My good mood kept up to the meadow where I'd scattered half of Ragna's ashes under the red oak. My eyes skirted to it, and my mind slammed to the other half stored in my saxophone case.

I forced my thoughts elsewhere. Nothing would ruin this day.

Up ahead, I listened to the happy bustle of the tribe around the manor. The air smelled calmer. Tribe Night worked.

The light feeling in my chest soared.

"*Rhona said she knew for weeks before Sandstone.*"

I stopped short. "Wait."

Wade spun back. "Huh?"

Holding a finger to my lips, I crept forward, tilting my head.

"*Keep it to yourself. Hardly anyone knows. Andie's working really hard to tear Rhona down. We have to strike at the right time.*"

My mouth dried, but the whispered conversation was apparently over. "Rhona's been at work."

Wade glanced around for company. "What?"

"I just heard people talking about me in Sandstone. They said to keep it quiet and that they're waiting for the right time to strike."

His eyes widened. "You're fucking joking. She's told people about Herc? Why now? She's kept quiet all this time."

I shared my theory. "She thought she could win without it. In the first head team meeting, she realised it wouldn't be that clear cut. Guess demoting her after Clay was the final straw. She's going for the throat."

"You need to stomp on this, Andie."

We picked up the pace to the manor.

"I'm not sure who was speaking."

He hurried after me. "You can guess from those who took real guns to Clay."

"Proof, Wade. I won't accuse anyone without it."

I waved at a group of training stewards, beaming. My smile dropped the second I passed.

Yeah, my good mood was officially gone.

Wade was breathing hard when we entered the manor. He lowered his voice. "What will you do?"

I turned to him in the hall. "The stewards have settled down after Clay. I can't upset things so soon, particularly after overhearing a conversation from *two hundred metres* away. How do I explain that? Whatever I do has to be done quietly."

Just what, I had no idea.

"In the meantime," I said, "we ramp up the one-on-one introductions with stewards. I can smell those who don't like me. It's a start to get a list going. And me strengthening the bond with tribe members might help to counteract Rhona's efforts."

"Are *you* prepared for this to come out, baby girl? You can't only think about countering her efforts. What will you do if you wake up tomorrow and every steward knows the truth?"

I tilted my chin. "Exactly what I did the day after telling Rhona the truth. I'll face the music and do whatever I can from whatever capacity I'm given. Every person plays a part in the win, no matter how big or small. I never wanted to play the big part, Wade, and I have no problem with playing a small one."

His salted caramel scent was bittersweet. "But that's exactly why you *have* to play the big part, Andie."

Nathan stared across the table. I smelled the sourness to his apple scent.

He knew the truth.

Rhona was digging at the head team—probably via Valerie, who I could almost say with certainty was in on the truth as well.

The scent in the manor had changed, gaining the sourness and decay I'd learned meant nothing good.

"Sandstone is a big one for us," I said calmly. "This win is important for morale and to honour Herc's memory."

Nathan's sour apple scent tripled.

Yep, he knew for sure.

I scanned the head team. Should I confess everything before Rhona could completely turn them against me?

Their reaction would be a good indication of the tribe's possible reaction. Except I couldn't play the game without this team. If I wasn't head steward, I wouldn't care as much, but I still held the position and if these people stopped listening, the tribe would suffer.

"I'll see you tomorrow afternoon." I stood.

At least I'd reached a new level of trust with my wolf. We'd gone through the new moon without mishap, and that relieved the last of my lingering worry. I mean, who wanted to black out for an entire night?

But we woke up where I'd requested, and she'd slumbered for most of the last few days, recovering and only speaking here and there.

I strode down the hall.

We need to keep going with the mating meets, I told her. *If the tribe finds out about our link to Sascha and Greyson, at least then I can tell them it's over and I turned him down.*

I smiled at Heather from security, who barked a nervous laugh in return, hurrying past.

Entering Herc's office, I settled into his chair. Over the last few days, I got a big chunk of my assignment done. Yes, the bad grades to weekly tests rankled, but if I could scrape through a pass, this degree would be the first accomplishment on my own. That meant more each day when so many wanted a piece of me or my time.

Before this, you've delayed the kiss meet, my wolf answered. *Why?*

The thing about having another being inside of you... lying was pretty pointless and hard. The reply of *it means so much to Sascha* died in my mind.

I leaned back. *I can't stop thinking of him.*

You want the kiss to mean something too.

That sounded so stupid. A silly kiss. *I don't know what I want.*

You fear that forming a deeper connection to him will lead to pain.

I lifted a shoulder. *I've formed deeper connections in normal situations that have led to pain. The situation between me and Sascha is definitely not normal. It's almost assured to end in ruin and hurt. Why would I do that to myself? Plus, he doesn't want to sleep with me after the kissing meet, so I'll need to reject him again, and that doesn't actually make me feel great.*

So don't do it.

My jaw dropped. *Are you serious? I can't give in to the heat. Are you insane?*

Having sex with him after a meet doesn't mean you'll become his mate. That is only decided after all seven meets in a ceremony.

But Mandy told me... She told me that to deny the heat, I had to do the cleopatra thing. She didn't say a thing about sex sealing the deal.

Likely on purpose to limit how much I knew about the mating process.

I'd just assumed the rest.

Sex with him will complicate everything more and he's already said no, I told her.

Seems like your issue is more that he said no than anything else.

Whatever. Opening my lectures for the day, I played the recording, but my eyes soon drifted to my phone.

I picked it up and sighed.

We need to do the next meet.
Things are heating up here.

Three dots appeared as he read the message and typed back.

What's happening?

What *wasn't* happening?

Rhona's telling people what happened in Sandstone.
She's planning something.

Rhona wasn't the subtle sort. Aside from this latest move, her efforts had proved clunky, loud, and explosive.

Would her next move be loud though? She wasn't unintelligent by any means. Somehow, I expected a different approach.

What do you propose?

Reading his text, I rubbed my forehead as the lecturer droned on about enterprise development. Nothing could be further from my mind.

My answer really came down to one question: Did I believe Rhona would be a better leader than me?

If I put my pride and love of a challenge aside, was I the *best* possible leader for the tribe? At first, I'd leaned on Rhona's confidence so much—in awe of her strength. She didn't bat an eyelash before confronting a crowd who may disagree and dislike her. People looked to Rhona as a role model and a woman of power.

They *knew* her. With Rhona, they were sure. There wasn't this need for her to convince the harder-nosed stewards.

And yet.

I sometimes wondered if Rhona valued the title of head steward more than the responsibility the role demanded. And sometimes her actions weren't in the tribe's best interest.

... Or was that just my pride talking? Did I just want to believe those things?

I picked up my phone, replying:

Kiss meet tonight
Bite meet tomorrow
Sex meet on Tuesday.

Until certain that Rhona was the better bet, I had to keep moving forward as head steward.

The meets could be over by Sandstone on Wednesday. There was no need to have days or weeks between times. We'd only waited so long between others because of me—and Sascha recently.

Three dots appeared, and I waited for his reply.

When it didn't come, I jotted down notes on enterprise development, trying to tune into the lecture. This degree was important. I couldn't waste money paying for a re-do semester. Maybe I wouldn't set up my own business as I'd once thought, but I had a whole heap of businesses in the grids to manage.

The lecture finished.

I managed a second lecture on business research methods.

I checked my phone.

No reply. Sascha was probably caught up or having a day off without our usual Sunday grid announcement on the cards today. I'd give him an hour.

Wade walked in after knocking. "Hey, beautiful. Ready to go?"

"Thanks so much for doing this on the weekend." I gathered my things and locked the office door behind us.

"I have no social life anyway," he said. "This is more important."

We set out to meet the next stewards on the list. The questions were different this week.

Why is Rhona so angry?

How are things between you two?

She's a Thana. We hate seeing her so upset.

Would we have lost the grid if you didn't forfeit?

None of the questions were easy, but I seized the opportunity to answer them in this private setting, thankful to get a chance at all. I was happy to notice the change of scent with a few who'd been on the fence about me.

"Who's next?" I asked.

Wade exhaled. "Are you sure you want to visit anymore? How do you not get angry with that bullshit?"

"Because they deserve to know the truth. Or as much as I can give them."

"It's not a guilt thing, right?"

I gripped the wheel. "Maybe there's an element of that. You

know how much I love being lied to. I hate doing that to others. Mostly, I just want to do the right thing by them."

He peered out the window. "Did you notice none of the stewards have asked how the shot Luthers are recovering?"

That hadn't escaped my attention. "I can't decide if that's callousness or fear of showing sympathy—*or* if they want to show me that sympathy for Luthers isn't okay after my forfeit."

"It's so fucked up," he said. "If the game was just Grids, things would be so much easier."

Yep.

Which was why I had to get the meets done. Sascha hadn't made a peep. He always texted back within minutes.

He was ignoring me on purpose.

"Just here on the left." Wade pointed.

Parking, I strode to the front door. A man no more than ten years older than me opened it before I could knock.

"What do you want?" He crossed his arms.

Wade spoke over my head. "Do you know who you're talking to, Mark? Have some respect."

I rested a hand on his arm. "Mark, Wade is introducing me to the tribe. Do you have five minutes for us to better know one another?"

Whoa, only Valerie put out this much dislike. She generally made the effort to keep it from her expression too.

"I'm busy," he replied coolly.

I smiled. "No problem. I'm sure you're hard at work for the tribe, and I commend you for that. Is there a time that suits you for me to return?"

He looked me up and down. "I'm busy every day, *Head Steward.*"

I blinked as the door slammed in my face. *Okay, then.* "I think he likes me."

Wade was scowling so hard at the wooden entrance I worried it might burst into flame.

"Come on," I said. "Not here."

We'd barely pulled out of the driveway, when he slammed a fist on the dash.

I slanted a look at him. "We knew that would happen with some stewards. Put his name on the list and forget about him."

"He's such an asshole. I hate that guy."

"History?"

"We kissed in secondary school. He freaked out after and was a dick to me for years along with all his friends who had no idea what happened."

"You never told them?"

"I have a heart."

"You do. And I love you for it. Even if I find you grossly unattractive."

Wade lifted his head. "How unattractive?"

"I found a mouldy onion in my fridge and for a second thought it was your face."

He squeezed my hand. "At least one thing is right in the world."

No kidding.

I pulled up in front of my cabin. "You go ahead. I've got to call Sascha."

Wade obeyed—after gyrating his hips.

Things would be so easy if we lusted for each other. I'd marry him in a heartbeat.

Instead, I just wanted Sascha's hands all over me in the worst, borderline painful kind of way.

I dialled his number and waited.

One ring.

Two rings.

The ringing cut off, and I gaped at the screen. "You mother*shitter.*"

He screened my call.

Furiously, I typed a text, but his message came through first.

Busy today and morning, but Tuesday works for a meet.

A meet. Any ol' one?
And he was *not* that busy.
Liar.
Eyes narrowed, I sent my reply.

No problem. We can do them one after another.
One second for a kiss. A few seconds for the bite. And a minute for sex?

Suck on that, Sascha Greyson.

24

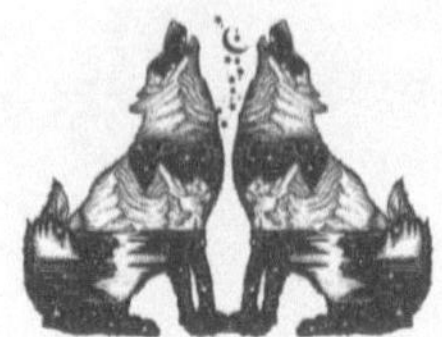

"Lovely to have met you, Darryl," I said, clasping his hand in both of mine.

The *politician* handshake cracked Wade up for some reason.

My phone rang as we returned to the car, and I nearly didn't answer. There was only an hour before the tribe's Tuesday night gathering, and Sascha was meeting me at Lake Thana to finish this meeting crap once and for all.

"Hello." I tossed the keys to Wade.

"Andie," Pascal said. "We've heard some alarming news. The head team thinks it's best to discuss the matter without delay."

My stomach dropped as I fastened my belt. "Is everything alright?"

"I'm sure it will be, but its best that you're here."

Shit.

They knew.

They fucking knew.

"Be there in ten." I hung up. "To the manor. Shit has hit the fan."

Wade stepped on it. "What's she done now?"

"The head team received some alarming news. They must know."

"We can't assume that, baby girl." He sped between the cabins to the nearest major road.

I could. "What else could alarm them enough to ask me to come in?"

"It might not be about you. Maybe a marmot got into the pantry again. Just, please don't panic."

Closing my eyes, I took deep breaths while wishing my wolf was more into *human politics.* I could use her insight right now.

She surprised me by giving it. *Fight them all to establish hierarchy. Sniff each other's buttholes after.*

Maybe I'd go this alone.

Crap. Sascha.

I'd have to postpone the damn meets. Just what I needed.

Can you do tomorrow morning?

His reply was instant.

Not tomorrow.
I can meet on Friday for the one minute and four seconds we need.

"Smartass." I growled, messaging back.

You can do earlier than that.
You're being selfish.

Strangling my phone, I tried to reset my focus as Wade parked in front of the manor.

"Need me in there?" he asked.

"That will make me look extra guilty. I don't want to implicate you like that. Meet you at the gathering?"

He kissed me on the cheek, and I walked into the manor to face my doom.

This was what I expected after telling Rhona. I smiled at one of the younger stewards and received a stony stare in reply.

The same happened with Gerry, the trainer, just down the hall.

I was right.

Everyone knew. My heart pounded as I received snub after snub.

The head team had assembled in the meeting room.

I sat. "Someone put me out of my misery. What's happened?"

Wade was right. I shouldn't blab everything.

Maybe a marmot did get in the pantry.

They avoided my gaze—all except Nathan who'd appeared around one second from exploding.

Roderick cleared his throat. "Rhona sent a message through the tribe SMS system an hour ago."

We had that? "It said what exactly?"

"She gave the details of money stolen from the manor to cover a debt racked up before coming to the valley. Your debt."

I stared, genuine outrage flooding me. "She said *what*?"

Relief plastered over his face. "We knew it wasn't true."

"No," I said slowly. "It's true that I *borrowed* money from the manor—I did so at Rhona's urging. Ragna left me a large debt that the sale of our house in Queen's Way didn't cover by five thousand dollars. I hesitated to take the money, but Rhona assured me borrowing the funds wasn't a problem. She said that ridding myself of one problem would allow me to focus more on the tribe."

I couldn't believe this!

She'd been working against me back then?

"I had a contract drawn up," I glanced up, "by a tribe lawyer."

Trailing off, I recalled that the money wasn't meant to transfer into my account until the house sale recently. I didn't think anything of the money coming in earlier but looking back Rhona played me well and truly.

Was *anything* between us ever real?

"That's certainly a different story from what she outlined,"

Pascal said in the silence. "The problem now being that every steward in the tribe has heard the incorrect version."

Stanley leaned forward. "You shouldn't have borrowed that money, Andie. It looks bad no matter the angle."

His words stung extra bad because I'd known that at the time too. "We need to do damage control."

Nathan glared daggers.

"Do you have something to add, Nathan?" I asked.

"We've never had so much tumult with a leader," he said. "I can't help but wonder if you're the right person for the job."

The others fell silent.

His words were nothing I didn't ask myself each day. "I don't know if I'm the right leader for this tribe or not, but if Rhona were in this seat, I wouldn't spend every waking moment trying to tear her down. Her methods—texts like this—the rumours I've heard spreading, her acts of violence in Clay, none of that helps our people. That's what I know."

His scent remained the same. Nathan was Herc's best friend. If he believed me guilty of Herc's death, nothing I could say would reach him.

Trixie broke the tension. "We'll need to corroborate your story to convince the tribe. Which lawyer did you use?"

I related the details, and Pascal left to call Neve.

"I need to clear up the truth at the gathering," I said in the quiet wake.

"I think so," Roderick said.

"The night before the game." *For fuck's sake.*

Waiting would be worse.

Pascal returned. "Neve is on board. She verified that Rhona was present at the time and that she witnessed the document. She also said that you seemed reluctant to take the funds at the time but did so at Rhona's urging. She mentioned that Rhona called her and said you'd asked for early transfer of the funds and to amend the contract."

"I did no such thing." It must have been directly after she

watched the camera footage outside my cabin and caught me out. Or earlier. At worst, Rhona had despised me from the reading of Herc's will. At best, she started moving against me the day after my confession.

Stanley returned from the window. "Everyone's here."

"Do you have bank details for the manor trust?" I drew out my phone.

He consulted his tablet, reading the account number.

I transferred the exact loan amount back to the tribe. I hadn't closed the mortgage account yet.

Back in the negatives.

Always so close.

"The money should appear in the account within a day."

"Doesn't that put you back in debt?" Trixie asked.

"I'd rather be in more debt than be called a liar and a thief," I answered quietly.

Standing, I smoothed down my sweater and looked at the faces of the head team, reading them loud and clear.

I was on my own.

The trust I'd cultivated with this team was void and gone, and what made me most angry was that accepting the money was stupid beyond reason. *No one* gave money away like that.

Clearing the debt was too good to be true.

I was a fucking idiot.

I went directly outside, ignoring stewards who abruptly stopped talking at my approach.

Walking through their whispering midst, I caught sight of Wade in terse conversation with Cameron. He peered over and I saw his fear for me.

Yep, that about summed it up.

This betrayal hurts you, my wolf said.

With all that Rhona had done, this was such a stab in the back. She'd offered me the money so sincerely. She knew how sensitive I felt about Ragna's gambling problem. And now I'd have to convey that to the tribe.

Rhona hit me across the face in Clay, but this was a dagger to the heart.

I climbed the stairs and stood at the mic, studying the sea of stewards.

The head team filed into the front row, and I spotted Neve beside Pascal. At least there was an impartial witness to back me up.

"I was informed less than an hour ago of a text sent out to the tribe by my sister, Rhona." She was nowhere in sight, surprisingly. "I haven't seen the text itself, but I'm told it details funds stolen from the manor accounts to cover my personal debt. I cannot express how hurtful this was to hear. One, because our tribe is still recovering from what happened in Clay and this is another blow to deal with. *Two,* because the message brings up personal and painful memories of mine that I'd rather keep in the past. And three, because there is some truth to the matter."

I let their outraged murmurs flow for a minute. "Let me give you an accurate recount of this transaction. You deserve no less, and if I'd known this would be an issue for the tribe, you would have known this long ago."

There was a downside to having great senses.

As a human, I could feel my heart race and my chest tighten—maybe sweat rolling down my temple. As a Luther, I could hear the pounding beat of the hearts closest to me. I could smell *their* sweat and sour decay.

I could hear every gasp and mutter and whisper.

"My mother, Ragna Thana, or the woman I believed to be my mother for twenty-one years, died of cancer shortly before I came to this valley in search of her origins. Unbeknown to me, she'd relapsed into her gambling addiction a year and a half prior to dying, and upon her death, I inherited a debt upward of four hundred thousand dollars."

The gasps weren't entirely outraged this time.

"I immediately put our house up for sale, hoping this would cover the outstanding amount."

I detailed the conversation between myself and Rhona and outlined what followed with the lawyer.

"You are about to hear from Neve, the tribe lawyer who oversaw this contract. A copy of this contract will be sent to every steward after this gathering because despite my intentions when accepting this money, I see that my actions weren't transparent enough, and I know many of you will be disappointed in my conduct. Before this gathering, I transferred the entirety of the loan amount owed back to the manor. From today, a head team member will be granted access to all manor accounts to audit the use of funds by members of the Thana family. I assure you this will never happen again."

For a lot of them, one mistake was all they'd needed to make up their mind about me.

But one point was crucial.

"We've faced so much in recent times," I spoke. "Most weeks of every year for *centuries*, we and our ancestors have faced a battle from the outside. More and more, I worry that the actions of a small group in this tribe are creating a battle from within. This is not a plea for that group to stand down. If what I showed them after Clay hasn't stopped their movement, then this plea won't work. I'm telling that group, very clearly, that we cannot survive the outside battle if we're fighting another within. If you're one of the stewards who knew this text would be sent, and if you're one of the stewards who shot a real bullet at a Luther and continue to spread rumours about my past, then that's my message to you. *You* are going to lose Victratum for us."

I couldn't tell if that was enough.

"Before I hand this mic to Neve, a word on tomorrow. Sandstone is a sore reminder of the leader we lost not long ago. Returning there will be a source of hurt and pain for us all. Tomorrow, we show Luthers that Hercules Thana did not die in vain. We fight for him. But we fight the right way. This is my declaration to the tribe that any extreme violence of *any* kind will result in me immediately forfeiting the grid to our opponent."

Yep, I was little miss popular today.

"Those who maim and seriously injure a Luther are putting themselves before the wellbeing of this tribe. We will win this game with dignity and a fairness that future tribe members will remember with pride instead of shame. Don't let your hate for the opponent change who you are—who *we* are."

If I had to forfeit tomorrow, then that was me done as head steward. But at least I wouldn't have blood on my hands.

Forfeiting would put us back at two grids, but if Rhona was smart, she'd ask one of her plebs to take the risk anyway, so she could swoop in to shove me off the throne.

"Neve," I said in the tense aftermath. "Over to you."

The lawyer passed me, shaking my hand in a show that nearly brought tears to my eyes.

I was hanging on by a literal thread.

And I had a sick feeling that thread was about to snap.

25

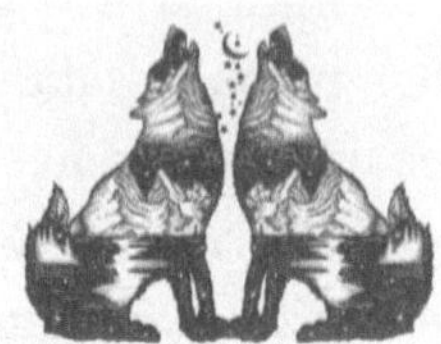

"Phone me back, and I'll say baby boy *once,*" I said to Wade's voice mail.

Since when did he not answer my calls?

I tried his home number. His mother answered.

"Hey, Andie. Wade left for yours a while ago. At least an hour. He's not there?"

I frowned, peering out the window. "Not yet, but maybe he stopped somewhere."

"I'm sure you're right. And just so you know, dear, we're on your side. Rhona's treating you horribly, and those of us with sense won't stand for it."

I thanked her, trying not to cry again. Hanging up, I pulled on hiking boots that once belonged to Rhona. Maybe I should give them back before she accused me of stealing these too.

Out on the porch, I listened for Wade's footsteps.

Nothing.

He made the trip in less than an hour usually. A leaden feeling weighed in my stomach.

I grabbed a jacket and jogged down the trail.

Is your Wade in danger? my wolf asked.

Probably not, I replied. *Best to check.*

He wouldn't worry me on purpose. Not on a grid day, but also not ever.

"Wade?" I called.

Inhaling, I froze, crouching as the faintest strand of spice reached me. *Smell that?*

My wolf checked the scent. *He's no longer here. Recent scent.*

Fear climbed my throat.

I ran toward the scent and Wade's salted caramel hit me.

No.

Bursting up the rise, I paused where the scents grew strongest, noting a rusty tang.

Blood. Human blood.

Red smeared the stone at my feet. A low cry fell from my lips as we circled, searching for more.

Wade was wounded.

Not badly, my wolf said.

Sprinting, I chased the trail, surging out of the tree line and onto a dirt road.

The scents stopped.

My eyes fell to the thick tire tread embedded in the soft mud of the roadside.

Blood rushed into my ears, and I gripped my hair. *They have him.*

Wade is your pack, she answered. *We must find him.*

I ran back the way we'd come, giving control to my wolf as I turned over the problem.

I couldn't take his disappearance to the tribe. The news would cause an all-out war and telling anyone what I knew about the black wolf would inevitably lead to uncomfortable questions and the risk of them uncovering my Luther nature.

If I told Cameron, that could put her at risk.

Only Sascha could help.

Panting as I reached the cabin, I called him.

He screened the call and I screamed, nearly hurtling my phone into the trees.

I typed:

This is urgent. Call me back.

Sascha's name popped up without further delay, and I didn't waste time.

"What's wrong? Where are you?" he said.

I clenched my teeth against the urge to tear a chunk out of him for avoiding me. "Are you alone?"

"Yes."

"Wade was taken by the black wolf. He was supposed to be at mine half an hour ago. I found their scents on the rise behind my cabin. The scents stopped at a road. There were tread marks from a truck."

Sascha's growl echoed down the line.

"The tribe can't handle this right now." I paced on the porch.

A snarl rode his voice. "The wolf is from my pack. He's my responsibility."

"Where do we start?" Wade could be anywhere.

"I'll call a pack gathering. I'll force the truth from my black wolves."

Something he really didn't want to do.

"I know what he smells like. I can tell you who it is."

"Outsiders aren't allowed in pack gatherings."

"You'll be a whole lot less popular for bursting into the minds of eighty wolves, Sascha."

He was silent for a beat. "You're right. Formality must be put aside. Most of the pack work until four. I'll call the gathering for then."

"That's six hours away!"

"I don't like it any more than you do, but all black wolves need to be here. No one can be absent, or this doesn't work, and Wade pays the price for our impatience."

Tears sprang into my eyes. "He may not live that long. There was blood."

Sascha swore. "How much?"

"Not much, but he's injured. This Luther knows what Wade means to me. He'll hurt him."

"We'll get him back, Andie."

I covered my wet face. "I can't lose him, too, Sascha. I just can't take any more of that."

"I'm here, little bird, and I'm not going to let anything happen to Wade. Okay? I'm going out right now to search for him."

"I'll come too," I said.

"We can't let this wolf know anything is amiss," Sascha said. "I need you to stay at the manor today. Until the gathering. It's normal for me to run between our grids and around the pack lands over the day. No one will think twice about seeing me in wolf form. They will if you're there."

I couldn't sit in stupid meetings all day with Wade hurt. "I can't just do *nothing*."

"It's not nothing. Wade needs you to be smart and calm. Can you do that for him?"

That didn't feel smart. It felt cowardly and uncaring. But there was logic to Sascha's words.

"If you find him, please tell me straight away. Tug on the bond like I've done," I whispered.

His voice was harsh as Greyson climbed in. "You know I will."

Fresh tears spilling over my cheeks, I ended the call.

I couldn't go to the manor.

I couldn't.

But I did.

Washing my face, I dressed on the comfortable side of professional in case I had to run on short notice.

The cold shoulders of those in the manor bounced off me as I walked to the office. I inserted the key and turned it.

She'd changed the fucking lock again.

Standing back, I kicked the entrance in. Today was not the day to fuck with me.

No one was inside—lucky for them—and I propped open the splintered door as best as possible before settling at the desk.

I stared at my phone, willing Sascha to call. I could feel the elastic sensation pulling tighter, moving systematically as he searched for Wade.

"Hey, Andie?" Eleanor said from the door. "There was a call for you. Something about a problem out at Sandstone."

"Thanks," I replied. "I'll call them."

I swallowed hard, checking the desk clock. Time for my first meeting. I stood on autopilot.

This day would drag forever.

As long as Wade was safe at the end of it, I didn't care.

2:00 p.m.

Sascha hadn't replied to my string of texts. He could be out of reception, but I was one more text from losing my cool.

Hands shaking, I gathered the reports and filed them in my drawer.

Nope. I couldn't stand it.

I had to go to pack lands now.

"Hey, Andie," Eleanor said from the door. "Sandstone called again. They didn't hear from you."

I groaned. "Totally forgot. I'll give them a call now. Did they say what the issue was?"

"There's something they needed you to sign off on. That's all I got."

Grids was there tonight. I couldn't ignore this. Reaching for the phone, I looked up the number for Sandstone reception and dialled.

It rang out.

I tried again.

"Fuck." I jammed the phone down.

2:10 p.m.

Driving there took forty minutes. I could make it there and back for the pack gathering at four.

Just.

And it would give me something to do.

Entering the Sandstone number into my personal phone, I dialled again, jogging down the hall to my car.

No answer.

Ella F came to life and I stilled. What if the problem in Sandstone had to do with Wade and the black wolf? Surely not.

There were over a hundred workers in the quarry. There's no way one Luther overthrew all of those trained stewards.

Shaking panic off, I started the drive to the quarry.

Panic won't help your pack, my wolf said.

I don't know how to stop feeling panic.

We'll tear out the throat of the Luther responsible for this. Focus on that.

I gripped the wheel, trying the thought of murder on for size, but I wasn't much for seeking blood. I just wanted Wade back.

Driving through the quarry car park, I scanned the other cars. Some stewards had left to prepare for the game, but there had to be at least fifty vehicles around.

My chest loosened. *I'm way too on edge.*

Locking the car, I checked my phone, frantically opening Sascha's message.

Searched the south side. He's not here.
See you soon.

The black wolf would be a fool to hide Wade on pack lands. I'd known that and still hoped.

I opened the reception door. "Hello?"

Hanson was head admin for Sandstone. I looked into the staff and storage rooms. Closing the door behind me, I walked toward the sheds, ignoring staring workers.

"Andie!"

I silently berated myself for jumping as Hanson approached. "Hey. Eleanor got a call from someone here who needed me."

He frowned. "Did she say who called? Oh." He straightened, "It was probably about approval to clear the next quarry zone. We need the proposal assessed to make sure care for the land is displayed before work starts."

Dammit, this wasn't urgent at all.

"Who should I speak to?"

"Foley's in the far shed. He's your guy."

He wasn't my guy, and he certainly wasn't my favourite guy after Clay.

I'd arrange a time to return after Wade was found. This wasn't a priority at all. And assessing their proposal would take longer than the twenty minutes I had before the drive back.

Colour me a hypocrite, but Wade's life was far more important to me than tribe matters.

I entered the large shed that housed the cherry pickers.

"Foley?"

"Yeah?" came a shout.

"It's Andie. Hanson said you had a proposal for me?" I moved into the shed and spotted him in the back office.

The stench of oil overwhelmed my senses and I covered my nose with my tank top. *Gross.*

Foley appeared, wiping his hands on a rag. "Hey, yeah. It's back here."

How did he stand this smell all day? My eyes watered. "I'll take it with me to review. I should have it back in a few days tops."

"There's no real rush."

I don't like him, my wolf said.

Yeah, he's kind of spineless.

Not that. Look at his eyes.

Foley handed me a bound document, eyes never lifting higher than my chin.

Right. I see what you mean.

He's jumpy.

"Foley," I called as a machine started up behind us. "Is everything okay?"

He licked his lips. "It's just… I'm sorry about my part in what happened in Clay. I can't stop thinking about it."

There was so much stink in here, I couldn't tell truth from lie. He did look sheepish. "That's why you were put on probation instead of exiled from the tribe. I know—I *hope*—that those involved will see the error of their decisions. Everyone deserves a second chance."

Though, in my experience, most people blew it.

Ragna.

Herc.

Murphy.

Rhona.

Me.

I jerked at a sharp pain in my back. "What?"

Spinning, the world slanted as I stared into Rhona's emerald gaze. My gaze dropped to what she held.

A tranquiliser gun.

I stumbled to the side, knees buckling. Sliding across the floor, unable to support myself, my blinks became heavier.

So heavy.

Rhona crouched over me. "It's time for the truth, *sister,* don't you think?"

26

Ouch.

My head.

Hands.

Body.

I tried to speak, but my lips couldn't open. Jolting awake, my eyes flew open. I couldn't move my hands!

Oh my god.

Was there duct tape over my mouth?

The world swayed like an ocean, and I choked back rising bile that couldn't escape with the tape over my mouth.

Are you okay? I asked my wolf.

Don't feel good.

Rhona shot me with a dart. A fucking *dart*. That she hated me enough to resort to that method nearly brought forth a free surge of vomit.

I really didn't feel so good.

Where was I?

My feet were bound with rope. They'd bound my hands in front of me with rope too. I was lying on a metal floor. The small platform had rail sides. A remote-control panel sat above my head.

I was in a cherry picker tray.

Blinking, I studied the twilight sky above me.

We're not in the shed, I thought at her.

How long had passed?

I tensed at the telltale *boom* of the cannon. *Shit.* The game had started? We'd been out for hours. Or they'd shot us multiple times.

I struggled against my bonds. This couldn't mean anything good. Rhona wanted me out of the game. She had something planned.

The tray jolted down, and I choked back fresh nausea.

We cannot shift, my wolf slurred.

The sedative affected her more than me, but she was right. I couldn't feel my wolf form. I should be able to hear and smell far better than this. We needed this tranquiliser to wear off, which meant not getting shot again.

These human limitations were debilitating. I felt so vulnerable.

Head lolling, I closed my eyes and relaxed my body as the tray continued to lower.

"She still out?" someone asked.

Valerie.

What a cow.

A hand gently slapped my face. The male sighed. "Yeah. She's out."

Billy.

Let's make a coat out of their skin after this, my wolf said.

The thought nearly overturned my stomach again. *Not happening.*

You have coats made of other animals' skin.

Fake leather, but... *Can we discuss this another time?*

"Maybe we should give her another dose just in case," Valerie said. "We don't want her to wake during Rhona's speech."

"It doesn't matter if she's awake or not during the Stabattse. She's tied up."

What the hell was a Stabattse?

It was kind of familiar. Had I read the term before? Billy placed particular inflection on the word. It was important.

Ceremonial.

And it contained the word *stab* so it couldn't be anything great.

Valerie nudged my thigh. "Maybe I just feel like shooting her."

Billy said, "The plan seemed simple but seeing her tied up makes me feel crap. There must have been a better way to do this."

"Tell that to Herc."

He didn't reply, and my hopes for release vanished. One of them checked the bindings on my hands and feet.

"Okay," Valerie said, excitement tinging her voice. "Let's take her over."

Her footsteps faded, and Billy crouched at my head, prying the tape off my mouth.

"They shouldn't have put this on. What if you vomit?" he said.

I deserved a damn Academy Award for keeping the act up during *that*.

I could move my mouth again. Should I give up the act and reason with him?

Wait until I can help you, my wolf urged.

Obeying, I didn't budge as Billy left the tray. The tray rose once more, and soon after the cherry picker truck drove forward with us suspended high above.

At least we could be certain Rhona hadn't learned about my Luther status or she never would've left me alone.

I cracked open my eyes.

We were still in Sandstone, moving across the ground level of the quarry. Where were the stewards? The cannon had boomed. The first one, I assumed, for no reason other than Billy and Valerie were with me. Stewards should be on the tier just above my tray by now. Others should also be rock-climbing into position.

Whatever this Stabattse was, it wasn't good.

How are you feeling?

Her voice was still weak. *Can't stay awake.*

Lifting my bound hands to my mouth, I tugged at the rope knotted around my wrists.

Whoever tied this was good. Without access to my fangs, I wasn't getting anywhere.

The sounds of a crowd reached my feeble ears. The temptation to roll and look over the edge was real, but I couldn't risk alerting anyone to my conscious state.

My heart pounded as I strained to listen.

A *large* crowd.

There was a definite edge to their murmurs and whispers. Suspense? They didn't know what was happening, perhaps.

I'd wager a guess every fighting steward was in attendance by the volume.

Someone tapped a microphone, and the volume of the crowd surged before dropping away.

"We, the Ni Tiaki tribe, ancient guardians of this land, call a Stabattse. Luthers, come forward as witness to our words," Rhona said.

I stilled. *Oh, fuck.*

Was this like a cease-fire thing?

Her voice was serene, not defensive or angry, and that couldn't mean anything good. What was she going to do to them? It had to involve me. Or did she just want me out of the way?

Sascha would be down there too. If he'd replied to Rhona, then my human ears were too weak to pick it up.

He'll feel where we are, my wolf said.

He would have known something was wrong when I didn't show for the meeting at 4:00 p.m.

My eyes widened.

Wade!

I renewed my efforts on the ropes.

"Stewards." Rhona's magnified voice boomed through Sandstone, though I couldn't tell exactly where she was. "I have a confession to make. I am not Andie as I've led you to believe."

Shocked outcries rang out.

"I apologise for the subterfuge, but as you'll soon hear, the leader, who I have the misfortune to call sister, is unworthy of her position."

Giving up on the rope, I listened over my erratic breaths.

"Some of you have found my recent behaviour selfish and dangerous. Many of you blame me for the loss of Clay. You see my actions as intended to divide and split the tribe. But you'll see that my actions were in response to learning something horrific, something *heart-breaking*, not long ago."

The stewards were quiet. It was the attentive silence I'd experienced once before. The type where people were deathly curious.

She'd tell them, and then what? I had to assume they'd drag me out for show and tell, otherwise what was the point in bringing me at all?

"In this grid, mere months ago, I ran through the forest to find Andie crouched over my father. His neck had been broken by the Luther standing right there. At that time, Andie worked in The Dens on our orders—or so we thought. She'd conveyed her worry about a new tension from the Luthers at work. I was concerned but accepted her word when she told me it was being handled."

I closed my eyes, heart sinking.

We'll get through this, my wolf whispered.

Rhona continued. "My father was dead, and I sat beside Andie in his office before the will reading, wondering how I'd ever fill his shoes. Andie sat beside me and convinced me I was ready."

I had. Lying all the while.

Clearly, she thought back on that moment as much as me.

"You saw my shock at the will reading. I'd been lied to my entire life by my father. By my mother too. At the same moment, the role I believe myself born for was swept away. I was afloat with no idea where to go next. But there was an upside. I had a sister. If anyone could do the job, it was her."

A lump rose in my throat.

"You saw her that day too," Rhona said. "The way she stood by my side. The way she accepted these huge changes without tears or fear. You saw how she effortlessly slid into the role of head steward—after mere *weeks* playing the game. Like me, I'm sure you marvelled and rejoiced that, even if we'd lost an unforgettable leader, somehow, *somehow,* we'd found another."

My nose twitched. The muted scents of those below ticked my awakening senses. The scents grew stronger, and soon I could identify the massive group of Luthers standing on the edges of Sandstone.

I had my nose back.

"I started to notice things," Rhona said, and no one stirred beneath my tray. "I started to notice Sascha Greyson's behaviour around my sister. We all witnessed the way he went for her in Sandstone that day. We believed he sought vengeance for her subterfuge at The Dens. Something he couldn't seek outside of the game without risking penalty points. But the more I looked, the more I saw that wasn't the case. There was something else happening."

A Stabattse had to be a takeover. A change in leadership. That was Rhona's aim here.

Rhona's voice was hoarse. "My only defence for not putting everything together at that moment is that I loved my sister. I trusted my sister. The terrible truth never occurred to me. Instead, foolishly, I told her my growing theory in excitement for how we might use it in the grid." Her breath hitched.

Shame spread through me unchecked.

I'd treated Rhona so badly.

My ears sharpened, and I sorted through the sudden onslaught, absorbing the sound of shuffling feet and whispered comments between stewards.

I felt the tug of Sascha's presence beneath my ribs.

He was here and watching.

"Andie cautioned me though," she said. "We had to be careful with how we used this theory of mine. It could give the wrong impression to the tribe. I wanted her to succeed, so I listened. But even at that point, my instincts told me something was amiss. I began to watch her, fearful that something more was happening, and she was in danger. I watched as she asked to be removed to a cabin on the outskirts of our tribe. I worried about her lack of protection out there. I'd just lost my father. I couldn't lose her too."

I couldn't take it.

Rolling very slowly, I peered over the edge.

There she was, back to the Luthers as she addressed the tribe. One hundred metres separated the wolves from us. The Luthers stood in their usual rows, faces impassive as they watched on.

I dragged my eyes to the middle of the front row and looked into honey eyes. Sascha stared up at me, and blinking a few times to focus, I took in the scent of his utter fury.

He tore his gaze away, and I did the same, rolling flat in case Rhona glanced from the pile of sandstone bricks she stood upon.

"My worry turned to suspicion at last," Rhona called. "Hating myself for doing so, I watched the camera footage from around her cabin. On it I caught her in a lie. And so I confronted her. I like to think Andie's words then were honest, though with how thoroughly she'd fooled us all, I'll never be sure."

Ouch.

I feel stronger, my wolf said.

Fangs and claws stronger?

Soon.

I shoved back my urgency, knowing it wouldn't help.

"Andie Booker is Sascha Greyson's mate. His one and only mate. And she has known it since the first day she entered the valley."

That was a stretch of the fucking truth.

Maybe the stewards didn't really know what a mate was, but it wasn't hard to guess, especially with the amount of venom Rhona injected into the word.

"I'd told her that Sascha Greyson wanted her. *That* was my theory. I thought he was obsessed over her and it could be used against him in the grid. My sister looked me in the eye and said she'd work on it. That's why she moved to the cabin. So he could visit. The day I showed up at the cabin unannounced, she answered the door *naked*. A half-dressed Sascha Greyson was also inside."

That got them.

A wall of sour decay rose up from the one thousand stewards beneath me that consumed me.

I swallowed hard, and a tear trekked across my temple into my hair.

"The cameras confirmed my theory," she said. "My sister was having sex with the monster who killed my father. Our beloved leader."

The crowd couldn't keep silent anymore. They shouted, voices filled with fury and disgust.

Not at Rhona.

At me.

The woman who would have sex with a werewolf.

What's our status? I asked. Did escaping even matter anymore?

I'm trying.

I know. Don't worry. The damage is done.

The crowd simmered down eventually. I inhaled their horror and disbelief, their nausea and hatred.

"The day my father died," Rhona shouted, "something called the capture meet occurred between Andie and the leader of the Luthers. She knew about this in advance and told *no one*. She knew that the Luther would attempt this meet in the grid, but she did not reach out for help or aid. She did not tell my father who came upon them during this meet. When Sascha Greyson immediately attacked, my father managed to draw his gun. *Managed* to fire shots into the beast. But it was too late. He'd arrived unprepared to fight because Andie never thought to tell any of us about the danger."

Some in the crowd were crying.

Was Cameron down there?

Roderick?

Pascal and Stanley?

Eleanor and Heather?

I'd never felt smaller in my life. I just wanted to stay up here in the cherry picker and crawl away when darkness fell.

"Even then, I tried to convince myself it was all a mistake." Her voice broke. "But excuses for her ran dry as I thought back through it all. I finally realised the person she was. The Luther might have snapped my father's neck, but Andie killed him well and truly. Her own father. You've seen her attempts to shut me up since. You've seen the way she's belittled and shoved me aside. But there's one thing I will never give up fighting for—and that's the wellbeing of this tribe. Andie Booker is no Thana. She is no sister of mine. Tonight, knowing all, I implore the Ni Tiaki to follow a new leader —their rightful leader. I ask you to follow me, and not this..."

The cherry picker began to descend, and I squeezed my eyes tight.

You can leave with your dignity, Andie Thana, my wolf hushed. *Show them what a real queen looks like.*

Billy and Valerie climbed into the tray and dragged me upright.

Whoa.

I stumbled into Billy, head thumping against his chest. He righted me, and Valerie jerked me back. The world spun, and I thumped against the railing and crumpled to the ground again.

"What have you done to her?" someone yelled.

I was dragged up again and, this time, held upright.

Ugh, gross.

Cameron shoved through to the front. "What did you give her? And why the hell is she tied up like that? Jesus, Rhona, you can disagree with someone without treating them like this."

"Cameron." I licked my lips.

She cut off, looking up at me.

"It's okay. Thank you, but I'm okay."

She scanned my face in a way that made me realise I must look pretty fucking rough. I inhaled, finding my feet.

"Cam," I told her, though others were bound to hear. "This one is on me. Stand down."

Tears coating her cheeks, Cameron nodded.

I tilted my chin and regarded the tribe. The sour decay thing *really* wasn't helping my wooziness. "I think you all deserve the truth."

"They've *heard* the truth," Rhona said into the mic.

I ignored her. Only because turning my head made the world wonky. Pitching my voice higher, I called. "I'm engaged in a series of meets with Sascha Greyson at the end of which I will be able to choose him or not choose him as a mate. He also holds the power of this choice."

No one made a peep. Probably because most couldn't hear me.

"That night in Sandstone, I had knowledge that could have saved the life of Hercules Thana. I made a mistake and live with that immense regret. In hindsight, concealing the truth of what happened from those who knew him best was cowardly. My only excuses are fear of your reaction and shame. I knew if the truth was known that I would lose a sister. I wanted to delay that moment."

"We've heard enough," Rhona scoffed, turning away.

"Just one more thing." I shoved away every shred of my pride.

Taking a steadying breath, I said, "I hereby abdicate the position of head steward and nominate Rhona Thana in my stead. In her, you will find a leader you can be proud of. But you *must* unite behind her. Enough of this mess. When you leave Sandstone today, forget your problems with those around you. Division has and *will* weaken this tribe. Support Rhona completely. Do it for her or do it for this land but ensure you do it."

I nodded to Valerie and Billy. "You can take me away now."

That earned me an angry shove from Valerie. I grinned as Billy released the ropes around my ankles.

"Return her to that shitty car," Rhona said into the mic. "Andie Booker, you have two hours to pack what you need. After that, leave this valley and never return."

Wow. She was exiling me?

One tiny problem with that.

I cast a look at Sascha.

"See how she watches him?" she hissed.

I met her emerald eyes, so like my own. "I love you, Rhona."

Her grip on the microphone tightened.

Turning on my heel, I lead the way through the crowd. Valerie did her best to stride beside me, but Billy didn't seem to have his heart in it.

It's over, my wolf said.

It is. That was about five times as horrible as my worst fears.

But it was over.

My awareness of my wolf strengthened with every step. The movement was helping push the drug out of my system.

We can free our hands if you want, she said.

There was a slight push at the base of my nail beds. I could cut through the ropes with my claws, but there wasn't any point. *Nah, they'll remove them soon anyway.*

We're leaving? It's a risk.

No. We've got to find Wade. I won't leave before then. After that... we'll cross that bridge when we come to it.

I didn't really want to see Sascha again before going, but I probably had to if I wanted to have the best chance at finding Wade.

My wolf wrenched us to a halt.

Her growl ripped through my mind, and then I smelled it too.

"What are you doing, dog lover?" Valerie spat. "Keep moving."

Spice.

The black wolf was here. Behind me. Behind the stewards. With the Luthers.

As I inhaled again, my insides froze to ice.

He was moving closer.

To the scent of vanilla and cut grass.

To *Rhona*.

"Come on, Andie. We've got to go," Billy said, half apologetically.

Ears buzzing, I stumbled forward, hunching slightly as I extended a claw and began to saw at the ropes. The angle was awkward, but my claws were powerful and sharp, capable of slicing through bones.

Picking up the pace, I sawed harder.

"Slow down," Valerie snapped.

"I only have two hours. There's packing to do," I caught the ropes as my hands came free.

Ready? I asked my wolf.

Rhona betrayed you. Leave her.

But my mind was cast back to that moment after Herc's death when we sat together in his office, holding hands. The split second where Rhona decided to take a tranquiliser dart for me rather than save herself. We'd climbed under the blankets after scattering some of Ragna's ashes and spoke of our mothers until near dawn.

I can't, I thought to her.

Whirling, I ripped the guns from my captor's clutches, bursting forward at a speed just within human confines.

Their shouts rang after me, but I ignored them, sprinting toward Rhona.

The spice grew stronger.

He was closing in on her.

The stewards turned at the shouts behind me, rearing back and eyes wide as I catapulted through their midst.

"Move," I told them in a voice only half mine.

He was too close.

But how was he getting so close to Rhona while Sascha remained back with the other Luthers?

I shoved through the final row of stewards.

27

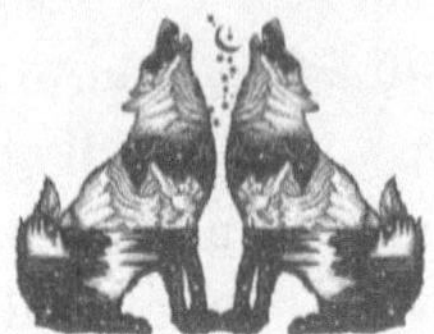

The Luther marshal.

His spice scent filled my nostrils. My body ached with the need to shift and protect.

His yellowed eyes locked on mine.

"Rhona," I called low.

She turned, furious as she spotted me.

"Rhona. Run. Right now."

She drew herself taller. "The transfer of leadership is being witnessed. Leave this place."

The marshal picked up his pace, and I strode forward, throwing off hands pulling me back.

"Rhona, I'm not kidding. Get away from him."

Looking at the Luther, I saw his sudden smirk. The same as in Water.

With an explosion of cracks and pops he shifted into a black wolf.

The stewards cried out, scrambling over each other to get away. I ran for my sister.

"Run!" I screamed at her.

The black wolf would reach her first. Unarmed, Rhona was turning to race backward to the tribe, but she wouldn't make it.

I wouldn't make it to her in time.

Not like this.

My teeth set, and I picked up the pace beyond human capabilities. *We need to shift.*

You're sure?

For Rhona? *Yes. I'm sure.*

She was twenty metres away. The huge black wolf bore down on her as I threw myself headfirst in a spiral, sliding into my wolf form. We hit the ground on all fours, hurtling forward with supernatural speed.

I soared over Rhona's head and took the black wolf to the ground.

Rolling to my feet, I dodged backward until I stood between my enemy and Rhona.

The other Luthers were here now. Sascha had shifted and charged for me, but wrenched to a halt, gaze on the black wolf.

Hackles raised, Greyson swung his head to me. *Daniil has formally challenged you. I cannot interfere. Our lives will be forfeit.*

Are you fucking serious? I moved back from the black wolf. *I'm not part of your pack.*

I'd never heard snarls of the like rip from him. A wall of wolves advanced to separate him from me and the fighting circle they'd formed around us.

Glancing back, I noted Rhona sprawled on the ground and looking at me in horror.

The tribe stared on with the same expressions.

They knew what I was.

Now, I was the monster.

What if I lose? I asked Greyson.

He can choose to spare you. He can choose to kill you.

I knew even as the words left him that Greyson wouldn't allow that to happen. He'd break tradition. He'd fight to reach me.

I'll need to spare or kill him? I asked.

Yes. But we don't know where Wade is.

Fuck.

My wolf cut in. *Are there any other rules we should be aware of?*

None, Greyson said.

The black wolf and I circled each other, and though I had no idea how to fight, this was instinctual to my wolf.

Giving her control of everything, I didn't sit back but sat ready to assist when needed. As she'd done with Greyson, we danced back, darting in and out as the circling continued.

My wolf's assessment flowed into me. He'd be a slightly weaker opponent. He'd passed his prime years.

He was older. In appearance too. Unmated.

Not immortal.

His yellow eyes bore into mine, and my wolf didn't back down from the battle of will. It was crucial to win this too.

We launched across the divide and slashed at his hindquarters. Rounding back, we slashed the other side.

He was hot on our tail, and we faked one way, dashing around him. He didn't relent as expected, continuing to chase us, a close match for our speed.

Shit.

My wolf changed direction, widening the distance. He wasn't as agile on sudden turns. Spinning, she clawed down his side, eliciting a yelp.

Teeth sank into our hind leg. Pain shot through us and we rolled away. As my wolf recovered, I slid forward into the driver's seat and kicked at the black wolf's underbelly.

His fangs gleamed over us, and without thinking, I *shifted* to my much smaller human form. Staring up at his belly, I extended my claws and punched them into his gut.

I rolled out and stood, naked.

The black wolf staggered to the side, blood pouring from the deep puncture wound in his stomach.

We could heal fast.

So could he.

"Where's Wade?" I asked him coldly.

He growled back.

I slid into wolf form again and padded closer. She pressed our advantage, darting around him to inflict wounds meant to tire and weaken.

He slashed back, returning the favour when possible.

There.

With no idea which of us said the words, we both leaped for our chance, pouncing to grip the Luther's throat in our fangs.

Where is Wade? I forced at him.

His laughter rang back. *He's dead.*

I smelled the lie but couldn't help tightening my fangs. His back legs folded, and I shook him roughly.

Tell me now.

If I tell you, I die.

If you tell me, you live.

The black wolf wrenched his body away, and my teeth tore through his fur and flesh. Blood coated our tongue, and we scrambled back in preparation of his attack.

Red spurted from his neck.

He killed himself, I gasped.

The black wolf collapsed in a heap, and I approached warily to stand over him. Pressing a large paw against his bleeding throat, I lowered my head to stare into his eyes.

This fucker couldn't die without telling me what I needed to know. *You will tell me where he is.*

I almost jumped at the booming quality to my voice.

Some of the other Luthers skittered back.

Had they heard it too?

The wolf beneath me stilled, and I latched onto the power spreading in my chest.

You are no match for me, old wolf.

The marshal whined, trying to escape, but I didn't release him from my stare, shoving the power inside at him in waves.

It hurt him, I could tell, and I redoubled my efforts even as I could feel the toll on my body. My energy, or whatever magic made me a Luther, was flooding away.

Like a shattering champagne glass, his mental defence shattered under my onslaught.

We had him.

My wolf rode my voice. *Tell me where her Wade is.*

The answer came to me in a torrent of images, and I blinked through them, scenting their truth.

Like the snap of a rubber band, I released him. He shuddered as a thick wave of blood pulsed from his neck.

Life drained from his eyes. With a rattling breath, he was gone.

Wobbling on shaking legs, I toppled into a heap.

Ah crap, I said.

Crap, my wolf agreed.

Hands found me and my warning growl snapped off as warmth flooded through me. I stared up at a trembling Sascha.

"You're okay, brave wolf. You'll be okay. Shift back now."

His voice soothed me, and though weak, I felt his power ready to help me.

Crack.

So slow.

Pop. Crack.

My legs lengthened and, in human form, I panted hard on the ground.

Sascha scooped me into his arms, and I had nothing in me to do anything but rely on him.

"She is to leave within two hours," Rhona's voice shot across the gap.

Oh... apparently, I *could* hurt more.

A savage snarl left Sascha's mouth. "She is no longer yours to command."

"That's Head Steward to you, Luther."

Sascha's laughter rattled me. "No one believes that, young Thana. Not even yourself."

With that, he turned from her, carrying me away from my sister and tribe.

And I surrendered to the darkness.

28

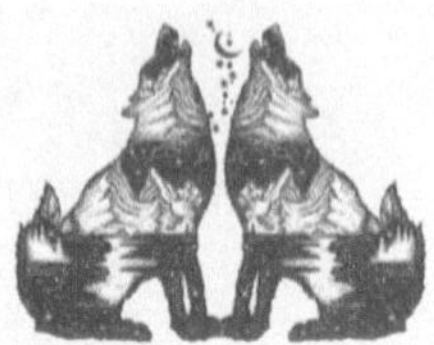

A warm body curled behind mine. Scalding hands splayed across my lower belly. His knee was between mine.

I forced my eyes open and took in Sascha's bungalow.

How long was I out? I asked my wolf.

She yawned. *It's the next day. Nap time.*

The sun was at its highest. Her nap time, not mine.

"I thought it best to keep close overnight—you know, with the healing thing," Sascha said in my ear.

I shivered. "Is that right? This was for medicinal reasons?"

He hummed against my shoulder and I shivered again. "I'm not sure medicinal is the right word. How do you feel?"

Fantastic. "Far better than expected."

It's because we're with him, my wolf said breathlessly.

I rolled my eyes. "Yes, it's because we're with him."

"Yes, it's because you're with me."

Dammit. "I was speaking to someone else."

His shoulders shook. "Does she like me?"

My eyes narrowed in response to my wolf's exuberant *yes.* "She has a crush on you. I can't see the appeal."

His hand swept down the curve of my waist and hip, coming to rest on my thigh. I resumed breathing a beat too late.

"I have a strong feeling, little bird, that you can see the appeal."

I rolled onto my back. It should be illegal to be this close to Sascha Greyson. How the heck was a person meant to think straight? "I don't think I'm head steward anymore."

He didn't laugh as I'd intended, perhaps because he could smell exactly how I felt.

Discarded.

Mostly, I just felt like it was justified.

Sascha's honey eyes burned. "No one deserves to be treated like that, no matter their circumstances. Your part in Hercules Thana's death was miniscule to the point of insignificance. Rhona has twisted that night to her favour. She is playing on the guilt you feel. You *don't* deserve this."

I closed my eyes and tried to absorb his words to no avail.

He kissed my nose and forehead, whispering more kisses on my cheeks and jaw. "When you didn't show, I assumed the black wolf took you, too, but all black wolves were accounted for and I could feel you around Sandstone. I cancelled the formal gathering for fear of alerting the wolf that I knew something more and left for Sandstone. You were well guarded by Rhona's force. I couldn't get to you."

"Thank you for trying. It's done now. Is there a way for me to leave the valley?" I peeked up at him.

Sascha froze. "You can't leave the valley. It's too dangerous."

That put me in a pickle to say the least.

"Andie," he said. "We'd be honoured if you remained on pack lands."

My brows shot into the stratosphere. "There's no way your pack wants me here."

He didn't answer.

Yep.

"Whether you wish to stay or not, there's no other place for you now. The pack has acknowledged that."

Tears clogged my throat.

Sighing, Sascha gathered me close.

After a moment, I sniffed. "I'm naked."

His voice dropped. "I realise that. I thought you'd be more concerned about how Wade's doing."

Gasping, I shot upward. "Wade!"

Sascha caught my hand before I could launch out of bed, assemble an army, and find a flamethrower.

"We have him." Sascha rushed. "I saw the images Daniil showed you. Hairy and Leroy found him last night. He's okay. Tired."

"I need to see him."

He tugged me back a second time. "We returned him to tribe lands."

My face fell. I stopped pulling away. "You did? I mean, that makes sense. He'll be okay there."

"We don't have medicine here. We'll lose points for one of our wolves harming Wade. The penalty would be greater if we held Wade here."

Of course. "I can message him."

My phone.

Was in my car.

"I need to get my car."

"It's in tribe territory," he said. "I can ask for it, but you cannot enter Sandstone without sanction."

I sat on the bed. "Right. Okay."

"I'm so very sorry, Andie," he said after a beat. "You must regret the day you ever met me."

Did I?

I'd certainly told him that numerous times.

Did I regret that day in Timber when we met?

If that never happened, I wouldn't have my wolf, and I could never give her up. Cut off from her with the tranquiliser, I'd felt less than half of myself.

My regrets could fill a book—maybe more. But I couldn't regret the end result.

I wouldn't be this amazing being if Sascha hadn't caught a sniff of me.

And I wouldn't know Sascha Greyson.

"If anything should be blamed, it's the mating call. Blaming nature for the state of my life seems ludicrous. I just know you weren't responsible for the way I chose to handle everything. You've respected my choices, Sascha. I haven't missed that even if I threw stuff in your face along the way. It was just a lot. I'm sorry too."

Sascha shoved back the blanket to expose his bare torso and low-slung sweats.

He drew me onto his lap, and I craned my head to meet his beautiful eyes.

"I just want to give you everything you want and need," he said softly.

My chest rose. "Should I give you a list?"

He gripped my jaw between his thumb and forefinger. "Yes."

In a blur, I was straddling him, pinned by his unrelenting grip on my chin.

I stared up in challenge, gaze dipping to his lips—that full bottom lip that haunted my dreams. Warmth pooled between my thighs, and something thrummed between us.

A heartbeat.

The tugging sensation beneath my ribs was almost painful as it urged me to close the gap. To put my mouth to his.

We'd played a dance in recent weeks, both of us delaying the kissing meet with weak excuses.

When I kiss you because no one else exists for me any longer, I want you to kiss me back just the same.

His words at the waterfall had entered my heart that night, and since then, a growing part of me cared about Sascha's dreams.

About not breaking more of them.

This kiss was more than a kiss. It could be more than anything I'd ever shared with another.

If I let it.

"No one else exists for me any longer, little bird." Sascha lowered his head, eyes blackening.

Mine were the same.

Did anyone else exist for me? I opened my mouth.

"Boss?"

I jerked, dislodging Sascha's grip.

Twisting, I glared at a grinning Leroy.

"Bad time?" the blond alpha asked, his grin wiping clean when Sascha began to growl. He straightened. "There's a steward here to see Andie. It's the tribe's marshal."

"Pascal?" I slid off Sascha, really hoping Leroy didn't make a comment about this place smelling like a sex den.

Because it definitely did with what we were giving off.

I glanced down. "I'm naked."

Leroy shrugged. "Normal here."

Sascha strode to a wardrobe and tossed me sweatpants and a huge shirt. The sweatpants didn't work, so I shrugged on the shirt and followed Leroy out, Sascha at my back.

I looked from Ella F to the grey-haired marshal just beyond. "Pascal. What are you doing here?"

She'd turned from her vigil over the harvest fields visible in the distance. "Andie, how are you?"

"Alive. How is the tribe?"

"Alive."

My heart sank. "Is Wade okay? And Cameron." She'd spoken for me—who knew what Rhona might do to her.

"Wade is awake and healing in your cabin. He asked me to convey that he'll bring over your things when he's up and about. He's very unhappy with how you were treated."

I waved a hand. "Cam?"

"She's fine. Rhona's battle was with you."

I paused. "Is she okay?"

"Rhona hasn't been okay for a long time."

A sigh left my lips. "Thanks for bringing my car."

"I thought it best before angry tribe members got a hold of it. I wanted to come to explain a few things that may be unclear."

She glanced at Sascha and Leroy. "If I may?"

Sascha's eyes skirted her frame. "Don't upset her, marshal. She's dealt with enough from your kind to last a lifetime."

"To my memory, both sides attacked her," Pascal replied.

Stepping between them, I gestured to the stream. Not that every pack member wouldn't listen in.

We walked to the water side by side.

"Is there more to what happened with Murphy?" I asked.

She smiled. "I've become rather a good liar after all this time, but you inherited Herc's uncanny knack for sniffing out the truth. Something Rhona unfortunately inherited without the reasoning ability."

I slid a look at her. "That's your head steward, Pascal."

"Your loyalty though. That's all Charise. Neither Savannah and Herc possessed much of that."

A bench faced the stream. The overhead sun gave it a golden hue that was so at odds with how cold I felt.

"Tell me." I sat.

She joined me, fixing her unseeing gaze on the water. "My story happens before what happened with Murphy. I met a Luther during Grids forty years ago and something happened to us. It continued to happen to us, though neither of us wanted it."

My mouth dried.

She stole a look at me. "The mating call."

Oh my god. "What happened?"

"The process was only slightly less messy than your own, I'd say. With the difference that Daniil and I hated each other well and truly."

Daniil. The black wolf.

She clasped her hands. "Though we detested each other, we had to continue the meets to the end when we could both go our separate ways."

I felt the *but.*

"The grid was the easiest place to complete the meets. Cars weren't a common thing in the valley back then. To drive a car to pack lands would be obvious to his people and mine. To walk would take too long. During one game, we were seen during the kissing meet by Murphy."

She broke off, then took another breath. "Daniil bit Murphy, certain it would keep him quiet. Murphy could scarcely point the finger if he became the very thing he hated. And so it appeared to work for a time. Daniil and I got through the remaining meets. But at the end, Daniil pleaded that I change my mind. He'd... altered his stance on things between us."

I'd smelled the black wolf during our fight. He was single and not immortal. Pascal didn't change her mind.

"You can imagine my relief when it was done," she whispered. "Murphy had disappeared too. Against the odds, I'd kept the truth from the tribe. I was free. Overnight, I felt young again."

I'd so often yearned for the same thing. "But Murphy returned."

She nodded. "Murphy returned. He met with Herc, as was later divulged to me. He confessed that a Luther bit him years before and that's why he and Ragna ran. They never intended to steal you, but Savannah was hospitalised in Frankton Gorge due to an exacerbation of her multiple sclerosis. Ragna was left in charge of your care just as she'd planned to run. To make matters worse, she'd just posted an explanatory letter to Herc that would arrive at the manor in a matter of hours. She had no way to communicate a change in plan to Murphy, and there was no plan B. So she raided your parents' room for necessary documents and clothing and took you too."

I could imagine Ragna's cold terror at the thought of never seeing Murphy again. There was no doubt about that after reading her journals that he was her everything—the single person that could have compelled her to steal a child.

"Murphy couldn't condone what they'd done," Pascal continued. "Ragna was unhappy away from the valley, and he wanted to broker a deal for them to safely return. You would be returned to your parents. He and Ragna would live with the tribe in whatever working capacity Herc deemed fit." She glanced to the clear sky. "Herc agreed. He hardly had any other choice if he wanted to get you back."

"But Murphy would have smelled Herc's dislike."

"Of course Herc disliked him. Murphy couldn't expect anything less for taking his daughter."

I supposed so.

"Herc searched Murphy's belongings during a tribe night. He found a letter from Bluff City with an address on it. It was filled with baby photos. Of you. He'd found where you and Ragna were hiding. He no longer had a need for Murphy—a Luther in the tribe. Preposterous. I'm sure you can imagine Herc's sentiment on that front."

I arched a brow. "Yes."

"He asked if I could go rock-climbing with them. He'd sold it to Murphy as a bonding activity, I think. I didn't want to go for obvious reasons. Murphy knew too much about my past."

He had to have suspected something was up, but he'd come to the valley eager to build bridges for him and Ragna. Maybe even me.

"I was setting anchors," she said. "I heard a commotion and ran around the corner just as Murphy fell from the very top. Straight onto his back."

Horror crept over me.

"He wasn't dead. I raced to help as Herc reached him, shouting for help. Murphy looked straight at me and said, *This is because your mate bit me. This is what he did to me and Ragna.*"

Shit. He'd dropped Pascal in it.

She sighed. "Herc put it together. He dropped the act and got down to business. I would keep my mouth shut and help him. If I didn't, the tribe would learn the truth. Herc had sprayed him with wolfsbane and cut the rope. We switched the ropes and tampered with the belaying station to make our story plausible. He wasn't dying fast enough, so…" Pascal swallowed. "Herc smashed the back of his head against the rock until he was gone."

A crawling sensation crept over my skin.

"I should have been stronger that day," she said. "That one experience shaped me so completely. After that day, I realised that Luthers weren't the only monsters in this valley. Seven mating meets didn't achieve that, but Herc's actions did."

That wasn't all. "I've never lived in Bluff City."

She arched a brow. "It was a nice day when Herc made the discovery. The address never gave him any lead. It made me happy that you and Ragna could be free of this."

"She was never free after Murphy left."

"No. His words played in my mind often as you can imagine. *This is because your mate bit me. This is what he did to me and Ragna.* For a long time, I assumed he meant that Ragna had to leave the valley for him. But they always shared a bond unlike any other I'd seen, even while he was human. How did Murphy know what a mate was?"

"They mated," I said.

"You know this for sure?"

"I think his death broke her. His absence broke her to a degree that I can now see was unnatural. When he died, she stopped doing mostly everything and started gambling. She always tried her best but could never quite manage it. I guess that makes sense now." Tears burned behind my eyes. This was the truth. I felt it. This was why my mother did those things. To herself and me.

Pascal rested a hand on my shoulder, and it felt strange coming from the composed woman. "It's a good thing when the world makes sense. Often, it doesn't."

We sat for a time.

"Why did you tell me all this?" I asked.

She looked at me. "When I turned Daniil down, he was never the same, but his change in behaviour not long after you entered the valley was startling. I believe when he learned of the connection between you and the pack leader, the information changed him."

"What happened that day in Water?"

"I found an empty boat waiting at the bottom. There was no one in sight, so I took it, believing a steward left it for my use. Daniil met me later after confirming some of the underwater points. I didn't think anything of it."

He'd come to meet her and then jumped overboard. *Clever bastard.*

"But then Rhona forced you to bring the theory of Sascha Greyson's obsession to the head team. I knew what that meant. You were going through a mating call together. At that point, I wondered if that explained Daniil's sudden change. But rather than come clean, I decided to monitor the situation and swallowed my concerns."

I'd never told the head team about the black wolf's other attacks. She wouldn't have known about anything other than what happened in Water. "It's not your fault. He chose to act that way."

Pascal dipped her head. "He did."

I inhaled her pain. "You're mourning him."

"Strange thing that mating call," she said quietly. "It never quite leaves you. I wasn't able to complete one of the meets—the scenting meet. Daniil believes this might have disrupted the process for us and left us in limbo."

Standing, she dipped her head and turned away.

"Pascal?" I called.

She peered back.

"If you could go back to that moment with Daniil. Would you change your mind?" I didn't bother specifying which moment.

The older woman regarded me. "It was harder to choose him than not. I found out later that the hardest path is usually the one worth taking. A few decades bring clarity that youth doesn't have."

Nature was so very cold. Really, we had no choice in the mating call at all.

To create a Daniil.

To become a Pascal.

To end as Murphy.

To exist like Ragna.

I searched her face. "Daniil attacked Rhona to force me to shift. Other times, I was sure he wanted me dead."

"I'm not sure Daniil knew what he wanted. Did he want to force you and Sascha together or tear you apart? I'm undecided."

Daniil turned me into a Luther. That would only help us to progress through the mating call.

But he took Wade to lure me out alone.

In my mind, he attacked Rhona to reveal my true nature to the tribe. Something that landed me here.

His scent was spicy to me and not to Sascha.

Of course, Daniil then tried to kill me in the challenge.

No one would ever know the truth.

Part of my heart ached on Daniil's behalf, which only proved I'd lost my damn mind. "I'm sorry you lost someone you loved, Pascal."

She blinked several times. "You deserved more from a tribe and sister that you broke your back to help, Andie." She turned toward the bungalows. "My condolences to this pack who lost someone they loved dearly."

The marshal walked slowly away, and a huge part of me longed to follow and comfort her.

Sascha joined me on the bench and pulled me onto his lap. "Are you alright?"

Am I?

I hadn't paused for breath since Ragna's death. I certainly hadn't processed what happened in Sandstone.

For the first time maybe *ever,* I had absolutely no plan or idea of my future.

I did recognise that this moment was a happy bubble in what was a harsh, centuries-old war. That war wouldn't stop just because the tribe had cast me out.

At any second this happy bubble could pop.

"I'd given up on getting any answers about Ragna and Murphy." I looked up into gorgeous honey eyes.

Sascha held me close. "Then I'm happy for you. Pascal gave the pack closure, too, and I'm grateful to her. We never had any idea Daniil had entered a mating call, but it explains a lot."

I toyed with the ends of his dark-brown hair. Something I'd always wanted to try, but never dared do with so many barriers between us.

In this bubble though, I could do such things.

I rested my cheek against his chest. "Sascha? What happens tomorrow?"

He kissed my temple. "I'm not sure, beautiful wolf. But we'll get through it together. How about that?"

Another happy bubble.

Forcing the thought away for now, I closed my eyes. "That sounds like a dream I'd like to share."

WOLF ROULETTE

SUPERNATURAL BATTLE: WEREWOLF DENS, #3

Grab Your Copy Today!

BOOKS BY KELLY ST. CLARE

<u>**Supernatural Battle**</u>

Vampire Towers (Paranormal urban romance)

Blood Trial

Vampire Debt

Death Game

Werewolf Dens (Paranormal urban romance)

Shifter Wars

Moon Claimed

Wolf Roulette

The Darkest Drae (Dragon shifter romance)

with Raye Wagner

Blood Oath

Shadow Wings

Black Crown

The Tainted Accords (Royal fantasy romance):

Fantasy of Frost

Fantasy of Flight

Fantasy of Fire

Fantasy of Freedom

The Tri-World Exchange

(The Tainted Accords Novellas):

Sin

Olandon

Rhone

Shard

The Tri-World Exchange Set

Pirates of Felicity (Pirate fantasy romance):

Immortal Plunder

Stolen Princess

Pillars of Six

Dynami's Wrath

Veritas

Eternal Gambit

Mortal Trinity

Last Battle for Earth (Dystopian romance):

Earth's Warrior

Rebel's Crusade

Traitor's Mandate

www.ingramcontent.com/pod-product-compliance
Lightning Source LLC
Chambersburg PA
CBHW020932310726
48980CB00007B/745/J